Globalization, Utopia, and Postcolonial Science Fiction

Globalization, Utopia, and Postcolonial Science Fiction

New Maps of Hope

Eric D. Smith

First published 2012 by
PALGRAVE MACMILLAN

Palgrave Macmillan in the UK is an imprint of Macmillan Publishers Limited, registered in England, company number 785998, of Houndmills, Basingstoke, Hampshire RG21 6XS.

Palgrave Macmillan in the US is a division of St Martin's Press LLC, 175 Fifth Avenue, New York, NY 10010.

Palgrave Macmillan is the global academic imprint of the above companies and has companies and representatives throughout the world.

Palgrave® and Macmillan® are registered trademarks in the United States, the United Kingdom, Europe and other countries.

ISBN 978–0–230–35447–0

This book is printed on paper suitable for recycling and made from fully managed and sustained forest sources. Logging, pulping and manufacturing processes are expected to conform to the environmental regulations of the country of origin.

A catalogue record for this book is available from the British Library.

A catalog record for this book is available from the Library of Congress.

10 9 8 7 6 5 4 3 2 1
21 20 19 18 17 16 15 14 13 12

Transferred to Digital Printing in 2013

For Alyssa Mackenzie, who teaches me about the future

Contents

Acknowledgments

This book owes its existence to the expertise and encouragement of far too many wonderful friends and colleagues to name here. Special thanks are reserved, however, for Alanna Frost, Philip Kovacs, Jason Richards, Rashna Wadia Richards, Christine Sears, Joey Taylor, Angela Balla, Holly Flint, Brian Martine, and Rolf Goebel, who offered helpful insight and advice or simply a sympathetic ear during the book's composition. I am equally grateful to those students, past and present, with whom I have had the privilege to discuss many of the ideas presented here while yet in their earliest and perhaps least coherent form. In particular, I thank former student Tim Farrell, whose sharp eye and generous assistance in preparing the final manuscript were invaluable and whose friendship has proven even more so. I owe a tremendous and irredeemable debt of gratitude to those who have influenced my thinking and who have over the years provided me with intellectual inspiration as well as vibrant models of scholarly aspiration: Brandy Kershner, Malini Schueller, Leah Rosenberg, Kelly Marsh, Al Elmore, Penne Laubenthal, and especially Phil Wegner, who introduced me to utopia's inexhaustible worlds. Sincerest gratitude also goes to my late mentor and friend Richard Patteson, whom I will ever remember, after the character of his favorite novel, in his prime. I am grateful to the editors at Palgrave Macmillan for their interest in this project as well as for their patience and guidance during the publication process. I am likewise indebted to the anonymous reader, whose generous insights and eminently constructive criticisms helped to make this a much more coherent book than it might otherwise have been. What flaws and infelicities remain are, alas, my own. Versions of chapters 1 and 2 originally appeared in issues of *Twentieth-Century Literature* and *Genre*, respectively, and I thank those editors for graciously allowing that work to be reprinted here. Foremost, I thank Sangreal, my wonderful wife of 14 years, whose love and steadfast faith never fail to reveal hope in those moments when I most fail to find it. Without you, they're only words.

Introduction: The Desire Called Postcolonial Science Fiction

In his 2007 Pulitzer Prize-winning novel *The Brief Wondrous Life of Oscar Wao*, Junot Díaz has his tragic protagonist, the son of Dominican immigrants living in New Jersey and an aspiring writer of science fiction (SF) and fantasy, pose an arresting analogy – startling in its frank, unqualified delivery – between the traditionally Euro-American genre of SF and the political and cultural realities of the Caribbean: "[Oscar] was a hardcore sci-fi and fantasy man, believed that that was the kind of story we were all living in. He'd ask: What more sci-fi than the Santo Domingo? What more fantasy than the Antilles?"[1] A wealth of political, cultural, and aesthetic claims is advanced in this peculiar juxtaposition. For how can the "underdeveloped" nations of the postcolonial Caribbean be said to recall in any reasonable sense the quicksilver lozenges, crystalline skyscapes, or, indeed, even the gutted, post-industrial, dystopian wastelands of canonical SF? The book that follows is, in short, an attempt to explore the conditions, both political and aesthetic, that make possible Díaz's unqualified comparison of the seemingly incongruous and even incommensurable domains of the postcolonial third world and the genre of SF, particularly as expressed in the recent phenomenon of visionary SF narratives originating in these "marginal" national cultures.

The imperialist preoccupations of traditional SF have long been a topic of discussion,[2] and many scholars have recognized that, as John Rieder recently puts it, the period witnessing the "most fervid imperialist expansion" in the late nineteenth century coincides exactly with the rise of the genre.[3] Following Edward Said's famous claim that the novel as cultural artifact is quite literally unthinkable outside its proximate relation to imperialism, Rieder argues that SF must likewise be contextualized as a product of imperialist culture, finding its original expression in late-nineteenth-century British and French fantasies of global conquest before emerging in the "new" imperialist cultures of Germany, Russia, the United States, and Japan in the twentieth century. Patricia Kerslake likewise contends that "[t]he theme of empire ... is so ingrained in SF that to discuss empire in SF is also to investigate the fundamental purposes and attributes of the genre itself."[4]

Istvan Csicsery-Ronay Jr. therefore observes that canonical SF emerges from the juncture of three requisite conditions: the technological expansionism of the imperialist will to power; the intercession of a mediating popular culture at home to absorb and transcode the contingent trauma of the imperial project; and the pseudo-utopian imaginative projection of an "achieved technoscientific Empire."[5] Despite, however, this historical complicity with the encompassing and hegemonic "imaginary world-model of Empire," Csicsery-Ronay holds that SF need not mechanistically replicate imperialist ideological structures. The genre may also, in its deployment of the globalizing models of Empire, provide the means for us to detect and decipher the ideological mystifications of global capital, the unique manifestations of globalization in particular national cultures, the emergence of technology as a cognitive mode of awareness, and the processes whereby individual national cultures exist alongside and engage the polymorphous *bad infinity* of the new global habitus. Likewise, Rieder contends that "while staying within the ideological and epistemological framework of the colonial discourse, [SF] exaggerates and exploits its internal divisions" such that the occlusions and occultations that subtend them are (however metaphorically or allegorically) rendered apparent and available for critique.[6]

SF's unique generic tendency to replicate at the level of form as well as content the constitutive contradictions of empire and imperialist culture (including its more recent phase of globalization) may therefore reveal a deep structural affinity with the discourses of critical theory, specifically the latter's deployment of the dialectic. Appealing to Darko Suvin's now indispensible Brechtian definition of SF as the literature of "cognitive estrangement," Carl Freedman advances the provocative claim that SF and critical theory may in fact be read as "versions" of one another in their structural predisposition for dialectical formulation, for exposing the apparently unassailable whole as an uneasy unity of antagonistic forces or tendencies (and vice versa). The genre of SF, Freedman notes,

> is determined by the *dialectic* between estrangement and cognition. The first term refers to the creation of an alternative fictional world

> that, by refusing to take our mundane environment for granted, implicitly or explicitly performs an estranging critical interrogation of the latter. But the *critical* character of the interrogation is guaranteed by the operation of cognition, which enables the science-fictional text to account rationally for its imagined world and for the connections as well as the disconnections of the latter to our own empirical world.[7]

For Suvin, the sustainment of this foundational dialectic is crucial for our understanding of how an SF text *works* as well as for the classification of exemplary SF narratives. An overbalancing or neutralizing of this dialectical tension in favor of cognition results in the mundane familiarities of an aesthetic "realism," while one in favor of a mere estrangement not cognitively tethered to the present (and thus not critically charged) yields the irrationalist projections of purely generic "fantasy." However, Suvin's categories should not, Freedman cautions, be taken as objective criteria by which one may submit a given text to a merely superficial valuation. Rather, he suggests, we should consider the "attitude of the text itself to the kind of estrangement being performed."[8]

Freedman's primary contribution to Suvin's influential model of SF is thus the unbinding of the form from the constrictively empirical categories of routine generic classification. We must learn to rethink genre, he offers, as a tendency (perhaps only one among several simultaneous, conflicting tendencies) active within the text rather than as a categorical master-list of cosmetic features by which one always provisionally assigns a work to the most appropriate taxonomic grouping: fantasy, science fiction, realism, modernism, novel, epic, and so forth.[9] In this way, Freedman also provides a useful corrective to Suvin's notorious dismissal of generic fantasy as "just a subliterature of mystification."[10] Positing genre as a kind of cognition and form as already a kind of content, Freedman's dialectically tendential theory of generic classification privileges genre as "a more fundamental category than literature itself."[11] So while genre may be understood as "a substantive property of discourse and its context," the *literary* is simply the functional designation of a "formally arbitrary and socially determinate category," the constitution of which can be traced to the thoroughly ideological practices of canon formation and hegemonic culturalization.[12]

As Freedman demonstrates through a close stylistic analysis of Philip K. Dick (whom Fredric Jameson famously nominates the "Shakespeare of science fiction"), the typical academic disregard for the genre, based traditionally on its presumed stylistic infelicities or inferiorities, ultimately reveals an enduring bourgeois "celebration of personal subjectivity" and its canonical array of technical virtuosities as well as a deep aversion both to SF's inherently *public* orientation and to its fundamental dialecticism, qualities which Freedman productively identifies with the Bakhtinian dialogic principle and the latter's criticism of literary formalist interpretive practice as "precritical" discourse.[13] The overriding formal tendency of SF, by contrast,

> is above all critical and dialectical; its "prosaic" quality may signal substantive, as opposed to merely technical, complexity. Indeed, the entire category of the dialogic in Bakhtin's sense is in the end nothing other than the (primarily Marxian) dialectic as manifest in literary (and linguistic) form.[14]

Freedman can, therefore, justifiably make the somewhat surprising claim that, inasmuch as SF maintains a unique structural fidelity to critical dialecticism and a historicizing, demystifying commitment to the embattled Marxian concept of totality, Marx himself may be read as "a theorist of science fiction *avant la lettre*" and SF as the privileged literary expression of critical theory.[15] For just as Jameson suggests of dialectical thought more generally, SF undertakes the imaginative linking together of two or more "incommensurable realities" (subject and object, spirit and matter, self and world, and so forth) so that "for a fleeting instant we might catch a glimpse of a unified world, of a universe in which discontinuous realities are nonetheless implicated with each other and intertwined, no matter how remote they may at first have seemed."[16] Imbued then with what we might call a *dialectical intelligence*, SF takes as its point of departure not the monadic and discrete but rather the point at which the identical and non-identical have yet to abstract themselves from this fundamental, mutual interpenetration and/or antagonism. SF, like the dialectic, is thus "comparative in its very structure, even in its consideration of individual, isolated types."[17] Born in the imperialist collision of cultural identities and taking as its formal and thematic substance the spatial dislocations that inhere in the imperial situation, science fiction would seem the ideal instrument with which to engage critically the transition from the postcolonial condition to that of globalization.

However, despite both Freedman's claims for the inherently critical tendencies of SF and Darko Suvin's now widely held assertion that the estranging function of the genre provides the utopian means to "redescribe the known world and open up new possibilities of intervening into it,"[18] the disproportionate bulk of science fiction continues to be both produced and consumed, much as it has always been, in European and American imperial centers. The overwhelming impression left by this global disparity in the production of speculative narrative, Csicsery-Ronay observes, is that "only the technohistorical center will have a future."[19] It remains as yet uncertain, he argues, whether "writers and readers of the less central nations" will choose (or even be able) to appropriate the estranging devices of SF – perhaps themselves "precisely the tools of hegemony" – to imagine the alternative social horizons that Suvin, Freedman, Jameson, and others celebrate.[20] Thus, Csicsery-Ronay finds that, in full accord with globalization theory's (perhaps premature) diminishment of the nation-state, the genre's propensity for imagining denationalization and elaborating fantasies of "global management" are less the result of emancipatory political anticipation or logical extrapolation than they are allegorized projections of "the political perspective of the dominant technopowers, for whom national cultural identity represents an obstacle to political-economic rationalization, the foundation upon which their hegemony is based."[21]

The first decade of the new millennium in particular has witnessed, however, the phenomenal efflorescence of narratives written within a speculative framework that radically reconfigure the conceptual machinery of SF and utopia to address the exigencies of postcoloniality and globalization in a way that challenges the hegemonic order to which Csicsery-Ronay refers. Beginning with Salman Rushdie's underappreciated 1975 debut novel, the genre's organizing engagement with globalization arguably reached formal consolidation with the 2004 publication of *So Long Been Dreaming: Postcolonial Science Fiction*, a collection of short fiction edited by expatriate Caribbean SF writer Nalo Hopkinson and postcolonial scholar Uppinder Mehan. From the Caribbean steampunk of the Grenada-born Tobias Buckell and the South African cyberpunk of Lauren Beukes to the host of African and Southeast Asian writers of speculative fiction, these national cultures, consigned to the absolute past of first-world post-industrial progress, are increasingly exploiting the critical and utopian resources of the genre of the future to re-imagine and redefine their place in an uncertain present. As Hopkinson puts it in the introduction to *So Long Been Dreaming*, writers of postcolonial science fiction appropriate "the meme of colonizing the natives and, from the experience of the colonizee, critique it, pervert it, fuck with it, with irony, with anger, with humour, and also, with love and respect for the genre of science fiction that makes it possible to think about new ways of doing things."[22] And as Irish SF writer

Ian McDonald reminds us, "The future comes to Kenya or Kolkata as surely as it comes to Kansas."[23]

Perhaps more consequential, however, than the arrival of *the future*, whatever that concept may now mean, in the Kenyas and Kolkatas of the world (a formulation that merely replicates the rhetoric of developmentalism it seems designed to contest) are the array of futures emanating *from* these sites of production. Indeed, I argue that it is only in the recognition of what I want to call postcolonial SF's "new maps of hope" that we may ultimately justify recent claims to science fiction's status as a properly *historical* genre. As the account goes, in one of the more fascinating moments of juncture and transition in all of literary history, the decline of the great historical novel of Walter Scott coincides almost exactly with the emergence of narrative science fiction. Only four years after the publication of *Waverley* in 1814, Mary Shelley's *Frankenstein* marks the publication of what some claim as the first science fiction novel or, as Freedman argues, at least "the first work in which the science-fictional tendency reaches a certain level of self-consciousness, thus enabling a line of fiction that, at least in retrospect, can be construed as the early history of science fiction proper."[24] For Freedman, *Frankenstein* is particularly noteworthy as a threshold text in that it also formally embodies this moment of historical and generic transition. The reader, for instance, initially identifies Captain Walton, the typical "hero of an old fashioned travel narrative" and author of the letters that compose the novel's opening pages, as the book's protagonist.[25] What appears to be Walton's arctic travel narrative is disrupted, however, with the sudden appearance of Viktor Frankenstein, "the properly science-fictional hero, whose emergence as protagonist transforms the narrative into a predominantly science-fictional one."[26] This narrative displacement marks the exhaustion of the estranging function of the travel narrative or quest romance in the moment of bourgeois modernity. Exotic locales, made commonplace in the nineteenth century by the omnivorous cultures of imperialism, are no longer alien enough to induce a truly dialectical experience of identity and difference, so that the foreclosure of spatial dislocation as an estranging mechanism is accompanied by the near-immediate ascendance of the temporal.

This formal displacement can occur, as the work of H.G. Wells most readily demonstrates, in either of two directions, the past or the future. In either case, the achievement of imaginative distance from the present allows for its critical historicization, and it is precisely this estranging function that is central to Lukács' privileging of historical realism. The ruptural event of capitalism, as Jameson points out, requires a new, *progressive* relationship to time than that of previous social and political formations like those of tribal or feudal systems or even of the ancient city-state: "it demands a *memory* of qualitative social change, a concrete vision of the past which we may find completed by that far more abstract and empty conception of some future terminus which we sometimes call progress."[27] Positioned as he is amid the fraught interstices of a rapidly transitioning world, "between two modes of production, the commercial activity of the Lowlands and the archaic, virtually tribal system of the surviving Highlanders," Scott is uniquely positioned to imagine into being a genuinely historical consciousness by constructing the present as the telos of a determinate past that has been successfully superseded.[28] Equally central to Lukács' account of the historical novel, however, is the gradual decline of the form, its faltering ability to fix its critical gaze on the present due to formally inherent tendencies toward escapist nostalgia and technical complexity. Thus, the post-1848 arrival of Flaubert and proto-modernism signals for Lukács the exhaustion of the historical novel as a vital form and the beginning of its swift descent into the aesthetic decadence and bourgeois ahistoricism of high modernism on the one hand and the stoic resignations of literary naturalism on the other.

Jameson likewise observes that the devitalization of Lukács' historical novel is coterminous with the rise of SF, which he marks not with the publication of *Frankenstein* but with the early novels of Jules Verne. Narrative SF continues the estranging work of the historical novel albeit, Jameson argues, in the opposite temporal direction:

> We are therefore entitled to complete Lukács' account of the historical novel with the counter-panel of its opposite number, the emergence of the new genre of SF as a form which now registers some nascent sense of the future, and does so in the space on which a sense of the past had once been inscribed.[29]

With the site of its temporal estrangement located in the space of the future, the genre of SF at once avoids the alluring encumbrances of nostalgia that compromised the historicizing force of the historical novel and assumes a definitively utopian vocation through its inevitable failure to imagine a radical future that is not simply a protraction (or what Rushdie, as we shall see, might call an "anagrammatical" reconfiguration) of the present in which it is written. For Jameson, this *necessary* failure constitutes the most important pedagogical function of the utopian genre, one that has re-emerged in our world of "post-" inflections and global finance as a "sub-variety of SF in general" and, I suggest, of third-world SF in particular.[30]

Such productive failure Jameson associates with the comprehensive and ongoing project of aesthetic modernism itself. Contrary to Lukács, who views the modernist aesthetic as fundamentally dehistoricizing, Jameson seeks to restore to our understanding of modernism a political imperative that the ideological solidifications of "late modernism" and New Critical formalism actively obscured or reterritorialized. Characterized by a Lukácsian aspiration to totality and enacting a "Utopian metamorphosis of forms" that resists tendencies of formal reification, aesthetic modernism produces works that increasingly defy traditional classifications "at the same time that they invent various mythic and ideological claims for some unique formal status which has no social recognition or acknowledgment," thereby establishing what Jameson (like Alain Badiou) terms "the void" that necessitates modernism's characteristic auto-referentiality, or its reflection on the conditions (and limitations) of its own production.[31] Having redefined modernism as a utopian project that "re-emerges over and over again with the various national situations as a specific and unique national-literary task or imperative," Jameson declares the need for "a wholesale displacement of the thematics of modernity by the desire called Utopia."[32] Aligning the ongoing global project of aesthetic modernism with the generic preoccupations of SF (and anticipating his subsequent book on the subject), Jameson concludes *A Singular Modernity* (2002) with the strident assertion that "[o]ntologies of the present demand archaeologies of the future, not forecasts of the past."[33]

In a perspicacious assessment of the extended treatment of SF offered in Jameson's subsequent *Archaeologies of the Future* (2005), Phillip E. Wegner claims that one of the book's most "original contributions is that it enables us to understand science fiction itself as a *modernist* practice."[34] Following Jameson's endorsement of Suvinian cognitive estrangement as a way of grasping "the formal specificity of science fiction" as critical and utopian praxis, Wegner adds that one of the genre's unique characteristics is its ability to realize the dialectical convergence of two seemingly antipodal, if not irreconcilable aesthetic forms: realism and modernism.[35] While works of classic modernism achieve their estranging effect through manipulations and distortions of formal and linguistic norms, SF does so precisely "through its 'realistic' content, a realism whose referent ... is an 'absent' one."[36] Thus, SF might be said to achieve a paradoxical "realist (cognitive) modernism (estrangement)" capable of overcoming the formal contradiction in which the historical novel of Scott eventually becomes mired – and able, therefore, to fulfill the latter's critical and imaginative vocation for a new epoch.

The study that follows argues that the recent surge of SF production from the marginalized sites of third-world national cultures may be read as a continuation and enduring validation of this unfinished modernist/ utopian project. An objection might be raised at this point, however, to the assertion that the fantastical estranging devices of SF are singularly or, at the very least, especially equipped to address the desperate realities and historical paradoxes of contemporary postcoloniality. For what of that celebrated genre of magical or marvelous realism and its formal propensity for the ludic transformation of the material and the mundane, its willful disregard for the western dogma of an inevitable, implacable History, and its liberation of the powers of perception and the imagination from the linear, binary strictures of European cognitive and aesthetic modes? Díaz provides us a clue with Oscar Wao's assertion that Santo Domingo, the wider Caribbean, and, by implication, the third world itself now inhabit a science-fictional narrative. In fact, Oscar's query – "What more sci-fi than the Santo Domingo" – rehearses almost exactly the final rhetorical flourish of Alejo Carpentier's apologia for the aesthetic practice of the *real-maravillosso* in his majestic 1949 prologue to *The Kingdom of This World*: "After all, what is the entire history of America if not a chronicle of the marvelous real?"[37] Announcing (somewhat belatedly) his break from the aesthetic practice of Surrealism, Carpentier's prologue assumes, for all its sharp economy, the function and gravitas of a manifesto in its programmatic and passionate declarations, not least of which involve the distinction between the imaginatively impoverished and thoroughly reified legerdemain of European Surrealists and the utopian vitalism of an authentic, American marvelous realism, the conditions for which he discerns as if for the first time on a 1943 visit to Haiti:

> After having felt the undeniable spell of the lands of Haiti. . ., I was moved to set this recently experienced marvelous reality beside the tiresome pretension of creating the marvelous that has characterized certain European literatures over the past thirty years. The marvelous, sought in the old clichés of the Broceliande jungle, the Knights of the Round Table, Merlin the sorcerer and the Arthurian legend. The marvelous, inadequately evoked by the roles and deformities of festival characters ...[38]

Carpentier suggests that formulaic attempts to force the arousal of the marvelous or to counterfeit its wildly protean powers within a sclerotic

European imaginary, whose structural integrity consists of an absolute disavowal of precisely the "alternative" realities of sites like Haiti (and their deep interdependencies), reduces the thaumaturge to the legalistic bureaucrat and visionary creation itself to mere technical or instrumental proficiency. He traces here a process of aesthetic reification comparable to Jameson's description of the hardening of an authentic modernist praxis into the ideological institution of late modernism. The marvelous, above all a kind of critical perception and ethico-political consistency, cannot be apprehended or fully even comprehended without the a priori commitment to it, which, in the face of all evidence to the contrary, perceives in the baleful and banal poverty of the present its immediate and utter transfiguration. Appropriating the tactic of Baudelairean shock, Carpentier writes,

> There are still too many "adolescents who find pleasure in raping the fresh cadavers of beautiful, dead women" (Lautreamont), who do not take into account that it would be more marvelous to ravish them alive. The problem here is that many of them disguise themselves cheaply as magicians, forgetting that the marvelous begins to be unmistakably marvelous when it arises from an unexpected alteration of reality (the miracle), from a privileged revelation of reality, an unaccustomed insight that is singularly favored by the unexpected richness of reality or an amplification of the scale and categories of reality, perceived with particular intensity by virtue of an exaltation of the spirit that leads it to a kind of extreme state.[39]

This imaginative alteration or critical intensification of our experience of the present, the enfeebling limits of which are thereby exposed as such, obviously has much in common with both the critique of ideology and the utopian project outlined above. Indeed, a consideration of Jameson's own tentative periodization of magical realism offers us a way to understand this essential linkage between the rhetorical question posed by Carpentier at one historical/aesthetic juncture and its deliberate re-authoring by Díaz at another. In his brief analysis of magical realist cinema, Jameson offers the

> very provisional hypothesis that the possibility of magic realism as a formal mode is constitutively dependent on a type of historical raw material in which disjunction is structurally present; or, to generalize the hypothesis more starkly, magic realism depends on a content

> which betrays the overlap or the coexistence of precapitalist with nascent capitalist or technological features.[40]

Like the historical novel of Scott, then, magic realism emerges as a narrative mode to address the structural doublings, dislocations, and diremptions of a constitutive shift or disturbance in the mode of production, in Carpentier's case, one that sees the uneasy cohabitation of capitalist and precapitalist forms in the interwar period of the 1930s and early 1940s. Crucial for Jameson is the recognition, however, that these "archaic" forms are not themselves reducible to the unruly supplement that disturbs (or enriches with a purely additive alterity) the normative "realism" of the present situation. Rather, magic realism lays bare for us the miraculous potentialities already present within the perceived limits of what we call "reality."[41] Following World War II and decolonization, however, came the growing influence in the third world of the Bretton Woods system and the abrupt decline of such visible precapitalist practices. If, as Brenda Cooper suggests, magical realism thrives in the complex zones of contest and negotiation between a precolonial past and a post-industrial present, between history and magic, what happens to it once capital has saturated the world system through the IMF and World Bank and the collapse of the Soviet bloc?[42] Díaz's reformulation might therefore be read as acknowledging the decline of one historical situation, and the narrative form to which it gives birth, and signaling the recognition of a new one, whose unique parameters demand an altogether different set of representational strategies than those deployed by Carpentier or even Gabriel García Márquez. Thus, it is not incidental that many works of postcolonial SF (especially those of Caribbean, Indian, and African origin, where an aesthetic of magic realism may be said to have achieved a kind of primacy of expression) seem formally preoccupied with the transition from magic realism to SF and often either dramatically "enact" this passage or pay anxious homage to this prior and deeply related aesthetic form, which, in the absence of its vitalizing context, becomes as empty and reified a set of formal practices as those of the Surrealism decried by Carpentier, calcifying into the properly ideological institution that Michael Denning denounces as nothing more than the "empty and contrived. . .aesthetic of globalization" itself.[43] It is precisely this point of exhaustion that Díaz's revision of Carpentier acknowledges as it gestures (not coincidentally from the same geospatial location) toward the imaginative capacities of postcolonial science fiction.

Such an historicist charting of postcolonial SF's filiations with magical realism also pre-empts developmentalist models of formal derivation that can often follow from Suvin's strict definitional framework, particularly from the hard distinction he proposes between the genres of fantasy and SF.[44] Elaborating on the central provocation of Mark Bould and Sherryl Vint's essay "There Is No Such Thing as Science Fiction," John Rieder offers five propositions about SF that are instructive in this regard and that will inform to some degree the readings that follow: (1) "sf is historical and mutable"; (2) "sf has no essence, no single unifying characteristic, and no point of origin"; (3) "sf is not a set of texts, but rather a way of using texts and of drawing relationships among them"; (4) "sf's identity is a differentially articulated position in an historical and mutable field of genres"; and (5) "attribution and identity of sf to a text constitutes an active intervention in its distribution and reception."[45] Rieder's privileging of the historical over the generic and taxonomic therefore radically prioritizes the form's fundamental dialecticism to the point that SF ceases to be a properly inert category of genre and emerges instead as a versatile and provisional praxis among and within genres, a field of articulation among "various communities of practice."[46] Some of the implications of such an aesthetic and political model for imagining otherwise in the moment of globalization it will be the broad task of this book to delineate.

Despite, however, the recent consolidation of what I argue must now be recognized as a genre in its own right, works of postcolonial science fiction have as yet received only scant critical attention and insufficient formal theorization. Among the first and most influential monographs devoted to the comprehensive study of third-world and postcolonial speculative/utopian production[47] is Ralph Pordzik's *The Quest for Postcolonial Utopia* (2001), an analysis that regards with telling suspicion the "embarrassing transformative scenarios" of previous utopian imaginings and applauds the "self-referential, disjunctive and detotalizing" heterotopic alternatives of the third world.[48] Pordzik implicitly locates the postcolonial utopia at the end of history, a moment characterized by "a certain degree of exhaustion" with "humanist or Marxist" totalizations, which he equates/conflates throughout the book with forms of *totalitarianism*.[49] This "growing body of speculative fiction written in a decade that has witnessed the demise of the last *grand récit* of western etatist philosophy" is thus presented as yet another postcolonial variant of postmodernism, and while Pordzik reveals the postcolonial utopia's capacity to generate "unexpected and revealing ways" to "make available perceptual alternatives to the poor future prospects of many postcolonial societies today," his reading equally disables the form by severing it from the specific material/historical matrices responsible for those forlorn prospects.[50] As Tom Moylan observes in an astute critique of the book,

> When [Pordzik] argues that these works avoid "a fixed counter-position or counter-ideology" and transcend national and ideological boundaries in order to produce a radical new cultural otherness (104), he risks eviscerating and de-valuing the very cultural and political plenitude and power of this literary tendency by stepping away from and thus effacing the historical conditions and political struggles that helped to produce such works in the first place.[51]

Pordzik's study, in other words, repeats the twin gestures of postmodern dehistoricist uncoupling and radical textualization that render the geopolitical present (and its potential transformation) unthinkable. What is needed, then, is a reconsideration of the postcolonial utopia that avoids replicating this valorization of the postmodern aesthetic on the one hand and that keeps clearly in view the material circumstances that both make possible and necessitate such utopian figurations on the other, forms that, far from celebrating an aesthetic of "inconclusive agency," instead imagine ever new possibilities for acting in the present.

Somewhat more promising in this regard is the recent critical anthology edited by Ericka Hoagland and Reema Sarwal, *Science Fiction, Imperialism and the Third World: Essays on Postcolonial Literature and Film* (2010), the introduction to which undertakes the definitional grounding of the key terms of the book's eclectic assemblage of essays: "postcolonial," "science fiction," and, perhaps most crucially and contentiously, "third world."[52] Acknowledging Adam Robert's sobering claim that SF – animated by a nostalgic attachment to the here and now that parades as a kind of ersatz futurity – functions merely as the "dark subconscious to the thinking mind of Imperialism,"[53] Hoagland and Sarwal concede that while the strategic displacement of the future by a nostalgic investment in the present might accurately define the creative impetus of popular science fictional texts like *Star Trek*, it does not exhaust the critical reach of the genre as realized in visionary artists like Wells and Bradbury, who rather reveal the stresses and contradictions internal to imperialist histories themselves. Thus, they contend, the "rewriting/revising of history and the recovery of the subaltern subject, integral components to postcolonial studies, are mirrors of science fiction's complex relationship with history and the haunting presence of aliens and others like Bradbury's Martians."[54] It is at this point of overlapping interest in the ethics of Otherness demonstrated in SF and postcolonial literatures alike that Hoagland and Sarwal introduce the "controversial" third term that begins to suggest, though never fully provides in their introduction, the essential materialist ballast for the other two categories.[55] Paying due heed to astringent critiques of "Third-Worldism" as advanced in recent decades by Aijaz Ahmad, Arif Dirlik, and Kumkum Sangari, the editors nonetheless insist on its critical utility as an "uncomfortable term" indicative, in the very dilemmas that accompany its always polemical appearance, of the "inequality of current cultural global dynamics."[56] Self-consciously courting the representational risks that attend the concept of the third world – that is, of imposing a too narrowly defined or prescriptivist function in which uniquely individual authors from singular cultural and ethnic subject positions are "stripped of their creative agency and subjectivity" – Hoagland and Sarwal maintain its value as a familiar conceptual landmark and point of articulated alliance between diverse and otherwise incommensurable localities of global struggle, thereby obliquely evoking a totalizing strategy that is never quite named as such.[57]

This reluctance might itself be read as symptomatic of that curious evolution in the ongoing intellectual parsing of the "third world" in which, as Neil Lazarus argues, "the critique mutates from a Marxist critique of 'Third Worldism' [such as we find in Ahmad's well-known appraisal of Jameson's use of the term] into a 'Third-Worldist' critique of Marxism."[58] That is, by privileging as central to the imaginative labor of the SF and postcolonial text (and certainly to the products of their recent cross-pollination) interventions in the rhetoric of a purely ethno-cultural Otherness, the editors of *Science Fiction, Imperialism and the Third World* occlude a sustained engagement with the material. While no doubt true, their observation that "[t]he 'Other' is one of the most well-known markers that science fiction and postcolonial literature share in common"[59] also circumvents a critical encounter with the obstinate fact of globalized capital, barring which, we are left with those merely involutional queries about cultural influence and derivation, hegemonies and counter-hegemonies, all of which, it seems to me, operate finally within the horizon of an insidious developmentalism masquerading as the progressivist countenancing of cultural plurality.

A comparable hesitation can be detected in the most thoroughly comprehensive study of the genre to date, Jessica Langer's groundbreaking *Postcolonialism and Science Fiction* (2011).[60] While Langer acknowledges the "materialist/discursive" divide that in so many ways defines the broad problematic of postcolonial studies, and while her critical survey offers rigorously historicized treatments of an impressive range of science fictional texts (her lengthy excursus on Japanese SF is especially insightful), the book's thematic organization reveals a clear overbalancing toward the latter term of this disciplinary binary: Langer follows the introductory chapter concerning history and geography with chapters devoted to "Diaspora and Locality"; "Race, Culture, Identity and Alien/Nation"; "Hybridity, Nativism and Transgression"; and "Indigenous Knowledge and Western Science," topics connoting the longstanding landmarks of identity, epistemology, and discursivity familiar to students of postcolonial analysis. While duly acknowledging the enduring necessity of such analytical frameworks, my aim here will be to redress what I view as a consistent absence from existing considerations of the genre of the initial term in postcolonialism's fundamental divide. Therefore, whereas existing interventions attempt to extend or apply the familiar conventions of postcolonial analysis to these new works of science fiction, this study will ask rather how the emergence of the latter serves to challenge the institutional limits of the former and to both reconfigure and reclaim the materialist stakes of an anti-imperialist resistance.

Such de facto capitulations to the new global order – out of which, Lazarus argues in a thoroughgoing critique of the field, "[p]ostcolonial studies emerged as an institutionally specific, conjuncturally determined response" – are predicated on the loss of the third world as the blazon of consolidated resistance to capitalist imperialism.[61] Neil Larsen observes that "we who once unself-consciously said 'third world' now hesitate, if only for a second, to utter it in the same contexts" and, moreover, that this hesitation is itself expressive of "the decline of the national liberation movements of the 'Bandung Era.'"[62] Lazarus insists, then, that the term "third world" must be retained or recovered today, when imperialism has boldly relinquished its ambivalent "post," not as "the descriptor of any actual place or historical location or, of course, mode of production" but as "the name of a political desire."[63] Arguing that there is in fact no third world in the "politico-ontological sense," Lazarus exhorts us to remember that "'Third-worldness,' as a regulative ideal, is born of anticolonialist and anti-imperialist struggle. It gestures towards a world in which autonomy and popular self-determination will be politically meaningful concepts, in which 'independence' will not correspond merely to 'flag independence.'"[64] Such a world, or the desire that claims such a world as its destiny, is of course already familiar to us as the no less maligned, if no less essential concept of utopia, which in the epoch of globalization, I argue, we can glimpse (particularly if not exclusively) in the emergence of postcolonial SF.

If, as Jameson claims, first-world fantasies of the third world "can have nothing whatsoever in common, formally or epistemologically, with what the Third World has to know every day about the First," if indeed, "subalternity carries the possibility of knowledge with it" through a stereoscopic vision of the world in full, what then might be learned about the unrepresentable totality of the present (and of its alternatives) from the speculative fictions of the third world?[65] Like Scott, SF writers of the "developing nations" of the third world occupy a unique position at the interstices of dramatic social, political, and economic transformation – between the former imperialist capitalist order and the no less brutal, if (from the vantage of the West) often less visible, contemporary realities of globalization. We thus find in the speculative production of these sites – and particularly in the recent turn to SF, which, as I have suggested, functions increasingly as the literary-aesthetic idiom of critical discourse – figurations that undertake the twin operations of a critical *cognitive mapping* of the present and an imaginative cartography of utopian possibility. The central assumptions of the book that follows are that, first, the rise of "globalization" in the mid-1970s is the result of a dramatic respatialization of capital entailing unprecedented geopolitical reorganizations in which, as David Harvey observes, many of the previously governing assumptions about the "natural" geographic and political order are suddenly rendered meaningless in the face of an altogether new logic, the operative rules of which have yet to be made legible.[66] Foremost has been the transformed nature and agenda of the nation-state. Once the hard-sought guarantor of political independence for those under the heel of imperialism, globalization's strategic "denationalizations" have refunctioned the nation to attend the complex demands of a more flexible capitalism: phenomena like the rise of the multinational corporation and of global finance, systemic deregulation, the widespread privatization of the public sector, and the increasing prominence and influence of international entities like the World Bank and the World Trade Organization are all symptoms of – as well as conditions for – this new political and economic dispensation.[67] Second, following Jameson's influential provocation that the dominant concern of contemporary SF has less to do with fluidities and paradoxes of time, technology, and the enduring fascinations of "otherness" than with a sustained critical engagement with the concept of space and its imaginative and physical production, I argue that as the literary and cultural expression of the habitus of globalization, postcolonial SF is formally equipped to offer critical mappings of its geospatial structures and to achieve, like the protagonist in the climactic scene of the recent "breakthrough" South African film *District 9* (discussed in chapter 5), the dialectical vision whereby the illusory membranes separating the first world and the third are dissolved and the deep, material interdependencies of the two stand finally revealed.[68]

In short, I contend that Harvey might well be describing the emergent genre of postcolonial SF when he writes in *Spaces of Hope* of the need, as well as the historically unprecedented potential, for a new, more robust critical vision:

> We are therefore faced with a historic opportunity to seize the nettle of capitalism's geography, to see the production of space as a constitutive movement within (as opposed to something derivatively constructed by) the dynamics of capital accumulation and class struggle. This provides an opportunity to emancipate ourselves from imprisonment within a hidden spatiality that has had the opaque power to dominate (and sometimes confuse) the logic of both our thinking and our politics. It also permits us to understand better exactly how class and inter-place struggles so often cut across each other and how capitalism can frequently contain class struggle through a geographical divide and rule of that struggle.[69]

Each of the works examined here undertakes precisely this critical exploration of globalization's enigmatic and elusive imaginative geography, manifesting what Alain Badiou calls an "urgent, phosphorescent writing" that is the impossible, but nevertheless *insistent* signature of the political subject in a posthistorical world.[70] For this reason, the growing number of global voices in SF can, like Carpentier before them, lay claim to the modernist dictum of the first-generation Surrealists: *Vous qui ne voyez pas, pensez a ceux qui voient*: You who don't see, think about those who can.

Looking first at Salman Rushdie's unjustly pilloried debut novel, *Grimus*, I suggest that what has often been criticized as the author's failed experiment in genre fiction may in fact be read as an early effort to train the critical and dialectical apparatuses of SF on the still emergent formations of globalization in the mid-1970s. The novel's spatial abstractions, which have so frustrated attempts to secure the book within a formalized and procrustean postcolonial hermeneutic, may be seen from this vantage as enacting an early mapping of globalization's disorienting geospatial effects. By situating Rushdie as central to this generic emergence, I do not simply replicate the canonical logic of the postcolonial cosmopolitanism rightly decried by Timothy Brennan and others; rather, what I hope to show is that the mutually sustaining constructs of "postcolonial studies" and the canonical Rushdie cannot tolerate the dialecticism and materialist interventionism of this earlier novel and so must regard it as an aberration and a failure, unreadable within these sanctioned interpretive frameworks. That is, while Rushdie cannot be said to speak without qualification for the interests of the third world, attention to this neglected novel as a work of science fiction can sensitize us to a certain submerged materialist project within cosmopolitan postcolonial literatures – one that, though absented from the institutionalized rubric of postcolonial critical praxis, returns to us today through the dialectical genre of postcolonial SF.

If Rushdie's early novel registers the transformations of time, space, and politics under the emergent global dispensation, Nalo Hopkinson's fiction more narrowly and specifically addresses the mechanisms by which these changes are still being wrought at the turn of the millennium. Touching briefly upon her award-winning first novel *Brown Girl in the Ring*, chapter 2 more thoroughly engages her ambitious follow-up *Midnight Robber* and its attempt both to localize and historicize the machinations of globalization in relation to colonial history and, more important, to ongoing practices and institutions of spatio-economic exploitation in the Caribbean.

From these diagnostic expressions, I turn in chapters 3, 4, and 5 to a series of texts that not only map the effects of globalization but that also undertake the creative harnessing of its fractious and frenetic energies toward the elaboration of new collectivities and a flexible array of articulating politics. First, I examine Vandana Singh's impressive debut collection of short fiction, which, in its form as well as its content, repudiates the tempting consolations of the domestic and effects the "long space" of a utopian transnationalism, an achievement that is the ideational and structural condition of possibility for the alternative subjectivities outlined in the chapters that follow.

I next consider Amitav Ghosh's widely discussed novel of science fiction and alternate history, *The Calcutta Chromosome*, as contributing to a revised and renewed Marxist historicism. Against prevailing assessments, I argue that Ghosh reformulates a specifically Hegelian cunning of history: one that does not simply posit a stereotypically unlinear progression toward a determinate end but that rather enacts the excavation and seizure of the future in the desolate field of the now, rethinking at once space, time, and the contemporary political subject. This chapter also examines briefly Manjula Padmanabhan's short story "Gandhi-Toxin," which simultaneously completes and helps make visible the deeply original implications of Ghosh's project, one echoed in recent philosophical and theoretical reclamations of Hegel.

In chapter 5, I suggest that the insistent occupant (at once subject and object) of the now-universal space of exception, whom Giorgio Agamben names *homo sacer*, is increasingly registered in first- and third-world cultures alike by the return of the monstrous subject. Here, I examine two recent popular films that encounter this monstrous subjectivity within the broad context of a late capitalist diminishment of the state and restructuration of social space. First, I look to *I am Legend*, a first-world representation that, while acknowledging a certain constitutive antagonism, finally mystifies it as a conflict of incommensurable lifeworlds and recontains it within the structures of religious allegory and the enclave community on the one hand and an orthodox multiculturalism on the other. By contrast, I read the recent South African SF film *District 9* as a more consistently dialectical intervention into phenomena of post-contemporary spatiality and globalization. Resisting consensus appraisals of the film as an apartheid allegory, I offer an alternative reading that provides more urgently contemporary contexts and imaginative stakes and acknowledges the film's allegorizing of an alternative political subjectivity.

The book's final chapter considers recent exemplars of postcolonial cyberpunk and steampunk. I read Lauren Beukes' South African cyberpunk novel *Moxyland* alongside and against William Gibson's cyberpunk classic *Neuromancer* as well as his more recent "departure" from cyberpunk, *Pattern Recognition*; next, I reflect briefly on Tobias Buckell's rehistoricizing Caribbean steampunk novel *Crystal Rain*. Situating the first as a utopian antipastoral for the cyber age and the second as a postcolonial rejoinder to the dehistoricizing meme of steampunk, I argue that attention to the novels' unique critical engagements with their source genres (which are themselves often figured as marking the imaginative terminus of traditional SF) illuminates their complex formal and political contributions even as it throws into relief many of the potential limits and necessary risks of postcolonial science fiction more generally.

1
"Fictions Where a Man Could Live": Worldlessness Against the Void in Salman Rushdie's *Grimus*

Read against the industry-inspiring success of his better-known works, Rushdie's 1975 debut novel *Grimus* is often regarded as the artistically tentative effort of the author who would, in his maturity, go on to write *Midnight's Children* (1981). The relative dearth of critical responses to *Grimus* in the more than 35 years since its publication seems emphatically to indicate a scholarly consensus, one which, perhaps given the recently recognized emergence of the genre of postcolonial science fiction, invites renewed consideration. Indeed, what if we resist this broadly dismissive critical approach by suggesting that Rushdie's unique appropriation of SF provides for both a critical/aesthetic intervention – among the very first – into the global order just making itself visible in the mid-1970s and, perhaps more important, for the utopian *neutralization* of that order? To reposition *Grimus* within the rich tradition of utopia/SF is therefore to overcome the ideological limits of previous scholarly appraisals and to restore a properly historical context against which the novel's deep political and pedagogical tendencies – as well as its considerable aesthetic accomplishments – may be fully revealed. What is more, such a recontextualization may cast new light not only on the critical history attending Rushdie's celebrated body of work but also on that generic line of postcolonial SF in which his first novel, much to the consternation of postcolonial scholars, unapologetically participates.

A common justification for the critical neglect shown to *Grimus* is its apparent obliviousness to the disciplinary shibboleths of what was, throughout the 1980s, the yet-emergent field of postcolonial studies. From the vantage of the early 1990s institutionalization of the discipline, *Grimus* is not a successful novel because it is not yet an identifiably *postcolonial* one. Mujeebuddin Syed writes in 1994 that "In spite of its brilliant attempt at creating an ironic *meta-histoire*, a sardonic *philosophia perennis*, *Grimus* falters in its failure to countenance post-colonial concerns."[1] Rushdie's Joycean narrative experiments, Syed further argues, "prove inadequate in providing *Grimus* with a mooring, an anchor that can provide its high profile a well-defined identity."[2] Similarly, Catherine Cundy suggests in 1992 that the true value of *Grimus* is simply that it "offers an important insight into the stylistic and thematic preoccupations developed more fully in the author's later work," thus allowing us to see *in embryo* the "areas of debate which are handled with greater depth and maturity in Rushdie's later work."[3] At this apprentice stage, it is suggested, the thematic concerns that will inform subsequent novels (hybridity, the émigré experience, the quest for postcolonial identity, and the ambivalent cultural legacies of imperialism) appear as yet frustratingly inchoate: "the diversity remains just that; the elements insufficiently blended to make the novel appear a skillfully amalgamated whole."[4] *Grimus* is, Cundy contends, "clearly a novel from a period when Rushdie had not yet achieved the synthesis of diverse cultural strands and narrative forms," and it takes only "tentative steps towards an examination of post-coloniality," a question that she describes as "submerged" in the novel's mercurial structure.[5]

Yet, what if these readings assess Rushdie's literary debut according to the wrong criteria, that is, by standards derived from the disciplinary habits of thought that his later work helped to instantiate? Indeed, the above approaches all consider *Grimus* in the light of both *Midnight's Children* and a poststructuralist-inflected postcolonial hermeneutic. If, however, we disregard this interpretive consensus and its fundamental narrative of authorial entelechy, might we then read the novel's unapologetic rejection of a national-cultural habitus not as a failing – as Rushdie's reluctance or, worse, callow inability to situate the book's multiple dislocations within the ambit of the postcolonial nation-state – but rather as the register of an altogether different creative aim?

At least one recent critical response to *Grimus* has taken important steps toward such a reconsideration and provides us a useful point of departure. In an essay tellingly titled "From Science Fiction to History," Andrew Teverson attempts to reclaim *Grimus* as a politically interested work of fiction by distinguishing (some might argue unnecessarily) between the thematic preoccupations of "science fiction" – expressed variously in its futuristic effects, its exposition of alternative causalities, and its "desire to postulate and explore the existence of parallel dimensions" – and the imaginative interventionism of the SF subgenre "speculative fiction," the techniques of which, Teverson notes, "fulfill distinctive political aims" through the operation (though he does not use the term) of a Suvinian *cognitive estrangement*.[6] Rushdie, Teverson points out, does not regard SF "as an end in itself, however, but as a springboard for the exploration of philosophical and political concepts."[7]

Recognizing in the novel's "Conceptualist" philosophical system – by which the Gorfs "create" by simply reconfiguring the sequence of what already is – elements of a familiar poststructuralist epistemology, Teverson suggests that the novel might be read as a self-reflexive "covert analysis" of the limits of poststructuralism itself. The poststructuralist privileging of discourse as anterior to and thus constitutive of both the self and experiential reality is "only a whisper away from the Gorfic assertion that reality is constructed by thought forms and can be transformed by the anagrammatical rearrangement of these thought forms."[8] To this philosophic trend, which was by the mid-1970s rapidly becoming the dominant critical and philosophical discourse in the West, *Grimus* thus poses the central question: "if post-structuralist thought does describe reality as it is, what is that reality and what are its implications for the human condition?"[9] Teverson's analysis here begins to uncover, I think, the primary formal and political contribution of *Grimus* – and perhaps a substantial reason for the book's neglect – though even he reads it as a literary experiment that remains too generalized and culturally incoherent to realize its greater ambitions: "the intellectual explorations conducted in this fiction remain abstract, because they are never explicitly connected to a coherent, identifiable, historical moment."[10]

Thus confronted with the same impasse as previous commentators, Teverson offers the compromise that *Grimus* distinguishes between two conflicting forms of post-structuralism, one that is politically enabling and one that is politically disabling. The differences between these can be most clearly perceived in the Gorf's Divine Game of Order and its important lesser branch, Conceptualism, which originates in a response to a "rare" philosophical pronouncement from the Gorfic leader Dota: "*I think, therefore it is.*"[11] As Rushdie writes, "Dota had intended it to mean simply that nothing could exist without the presence of a cognitive intellect to perceive its existence."[12] The heretical Gorf Koax cleverly "reversed this to postulate that anything of which such an intellect could conceive *must therefore exist*," after which he conceives into existence other dimensions (Endimions) populated with various forms of life, an unprecedented act that understandably unnerves his fellow Gorfs.[13] For Teverson, working through the philosophical divergences and political implications of these primary postulates is the central concern of the book. Thus, in the orthodox model of Dota, he claims, "we engage with an independently existing material world using the structures of thought and structures of narrative that we have available to us," whereas the more heterodox locution of Koax "represents a dangerous form of self-delusion, because it detaches human actions from a material reality, and so relieves human beings of the need for a responsibility to that reality."[14] The problem posed by the novel, Teverson rightly suggests, is clearly that of political agency in the emergence of the postmodern, where, as Rushdie articulates it, "Then, everything was possible. Now, nothing is."[15]

While Teverson's reading does much to illuminate previously overlooked dimensions of the book, both repositioning it as a politically engaged fiction and underscoring the importance of material history in our understanding of it, I recommend that we might also recognize in Koax's radical founding of Conceptualism the initial step in the novel's dialectical unfolding of a specifically utopianist figuration, one that takes place against the "worldless" backdrop of an emergent globalization, the acknowledgment of which restores for us the novel's "missing" cultural context and hermeneutic ground.

Prior to the heretical pronouncement of Koax, our narrator informs us, Gorfic reality consisted of a vacuum-like stasis in which the stony beings sat trapped in "near-immobility and total isolation."[16] Because they lacked a self-substantiating other, the Gorfs could scarcely even verify the presumed superiority of their own culture and so succumbed to a "philosophy of despair" summed up in another of the celebrated utterances of Dota: "*And are we actually to be the least intelligent race in our endimions?*"[17] In a move that anticipates his subsequent major revision of the Divine Game of Order, Koax rejects the inherent pessimism of this worldview in an anagrammatical reformulation of the question: "*Determine how catalytic an elite is; use our talent and learning-lobe.*"[18] This response, our narrator observes, is

> a perfect use of Anagrammar; for not only does it contain all the letters of the Chiefest Question and only those letters, but moreover, it enriches the Question itself, adding to it the concept of elitism and its desirability, the concept of catalysis and its origins, and instructions about how the question should be answered.[19]

That is, Koax's response, while admitting nothing materially extrinsic to the given framework of the original, nonetheless allows, in true dialectical fashion, for the faint recognition of a potentially contradictory impulse within it.

Perhaps even more useful here is the concept that contemporary French philosopher Alain Badiou calls the *void*, the indiscernible excess that "inexists" in the field of the known as the "non-term of any totality."[20] Badiou contends that any situation or field of knowledge also contains within it the not-yet-known, that which can figure into the existing structure only as the unaccountable or impossible. He notes, for instance, that for the ancient Greek Pythagoreans, the numerable domain was composed solely of whole, rational numbers. The discovery that the diagonal of a square to its side is a number neither whole nor rational therefore presents a particularly vexing aporia, especially given that Pythagorean ontology is built on the premise that *being* is consonant with *number*.[21] The paradoxical existence of that which is not denumerable within the ontological realm of number figures a void, or that which exceeds the existing symbolic order and therefore provides an alternate perspective on the present situation, now revealed as contingent and unfinalized, even as it beckons toward an as yet unsymbolizable future configuration. For Badiou, the unnamable nature of the void has specifically political implications because the emergence of the politically agential subject can occur only, as Oliver Feltham glosses it, "through an act of nomination that baptizes the point of impossibility in a structure and forces the latter to accommodate it."[22] The properly political subject is thus the *excess of the existent order*, the uncompromising and impossible demands of which at once rend the fabric of the social totality and clear space for the production of a new one.[23] This is Badiou's (early, Maoist-inflected) version of the *historical* dialectic, a structure, I believe, also very much at work within the narrative composition of *Grimus*.[24]

Calf Island, anagrammar, and the return of the subject

We can first observe the utopian operation of the void in *Grimus* as a philosophical dilemma borne out of the construction of the novel's primary setting, the chronotopically circumscribed, explicitly "utopian" space of Calf Island. Following his rogue act of Conceptualization, Koax reassures his grousing fellow Gorfs by conceiving an Object for each new Endimions that allows its possessor to control access to all other Endimions, a kind of networking system that secures the authority of the Gorfs over their creations. The Object created for Earth, fortuitously discovered by Virgil the gravedigger, is the Stone Rose, contact with which allows Virgil and his later associates Deggle and Grimus to discover the secrets of trans-dimensional "travelling," obtain the elixirs of eternal life and death, and ultimately construct and populate Calf Island, a haven where those "who tire of the world but not of life" may spend eternity indulging their respective intellectual and physical passions.[25]

Serving as the Dantean guide to protagonist Flapping Eagle – who is on a quest to find the now tyrannical Grimus and to rescue his lost sister – Virgil disagrees with Grimus, his erstwhile partner, on the crucial philosophical nature of Calf Island's creation. As Virgil notes in his journal: "We have been building a world. Impossible to say whether we *found* the island or *made* it. I incline to the latter, Grimus to the former. He holds that Conceptual Technology merely reveals existences which mirror your concepts. I am not so sure."[26] Grimus' view, that is, corresponds to the orthodox one delineated by the Gorfic law of Anagrammar, which, until the dramatic reformulation authored by Koax, limited the act of creation to the meager reshuffling of an already existent content. Conversely, Virgil allows for the radical act of creation *ex nihilo*, for the emergence of the pre-theoretical or pre-conceptual, that which has not yet, in Lacanian argot, been inscribed into the Symbolic order but rather bursts upon it as a traumatic irruption of the unsymbolizable Real. Badiou offers us a useful concept here as well, for Koax's revolutionary revision of the divine law of Anagrammar, as progressive as it seems in its immediate context, bears a striking resemblance to what Badiou criticizes as the "structural dialectic," which, through an overly deterministic theory of transformation that privileges the immobilizing circular symmetry of the dissolution of opposites, disallows both contingency and novelty and limits the process of (periodizing, historical) change to local modification rather than systemic transformation.[27] Such a mechanistic/formalistic model collapses the evental void of the situation that marks the site of the subject and thus of authentic political agency. Structural dialecticism, which Badiou comes to associate primarily with the thought of his mentor Althusser,[28] serves only as a way station in the more comprehensively dialectical trajectory (the historical) charted by Badiou's ongoing project and, I want to suggest, Rushdie's first work of fiction. So while Koax's revision is a necessary first step, the novel cannot allow it to be the last.

In what is perhaps the most thorough critical treatment of *Grimus* to date, Roger Y. Clark reads the novel's self-conscious appropriation of various cyclical cosmologies as an index of its poststructuralist sympathies, of its presumed repudiation of the linear and dichotomous in favor of the circular and the plural.[29] Flapping Eagle, whose birth name is Born-From-Dead due to his mother's expiration during childbirth, completes the cycles of his life and of the universe, symbolically returning the latter to a state of cosmic nullity out of which the next age can rise and likewise decline. Thus, according to Clark's interpretation, the novel rehearses a characteristically postmodernist cynicism with regard to emancipatory grand narratives: "Thinking in terms of the *Divine Comedy*, one might see Eagle's fate as a return from the light-filled realms of Heaven to the obscure forest of this world."[30] For Clark, Rushdie's patchwork interpolation of global mythologies simply reinforces the dominant motif of an inescapably recurrent historical cycle:

> Keeping in mind Attar's Qaf, one might note that Attar's pilgrim returns to the mundane world after his union and annihilation. Given the Hindu references in the text, one might conclude that Eagle remains on the wheel of death and rebirth, and that after his heavenly experience with Media he will proceed to a less exalted state of being. This fits with the references to Germanic myth as well, for the afterlife of Gimle is not nearly as exciting as the heroic battles and the eschatological chaos which precede it.[31]

Yet, what if this cyclical worldview, as perfectly consonant with the non-linear, perpetual present of postmodernity (and the structural dialectic) as with the Gorfic doctrine of Anagrammar, is precisely what *Grimus* undertakes to challenge? Applying Badiou's concept of the void, we can determine that the governing structure of the novel is not that of the cycle but rather that of the spiral. As Ernst Bloch reminds us, the cycle, which flatly refuses the radical alterity of the novum, and in which "the Last thing appears simply as the attained return of an already completed First Thing which has been lost or relinquished," is a favored trope of conservative, pseudo-utopian discourse.[32] Conversely, Flapping Eagle's journey to (and beyond) the stronghold of Grimus is punctuated by a series of transgressions and traversals of the dominant structure that Badiou might recognize as the spiraling arc of a truly *political* subject. By positing and then pointedly violating a series of "absolute" horizons, the novel establishes a dialectical pattern that grows increasingly more elaborate as the narrative unfolds and as Flapping Eagle approaches the object of his quest. Moreover, Rushdie's (yet abstract) figuration of this spiraling subjectivity will serve as the archetype for the elaboration of future subjects within and against a fully consolidated globalization, the particulars of which I explore further in chapters 4 and 5 by way of more recent science fictions of India and South Africa.

To begin his journey, Eagle wrenches himself free of the exclusive and static order of the Axona and attains a consciousness of the present *as present*. The opening of chapter two introduces us by way of flashback[33] to the young Eagle as he drowses in the effectively timeless enclosure of the Axona: "The day had begun well enough. That is to say, it resembled the previous day sufficiently (in terms of weather, temperature and mood) to give the half-sleeping young man the illusion of continuity."[34] This sense of continuity is tempered by just enough superficial variation "to produce an equal and opposite illusion of temporal movement."[35] Flapping Eagle basks "pleasurably in these conflicting and harmonious mirages, drifting slowly up towards consciousness, which would banish both and substitute a third illusion: the present."[36] The seeming whole of the present is therefore unmasked by the narrator as a conflict of oppositional tendencies (difference emerging here out of repetition), and Eagle's fleeting meditation on this constitutive contradiction signals the emergence of a discerning historical consciousness, one which will eventually lead him to violate the foremost Axona prohibition: "to be a race apart and have no doings with the wicked world."[37]

In fact, Flapping Eagle himself *embodies* the indiscernible within the Axona community. While the troubling circumstance of his birth from his mother's dead body marks him as ill-omened and his indefinite sex as a child proves an irreducible complication for the Axona's binary gender categories, it is his pigment that ultimately alienates Eagle from his tribe. A dark-skinned people who have never before encountered outsiders, the Axona can interpret Eagle's whiteness only as a horrifying sign of his absolute difference, the acceptance of which would require the utter dismantling of the Axona doctrine of homogeneity. This early exclusion prepares him, he later admits, for his long journey to Calf Island, the first step of which is a willful transgression of the obsessively guarded Axona border. Thus, when the Whirling Demons who, according to Axona legend, both defend and define the tribal boundary are exposed as "nothing but air" (or ideology), what Eagle previously perceived as an absolute limit is revealed as merely the first in a series of barriers to be overcome.[38] It is not then surprising that the first stop on his journey is the city of *Phoenix*, the significance of which would seem to validate the cyclical reading offered by Clark except that we are given no return here but instead the passing of yet another horizon, the forcing open of another asphyxiating circuit into a new space.

Eventually, after many years of travel, the outer boundaries of the world itself become confining, and Eagle imagines himself into the dimension of Calf Island through an impossible hole in the sea. Even on the island, however, he is confronted with complex strata of supposedly unbreachable boundaries. Virgil and Dolores occupy the lowest such stratum of

Calf Island along the coastline, where they have come to escape the steadily spreading Grimus Effect, a kind of debilitating hyper-awareness of both the existing and potential inner and outer dimensions, a condition that can result in mental derangement or even death.

Higher up on the forbidding slopes of the mountain is the island's single settlement of K. To approach K, Eagle must overcome the paralyzing delirium of the Grimus Effect, and his efforts to do so both indicate the novel's self-conscious engagement with poststructuralism and an incipient postmodernity at the same time that they reveal the utopianism inherent in Virgil's guiding philosophy. In explaining the novel properties of interdimensionality, Virgil notes that Eagle must cultivate "a different set of tools of perception," that he must come to the recognition that "the limitations we place upon the world are imposed by ourselves rather than the world."[39] Inherent in such recognition is the perception of the myriad potential realities present within the visible limits of the actual:

> Is it not a conceptual possibility that here, in our midst, permeating all of us and all that surrounds us, is a completely other world, composed of different kinds of solids, different kinds of empty spaces, with different perceptual tools, which make us as non-existent to its inhabitants as they are to ours? In a word, another dimension. ... If you concede that conceptual possibility, said Mr. Jones, you must also concede that there may well be more than one. In fact, that an infinity of dimensions might exist, as palimpsests, upon and within and around our own, without our being in any wise able to perceive them.[40]

Eagle's arrival on Calf Island, one of these "million possible Earths with a million possible histories," signals his special receptivity to such unseen possibilities, a characteristic that, even as it reveals the existence of the Calf Island Endimions also renders him acutely vulnerable to the disorientations of the Grimus Effect and its accompanying "dimension-fever."

Virgil recognizes in Eagle's unique sensitivity, however, the essential utopian characteristic of "unfinishedness," or what Bloch calls the "prospective horizon," the critical vantage of which "incompletes" the inert structure of the present and disturbs what Badiou might call its isotropic vectors. As Virgil informs the young hero, "Mr. Eagle, you are not a realized man. That is your weakness and also your power."[41] It is, we learn, only their relative "completion" that insulates the inhabitants of K from the maddening Effect even as it renders them incapable (indeed, *because* it renders them incapable) of resisting the quiet tyranny of Grimus, who resides on the mountain's peak behind an impenetrable "wall of cloud" that "never lifts."[42]

Mounting the slopes of Calf Mountain with Virgil as guide, Eagle is suddenly overcome with the dimension-fever, significantly described here as a "temporary loss of imagination," and faces his next major challenge in the form of the Abyssinian twins Mallit and Khallit, who are engaged in an argument "without beginning or end, its very lack of purpose or decision undermining Flapping Eagle's ability to think clearly."[43] The mystifying closed circuit of this interminable debate, in which the twin interlocutors exchange positions and perfectly rebut one another, creates yet another airless enclosure, an absolute limit and seemingly insuperable deadlock. As Clark describes it, the twins "throw irreconcilable opposites at Eagle and then make his survival depend upon reconciling them."[44] In so doing, Mallit and Khallit rehearse the defining conflict of Flapping Eagle's existence as well as the formal preoccupations of the novel: "But here's a paradox, said Khallit. Suppose a man deprived of death. Suppose him wandering through all eternity, a beginning without an end. Does the absence of death in him mean that life is also absent?"[45] Thus, they determine, Flapping Eagle is one of the living dead, "Incapable of influencing his own life" and utterly without purpose.[46] But for the timely intervention of Virgil, whose whirling "Weakdance" dissolves the conceptual doublebind, Eagle would certainly have succumbed to the ensnaring and enervating logic of this most postmodern of puzzles, the effectiveness of which derives from a simple paucity of imagination, from Eagle's inability to deny the intolerable terms given him and to choose the seemingly impossible option. After he is rescued and reflects on the anagrammatical rationale of the Mallit/Khallit puzzle, Eagle realizes that the way out, based on a pun told him by the trickster figure Deggle many years earlier, was before him all the time: "Ethiopia ... Abyssinia ... I'll be seeing you ... Goodbye. All he had to do was say Goodbye and the puzzle was solved."[47] In other words, confronted with the absolute foreclusion of agency, all he need do is assert it.

Flapping Eagle's passion for the real

Upon finally arriving in K, Flapping Eagle is obligated by the Doctrine of Obsession to declare a specific personal interest. Under the instruction of resident philosopher Ignatius Quasimodo Gribb, the "petrified" people of K, whose collectivity is defined by national-cultural plurality as much as by the unifying "absence" of Grimus, have devoted themselves single-mindedly to the objects of their respective personal "obsessions," which, as Virgil notes, "close the mind to dimensions" and their array of social alternatives: "Often [the people of K] fix themselves a time in their lives to mull over. Live the same day over and over again. ... Still. If a false front's thick enough, it serves. To protect."[48] As he is told by one of the inhabitants, "We in K ... like to think of ourselves as complete men. Most, or actually all of us have a special area of interest to call our own. I don't think we could accept anyone otherwise."[49] The paralyzing inertia of K (as well as the utopian agenda of the novel) is most clearly and poignantly epitomized by the arrested pregnancy of Irina Cherkassov, who, after drinking the blue elixir of eternal life and retiring to Calf Island, discovered that she was with child: "Can you understand, Flapping Eagle, how that feels? What it is to have a second life stagnant within one's womb, perhaps a genius, perhaps a second idiot, perhaps a monster, as frozen within me as the lovers on the grecian urn?"[50] I.Q. Gribb's personal obsession of choice, the cliché, likewise reinforces the circular (and circumscriptive) logic that characterizes the town of K, its foreclusion of invention: "This, said Gribb, jabbing a finger at the pages, is my great endeavour. The All-Purpose Quotable Philosophy. A quote for all seasons to make life both supportable and comprehensible. A framework of phrases to live within, pregnant with a truly universal meaning."[51]

While this obsessionalism and lack of historical consciousness is conspicuously concentrated in the settlement of K, it defines more broadly the postmodern reality of Calf Island as a whole. Before the catalyzing advent of Eagle as the island's unassimilable surplus, Virgil, along with his lover Dolores, had succumbed completely to the torpor and absolute relativism of the island's perpetual present: "We live wholly in the microcosm, you see; the state of my corns and the state of nations are to me of equal concern. I don't want to preach but I would recommend that you adapt yourself to minutiae; they are so much less confusing."[52] Virgil's worldview rehearses here almost exactly Fredric Jameson's observation that the ideally schizophrenic postmodern subject is "easy enough to please, provided only an eternal present is thrust before the eyes, which gaze with equal fascination on an old shoe or on the tenaciously growing organic mystery of the human toenail."[53] As Virgil goes on to council, "Concentrate on the *here*, Mr. Eagle, that's my advice to you. ... Don't worry about the *there*. Or the Past. Or the Future. Worry about dinner and your corns. Those are things you can affect."[54]

It is Eagle's threat to this perpetual present that most troubles Dolores, who keeps history safely contained in a locked trunk that is never opened:

> Sure, sure, sure, as fixed in the fluid of the years as her immortal body, immortal now as souls, replenished daily, neither growing old nor young, static. The present is tomorrow's past, as fixed, as sure, the trunk would tell her so. ... There, the past. Put him in the trunk, dear gravedigger poet, put him there to stay unaltered, put him in the trunk and keep him, folded, enfolded, the same for ever and ever, world without end, our men.[55]

Dolores' fears prove justified in that Flapping Eagle's arrival almost immediately rouses Virgil both to recall the history of the island and to risk what he later describes as "a return to a long-lost war," thereby abandoning the crippling and ahistorical monotony of his life on the shore with Dolores, who subsequently loses what is left of her tenuous mental equilibrium and commits suicide, the first of several deaths on this island of eternal life.[56]

To the astonishment of everyone in K, Eagle declares his obsession to be Grimus himself, the absent center (or Real) of Calf Island's existence. This choice is particularly disturbing to Gribb, who understands that the pluralistic, individualistic society of K depends for its structural integrity on the amnesiac suppression of the very force that subtends it. The people of K, rapt by the enervating euphoria of their individual obsessions, have so successfully forgotten the existence of Grimus that he has become *myth*, his disavowed phantasmic presence concealed as much by the perceptual limits of cognitive specialization as by the invisible wall of his subdimension. In a structural analogue to the anagrammatical snare of Mallit/Khallit, Flapping Eagle must then search for the symptoms that reveal Grimus' presence while resisting the powerful temptation to succumb to the comforting oblivion of K's perpetual here-and-now.

Eagle's task thus exhibits striking parallels to the "impossible" operation of ideology critique within the smooth space of postmodernity, where reification has pierced every dimension, where no uncolonized locus remains from which one can launch a proper critique, and where the vocabulary of ideology is merely a quaint curiosity. Noting this crisis in his seminal discussion of postmodernism, Jameson writes that with the collapsing of a "minimal aesthetic distance" and the lost "possibility of the positioning of the cultural act outside the massive Being of capital, from which to assault this last," "some of our most cherished and time-honored radical conceptions about the nature of cultural politics may ... find themselves outmoded."[57] The limitations of the traditional leftist critique, the perceptual apparatuses of which are no longer commensurate to the enormity and plasticity of late capital and its penetration of the formerly extrinsic spheres of nature, culture, and the unconscious, are revealed (uncannily, almost a decade before the appearance of Jameson's essay) in the character of P.S. Moonshy, whose Marxist burlesque functions not as an absolute dismissal of the leftist critique but rather as a critical dramatization of the insufficiency of the structural model (Marxism as a "science of history") to address the as yet untheorized problematic of globalized capital. In fact, the amnesiac settlement of K is founded upon a nostalgic preservation of the former model of imperialist/monopoly capitalism and its structural preference for the nation-state: "To be in K was to return to a consciousness of history, of good times, even of nationhood. O'Toole, Cherkassov ... like them or not, the names conjured a past world back to life."[58] But as Eagle's quest reveals, this reality is already obsolete, its old certainties and "structures of feeling" secured only by the absent center of Grimus, who later makes explicit his immanently *material* relationship to the fantasy-space of the island: "And who do you think it is that watches over K? Do you not think those aged houses would have fallen down by now? Do you not think that much-tilled soil would be exhausted by now? Did you ever wonder why Mr. Gribb never ran out of paper or where the metal hinges which held the doors on were made?"[59]

Grimus thus reveals itself as an allegory not of postcolonial national or cultural identity but of the perceived decline of the statist problematic and the rise of what would gradually reveal itself as the new global order. The structural crises of the capitalist system in the late 1960s and early 1970s, characterized by precipitous global stagflation, the waning influence of the Bretton Woods regulations, and the ultimate abandonment of the Keynesian compromise between labor and capital, led finally to the rise of the neoliberal policies and institutions that, by the late 1970s and early 1980s, had achieved full consolidation. From Nixon's abandonment of the gold standard in 1971 to the conclusion of the last imperialist war in 1974[60] to Milton Friedman's Nobel Prize for economics in 1976, the early 1970s saw the end of the old order and a seismic shift in global economic practice that would establish the foundations of the transnationalist capitalism we now call globalization. In Calf Island's deluded orientation toward an outmoded political and economic model, *Grimus* offers both a pre-conceptual mapping of this new global order – taking shape at the very instant of the novel's composition – as well as a necessarily critical engagement with forms of resistance now rendered structurally obsolete.

In his perfunctory protests against the island's aristocratic Cherkassov family, the limits of Moonshy's resistance are thrown into pathetic relief, as are the ways in which that resistance is itself both complicit in and determined by the encompassing system by which this older antagonism has been subsumed. As Badiou notes, what eludes those Marxists who, like Moonshy, honor the ineluctable laws of "bourgeois society" and the "science of history," is the fact that the politicized "proletarian society" for which they wait is determined by the inert structural whole of bourgeois society itself as its internal and sustaining contradiction.[61] Such a dialectical perspective ultimately dissolves its "weak" constitutive contradiction and favors/anticipates the return of the Whole. This, Badiou writes, is a "dialectical materiality without leverage" because it cancels the force of the contradiction and, in its renewing plenitude, forecloses the radical possibilities of the void.

Nonetheless, Eagle is inevitably drawn to Moonshy because he is the only inhabitant of K to doubt openly Gribb's blithe assurance that Grimus does not exist. As Moonshy observes during a characteristic pantomime of slogan-wielding protest in which he declares (presumably not for the first time) his impossible departure from Calf Island, "It is your ideas, Mr. Gribb, that are chiefly responsible for our bondage."[62] Moonshy's "faith" in an invisible oppressor is quickly dismissed by Gribb, who notes that he had always understood the Marxist position to be that it was "superstition that was supposed to provide the opiate of the masses."[63] This exchange is especially remarkable in its anticipation of the work of recent thinkers from the left like Žižek and Badiou, both of whom in fact reclaim the radical structure (if not the substance) of Pauline Christianity as a way to counter the postmodern condition of fragmentary contingency.[64] It is significant then that Eagle's sympathies, revealed here by way of interior monologue, clearly lie with Moonshy's conspiratorial suspicions: "*Unless the superstitions are grounded in fact. In which case, to deny them would indeed be a form of bondage.*"[65] Thus, following a final discouraging exchange with Gribb in which the diminutive collector of clichés rehearses the standard postmodern prohibition against origins ("... origins, beginnings, are valueless. Valueless. Study how we live, by all means. But leave, for goodness' sake, this womb-obsession of yours, this inquiry into birth"), Eagle seeks out Moonshy, who "has struck [him] as a man worth talking to, if only because he had questioned the sovereignty of Gribb's ideas."[66]

However, upon visiting his home and observing the fading placards on Moonshy's walls, "screaming defiance at long-gone tyrannies," Eagle comes to the crucial realization that Moonshy "differed from the rest only in his choice of obsession," that his predictable challenges to the system were, first, challenges to an already superseded system, and, second, already assimilated within the routine operation of the existing one.[67] As Eagle observes of Moonshy's presumably endless deferral of revolutionary action, "He was secure in his attitudes, as he would never have to carry them to their logical conclusion."[68]

Awaiting the vulgar Hegelian evolutionary transformation/politicization of K's inhabitants, Moonshy's complacency recalls Žižek's reformulation of Lacan's knave/fool opposition. The knave, which Lacan defines as the "conformist who considers the mere existence of the given order as an argument for it," could formerly be identified with the conviction of the traditional Right that there could be no viable alternative to free market neoliberalism.[69] On the other hand, the traditional Leftist (Moonshy) assumes the role of the fool, who, while exposing the limitations and contradictions of the existent order, "suspends the performative efficiency of his speech."[70] In the moment of postmodernity, however, Žižek contends that these traditional roles have been complicated if not wholly inverted: the "radicalism" of the postmodernist Left (for Žižek here, manifest in the work of Laclau and Butler) results in a "cynical resignation" to the unalterable fact of global capital, while the Right assumes a "more attractive" Pascalian commitment that simultaneously reveals the essential hidden mechanisms of the system.[71] The way out of this crippling impasse, Žižek argues, is for the postmodern Leftist knave to reject the pseudo-activity of a merely revisionist hegemonic struggle within the horizon of the present system and to "*hold this utopian place of the global alternative open*, even if it remains empty, living on borrowed time, awaiting the content to fill it in."[72] If Moonshy's traditional Leftist position of the fool is insufficient to address the situation of an emergent globalization, so too is the knavist strategy of the postmodern Left. Once more, Eagle must resolve an impossible deadlock and manifest what Badiou might characterize as the lack of that which is lacking, the dialectical exposure and abolition of the disavowed founding exclusion (Grimus himself) upon which rests the existent order.

Thus, while Teverson recognizes the way in which the "logic of the novel seems to reflect the charge leveled against postmodernism and post-structuralism" (118) by thinkers like Jameson and Aijaz Ahmad (the two he cites), allowing for a reading in which a totalizing political agency is not wholly abandoned, by framing Eagle's activity as a form of "good" postructuralism, he reduces Eagle's disappointing encounter with Moonshy to a metonymic recapitulation of what he implicitly identifies as the novel's ultimate thematic imperative, the futility of resistance:

> Eagle believes that he is acting according to his own free will. When he reaches Grimus's home, however, it is revealed to him that his entire adventure, from the moment he left home to his confrontation with Grimus, has been plotted by the magician. Even his revolutionary desire to destroy Grimus and liberate the people of Calf Island, Flapping Eagle discovers, is part of Grimus's plan to complete the mythic structure of his life by making Flapping Eagle his 'death.' Flapping Eagle's act of resistance is, thus, like Moonshy's, because it becomes nothing more than a confirmation of Grimus's absolutist agendas. (118)

We can identify this tendency in many postmodern SF narratives of the West, including the *Matrix* trilogy, in which the revolutionary promise with which the first film concludes is betrayed by the realization in the two sequels that Neo's resistance is a function of the system's routine self-maintenance, reducing "revolution" to merely cyclical "revolutions." It is precisely at this point of what appears to be a purely negative dialecticism, however, that a reconsideration of the book's generic link to utopia/SF can offer an alternative perspective on the seemingly forlorn conclusion of *Grimus*. To this end, I offer, the lesson Eagle learns from his encounter with Moonshy – that the terrain has fundamentally shifted – is indispensable for our understanding of Eagle's final, heroic act.

Space, subsumption, neutralization

After visiting Virgil's ex-wife Liv[73] and enduring the requisite sexual humiliation (Liv's indirect vengeance on Grimus for a previous slight), Eagle receives a startling invitation to the otherwise inaccessible fortress of Grimushome itself:

> The house was wildly irregular, its walls anything but straight, no corner at a right angle, but it was a designed eccentricity, a deliberate folly. The zigzag patterns it wove on the mountaintop were purposeful, reflections of their creator.

> Reflections: the house gave them off in all directions, for every window in its wondering walls was also a mirror. This combination of undulating stone and blind, gleaming windows made the house curiously difficult to focus upon, as if his eyes refused to accept it, as if it was an illusion that would not harden into fact.[74]

This incredible description recalls *avant la lettre* postmodern architecture's much-discussed production of hyperspace, the structural bewilderments of which impose a disjuncture between the individual and her (social or natural) environment. Like the reflective "glass skin" of Jameson's famous Bona Ventura Hotel, the exterior of Grimushome also "achieves a peculiar and placeless dissociation" from its surroundings, making it impossible to fix one's gaze on the physical contours of the building, reflecting instead "only the distorted images of everything that surrounds it."[75] As Jameson observes, this disconnection "itself stands as the symbol and analogon of that even sharper dilemma which is the incapacity of our minds ... to map the great multinational and decentered communicational network in which we find ourselves caught as individual subjects" in the cultural moment of late capital.[76] In the architectonic complexities of Grimushome, Eagle confronts physically the "deliberate folly" of an emergent globalization's disjunctive spatial logic and reveals the novel's tendency toward a critical cognitive mapping of postmodern space itself. Thus, when Grimus reveals to him the Rose Room at the hidden geometric center of Grimushome, Eagle observes of the structure's obfuscating design, "So that was why the house was such a crazy shape. Its labyrinthine excesses fogged the brain to such an extent that the presence of this small room went completely unnoticed."[77]

The novel's *mise en scène* is again revealed at the nexus of postmodern space, ideology, and resistance. Just as he has violated the inviolable taboos of his Axona home and ventured beyond the whirling demons to the ends of the earth only to pass beyond even that absolute boundary, just as he has entered the invisible fortress of Calf Island's non-existent oppressor, Eagle makes his way past the mystifying veils of Grimushome to the totem object and source of Grimus' power, an object that represents both the island's link to myriad potential dimensions and its assimilation within the multidimensional dominion of the Gorfs: the Stone Rose.

Naturally, Eagle's first impulse is to destroy the object that has generated so much grief, a course of action not without considerable risk, as Virgil forewarns: "It is possible that this dimension cannot survive without the Rose. What is certain is that no-one will survive here, except for spiders, flies and animals, unless the Rose is broken. So it is a risk we must take."[78] Led to the secret chamber of the Rose, Eagle announces his intent to destroy it, to which Grimus responds with a curious final plea: "I foresaw I would have great difficulty in getting you to see my point of view, he said. It was for this reason that I conceptualized the Subsumer. If you take the other handle, we can communicate telepathically. Through the medium of this sphere."[79] Grasping the handle of the device, Eagle's mind is immediately penetrated by the invading consciousness of Grimus. As their psyches inextricably combine, his last coherent thought is of Grimus' smug words: *"My old mother always told me you've got to trick people into accepting new ideas."*[80]

While ideological manipulation and the mechanisms of cultural hegemony clearly inform Grimus' strategy here, most striking is Rushdie's choice for their vehiculation. Closely following Eagle's disillusionment with Moonshy's obsolescent model of the gradual politicization of the proletariat, the violent sublation of his mind by Grimus's machine explicitly anticipates the recent resurgence of interest in Marx's theory of *subsumption*. Describing the process by which capital internalizes that which is exterior or autonomous, Marx distinguishes between *formal* and *real* subsumption. The former he designates as the requisite expansion of capitalist markets and the incorporation of the means of production outlying capital's immediate reach. The latter, however, marks what Hardt and Negri characterize as an "intensive" rather than "expansive" integration of labor such that capital folds in on itself and thoroughly penetrates and transforms its own relations of production.[81] Comparing Foucault's account of the passage from the society of discipline to that of control to Marx's theory of subsumption, Hardt and Negri note that the radical internalizing force of real subsumption incorporates "not only the economic or only the cultural dimension of society but rather the social *bios* itself."[82] By reconfiguring the "linear and totalitarian figure of capitalist development," the real subsumption of globalization/postmodernity sees the full absorption of global society in the transition from imperialism to Empire and the consequent relocation of resistance from the former margins of the centralized power structure to the "thousand plateaus" of its now thoroughly deterritorialized network.[83] Simply put, under postmodernity, Hardt and Negri claim, "there is no more outside."[84] And this is the crucial (and, for some, controversial) point for Hardt and Negri's theorization of a "postmodern" political agency: real subsumption is not the victorious culmination of the internalizing processes begun by an earlier formal subsumption; rather, formal subsumption itself creates the conditions of emancipatory struggle, in the form of "class" consciousness, which its disciplinary practices and institutions then prove insufficient to contain. The emergence of real subsumption is thus a consequential – and necessarily defensive – response to the new desiring subjectivities brought about by the processes of formal subsumption. Moonshy's resistance is no longer effective because he continues to misdirect his political ire at the conscriptive forces "out there," because, unlike Eagle, he fails to recognize that the system has no exterior. Thus, after his consciousness is subsumed by Grimus, Eagle can no longer distinguish between himself and his foe; he has become the very thing he opposed and faces the last and most insuperable boundary, the suffocating closed circuit of the structural dialectic in which the apparently oppositional forces of Eagle and Grimus are reunited in a synthetic whole.

This impasse brings us then to the novel's ostensibly cynical conclusion. In the final confrontation with his adversarial double (just prior to his revealing of the Subsumer), Grimus details for Eagle the impossibility of resistance: "Since you do not know how to conceptualize the coordinates of your Dimension, you cannot leave the island. ... You cannot stay among the Kaf's inhabitants, bearing my face. Your only alternative is suicide, and once I have shown you my marvels you will not wish to do so."[85] In an explicit recapitulation of the cyclical motif identified by Clark, Grimus reveals that Eagle has been carefully selected and groomed as his replacement as ruler of Calf Island and keeper of the Stone Rose: "It is both psychologically and symbolically satisfying. The period of stability containing within itself the seeds of its own downfall. The cataclysm being followed by a new and very similar order. It is aesthetic. It is right."[86] Free will, Grimus goes on to say, is illusory. One's behavior is governed by a limited number of flux lines suggestive of a finite number of potential actions, all of which Grimus has anticipated through the power of the Rose.[87]

Eagle's response to these revelations is notable not simply for its obvious posture of defiance, but for the particular manner in which it rejects the delimitations of Grimus' forced choice: "But in the end it all depends on me, Grimus, in some way which you haven't yet explained. It all hangs on my choice and I tell you now that I am not going to play."[88] This refusal to (re)act both repeats the novel's fundamental debate regarding the possibility of radical agency in the vacuum of postmodernity and illuminates Eagle's dramatic final act of defiance: the unmaking of Calf Island. Faced with the futility of any action, either positive or negative, Eagle chooses the impossible option of refusing to act at all, a choice with profound political implications. In a recent exploration of the concept of violence, Slavoj Žižek discusses the revolutionary power concentrated in the mass repudiation of one of the essential "democratic rituals of freedom":

> What happens is that by abstaining from voting, people effectively dissolve the government – not only in the limited sense of overthrowing the existing government, but more radically. Why is the government thrown into such a panic by the voters' abstention? It is compelled to confront the fact that it exists, that it exerts power, only insofar as it is accepted as such by its subjects – accepted even in the mode of rejection. The voters' abstention goes further than the intra-political negation, the vote of no confidence: it rejects the very frame of decision.[89]

Eagle's act is thus not one of simple passivity, but rather one that violently refuses the constraints of a forced "pseudo-activity" the purpose of which is to secure the operation and legitimacy of the existent system.[90]

Rather than validate the terms of the status quo through either capitulation or reactionary negation, Eagle instead imagines a new set of terms. Momentarily tempted to preserve the Rose, to appropriate its limitless power for good, Eagle suddenly recalls the "people of K reduced to a blind philosophy of pure survival, clutching obsessively at the shreds of their individuality, knowing within themselves that they were powerless to alter the circumstances in which they lived."[91] Instead of acting in reformist fashion from within (and thereby perpetuating) the stable coordinates of an assumed ground, Eagle simply reimagines the ground itself, reconceptualizing Calf Island from scratch and dismantling the ideological obstructions of Grimus' sub-endimions: "I made a picture grow in my head, a picture of Calf Island as one thing, Grimushome at its peak, the steps leading down to Liv's outcrop. No Gates, no barriers."[92] Next, he carefully re-imagines into existence every molecular detail of Calf Island save one, the Stone Rose itself. Elated by their continued existence in the absence of the Rose, guarantor of Calf Island's former reality, Eagle and Media spontaneously make love on the mountainside as strange mists begin to gather:

> Slowly, slowly, they were descending, closing in upon the island on all sides, closer, closer, a dense grey fog now, closing, closing. And

> they were not mists. Deprived of its connection with all relative Dimensions, the world of Calf Mountain was slowly unmaking itself, its molecules and atoms breaking, dissolving, quietly vanishing into primal, unmade energy.[93]

By rejecting the fundamental framework of Grimus' system rather than merely opposing it (after the classic agonistic pattern represented by Moonshy), Eagle opens up the truly radical space of possibility, the literal "no-place" of utopian figuration or, in Louis Marin's terms, the space of the *neutral*, which he describes as a kind of consciousness that is not yet a consciousness of the definite. The virtuality of the neutral, in itself "unthinkable, imponderable," reveals the limits of thought within the lifeworld of the system and thus traces a kind of "zero" that is not yet the third term beyond binary opposition but rather the non-space out of which such a third term might emerge:[94]

> it is the synthesis of the contraries reduced to a state of pure virtuality. ... Neither one nor the other, waiting to be one *and* the other, it has the power (for it is no longer simply passage from one to the other) to allow both to recognize the figure of their superior unity and mastery. The neutral is also the sign of the absolute 'polemicity' and the mark of their mutual destruction.[95]

Thus, we might also recognize the neutralization of Calf Island (quite literally realizing a dialectical double negation) as the site of Badiou's void, what we have defined as the ruptural gap within a situation that marks the evental site, fidelity to which consecrates the new political subjectivity. Beyond the constraints of conventional or traditional significations, laws, and philosophies, the void is the pre-symbolic space of a situation yet to come. Necessarily founded upon the insubstantial and incommunicable, fidelity to the event demands a decisive act on the part of the subject, an act that, from within the enclosures of the present situation, appears nonsensical if not literally unimaginable. As the examples cited above demonstrate, this kind of fidelity to an unseen truth, punctuated by a series of impossible assertions, characterizes Eagle's quest from its beginning in Axona to its culmination on Calf Island, such that the no-place of the novel's conclusion realizes "a new coherence that is instituted by the interruption of the repetitive series that made up the whole previous social order."[96] By situating the novel's conclusion within the context of a radical utopianism, we therefore complicate politically cynical (and cyclical) readings – Uma Parameswaran observes, for instance, that "at the end Eagle and Media presumably return to the world as we know it"[97] – and discover instead ways in which *Grimus*, by periodizing or historicizing the "worldless" present, opens imaginative space for a world yet to be.

Liv's disclosure/recital of Virgil's journal to Flapping Eagle helps, for example, to contextualize an earlier passage, during Flapping Eagle's mortal struggle with the Inner Dimensions, in which the narrator alludes to Virgil's former partnership with Grimus and Deggle:

> There had been trips to the real, physical, alternative space-time continua. So close, yet such an eternity away. And there had been his own annihilating journey into the Inner Dimensions, like the internal inferno which now clutched Flapping Eagle, which had left him hollow and impotent and lucky to be alive. And there was the third kind.
>
> The Bridge between the first two kinds.
>
> With sufficient imagination, Virgil Jones had found, one could *create* worlds, physical, external worlds, neither aspects of oneself nor a palimpsest-universe.
>
> Fictions where a man could live.
>
> In those days, Mr. Jones had been a highly imaginative man.[98]

Virgil's theoretical "third space," a tangible, material reality that is neither the internal fantasy-space of individual wish fulfillment nor the zero-sum reality of Grimus, in which transformation is reduced to reorganization, defines for us the novel's underlying utopianist agenda. This gesture toward an interstitial third space, an *impossible* alternative situated beyond the terms of a constrictive binary formulation, announces the dialectical project at the novel's heart as well as its attention not to the defined problematic of postcolonial national/cultural identity, but to the as yet uncharted topoi of an ongoing globalization. Therefore, with Teverson, I argue that the tension between the opposed philosophical perspectives of Virgil and Grimus lies at the very center of the novel's sociopolitical engagement and, I would add, provides the fundamental contradiction from which emerges the book's radically utopian impulse. Unlike Teverson, however, I contend that the developmental trajectory of Rushdie's fiction is not "from science fiction to history" but rather *to* history *through* science fiction.[99] That is, *Midnight's*

Children is the result not of the hard-scrabble lessons Rushdie managed to salvage from the submerged wreck of his first, failed novel but of the narrative strategies and historical sensibilities *successfully* worked out through its composition. Indeed, it is tempting to claim that we cannot properly read *Midnight's Children* without first having read *Grimus* or that, having now read the latter, we can no longer read the former as the book we once thought it was. And inasmuch as this later work helped to instantiate the field of postcolonial studies, we must likewise consider the implications of its having been a work of science fiction all along.

2

"The Only Way Out is Through": Spaces of Narrative and the Narrative of Space in Nalo Hopkinson's *Midnight Robber*

If in Rushdie's unlocalizable structural abstractions we can recognize the mapping of a nascent globalization, then the work of Nalo Hopkinson provides, from the millennial vantage of the system's quarter-century maturation, a critical schematization more directly rooted in a lived experience of place. Notable for its novel injection of Afro-Caribbean mythology into science fiction (SF), Hopkinson's work is motivated by a dialectical formal logic that militantly opposes the discretionary binaries of mind/body, developed/developing, inner/outer, and so on and attempts to restore or invent a perspective capable of penetrating these perceptual barriers. Such a tendency is already evident in her award-winning debut novel *Brown Girl in the Ring* (1998), which considers the tenuous existence of a predominately immigrant Caribbean community residing in the decaying metropolitan core of a near-future Toronto (where the Jamaican-born Hopkinson has lived since 1977), a cityscape abandoned by governmental authority and private interest alike. The Burn, as this lawless core is called, is overseen by the gangster Rudy, whose authoritarian capacity for violence is achieved through the evil misuse of Afro-Caribbean Obeah to create zombified servants by separating the body from its animating spirit. The long-lost mother of Ti-Jeanne, the novel's young heroine, has been transformed into such a servant: divided from her wandering, insensate physical form, her spirit becomes a soucouyant, a vampire-like creature assuming the shape of a floating fireball. Cut loose from the material impedimenta of the body, these beings enjoy a kind of artificial autonomy, floating effortlessly through space, across borders and partitions, free from all privation and hunger and pain. Such liberatory delights tempt the young Ti-Jeanne in her climactic confrontation with Rudy, and she very nearly consents to the transformation just as she very nearly consents to leaving the Burn for the gated communities of the suburbs and their analogous assurances of freedom from material constraint. Thus, through its unique redeployment of the zombie motif, *Brown Girl* reveals the structural complicities obtaining in the fortified "satellite cities" of the suburbs – bastions of law and order, the capitalist dream come true – and the disavowed, but structurally essential wasteland of the Burn and also, therefore, between Rudy – the seemingly autonomous warlord – and an ineffectual government beholden to private interest. For Rudy's vile predations are merely at the behest of the Canadian Premier, whose withdrawal from the impoverished city core facilities a more efficient extraction of its material resources: in this case, the organs of its inhabitants, who, in the absence of governmental authorization, are no longer "citizens" as such. The utopian intervention of *Brown Girl* effects, however, the return of an obstinate materiality to the disembodied cerebrum of the post-industrial suburb (even as it indicates the paradoxical growth of "third worlds" in the first) through a possession that is not spiritual but emphatically physical. In the book's final chapters, the successful transplantation of (Ti-Jeanne's murdered grandmother) Mami Gros-Jeanne's heart into the body of Premier Uttley has unintended effects: simply, Uttley's literal change of heart results in a change of economic policy, one in which the rejuvenation of the city center is entrusted to the cultivation of the talents and creative energies of its inhabitants rather than to the venal seduction of private interests, one in which squatter's rights trump private property and in which government-provided interest-free loans build small, locally owned enterprises. It figures, in other words, the return of both the public and the political.

Hopkinson's more ambitious sophomore effort, much like the justly celebrated *Brown Girl*, is characterized by the innovative blending of narrative SF and Caribbean folklore and an attention to the spatio-ideological mechanisms of millennial capital. Elaborating on the basic dialecticism of her first novel, *Midnight Robber* attempts to restore a stereoscopic critical vision capable not only of registering simultaneously the *here* and *there* but also of discerning their structural interdependencies on a scale both more conceptually comprehensive and more sharply focused. Also in the tradition of the postcolonial *bildungsroman*, it presents the story of Tan-Tan, the pre-adolescent daughter of Antonio, the mayor of Cockpit County on the futuristic planet of Toussaint. Toussaint is home to a non-specifically Afro-Caribbean population[1] who colonized the planet well prior to the events of the narrative and has, in the intervening centuries, established an advanced, technocratic society monitored by omnipresent artificial intelligence. When Antonio discovers that his wife Ione has been having an affair with his best friend Quashee (one of Hopkinson's several nods to the famous Jamaican slave and folk hero Jack Mansong), he challenges Quashee to a version of the traditional Jibaro machete fight. To ensure that he receives satisfaction for the insult of cuckoldry, Antonio tips his machete with a poison (*woorari*) intended to slow the younger, more skillful Quashee. The dose proves fatal, however, and, to escape punishment, Antonio is forced to flee through a field called the dimension veil into New Half-Way Tree, an alternate "version" of Toussaint that functions effectively as the planet's own past: it contains the flora and fauna eradicated during the colonization of Toussaint and is used chiefly as a prison world from which there is no possibility of return. Antonio receives the *woorari* from Mako, member of a mysterious quasi-Luddite society of pedicab operators. These pedicab "runners" are in fact descended from a clan of computer programmers who have learned to mimic the language of the governing AI program and thereby disrupt its ubiquitous surveillance, a talent which also provides Antonio and Tan-Tan the means of escape.

After passage into New Half-Way Tree, Antonio begins sexually abusing Tan-Tan, coercing her into the role of his lost wife. On her sixteenth birthday, as he attempts to rape her, Tan-Tan fatally stabs Antonio and, to escape the undiscerning, retributive justice system enforced by sheriff One-Eye and his deputized cronies, flees into the forest, where she is sheltered by the primitive Douen, a tree-dwelling, indigenous species. Her guilt, homologous to the spatial logic of the novel, manifests in a psychic schism: good Tan-Tan and bad Tan-Tan.[2] To atone for the death of her father, caused by "bad" Tan-Tan, she adopts the powerful persona of the Robber Queen and engages in a series of daring, Jack Mansong-inspired raids, righting social wrongs, defending the poor and the weak against the predations of the powerful, and delivering her own version of justice to the various, often lawless settlements and townships throughout New Half-Way Tree. Her adventures, occasionally violent, are made all the more audacious by the fact that she is pregnant with Antonio's child, with whose redemptive birth the novel concludes as Tan-Tan ultimately finds love and happiness in the idyllic New Half-Way Tree settlement of Sweet Pone.

Utopian circumscription and the problem of history

Jameson maintains that a defining generic feature of narrative SF is its ability to dramatize productively the spatial, temporal, and narrative contradictions concerning the utopian problem of closure, the formal necessity of circumscribing an autonomous chronotopic totality while simultaneously maintaining some meaningful and interpretable connection with the present.[3] Thus, a common anxiety expressed by standard criticisms of utopia (and a common motif of the anti-utopia) is the fear of the loss of the familiar, the annihilation of the known world (including its insufficiencies and injustices) by that which is wholly and terrifyingly unknown. The torsion of this simultaneous impossible need for and fear of a formal break provides, however, the dialectical engine that drives the narrative utopia. The signature utopian gesture is therefore a conspicuous (often forced) spatial closure that is both an effect and a precondition of its narrative complement. In digging his trench and making an island of a peninsula, Thomas More's King Utopus effects the totalizing gesture that not only severs Utopia from the woeful constraints of history and geopolitical reality – allowing for new formations – but also results in the generic novelty and hence vexing formal problems of *Utopia*. This "constitutive secession" is a necessary one in that it avoids the compromises and potential complicities of a mere reformism and thereby clears imaginative space for the emergence of a fully mature consciousness of radical alterity.[4]

Midnight Robber achieves a no less dramatic and no less ambiguous severance from the realm of history with its construction of the extraterrestrial Caribbean utopia of Toussaint. At first glance, the syncretic, pan-Caribbean culture of Toussaint, named for the patriarch of the Haitian revolution, connotes an obsessive historical awareness; its culture is superficially aswarm with historical references and with invocations of luminaries from various anti-colonial and nationalist struggles throughout the archipelago: Granny Nanny and the Maroons, Marcus Garvey, T.A. Marryshow, "Three-Finger" Jack Mansong, and so on.[5] The reader soon discovers, however, that these figures are bereft of any but the most tangential and memorial historical significance. Even the traditional fete of Jonkanoo is a distorted and historically anemic variant of the subversive masquerade of its terrestrial ancestor. No longer a celebration of defiance, the historical significance of the festival and its attendant forms of cultural expression are either wholly forgotten or woefully diluted. The truth of the Toussaint carnival's ahistorical nature (its function as ideology) is revealed fully only at the novel's conclusion, when Tan-Tan attends carnival on New Half-Way Tree. Accustomed to the choreographed spectacle of the Toussaint celebration, she is initially unimpressed by the New Half-Way Tree celebration's random rusticity: "Truth to tell, nothing could be completely right about Carnival in this shadow land of New Half-Way Tree. Everyone here was an exile; this could only be a phantom of the celebration they would have had on Toussaint."[6] She quickly realizes, however, that this more unrefined celebration, populated by Pissenlit bands and long-forgotten characters from the carnival of Old Masque, possesses a crucial quality missing from its Toussaint counterpart: "Carnival was bringing people together on New Half-Way Tree" in a manner unimaginable on Toussaint.[7]

The traditional shipshaped hats of Jonkanoo, once crafted as symbolic reminders of the Middle Passage, are reduced on Toussaint to replicas of the Black Star Line II, the commercial fleet of nation ships that effected the colonization of the planet (and presumably others like it) some two centuries prior to the action of the novel. The ships are the property of the intergalactic Marryshow Corporation, named for T.A. Marryshow, a central figure in Grenada's fight for independence. The iconic leader of the Jamaican Maroons, Granny Nanny, has likewise been co-opted and banalized as the acronymic identity of the Grande Nanotech Sentient Interface, Hopkinson's matriarchal variation on Orwell's Big Brother, an omniscient and ostensibly benignant artificial intelligence that controls the planet through the perpetual surveillance and management of "earbugs," cybernetic nanotechnology that binds each subject of Toussaint to the Anansi Web.

The gulf of interstellar space thus proves a sufficient bulwark against history, leaving only its thoroughly evacuated and safely sublimated (if not overtly commodified) forms and providing the requisite spatial condition for "utopian" totality. As Hopkinson reflects in an interview:

> At some point, most of the way through creating the world I needed to write the story, I realized to my surprise that I had created a utopia. ... There are no poor people on Toussaint, and no wage slaves. And though Granny Nanny perceives all, she doesn't tell all, unless she thinks it's an issue of someone's safety. It really does feel like being mothered, and sometimes that's a good thing, sometimes it's a smothering thing.[8]

But the formal paradox of the utopian constitutive secession (in which also resides its pedagogical charge) is that it cannot and *must not* achieve a clean and absolute withdrawal from history. Utopian fiction, as Matthew Beaumont recently puts it, "necessarily remains anchored in the room in which it is written. ..."[9] If the utopian formulation manages too successfully this historical severance, if it figures an "otherwhere" that is not simultaneously an invested critical engagement with the present, it risks subjection to what Louis Marin terms "utopic degeneration" (or historical Disneyfication) and is summarily disempowered as an effective means of imagining otherwise.[10]

If utopia does not define a place discretely outside this one, neither does it script a specific political schematic, for "When utopia becomes a political project or platform for action, its content becomes a day-dream or a fantasy, even a trap in reality."[11] The authentically utopian narrative is therefore of necessity a failure, an alternative reality whose inability to exist in our own all the more emphatically enunciates its utopian call by making apparent the distance between the actual and the possible. Indeed, as Jameson declares, "Only in the cheapest generic Science Fiction does the revolution triumph" and succeed in surmounting and thereby merely supplanting the forces arrayed against it.[12] The operative mode of the SF and utopian text is not, therefore, merely predictive in the sense that it neither accurately forecasts nor even imaginatively prepares the reader for an *imminent* future. Rather, the "deepest vocation" of the SF text, Jameson vigorously maintains, is its ability "over and over again to demonstrate and to dramatize our incapacity to imagine the future" as such, and in so doing, to perform the crucial work of historicizing the present.[13] Utopia becomes in this formulation not a static locus of achieved meliorist or millenialist fantasy but rather the roving imaginative principle and restless dialectical figuration of social possibility itself.

It is for this reason that the futuristic, technocratic (even post-political) society of Toussaint, despite both its formal circumscription and Hopkinson's claims for its near-perfection, is exposed as a *false* utopia, as an ideological construct that replicates rather than interrogates the interests of the status quo. In declaring it as such, I offer an alternative reading to that of Ingrid Thaler, who identifies in the novel a recuperation and strategic refunctioning of the political utopias of the 1970s for the turn of the millennium.[14] Curiously, in a 2001 conversation with Elisabeth Vonarburg, Hopkinson unequivocally distances *Midnight Robber* altogether from the tradition of the narrative utopia, declaring, "Utopia is dead; dynamic tension reigns."[15] How does one reconcile this statement with her above-cited claim that she has in *Midnight Robber* inadvertently realized a functional utopia? If utopia in fact now exists, as Lyman Tower Sargent claims, "almost solely as a subtype of science fiction,"[16] we might revisit the curious question posed by Gordon Collier in his early critical assessment of *Midnight Robber*: "Does Nalo Hopkinson take science fiction seriously?"[17] Indeed, what might it mean for a Jamaican-born writer to take SF seriously at the threshold of the new millennium?

We might first more thoroughly explore Collier's justification for this query: Hopkinson does not, he points out, exploit in "futuristic" terms the ensemble of SF themes and tropes that her narrative effectively, if merely superficially, assembles. Rather, Collier deems Hopkinson a gifted "*bricoleuse* who gathers sci-fi elements and achieves cohesion not via a sci-fi vision but via a Caribbean enthnocultural dynamic," what Collier usefully describes as a "future, displaced Caribbean that can serve to explore socio-ethical ideas that are relevant to the character of present-day Caribbean societies."[18] If, Collier contends, SF "offers Hopkinson a set of counters to work with," she ultimately fails to "explore them as such, in a sense of working out forms of technological 'originality'."[19] While Hopkinson may therefore take the generic integuments of SF seriously, these are all merely "drawn from earlier science fiction which itself may have provided great elaboration of, and granted great centrality to, the devices and processes involved."[20] Taking SF seriously, Collier seems to suggest, means subordinating socio-spatial considerations and imaginative coordinates to temporal and processional ones. Even the technological dimension of Collier's implicit definition of SF is important primarily because of its association with a conceivable temporal future that can be charted by way of techno-scientific ingenuity and rational extrapolation. But as Louis Marin insistently cautions, "Utopia is not tomorrow, in time. It is *nowhere*, neither tomorrow nor yesterday."[21] And as Jameson reminds us, technology in itself is "little more than the outer emblem or symptom"[22] or "the result of the development of capital rather than some ultimately determining instance in its own right."[23]

Space, narrative, mapping

Collier's implied definition of SF might be read as a textbook example of what Jameson calls the "canonical defense of the genre," in which the SF narrative acts to mediate and mollify the alienating effects of modern life and the daily experiences of "future shock" that it precipitates.[24] According to this reading, SF texts "train our organisms to expect the unexpected and thereby insulate us, in much the same way that, for Walter Benjamin, the big-city modernism of Baudelaire provided an elaborate shock-absorbing mechanism" for the novel bewilderments of the nineteenth-century industrial metropole.[25] Against the canonical defense, Jameson proposes that SF is a genre increasingly preoccupied with and defined by its attention to problems of containment, closure, and form, in short, of the management and imaginative production of space. As he writes of SF in 1987,

> the more deliberate move, which we can witness everywhere in the genre today ... is less a matter of the extrapolation of forms of individual destinies onto collective histories ... than it is of the mediation of space itself; and the collective adventure accordingly becomes less that of a character...than that of a planet, a climate, a weather and a system of landscapes – in short, a map. We thus need to explore the proposition that the distinctiveness of SF has less to do with time (history, past, future) than with space.[26]

Here, Jameson explicitly declares the affinities of the imaginative and deeply pedagogical projects of SF and the narrative utopia with that of his own provocative intellectual/aesthetic model of *cognitive mapping*, of which he famously claims in its inaugural presentation, "I know nothing whatsoever, except for the fact that it does not exist."[27] The need for historicizing the opaque present, or fixing "the intolerable history of the present with a naked eye," is a familiar and well-nigh foundational utopian preoccupation.[28] Bloch calls this problem the *darkness of the lived moment*, of which he observes, "The Here and Now lacks the distance which does indeed alienate us, but makes things distinct and surveyable. Thus, from the outset, the immediate dimension within which realization occurs seems darker than the dream image, and occasionally barren and empty."[29] Similarly, Paul Ricoeur claims that his special interest in utopia is due to its utterly unique "capacity to break through the thickness of reality."[30]

For Jameson, the repudiation of totality characteristic of almost all strands of postmodern thought (including those elements of postcolonial and/or third-world studies operating under its authoritative imprimatur) is not "a thought in its own right but rather a significant symptom, a function of the increasing difficulties in thinking of such a set of interrelationships" in the epoch of late capitalism.[31] Hence, the structural limitation of Pordzik's critical hermeneutic is revealed: the inability to preserve the possibility of specific social transformation in local contexts that simultaneously imagines and confronts the global systemic structures that inform those local realities. While I do not wish to rehearse here the numerous critiques and counter-critiques of Jameson's reclamation of the concept of totality, I would like to explore ways in which Hopkinson's narrative figuration attempts to suture the growing chasm between the local and the global, between those oppressive structures visible in one's immediate cultural or national context and the invisible, unsymbolizable systemic conditions that generate and undergird that socio-spatial reality in the first place – in short, the ways in which the dialecticism of Hopkinson's imaginative cartography neither precludes the relevance of micropolitical struggles nor is bound or enfeebled by them. It is in this articulation of the local/global dialectic that Hopkinson advances and complicates the model of spatial and subjective abstraction offered by Rushdie's *Grimus*.

As with SF, the dominant concern of third-world literary production in the era following decolonization and the "poisoned gift of independence" is the problem of narrative itself.[32] Thus, when radical postcolonial writers like Ngugi wa Thiong'o "find themselves back in the dilemma of ... bearing a passion for change and social regeneration which has not yet found its agents," this utopian longing presents itself as a "crisis of representation" or as a problem of narrative form.[33] Phillip Wegner, who productively connects Jameson's thoughts on SF with the theory first developed in his controversial essay on third-world literature and national allegory, offers that narrative SF, like Jameson's third-world literature, also "eschews the pleasures and demands of canonical forms... in order to free itself for this operation of spatial figuration."[34] Plaiting these related threads of Jameson's thought within the context of what Amitava Kumar has provocatively designated "World Bank Literature," Wegner argues that Jameson's work in both SF and third-world narrative invites us to inquire

> in what ways might current efforts in the genre [of SF] present allegorical figurations of the contemporary processes and spaces of globalization? And even more significantly, what is the relationship between these mappings and any possible renewal of the capacity to imagine, and subsequently to produce new political agencies?[35]

By locating the source of Jameson's work on SF in the essay on third-world literature, Wegner helps to trace Jameson's thoughtful response to (and incorporation of) the substantial criticisms of third-world Marxists like Aijaz Ahmad, who counters what he views as the essay's homogenizing claim for a cognitive aesthetics of the third world with the "radically different premise" that "we live not in three worlds but in one" united "by the global operation of a single mode of production, namely the capitalist one, and the global resistance to this mode, a resistance which is itself unevenly developed in different parts of the globe."[36] This insistence upon what Jameson, in his book of the same title, later calls "a singular modernity" stands in stark contrast to the postmodernist postcolonial model deployed by Pordzik with its emphasis on subjectivity, plurality, and the cultural/aesthetic. Thus, while Wegner crafts a compelling reading of SF writer Joe Haldeman's *Forever* trilogy as an "early figuration of the utterly disorienting experience" of a nascent American postmodernity,[37] I suggest that Hopkinson's work, as a unique convergence of narrative SF and the third-world novel, offers a powerful instance – from the *margins* of modernity – of what Jameson terms a "conceptual instrument for grasping our new being-in-the-world."[38]

In one of the undeservedly few critical engagements with *Midnight Robber*, Bill Clemente offers crucial insight into the relationship between the novel's twin worlds when he suggests that the submerged or repressed history of Toussaint is revealed in the alternate dimension of New Half-Way Tree, where Tan-Tan "sees the violence Toussaint hides."[39] For Clemente, this violence is associated directly and singularly with the omitted sins of a colonial past and its forms of cultural inheritance: "The glorification of the Marryshow Corporation's achievements hides the violence and destruction behind the planet's transformation, and disguises the link to the horrors of the past the colonists have left behind."[40] Thus, when Tan-Tan and her father prepare to flee Toussaint for the prison dimension of New Half-Way Tree following the death of Quashee, we find the curious re-emergence of suppressed history as Tan-Tan significantly identifies this moment of transition between worlds with the Middle Passage of "the long time ago Africans."[41]

Additionally, the existence on New Half-Way Tree of the indigenous tree-dwelling Douen, named after creatures from Caribbean folklore,[42] as well as the persistence of other native flora and fauna, emphatically indicate their absence on Toussaint and imply what Clemente describes as "genocide on a scale that equals the European extirpation of the Caribbean native cultures" perpetrated by the Marryshow Corporation.[43] New Half-Way Tree houses even the revenant sins of Antonio, Tan-Tan's father, in the persons of Aislin, Tan-Tan's former nurse, and her disfigured daughter, Quamina. After Aislin conceives Antonio's illegitimate child, Antonio, fearing a scandal, has the nurse banished to the prison dimension. Passage through the dimension barrier, however, has devastating and debilitating effects on her unborn child. In ways such as this, New Half-Way Tree (named both for the midpoint between Kingston Harbour and Spanish Town, a customary resting place for newly transported slaves, and the point of intersection between the affluent and poor areas of Kingston) both contains and preserves the occluded historical content of Toussaint, which, on the prison world, is most emphatically *what hurts*. New Half-Way Tree might thus be said to function as the political unconscious of Toussaint, or what Sean Homer, *anent* Slavoj Žižek's engagement with the Lacanian Real, identifies as that persistent "nonhistorical kernel of a historical situation," the unsymbolizable (and thus nondiscursive) absent cause that is knowable only through its discursive effects, through the pressures that it exerts on the frames of its narrative reconstructions – a notion to which I return shortly.[44]

To read *Midnight Robber* as Clemente does, as a meditation on "the horrors of the past the colonists have left behind"[45] or even on the cultural echo-effects of colonization that linger into the present, is to neglect, however, Hopkinson's intervention into the utterly novel epoch of globalization. I argue that her work marks a new moment in Caribbean fiction, the genre in which she operates a new moment in postcolonial narrative, the preoccupations of which extend well beyond those formative nationalist and post-nationalist concerns that shaped according to their authoritative contours so much of the literary production of the decades following independence. Thinking new thoughts, as Mikhail Bakhtin teaches us, requires new forms through which to think them, new organs of perception with which to order, theorize, and conceptually crystallize the emergent and amorphous phenomena of the present – in this case, the global consolidation of the new imperial network and its spatial (and therefore narrative) articulations.

New Half-Way tree is described in the opening pages of *Midnight Robber* as the "dub side" of Toussaint, a shadow world, and "the planet of lost people":

> You never wonder where them all does go, the drifters, the ragamuffins-them, the ones who think the world must be have something better for them, if them could only find which part it is? ... Well master, the Nation Worlds does ship them all to New Half-Way Tree, the mirror planet of Toussaint. Yes, man; on the next side of a dimension veil. ... You know how a thing and the shadow of that thing could be in almost the same place together?[46]

The experiential and formal limit of Toussaint is the dimension veil, which, crucially, is traversable in only one direction. Elements may pass out of *this* reality and into the shadow, but elements from the shadow world may not intrude upon the "utopian" totality of Toussaint. In this way, Toussaint effaces its own history (that is, its fundamental social antagonism) in order both to construct and obfuscate the reality of its perpetual, post-political present.[47] This obfuscatory function is made strikingly clear early in the novel when Tan-Tan inquires of her "eshu" (or personal interface with the Anansi Web) about the long-extinct indigenous inhabitants of Toussaint, the Douen. After a rather suspicious period of delay ("Usually it could get information instantly from the web data banks"), the response from the official archives is simply "Indigenous fauna. Now extinct."[48] After Tan-Tan expresses dissatisfaction with this uncharacteristically succinct explanation and asks her eshu *why* the Douen became extinct, the web's response is equally circumspect: "To make Touissant safe for the people from the nation ships."[49] Thus, when Tan-Tan crosses the dimension veil and encounters a Douen for the first time, she thereby re-enacts (and recovers) a portion of the suppressed history of Touissant, that which lies outside the range of its ideological field. When Chichibud and his people reveal themselves to be gentle and charitable (he graciously provides Tan-Tan and Antonio guidance through the bush as well as food, water, and protection even though they have nothing of value to trade), Tan-Tan experiences a kind of ideological crisis: "Tan-Tan remembered Nursie's stories about how the douens led people into the bush to get lost and die. She started to feel scared all over again. She called silently for her eshu. Her headache flared, then quieted."[50] The absence of – or liberation from – her eshu forces Tan-Tan to reconsider both the authoritative narratives she has been told and the values they both manifest and obscure.

Thus, "the ones who think the world must be have something better for them," whose burgeoning spatial awareness is signaled by the qualifier, "if them could only find which part it is," pose a fundamental threat to the stable ideological enclosure of Toussaint. In fact, the novel strongly implies that it is their dissatisfaction with the world-as-it-is that constitutes the criminalization of the "restless people" who populate New Half-Way Tree in the first place.[51] Their crime consists perhaps of a coming-to-consciousness, of the emergence of a cognitive capacity to estrange the present in such a way that it becomes thinkable as a systemic whole. To put it another way, the dimension veil prevents the inhabitants of Toussaint from coming to a full realization of the social totality, of the deep connections that they share with New Half-Way Tree. To perceive the system in its fullness, one must press beyond this enclosure to the place where its ideological blinders fail. We see glimpses of this nascent ability to question in Tan-Tan's gradually evolving attitude regarding the social practices of the home world: *"She and Melonhead up in a wet sugar tree, arguing happily about whether it was humane for the Nation Worlds' to exile their undesirables to a low-tech world where they were stripped of the sixth sense that was Granny Nanny.*"[52] To imagine the constitutive limits of the social totality is simultaneously to project beyond it to the *terrific* no-place of the unimaginable, in this case outside the dimension veil, which, as the novel's metaphoric expression of the Real, functions as both "the Thing to which direct access is not possible *and* the obstacle which prevents this direct access."[53] As Hopkinson puts it, "Once you climb the half-way tree, everything change up."[54]

Traversing the fantasy: Tan-Tan's folktales and the real of history

It is precisely because of this historical suppression and dimensional partition that Hopkinson can claim that Toussaint knows neither poverty nor wage slaves; indeed, these are present on the planet, like the gentle Douen or the monstrous *mako jumbie*, only as an emphatic absence or erasure, as a fairytale about another world that no longer exists in the present – except as narrative effect. History persists on Toussaint as a spectral iteration of the Real, whose central paradox, according to Žižek, "is that it is an entity which, although it does not exist. ... can produce a series of effects in the symbolic reality of subjects."[55] The folktales that Tan-Tan sees come to life in New Half-Way Tree function precisely as such narrative and metaphorical expressions or obtrusions onto the ideological fabric of Toussaint[56] of an absolute horizon of nonidentity, or what Žižek describes as the "traumatic limit which prevents the final totalization of the social-ideological field," and, moreover, one that is perceived on Toussaint only as fantastic, as that which exceeds the limits of reality itself.[57]

It is within this context that we can read the interpolated folktales that both interrupt and disrupt the diegesis proper as a formal/spatial tracing of the persistent content of material history, as the spaces that prevent narrative closure by wrenching themselves free of the textual order in which they are enmeshed to comment on or to refashion its contents according to other generic conventions and other practices of writing-reading. The folktales function as autonomous gaps within the totality of the novel the very existence of which both allows us to think relationally (or dialogically) and forces us to develop provisional explanations in order to assimilate these departures back into the primary narrative. In short, the folktales enable us to perceive the narrative *as narrative*, as a systemic structure of meaning-making that is always unfinished or in process. Typographically, the tales signal that they are told by the same narrative voice that opens the novel, which at the conclusion of that enframing section explains its unique ability to perceive and relate multidimensional reality:

> I see both places for myself. How? Well, maybe I find a way to come through the one-way veil to bring you a story, nuh? Maybe I is a master weaver. I spin threads. I twist warp 'cross weft. I move my shuttle in and out, and smooth smooth, I weaving you my story, oui? And when I done, I shake it out and turn it over *swips!* and maybe you see it have a next side to the tale.[58]

The possibility of a "next side" to the hegemonic narrative is precisely the function of the folktales, which collectively define a kind of supplement that stubbornly exceeds the structural bonds of the novel and, in so doing, recalls Bloch's notion of utopian expression as the surplus (or "undischarged hope-content") that likewise exceeds the structural constraints of ideology and reveals social reality as in a perpetual state of becoming.[59] It is not surprising, then, that Bloch identifies fairytales and folktales as exemplary manifestations of this anticipatory excess. The vision of reality conjured forth from the "beautifying mirror" of bourgeois culture, he suggests "often only reflects how the ruling class wishes the wishes of the weak to be. But the picture clears completely as soon as the mirror comes from the people, as occurs quite visibly and wonderfully in fairytales."[60] This alternate perspective, through its distinctive set of aesthetic practices and its orientation toward the wishful/fantastic, revises and enriches the primary narrative as its unruly surplus.

The novel's first tale refashions a native etiological/ecological myth that nicely encapsulates the spatial and utopian preoccupations of the novel as a whole. Hopkinson's source for this tale is of Carib origin and concerns the emergent spatial consciousness of the earth's first people, who compare the dingy planet on which they live to the shimmering points of light that they assume to be other, better worlds.[61] In quintessentially utopian fashion, this imaginative projection of superior worlds too distant to be seen in detail reorients the relationship of the people to their own world and inspires them to clean it up.

The third tale is an adaptation of Jamaican folklore concerning the eighteenth-century historical figure "Three-finger" Jack Mansong, whose legend serves as both the inspiration for and primary intertext of Hopkinson's novel.[62] After killing the owner of the plantation on which he is a slave, Mansong led a group of rebels who terrorized and plundered plantations throughout the island. After his ambush and death at the hands of fellow Maroons turned bounty hunters, Mansong was resurrected in the theaters of England in the form of a popular pantomime, which presented him "as a kind of African Robin Hood."[63] This cultural harnessing of the revolutionary energies of Mansong's exploits would become a powerful vehicle for the expression of abolitionist sentiment in nineteenth-century England.[64]

The central-most of the three interpolated folktales is the most interesting for me here, however, largely because it is the most clearly divergent from (and in excess of) the primary narrative. "Tan-Tan and Dry Bone," a reworking of a West African Anansi story, is both the longest of the folk narratives and the least ostensibly relevant. It is connected only tenuously to the primary narrative through the topical coincidence of hunger. Dry Bone presents himself to Tan-Tan as a helpless old man, but once she picks him up, she cannot put him down and is immediately held thrall to his insatiable appetite, compelled by his peculiar power to spend her every moment preparing meals for him to devour without satisfaction.

Clemente suggests that the voice of Dry Bone "echoes the self-incrimination that weighs [Tan-Tan] down. Representative of the need to cast off the burden this excessive guilt causes, the narrative emphasizes the use of guile and the need for assistance," which presents itself in the form of Master Johncrow, the wily turkey vulture who functions as the trickster hero and ultimate nemesis of Dry Bone.[65] The text certainly bears out this reading, as when Master Johncrow tells Tan-Tan, "Like Dry Bone not the only monkey that a-ride your back, child. You carrying round a bigger burden than he," which is, of course, the debilitating guilt she feels over the death of her father.[66] At yet another allegorical register, however, Dry Bone might be seen to personify the restless and insatiable force of desire that initiates the transformation of her character from the victimized Tan-Tan to the potent agent of resistance, the loquacious and irrepressible Robber Queen. Read in this manner, Dry Bone's relentless hunger suggests a metaphorical iteration of the utopian imperative of "permanent revolution." As Bloch instructs, hunger is

> the force of production on the repeatedly bursting Front of an unfinished world. The Not as *processive Not-Yet* thus turns utopia into the real condition of unfinishedness, of only fragmentary essential being in all objects. Hence the world as process is itself the enormous testing of its satisfied solution, that is, of the real of its satisfaction.[67]

It is with regard to his role as the perpetually unsatisfied libidinal force of the *Not-Yet* that the narrator describes Dry Bone as "thin so *like the hope of salvation,* so fine him could slide through the crack and all to pass inside your house."[68] Likewise, it is not incidental that Dry Bone is the tireless scourge of the mythical Duppy Dead Town, "where people go when life boof them, when hope left them and happiness cut she eye 'pon them and strut away" and where the inhabitants "have one foot in the world and the next one already crossing the threshold to where the real duppy-them living."[69] Nor is it surprising that the vulture, symbolic of the utterly static negative plenitude of death, is Dry Bone's chief adversary. Dry Bone fears most the unbroken blue sky, the field of uniform totality without relative horizon that is the territory of his nemesis, Master Johncrow. As Bloch maintains, "everything real in general, because it is life, process, and can be a correlate of objective imagination, has a horizon" or a relative sense of the anticipatory *Not-Yet*: "Where the prospective horizon is omitted," Bloch warns, "reality only appears as become, as dead. ..."[70] Thus, it is only through her confrontation with Dry Bone and his transformative hunger that Tan-Tan finds the wherewithal to shrug off the paralyzing lethargy of Duppy Dead Town and to seek out Papa Bois, the "old man of the bush" who has the power to "look into your eyes, and see your soul, and tell you how to cleanse it."[71] The vitalizing power of this encounter, conspicuous in its departure from the primary narrative, is made explicit at the tale's conclusion: "Nothing would be trouble after living with the trouble of Dry Bone."[72]

Piercing the veil: space, labor, multitude

Perhaps the most definitive aspect of New Half-Way Tree, apart from its extant forms of primitive wildness, is its significance as a space of labor. On Toussaint, as Antonio is fond of observing, "Back-break ain't for people."[73] In accordance with the canonical convention that Bloch terms the utopian "primacy of rest," manual labor has been, through the benevolent intervention of technological innovation, superseded – with the singular exception of the pedicab "runners." Conversely, incessant physical work is a way of life on New Half-Way Tree, where as one inhabitant relates, "Granny Nanny sentence we to live out we days in hard labour" and where Tan-Tan notes that she "had never seen so much hard labour and so many tired faces."[74] When Aislin tells Tan-Tan upon her arrival that she and her father will now have to produce, hunt, and prepare their own food, to retrieve their own water and wash their own clothes, Antonio responds characteristically: "Back-break not for people."[75] Aislin's response, however, is telling: "We not people no more,"[76] articulating concurrently both the ontological limit and absolute social horizon of the degenerate utopia of Toussaint, where the labor and violent exploitation that built and sustain it have been so effectively repressed from cultural consciousness that to be a laborer is to be something other than human.

I offer that the historical amnesia of Toussaint suggests nothing so much as the pernicious first-world myth of the "'postindustrial society' from which traditional production has disappeared and in which social classes of the classical type no longer exist."[77] This fantasy is sustained in the first world by the requisite fluctuating unevenness of global capital itself, by the global dispersal of low-wage industrial production to the third world. Indeed, as Santiago Colás observes, for Jameson, the disappearance of the "third world" as a meaningful geospatial designation is in fact one of the central-most cultural indicators that a new phase of deterritorialized capitalist production has been successfully instantiated.[78]

Hopkinson's novel voices a powerful aesthetic rejoinder to this culture of forgetting that positions itself in relation to both local and global contexts; specifically, I recommend that we can profitably locate *Midnight Robber* at the site of their intersection in the international labor space known as the *free zone*. During the 1980s, under the economic restructuration policies overseen by the World Bank and the International Monetary Fund, Jamaica passed the Export Free Zone Act, which extended and expanded the original Kingston Free Zone Act of 1976. The free zones (or "EFZs") are spatially demarcated labor spaces, which the World Bank defines as "fenced-in industrial estates specializing in manufacturing for exports that offer firms free trade conditions and a liberal regulatory environment."[79] Raw materials are imported at a duty-free rate (Jamaican products have historically been textiles, though information processing and data entry services are now increasingly common), assembled at lowered costs due to relaxed labor law enforcement, and exported under a liberal tariff structure that relieves income tax on activities of international trade.[80] Free zones are thus spaces of exception in almost every sense. The Kingston EFZ, oldest of the Jamaican free zones, is a 44-acre concrete-walled compound, protected by barbed wire and armed guards, housing nearly 800,000 square feet of factory space and employing as many as 15,000–18,000 Jamaican workers prior to the NAFTA agreements of the 1990s, which freed multinationals to search out even cheaper labor sources in other parts of the Americas.

To appreciate fully Hopkinson's imaginative intervention in the spatial logic of this new world order – its global dispersions providing for the simultaneous, spatially dissociate existence of Marx/Engels's "kingdom of freedom" and "kingdom of necessity" – we might briefly compare it to another text from about the same period that likewise attempts to lay bare the devastating consequences of globalization in part through a consideration of the Jamaican free zones: Stephanie Black's powerful documentary film *Life & Debt* (2001). An unnamed commentator describes for Black's camera the Jamaican EFZ's unique spatial attributes: "The free zone operates in the theoretical [space] that is not even part of Jamaica. It is a separate entity. So the goods come in in a container and go through guarded gates. After it leaves the free zone, it goes back on a ship never in effect having touched the shores of Jamaica."[81] Reminiscent of the Toussaint/New-Halfway Tree dimensional barrier, the history of third-world production falls into the shadow-space of non-history (into the Jamaica that is not Jamaica) and helps to achieve in the first world what Wegner, in reference to the imaginary Boston of Edward Bellamy's *Looking Backward*, calls a "paradise wherein the dilemmas of industrialism have been wished away, a world of reified commodities from which every trace of labor has been expunged."[82] The finished Tommy Hilfiger, Brooks Brothers, and Hanes products (to name but a few) can therefore often technically retain the cultural cache of having been "Made in the USA," for as one of the supervising workers featured in the film declares, the product is "one-hundred percent USA-made materials, and we only assemble it."[83] It is likewise in this sense that another of the EFZ workers can claim that the zone functions effectively "like a state in our country."[84]

But the exceptionality of the free zone is, Sherrie Russell-Brown notes, "a *de facto*, not *de jure*, reality."[85] The zones, while not officially exempt from local and international labor legislation, are nonetheless under considerable external pressure to suspend the practical enforcement of such laws and to discourage the organization of workers' unions. Indeed, the free zones, into which the evanescent labor of the post-industrial first world vanishes, are among the only sectors of production in Jamaica that are absolutely *free* of organized labor.

Yet despite Black's admirable efforts, *Life & Debt* succumbs to certain structural and perceptual limitations. As Y-Dang Troeung observes,

> While such visual and discursive accounts paint a picture of the political-economic autonomy of the Kingston free zone from the rest of Jamaica, they also imbue the free zone with an aura of remoteness that casts the exploitation of workers within these zones as removed

> from the motivated and material agents of power responsible for this exploitation.[86]

Thus, for Troeung, the free zone is, in Black's film, estranged from history and generalized as a "broad symbol of globalization" that offers no effective means of exposing or confronting the transnational forces responsible for its existence.[87]

Troeung specifically criticizes Black's portrayal of the Asian workers (all female) who are shipped into residential camps inside the free zone to take over operations following the dismissal of the Jamaican labor force. Of a scene depicting a young Asian worker peering from the window of a bus entering the free zone gates amid throngs of protesting Jamaicans, Troeung inquires, "From where exactly, and under what circumstances was she, and the other 800 Asian labourers, displaced? What kinds of conditions were these labourers forced to endure once inside the free zone? What network of global alliances were responsible for bringing them there?"[88] Indeed, the film is surprisingly silent about the material circumstances of these homogenously nondescript "Asian" workers, who might be said in this case to represent the structural limit of class consciousness under global capital. As one of the Jamaicans in the film observes with undisguised envy, the Asian workers "don't object to nothing because they are getting paid in US."[89] One of the most troubling moments for Troeung is a scene depicting a group of workers laughing together, rehearsing, she argues, the image of the Asian female laborer as "a naturalized embodiment of transnational labour."[90] In this way, Black's film is itself subject to the same ideological and disciplinary strictures that it ostensibly seeks to contest. Black's attempt to imagine the dire realities of the Jamaican present is conceptually limited to the local, and the similar material circumstances of the geographically displaced Asian workers, likewise subject to the gyroscopic revolutions of global capital, are rendered incommensurable across an apparently insuperable racial/cultural divide, neatly replicating the grammar of postmodern pluralism.

This incommensurability is also, of course, the great dilemma facing any form of resistance in the postmodern era of Empire with its tendencies toward dispersion and fragmentation. As Amitava Kumar succinctly frames the problem, how are we to "elaborate a pedagogy that connects the 'here' and the 'there'?"[91] For Michael Hardt and Antonio Negri, the solution lies in the political arousal and mobilization of the multitude – what Hopkinson's novel calls "the massive-them, the masses that the Nation Worlds had dumped out here behind God's back"[92] – the consolidation of which is already provided for in the endlessly flexible and deterritorialized arrangements of Empire itself. According to their now familiar argument, "Empire creates a greater potential for revolution than did the modern regimes of power because it presents us, alongside the machine of command, with an alternative: the set of all the exploited and the subjugated, a multitude that is directly opposed to Empire, with no mediation between them."[93] This flexible collectivity of locally situated singularities and their common desires form what Hardt and Negri term "the virtual," the imaginary (and utopian) "*new place in the non-place,* the place defined by the productive activity that is autonomous from any external regime of measure."[94] The virtual is thus the latent "set of powers to act ... that reside in the multitude," of which they need only become aware.[95] Actualization of the power of the virtual can "put pressure on the borders of the possible, and thus touch on the real," effecting material transformation on an undreamed of scale.[96] *Midnight Robber* supplies an imaginative figuration of precisely this possibility in which New Half-Way Tree, as the repressed other of Toussaint and site of the multitude, can deform the unbreachable border and effect transformation in the "real" world; that is, it can reveal the ways in which the *two* worlds are actually *one*.

What is needed, therefore, is a language to give form to this restless, placeless longing, a "secular Pentecoast" which unveils the concrete universal that orients the multitude and marshals its desire in service of a new and as yet unimaginable collectivity.[97] This desired language is not unlike what Alain Badiou terms the "subject-language" that both articulates the fullness yet to come and constitutes a new subjectivity in and through its relationship (or *fidelity*) to what he designates the Truth-Event, the emergence of the impossibly new.[98] This fidelity, expressed in the subject language and the "act," represents, as Rushdie's Flapping Eagle demonstrates, an intervention in the present order that, as Žižek notes in specifically spatial terms, "does not merely operate *within* a given background, but disturbs its coordinates and thus renders it visible *as* a background."[99] This language is, however, from within the unperceivable totality of the present moment, necessarily *nonsense* in that it refers beyond to that which exceeds the horizon of experiential reality, to the metastructure of the Truth-Event, a concept that offers a unique way to imagine the interdependencies of the local and the global beyond the woeful limitations of postmodernism and multiculturalism. Like Badiou and Žižek, Hardt and Negri, Hopkinson's novel offers a spatial/narrative figuration (the *flash of another dimension*) that tries to imagine, from within the local and contingent, the present in its global fullness as well as the collectivity that can resist the inimical field of its gravity. If we read allegorically the novel's spatial exploration against the pervasive context of global capital,[100] how might *Midnight Robber* be said to succeed where *Life & Debt* so clearly fails; that is, how does Hopkinson's allegory offer a formal model for addressing the needs of the local that does not foreclose agencies of global resistance and the formation of new collectivities? What, in other words, is the subject-language of Hopkinson's multitude?

This question leads us finally to consider the pedicab runners, one of the few communities of laborers on Toussaint.[101] The runners are an embarrassing holdover within the post-industrial present of Toussaint because they archaically assume the measurability and valuation of their work. Hardt and Negri write that within the global domain of postmodern biopower, "every fixed measure of value tends to be dissolved, and the imperial horizon of power is revealed finally to be a horizon outside measure."[102] It is for their uncomfortable reminder of a measurable labor valuation that the runners are more heavily taxed than other citizens. As Antonio explains to one of the runners, "'Is a labor tax. For the way allyou insist on using people when a a.i. could run a cab like this. You know how it does bother citizens to see allyou doing manual labor so. Back-break ain't for people.' Blasted luddites."[103] With an equivalent emphasis on the visibility of labor, the runner protests, however, that "Honest work is for people. Work that you could see, could measure. Pedicab runners, we know how much weight we could pull, how many kilometers we done travel."[104] The runners differ in precisely this respect from their New Half-Way Tree counterparts, who, Tan-Tan observes, despite their incessant labor, "often never came into the full satisfaction of feeling their muscles work to move the world around them."[105] Furthermore, the runners are organized into what one of them calls the "Sou-Sou Co-operative," a clandestine union of pedicab operators who secretly lobby for the relief of the labor tax among other benefits.[106]

The runners are viewed with suspicion by the inhabitants of Toussaint not only because of their antiquated devotion to physical labor and their insistence of the material measurability of its value, but also because they operate beyond the authoritative ambit of the Web – like their counterparts on New-Halfway Tree, behind God's back. Exploiting the flexibility and programmed multicultural tolerance of the Web, they claim a religious right to refuse the injection of the nanomites and live in completely "headblind" communes, where there is "no way for the 'Nansi Web to gather data on them."[107] What is more, the runners have developed a method to subvert further the Web's gaze of power by appropriating the very language of the Web itself, known as *nannysong*. In the opening scene of the novel, a runner uses nannysong to disrupt momentarily Antonio's connection to the Web in order to offer the runners' clandestine service as conveyors of private messages (privacy being an invaluable commodity in this world of ubiquitous surveillance) in exchange for a reduction of the penalizing labor tax. Fittingly, Antonio can interpret the runners' singing, like Badiou's subject-language, only as nonsense:

> She hummed something that sounded like nannysong, but fast, so fast, a snatch of notes that hemidemisemiquavered into tones he couldn't distinguish. Then Antonio heard static in his ear. It faded to an almost inaudible crackle. He tapped his earbug. Dead. He chirped a query to his eshu. No answer. He'd been taken offline? How the rass had she done that? So many times he'd wished he could.[108]

The language of the 'Nansi Web, explicitly similar to the chirrups and whistles of a dial-up Internet connection, also recalls Hardt and Negri's discussion of the Web as both a metaphor and an instrument of Empire as well as a model for the resistance inherent in the formation of the multitude. The decentralized, rhizomic structure of the Internet, designed to withstand large-scale military attack, allows any of its individual nodes to function autonomously, through a nearly infinite network of potential relays and communication paths, as the whole. Thus, the structure that ensures the effectiveness and durability of the system of control, so they argue, is also what makes it impossible to govern since any single nodule may communicate with any other point simultaneously and through any number of conceivable pathways.[109]

It is fitting then that nannysong, the strategic misappropriation of which allows for Tan-Tan's arrival on the shadow world, provides the potential means of communication between the discrete mirror worlds of New Half-Way Tree and Toussaint. When Tan-Tan is adopted by the Douen following the death of her father, Chichibud confides in her the Douen secret that what appear to outsiders as the flightless pack-birds of the Douen traders are actually their wives (the hinte). Also, as Chichibud's wife Benta reveals, the hinte not only have large wings concealed within what appear to be stunted and useless wing-appendages but also speak a language that is remarkably familiar to Tan-Tan: "Benta gave a low, grumbly series of warbles that made Tan-Tan think of nannysong. But they were only nonsense phrasings."[110] The hinte language bears more than a merely superficial resemblance to the language of Granny Nanny, however, as the Douen are able to sense and interpret the high-pitched bursts of nannysong – undetectable to human ears – that mark the breaching of the dimension barrier and the arrival of the shift-pods to the prison world.[111]

Nannysong thereby functions formally as the persistent ligature between the two otherwise discrete dimensions, between the bourgeois utopia of Toussaint and the realm of its jettisoned but recalcitrant history. As the narrator makes clear in the beginning, this tale simply could not be told without such an intermediary mechanism, without some means of traversing the dimension veil and communicating the experience of New Half-Way Tree to the inhabitants of the home world: "Well, maybe I find a way to come through the one-way veil to bring you a story, nuh? ... Maybe is same way so I weave my way through the dimensions to land up here. No, don't ask me how."[112] It is fitting, of course, that the reader is here required to assume the subject position of an oblivious Toussaint (first-world) citizen. And while the novel remains necessarily ambivalent about the ultimate implications of this trans-dimensional language (might it be used to exploit further the resources and labor of New Half-Way Tree?), the presence of such a potentially emancipatory language, shared by communities of workers otherwise unknown to one another, gives expression to a social desire for collectivity (and a figuration of totality) to which Black's film is constitutionally oblivious.

But this language of mediation requires a mediator, this secular Pentecost an apostle of transformation. The tension of the novel's inside/outside spatial dialectic culminates finally in the opening forth of the hopeful space of the womb and the birth of Tan-Tan's son. In the novel's closing pages, we learn that the enframing voice of the narrator is in fact that of Tan-Tan's former house eshu relating the story of Tan-Tan to the child whom she is delivering. In this way, the body of the text is explicitly consonant with the body of the child, whose very existence threatens the formal totality of Toussaint. Tan-Tan's uncalibrated nanomites, we learn, survived the dimension shift due to her youth, and though the passage rendered them useless to Tan-Tan, the recalibrated nanomites later migrate to the fetus growing inside her. As the eshu informs the breaching child:

> You could hear me because your whole body is one living connection with the Grande Anansi Nanotech Interface. Your little bodystring will sing to Nanny tune, doux-doux. You will be a weave of she web.

> Flesh people talk say how earbugs give them a sixth sense, but really it only a crutch, oui? Not a fully functional perception. You now; you really have that extra limb.[113]

At his delivery, the eshu welcomes him into "one of the worlds," signaling his unique trans-dimensional nature, his ability to span not only the discrete mirror worlds of Toussaint and New Half-Way Tree but also the potentially unlimited other alternate dimensions, each of which might be said to represent either some fragment of lost history or an as yet undiscovered alternative to the social totality of Toussaint. As Tan-Tan's father informs her, "there were more Toussaints than they could count, existing simultaneously, but each one a little bit different."[114] The birth of Tan-Tan's child is therefore the bodying forth of an utterly new perceptual capacity, the eruption of Bloch's *novum* in the form of the child's surplus "limb." Significantly, Tan-Tan names the child "Tubman," which the eshu glosses as "the human bridge from slavery to freedom," reinforcing both his interstitial spatial orientation and emancipatory promise.[115]

Unlike Tan-Tan, who seeks and finally inhabits the hard-sought promised land of Sweet Pone, where there is no need for the intervention of her Robber Queen persona, where exploitative labor practices are largely unknown, and where the citizens erect a Palaver House for democratic government as well as a solar-powered library, Tubman's utopic promise lies in his potential to redress the historical amnesia of the home-world of Toussaint. Sweet Pone, as the exceptional promised land behind God's back, might be said to function much like the Icarian project of Etienne Cabet in the mid-nineteenth century, as a secession from history that leaves intact the logic of the dominant social system from which it flees. Marx's vehement objections to Cabet's Icarian project emphasize the impossibility of such facile utopian genesis outside of time and in the neutral space of non-history.[116] As Marx passionately enjoined potential followers of Cabet, "Brothers, stay at the battlefront of Europe. Work and struggle here, because only Europe has all the elements to set up communal wealth. This type of community will be established here, or nowhere."[117] The utopian promise of Tubman, however, is precisely not withdrawal but rather the perforation of the dimension veil and the reassertion of material history into the closed social matrix of Toussaint, in short, the transformation of utopic figuration into potentially revolutionary praxis. The only way to escape the encompassing global reach of Capital, Marx cautioned Cabet and the Icarians, is total systemic transformation from within, a pushing through to the shadow figuration of its other side rather than a withdrawal into the spatial fix of a perfected society located in a land far, far away. Antonio's earlier words to Tan-Tan, spoken as they prepare to enter the shift tower, are thus inadvertently prophetic: "The only way out is through," through not to another space but rather to the present space as other.[118]

Hopkinson's paradoxical disavowal of the narrative utopian tradition, her expressed preference for a dialectical "dynamic tension" over the socially inert, nonconflictual space of the bourgeois utopianism that has shaped so much popular SF production in the decades following World War II, is therefore hardly surprising. Its keen observance of the spatial effects of globalization might thus position Hopkinson's novel as a postcolonial response to David Harvey's call for a *dialectical utopianism,* a utopian expression that is explicitly attentive to concerns of space as well as those of social process in this era of universal capitalist supremacy.[119] The desire, Harvey suggests, is

> to find an alternative, not in terms of some static spatial form or even of some perfected emancipatory process. The task is to pull together a spatiotemporal utopianism – a dialectical utopianism – that is rooted in our present possibilities at the same time as it points towards different trajectories for human uneven geographical developments.[120]

Through its recalibration of the narrative utopia to address the dire circumstances of the Jamaican present in its relation to global contexts, *Midnight Robber* undertakes precisely the imaginative charting of these spatial and social possibilities against a mapping of the opaque present. Localizing the utopian methodologies of *Grimus* while refusing to compromise its totalizing, global reach, Hopkinson's novel provides a brilliant example of what it now means to take science fiction seriously.

3

There's No Splace Like Home: Domesticity, Difference, and the "Long Space" of Short Fiction in Vandana Singh's *The Woman Who Thought She Was a Planet*

Building upon the dialectical figurations of Hopkinson and Rushdie, Vandana Singh concludes the opening story of her luminous SF collection *The Woman Who Thought She Was a Planet* (2008) with the following passage:

> Meanwhile, she continued to read her science fiction novels because, more than ever, they seemed to reflect her own realization of the utter strangeness of the world. Slowly the understanding came to her that these stories were trying to tell her a great truth in a very convoluted way, that they were all in some kind of code, designed to deceive the literary snob and waylay the careless reader. And this great truth, which she would spend her life unraveling, was centered around the notion that you did not have to go to the stars to find aliens or to measure the distances between people in light-years.[1]

Here, the endorsement of the expansive social and imaginative vistas opened by narrative science fiction is bracketed by the temporal enclosure of the Andersonian "meanwhile." As Benedict Anderson claims in his influential study of the narrative dimensions of nationalism, such a synchronizing "meanwhile" temporality, in which diverse and unaware individuals nonetheless participate in the symbolic coincidence of their actions, is the hallmark of a novelistic realism that is itself indicative (if not largely constitutive) of the homogeneous empty time of the nation's "imagined community."[2] Homi Bhabha likewise notes in a postcolonial glossing of Anderson that this "steady onward clocking of calendrical time" imparts upon the nation's heterogeneous and far-flung subjects the impression of a "sociological stability" such that the political ideal itself comes to "work[ ] like the plot of a realist novel."[3] The illusion of coherence and continuity secured by this narrative belies, however, a "profound ascesis" of discontinuous temporalities and alternative subjectivities within, what Bhabha refers to as the minoritarian or subaltern voices that "speak betwixt and between times and places."[4] Therefore, I want to argue that Singh's invocation of this "meanwhile," while apparently incidental, is in fact illustrative of her collection's persistent formal and thematic engagement with both the dominant trend in contemporary Indian literature, domestic fiction, and its sociospatial analogues or extensions: home, city, and nation. In this chapter I explore the way in which Singh's unique SF intervention juxtaposes the abstract space and homogeneous empty time that characterize these deeply imbricated forms with a differential chronotope, Peter Hitchcock's transnationalist "Long Space," thereby reorienting postcolonial fiction toward a more urgent and comprehensive imaginative horizon: the creation of *a world* altogether different than the *one world* of globalization.

In *The Woman Who Thought She Was a Planet*'s brief coda "A Speculative Manifesto," Singh offers the observation that the "so-called Third World is undergoing vast and unpredictable changes, and the world at large – for we have only one world, after all – is beset by war and environmental catastrophe."[5] Incapable of grasping the complex material reality of globalization, "[s]o much modern realist fiction is divorced from the physical universe, as though humans exist in a vacuum devoid of animals, rocks, and trees."[6] Calling for a more materially responsive aesthetic to address the exigencies of this *one world*, she notes that speculative fiction, "dominated as it has been by white, male, technofantasies – Westerns and the White Man's Burden in Space ... has not yet fully realized its transgressive potential."[7] Speculative fiction, however, offers us the conceptual means to "rise above this pathologically solipsist view and find ourselves part of a larger whole; to step out of the claustrophobia of the exclusively human and discover joy, terror, wonder, and meaning, in the greater universe."[8] Though she does not further specify (beyond the broad descriptor "modern realist fiction") the culprit charged with the production of this pathological solipsism and abstraction from both materiality and the "greater universe," it is telling that of the ten stories that make up *The Woman Who Thought She Was a Planet*, at least half can be classified as domestic fictions, as narratives situated within (if critically engaging) the chronotope of the home. In this way, *The Woman Who Thought She Was a Planet* reflects the broader division of Indo-Anglian fiction into, on the one hand, epic and magical realist categories and, on the other, domestic realism. While there is certainly no dearth of the former, it is the latter that has – since the 1865 publication of the first Anglophone Indian novel, Bankimchandra Chatterjee's *Rajmohan's Wife* – achieved an undeniable primacy, if not hegemony, in modern Indian literature, this despite the very vibrant tradition of Bengali SF that precedes even the novels of H.G. Wells.

Pursuant his claim that "writing the home cannot be delinked from the adjacent project of writing the nation," Dirk Wiemann notes how internationally celebrated contemporary Indo-Anglian authors like Vikram Seth, Amit Chaudhuri, Arundhati Roy, and, to a lesser extent, Amitav Ghosh interrogate the domestic space as a site of the production and reproduction of modern subjectivities:[9]

> Far from evolving unaffected by these powerful discourses of imperial and national historiographies, these private histories of home prove to be rearticulations of various grand narratives with the particular experience of domestic lives. It is by their necessary dependence on, and porosity for, dominant discourses that their status as entirely idiosyncratic accounts is disclaimed. The house/home, in other words, appears finally as a palimpsest in which a wide range of diachronically emitted interpellations are superimposed upon the other.[10]

If, in these fictions, the home interpellates a national subject "in terms of gender, class and caste," they likewise call into question the logic of inner and outer partitioning on which the concept relies for its normative efficacy.[11] Nevertheless, through their formal reliance on "precisely that representational apparatus whose structural effects Anderson places at the center of the construction of the emergent imagined national community," the Indian domestic novel[12] "keeps stimulating and virtually producing exactly that kind of homogeneous empty time that, as Jonathan Culler paraphrases Anderson's argument, makes the novel 'a formal condition of imagining the nation – a structural condition of possibility.'"[13] Of central importance for Wiemann's argument is Mary Douglas' influential contention that the normative efficacies of the "tyranny of home" lie in the latter's unique ability to allocate a synchronous space-time that Anderson might recognize as that of the nation.[14] And it is precisely this confinement within the isomorphic spatiotemporal horizons of home and nation to which Singh's science fiction stands opposed or within which it figures radical alternatives by making domestic fiction over into the site of an estranging SF practice.

Thus, starting from the spatial and ideological enclosures of the domestic, the opening story of *The Woman Who Thought She Was a*

Planet registers the emergence of a faint speculative or differential impulse therein that will be developed more fully throughout the collection. "Hunger" is the story of Divya, a middle-class wife and mother whose ambitious husband has recently been promoted to junior vice-president of his company, an advancement accompanied by admission into a new social stratum and therefore a complex of new behavioral expectations. Resentful of these external pressures and secretly doubtful of the direction her life has taken, Divya seeks solace in "trashy science fiction novels," which seem to provide her models for understanding the increasing alienation she feels from her immediate social and material reality, models for the trying daily obligation to "learn the world anew."[15] The alienating strictures of Divya's domestic chronotope therefore recall what Henri Lefebvre theorizes as modernity's *abstract space*, wherein the public process of labor is isolated from "the process of production which perpetuated social life" and proceeds to function "'objectally' as a set of things/signs and their formal relationship."[16] Despite its enduring idealization as a "special, still sacred, quasi-religious and in fact almost absolute space" – as, for instance, in the "ontological dignity" granted it by thinkers like Gaston Bachelard – the putatively exceptional space of the home provides the means for social and political reproduction precisely *because* of its seeming exclusion from these public zones of activity.[17] Discussing the shift from a pre-capitalist monumentality, serving to integrate a disparate social multiplicity, to the simultaneously fragmented and naturalized *genitality* of the family unit under capital, Lefebvre writes,

> Familial space, linked to naturalness through genitality, is the guarantor of meaning as well as of social (spatial) practice. Shattered by a host of separations and segregations, social unity is able to reconstitute itself at the level of the family unit, for the purpose of, and by means of, generalized reproduction. The reproduction of production relations continues apace amid (and on the basis of) the destruction of social bonds to the extent that the symbolic space of 'familiarity' (family life, everyday life), the only such space to be appropriated, continues to hold sway.[18]

The home is thus foremost among producers of abstract space, at once the site "where contradictions are generated, the medium in which those contradictions evolve and which they tear apart, and, lastly, the means whereby they are smothered and replaced by an appearance of consistency."[19] In its capacity both to organize and manifest this abstract spatial configuration, the home may be said to assume the characteristics of what Alain Badiou names the *splace*, or the "space of placement" within the normative situational context against which the ruptural presence of the event and the emergence of its faithful subject[20] are given both visibility and substance.

Disruptive of the homogenizing and asphyxiating delineations of this abstract splace is what Lefebvre names *differential space* (or what Badiou calls the *site*), which inheres in the former as its internal limit-point or contradiction; for the constitutive instability of capitalist modernity requires the perpetual dissolution and reconstruction of social relations of production, the agitations or outright diremptions of which are mediated by the ongoing production of new space, that is, space that recognizes, accents, or creates difference within the homogenizing field of the abstract and thereby unifies (somewhat paradoxically, *as differential*) what abstract space first levels and then obliterates. In providing abstract space with this necessary point of release, however, differential space also admits the possibility for a radical *production of space*, for the profound acknowledgment that, as Phillip Wegner phrases it, space is not merely the inert and stable "*site* of politics, conflict and struggle, but also the very thing being fought over."[21] Perforce anti-dialectical, abstract space conceals this inner contradiction or differentiation and obscures all signs of the historical conditions that enable its smoothly immediate hegemonic functioning.

Singh's critical deployment of the dialectical genre of SF suggests such hidden fault lines and fissures of a seemingly homogeneous familial space when Divya conceptualizes in explicitly spatial terms the increasing estrangement she feels from her domestic reality. This differentiation begins, not surprisingly, in the kitchen. As both the functional and symbolic hub of domesticity, the kitchen, Divya acknowledges, "was never hers at night but belonged, for that duration, to the denizens of another world," specifically cockroaches, mice, and frogs.[22] This metaphor of internal spatial differentiation is immediately extended to intimate familial relations when, contemplating the figure of her sleeping daughter, Divya observes: "Her face was still so young, so innocent, and yet on the inside she was developing layers, convolutions; she was becoming someone that Divya as yet did not know."[23] The horizon of this subtle spatial variance is broadened once more to include the immediate neighborhood and, in particular, the uppermost stair landing of her building, upon which resides a "small, emaciated, bird-like man" incapable of speech, who is transformed in Divya's imagination into an "alien, speaking to her in an exotic tongue or in code, delivering a message that she had to try to decipher."[24] The old man's presence, like the kitchen vermin about which Divya obsesses and with which he is repeatedly compared, disturbs the fragile coordinates of her domestic reality with the unaccountably alien presence of difference; just as she has congratulated herself for hosting her first successful dinner party for her new social circle and for having "crossed an invisible barrier" to become "one of Them," the scream of a child disrupts the urbane festivities and beckons Divya and her guests to the upper landing, where the old man lay "curled in a nest of rags, clutching his throat with both hands, quite dead. His hooked nose, protruding from his too-thin face gave him the appearance of a strange bird; his heavy-lidded eyes were open and staring at some alien vista [Divya] could not imagine."[25]

Having convinced Divya's young daughter Charu to retrieve a vial of poison from her home under the pretense of keeping rats from molesting him in the night, the old man drinks its contents and ends his misery, further reinforcing the linkage between his spatio-ideological intrusion and that of the kitchen vermin. The man's death and the rupture that it occasions in Divya's domestic reality (her scandalized bourgeois guests leave at once) signals the story's nearly imperceptible departure from standard domestic realism via the *novum* of extrasensory perception, the acuity of which restores to the field of social vision the interstitial public spaces of a differential reality:

> When she went out, however, the gift or curse that had been left for her by the old man's death took its strangest form. When she looked upon the faces of strangers they appeared to her like aliens, like the open mouths of birds, crying their need. But most clearly she could sense those who were hungry ... Even in the great tide of humanity that thronged the pavements, amidst busy office-goers and college students with cellphones, or in the shadows of the high-rises and luxury apartment blocks, she could sense the hungry and forgotten, great masses of them, living like cockroaches in the cracks and interstices of the new old city.[26]

Here, the abstract horizon of the domestic is expanded once more to the domain of the city (which will become significant for what I identify as the collection's second thematic sequence), and just as she comes to suspect the discontinuities within the seeming solidity of the home, Divya's newly expanded sensorium penetrates the city's mystifications to the barely discernible social realities that they obscure: shadows in the alleyways and cracks in the walk, the erased traces of a forgotten *public* consciousness. Divya's "sixth sense" thus recalls Jameson's observation that SF's characteristic enlargement of the sensorium (such as the imagining of a new color) is always to be seen as allegorical of the ability to reconstruct the socium in its entirety and is not to be viewed as reified "innovation" or meager imaginative fancy. Rather, the elaboration of a new sensory awareness reintroduces as if for the first time "representational questions, which are somehow prior to the purely sensory ones" in and of themselves; thus, he writes, "a new quality already begins to demand a new kind of perception, and that new perception in turn a new organ of perception, and thus ultimately a new kind of body."[27]

The construction of such a new social corpus is significantly developed in the former story's companion piece "Thirst," which correlates a critical consciousness of the abstract domestic chronotope – one that acknowledges its complicity in maintaining the strict precincts of class and caste – with a comprehensive, "worlding" orientation.[28] Set on the eve of Naag Panchami, the Hindu festival of snakes, protagonist Susheela wakes from a vivid dream of serpents to find herself (like so many of Singh's female characters) inexplicably alienated from life as she has formerly known it:

> Even the familiar room, with the whitewash peeling off the walls and the summer dust on the sill of the open window, the sag of the bed, the curve of the man's shoulders as he lay in sleep with his back to her – all that seemed imbued with a remoteness, as though it had nothing whatever to do with *her*. Slowly her name came to her – Susheela – and with it the full weight of her misery returned.[29]

Like Divya, Susheela's estrangement extends to every dimension of her domestic identity, including her role as mother. Thinking of her young son, Susheela recalls that he is likely sleeping in his grandmother's bed, and despite her instinctive compulsion to hold him, she cannot bring herself to confront the reality of her family just yet.[30] Instead, she reflects on the much-needed monsoon rains, late this year, which provokes a deeper yearning, not wholly unrelated to the first, one that she cannot as yet name.

Susheela's indefinite longing is extended to a sympathetic physical environment in the "dead, spiny shrubs" and "withered grass" of the garden and courtyard and in the singularly thriving harsingar tree: "She felt the old hunger in her as though she was waiting for something. As the earth waits for rain, she thought, licking her lips."[31] If in a work of traditionally realist fiction the story's freighted juxtaposition of Susheela and the mysterious, proudly blossoming harsingar tree – which survives in the surrounding blight only "on a daily cupful of water and her love" – would be read simply as a moment of pathetic fallacy, metaphorically indicative of her inviolable individual spirit within the smothering confines of an oppressive domestic reality, here the correlation with the natural world is taken quite literally, and it is rather the individuating abstraction of the figurative that is gradually revealed as a tempting false identification.[32] The harsingar tree, which has only recently appeared in the garden, is "innocent of its origins," though it is rumored the work of a local gardener showcasing his skills in an effort to hire out his services.[33] Thriving unaccountably in the drought before the delayed monsoons, it "bloomed out of season, as though it obeyed the laws of some other universe."[34] Placing a bowl of milk beneath the tree, as she recalls having observed her mother do on the eve of Naag Panchami, Susheela collects fragrant harsingar blossoms to wear in her hair the following day and ponders once more the mysterious longing that this ritual arouses: "Let there be rain tomorrow, she said in her mind. She could not name the nebulous other thing she desired."[35]

The object of this unnamed/unnameable desire is already suggested, however, in the person of the gardener himself, with whom Susheela has previously exchanged a series of meaningful glances in the park that ultimately prompt his brazen proposition: "If ever there is anything you need ... I will be happy to serve you."[36] Aware that "respectably married housewives didn't wander about parks alone," Susheela is ashamed of her behavior, particularly when the gardener inquires as to the whereabouts of her son, whom she has intentionally neglected to bring along, thereby provoking memories of her own mother, who inexplicably abandoned her and her family when Susheela was a child.[37] While her interest in the gardener is clearly amorous ("For a moment, she imagined his fingers on the nape of her neck"[38]), such an explanation does not fully exhaust the content of Susheela's desire here in its overdetermined complexity.

After a dismal afternoon "blindly" performing household duties in the unyielding swelter of the late-summer drought, Susheela is tempted to break her self-imposed prohibition from the park and the lake (and therefore from the gardener), one that she confesses to having broken "many times before."[39] Compelled by the scent of water (another literalization), she looks in on her sleeping child and mother-in-law and admits, "I have not been a good mother," before hurrying to the lake.[40] In addition to the momentary rush of liberation from the crushing banalities of her home life, the encounter with the gardener (like Divya's old man) affords Susheela a more comprehensive social perspective. Indeed, Susheela finds most appealing his insouciant disregard for the regulatory codes of Indian civil society, here given a pronounced spatial inflection: "the way he said *namaste* so respectfully while his eyes looked at her in a way that dissolved all distance between them, all barriers of class, caste, and propriety."[41] While such a theme of forbidden inter-caste/inter-class romance is a staple of Indian domestic realism, "Thirst" presses this convention further in its relation to the story's fantastic or speculative core. On the morning of Naag Panchami the rains gloriously arrive, and as Susheela stands at the window transfixed by the drops needling the dust and gathering into rivulets that wash the old world away, she realizes with a flash of horror that her son Kishore is missing. Quickly deducing where he must have gone, Susheela finds him at the lake and carries the child home in her arms. But as she delivers him to the front steps, Kishore violently startles as though frightened by her appearance and dashes inside to his father. Just as she starts to cross the threshold and follow the boy back into the home, Susheela is arrested by a sudden *frisson* and observes in wonder as her skin takes on a nacreous, quicksilver sheen. Drawn immediately back to the lake by a "gravitational" force, Susheela enters the water and experiences at once the terrifying thrill of "something alien [invading] her mind and body."[42]

Finding herself transformed into one of the Naga, Susheela exults in the alien splendor of her "long, limbless and lithe new body" and its unfamiliar complex of sensory receptors. The metamorphosis is not merely physical, however, as soon "[m]emories that were not her own, yet belonged to her in some mysterious way came crowding into her mind: warm, narrow spaces in the earth, fluid darkness, the coilings of other bodies beside her. The earth, the womb, shutting out the wide emptiness of the world."[43] "[L]etting out all the needs and desires of her barren other life" within the welcoming space of this new community, amid the sub-aquatic ruins of its ancient history, she spontaneously mates with a cobra possessing "bright, ardent, questioning eyes" and comes to the realization that she must have been conceived in just this way, that her estranged mother's failure in maintaining a conventional domesticity was in fact attributable to the very "dilemma of choosing between two worlds," as was her own.[44] Frightened by the profound implications of this placeless new existence "in the twilight state between her two worlds" and of the choice of abandoning one for the other, Susheela is approached by the gardener, both now having resumed their human forms by the lake's edge. Initially receptive to his disturbingly familiar embrace, she "remember[s], with the suddenness of a thunderclap, the old fear and confusion" and, without warning, buries her still-serpentine fangs into his neck until he collapses in violent death spasms onto the ground, after which she quietly returns to her family and her former life, leaving no trace of this fantastical interlude.[45]

If Susheela's erotic fascination with the gardener violates at once the sacrosanctity of her domestic station and the integrity of its bourgeois foundation, her commune with the serpents and with Naga-consciousness represents a far more profound expansion of her lifeworld's frontiers. Here, the ontological barrier between human and non-human, individual and collective is suspended, and an experience of *deep history* is substituted for an alienated and individuated domestic angst. Simultaneously providing for a previously unimaginable sense of social solidarity and a radical identification with the natural world, the metamorphosis of "Thirst" thus enhances tenfold the tentatively utopian inclinations of "Hunger"; however, inasmuch as the former gives exultant free rein to the expression of this social desire, it likewise reveals the extent to which the abstract realm of the domestic is founded upon its violent suppression. Susheela's fear of the loss of the familiar motivates a reactionary, protective impulse that results in the concealment of difference itself: of poverty and exploitation fully as much as the ineluctable materiality of the natural world, both of which are figured here in the character of the gardener.[46]

Foremost among the story's remarkable features and expressive of the collection's defining literary-artistic agenda is the way in which it concretizes the thematic content of this ideological ablation at the level of narrative form. Having left the scene of the murder, Susheela initially finds unfamiliar the language of those she encounters along the road and wonders briefly if she will ever be able to return to her former reality, but as she nears home, the words become increasingly sensible, and her world gradually assumes features of a mundane familiarity:

> There was the house; the shisham trees, their round leaves glistening, the trunks dark with moisture. Through the open front window she could see her husband's profile as he waited, reading his paper, one brown hand on the sunlit sill. A picture came into her mind's eye: that brown hand scooping up earth, making a hollow like a womb for the roots of the harsingar tree, patting the soil in place. She trembled, as though a string had been plucked deep inside her. The door was open. She walked into the house as if for the first time.[47]

As her previous reality seals back into place around her, the presence of the gardener and of the radical possibilities he represents are wholly elided, and a new and complete origin of the harsingar tree is fitted seamlessly into position. Having restored Susheela to her proper role in a domestic fiction, the narrative, now deprived of the estranging force of its former novum, can provide only metaphorical or abstract evidence of that which it has heretofore expressed with unblinking literality. Indeed, as Samuel Delany teaches us, the valorization of the literal is one of the distinguishing stylistic features of SF narrative – such that even the most banal figural phrase, like "the world exploded" or "he turned on his left side," can take on vastly different significance in an SF text than it might bear in a naturalistic one.[48] Thus, the restoration of domesticity in "Thirst" (complete with newspaper) finds its formal complement or condition in a retreat to the abstract language of the splace – that is, to domestic realism – and its privileging of the merely figurative. Not only is Susheela's pregnancy metaphorized into inconsequentiality in the above passage ("a hollow like a womb"), but with the foreclusion of the unthinkable, the husband is symbolically reinstated in his default role as patriarch, and the differential threat posed by the illegitimate child – "an entity capable of existing in two worlds" – is neatly recontained within the homogenizing abstractions of a domestic fiction.[49]

Such intimations of radical totality, by turns restricted and neutralized in the domestic spaces of "Hunger" and "Thirst," are given uncompromising free play in *The Woman Who Thought She Was a Planet's* title story, in which the pattern of expression and containment established in the above works are finally overcome and in which a properly science-fictional narrative form may be seen to rise triumphantly from the delimiting enclosures of the home.[50] Taking up the splace of the restored domesticity where "Thirst" leaves off, "The Woman Who Thought She Was a Planet" opens on the scene of recently retired Ramnath Mishra likewise observing the daily "ritual" of reading the newspaper, the celebrated vector – along with the novel – of Anderson's meanwhile consciousness. His patriarchal repose is disturbed by an astonishing announcement from his wife, Kamala: "I know at last what I am. I am a planet. ... I used to be a human, a wife and mother. All the time I wondered if there was more to me than that. Now I know."[51] Putting aside his newspaper to scold her for the interruption, Ramnath is horrified to find her jubilantly disrobing: "'A planet does not need clothes,' she said with great dignity."[52] Fearing the scandal that might follow her being seen by servants or neighbors, Ramnath reasons with her, noting that planets are unimaginably massive objects orbiting stars, that they have their own atmospheres and provide habitation for innumerable living organisms: "You are not a planet but a living soul, a woman. A lady from a respectable household who holds the family honour in her hands."[53]

Singh's invocation of the wife/mother as faithful custodian of the family honor recalls Partha Chatterjee's important connection of India's late-nineteenth-century "women's question" to the nationalist project of constructing a domain of "inner sovereignty" with which to oppose the public/material rhetoric of imperialism.[54] As he notes, "the nationalist position was firmly based on the premise that [the home] was an area where the nation was acting on its own, outside the purview of the guidance and intervention of the colonial state."[55] Such a position, Chatterjee contends, necessitated the radical partitioning of sociospatial experience itself into discrete spheres of activity and authority:

> Applying the inner/outer distinction to the matter of concrete day-to-day living separates the social space into *ghar* and *bāhir*, the home and the world. The world is the external, the domain of the material; the home represents one's inner spiritual self, one's true identity. The world is a treacherous terrain of the pursuit of material interests, where practical considerations reign supreme. It is also typically the domain of the male. The home in its essence must remain unaffected by the profane activities of the material world – and woman is its representation.[56]

The home, Chatterjee goes on to suggest, is not merely one among other complementary loci in the broad formation of a nationalist identity "but rather the original site on which the hegemonic project of nationalism was launched."[57] Thus, we cannot think the domestic space of Indian modernity (*ghar*) without simultaneously thinking the nation (*bāhir*). Wiemann observes that

> the concept of house/home shares with pre-Derridean textual theories the assumption of a boundedness that allows for the distinction of inside from outside; it is in fact posited, in structuralist anthropology, on that very distinction. The concept of *ghar* as the site of the symbolic production of national culture interferes with this polarity in a historically specific manner, reinventing the domestic as a strictly circumscribed domain that achieves its political symbolism precisely by virtue of its removal from the public. While it thus may

> serve as an agency that produces a nationalist counter-interpellation polemically vying with colonialist modes of "being-called," it simultaneously constitutes the "new Indian woman" in strict domestic confinement. An immense body of contemporary Indian domestic fiction (not only by women writers like Anita Desai or Githa Hariharan) testifies to the longevity of this invented tradition[58]

Indeed, it is toward this canon of domestic fiction as well as its invention and circumscription of both nation and new Indian woman that Singh's SF orients its critical focus.

Ramnath, a recently retired government bureaucrat of more than forty years' service, implicitly appeals to the nationalist distinction between *ghar* and *bāhir* throughout the story. Comparing Kamala's apparent state of delusion to the "madness" that seized his great aunt, he recalls that the latter had "locked herself in the outdoor toilet of the ancestral home and begun shrieking like a sarus crane in the mating season," necessitating her forcible extraction at the hands of relatives and her shamed husband (whom she promptly bit on the arm after a feigned "meek surrender"): "What terrible dishonor the family had suffered, what indignity – a mad person in a respectable upper middle-class family – he shuddered suddenly, set down his newspaper and went to call Dr Kumar. Dr Kumar would be discreet, he was a family friend ...."[59] This class distinction is a crucial one, for while the rehearsal of such domestic values might seem to accord with those of the "indigenous" patriarchy of western stereotypes of Indian culture, Chatterjee insists that Indian nationalism's construction of the "new woman" is sharply to be distinguished from any notion of an anterior (presumably timeless) patriarchal authority. Citing Ghulam Murshid's study of the abrupt, early twentieth-century disappearance of the feminist agenda that had characterized Bengali politics for the previous five decades, Chatterjee contends that "[i]f one takes seriously, that is to say, in their liberal, rationalist and egalitarian content, the mid-nineteenth-century attempts in Bengal to 'modernize' the condition of women, then what follows in the period of nationalism must be regarded as a clear retrogression."[60] By identifying Ramnath and Kamala as members of a "respectable upper middle-class family," therefore, Singh invokes a particularly nationalist brand of patriarchy, one that delineates an absolute distinction not only between bourgeois Indian femininity and the "outside" world but also between the former and "the host of lower class female characters who make their appearance in the social milieu of the new middle class."[61] In her role as what Ramnath calls the "benign despot of the household" or "dutiful Indian wife," Kamala's respectable, bourgeois femininity is in marked contrast, for example, to the cook who serves the couple in reverential silence – to whose anonymous class presence "Hunger" has already sensitized us.[62]

Among the distinguishing characteristics of this middle-class femininity is a disciplined commitment to "the typically bourgeois virtues" of "orderliness, thrift, cleanliness, and a personal sense of responsibility, the practical skills of literacy, accounting, hygiene, and the ability to run the household."[63] Additionally, Chatterjee notes the shift in emphasis in late-nineteenth-century "feminist" discourse toward the "need for an educated woman to develop such womanly virtues as chastity, self-sacrifice, submission, devotion, kindness, patience, and the labors of love."[64] If Kamala's "shameless" disregard for physical modesty – most dramatically and humorously expressed in her frequent disrobings – clearly indicates her radical departure from this cultural ideal, only somewhat less troubling for Ramnath is Kamala's uncharacteristic disregard for domestic orderliness: "The blouse, petticoat and sari lay in crumpled folds on the bed. This in itself was disturbing because she was usually obsessive about tidiness."[65] More than a concern in its own right, this indifference to household dignity forces Ramnath to confront the discomforting reality of his own inability to care for himself in the wake of his wife's mental decline: "How would he manage now with nobody to look after him."[66] Indulging himself a moment of self-pity, he reflects that, despite his professional success and his having fathered two sons, "it would have been nice to have a daughter, somebody whom he could call on at times like this."[67] Thus, the crisis is one that throws into relief the strains, conflicts, and occluded alternatives that sit impatiently beneath the homogenizing surface of a normative domestic orderliness – and therefore beneath the official dispensations of the nation state itself in the post-contemporary moment.

One such alternative, the ontology of radical collectivity already prefigured in "Thirst," challenges the confines of the domestic narrative from which it springs by performing a spatial inversion that will provide the condition for the historical one that I will identify in Amitav Ghosh's *The Calcutta Chromosome*.[68] Rather than seek, as do the protagonists of "Hunger" and "Thirst," an exterior whole beyond the abstractions and occultations of the domestic enclave, "The Woman Who Thought She Was a Planet" heedlessly postulates a global totality *within* this abstract space itself (the transnational within the national) that explodes the determinate coordinates of the latter and opens onto an expansive horizon of the possible in which a binary spatiality of discrete inner and outer domains is discarded for an oscillatory or dialectical transpositioning,[69] where the one is revealed already to have obtained within the other. The story achieves this effect, unlike in the previous two tales, through an unremitting commitment to science fiction, revealed here not in the rigidities of a taxonomic purity but in the *practice* of a critical and dialectical defamiliarization. That is, here SF emerges as a point of internal differentiation within the domestic narrative, not only exposing its carefully disguised fissures but absolutely refusing its logics of containment. His patience with Kamala's "cunning" delusions now fully exhausted, Ramnath entertains for the first time the strangely liberating possibility of her death: "Now, as he watched her sleep, her hair in disarray and her mouth open like some hideous cavern, it occurred to him how easy his life would be if she would simply die."[70] This inevitably leads him to consider her murder, a prospect that becomes gradually more seductive until one night "he put his hand very gently on her neck" in preparation to strangle her, an act that is interrupted by Kamala's violent fit of coughing. Watching in amazement as she expectorates a dark, gelatinous gout that begins to gather about her chin with an apparent sentience, Ramnath leans in to investigate: "To his horror, he saw that the darkness was not blood but composed of small, moving things. One stood up on its hind legs for a moment, surveying him, and he drew back in horror. It was insectoid, alien, about as tall as his index finger. There was an army of those things coming out of her mouth."[71] The alien "army" furiously attacks Ramnath, protecting their new habitation from harm.

His behavior toward Kamala alters remarkably the following day, when, despite the fact that he has for many years prevented her from visiting her mother ("there was always something going on that needed her attention. The marriage of their sons, his retirement and the fact that *somebody* had to run the house and supervise the servants"), he unaccountably encourages her to make the trip to her ancestral village.[72] His new generosity of spirit is, of course, motivated by his fear of the incomprehensible legion that Kamala now houses in her body, a fear that reveals the carceral nature of a formerly tranquil domesticity, in which going home now "felt like going to prison."[73] When he works up the courage to ask her about the creatures, Kamala reassures him by declaring that her "alien" inhabitants are neither infestation nor invasion but rather an emanation from her person: "And these things, as you call them are not things but my own creation. They came from me, Ramnath."[74] Just as the global totality of a *planet* originates within and thus detonates the authoritative space of the home, the contestatory alien species (who, as we shall see, stage their own revolution of sorts) emerges from the seemingly homogenous singular subject presiding over that abstraction. Here is the "within and against" structural logic that conditions the effulgence of the multitude, whose radiance illuminates the underlying anatomy obscured by spatial abstraction and unveils the articulating ligatures of a common global struggle. Unlike the previous two stories, then, "Planet" successfully resists both the sanctuary of the domestic and the mystifications of metaphor and achieves an authentically SF departure. Though the reader may certainly be tempted to do so, Singh's story does not self-reflexively recontain the alien as a mere *figure* for a naturalized domestic disaffection and therefore gives free rein to the estranging and historicizing capacities of the genre. Even the characterological effects of the alien intervention, expressed in Ramnath's reconsideration of Kamala's personal complexity, lead us not back to the conundrums of personal psychology but to the broader material conditions for this domestic angst: "Looking at his wife over dinner, he began to wonder for the first time about her. What was she really like? What did she want that he had not given her? How had he come to this?"[75]

This new state of uncertainty, rendering the present unfinished, opens the enclave space of the domestic to an array of previously unimaginable exotopic potentialities. Kamala, perceiving the subtle change in Ramnath, invites him to become a part of her terrific new cosmology, the utopian thrust of which is made clear in her declaration that the "younger ones have been clamouring for a new world."[76] The culmination of this desire is figured in Kamala's ascension during a walk in the park as "[s]lowly and majestically she began to rise over the ground – an inch, two inches."[77] Stricken with horror and abject shame as he watches her ascend, casting off her clothing one garment at a time, Ramnath is nevertheless moved to contemplate the intoxicating possibilities of such a transfiguration:

> She was out of sight now. For a moment he almost envied her, out there among the stars. He imagined, despite himself, the little alien creatures running over the wild terrain of her body, exploring the mountains, gullies, and varied habitats of that mysterious and unknowable geography. What sun would she find? What vistas would she see?[78]

At precisely the moment that this slight receptivity to ontological alterity is registered on his consciousness, Ramnath hears the insectoid chatter of the aliens, and before he can react, finds them "already marching up his back, over his shoulder and into his terrified, open mouth."[79] Born of the half-conscious desire for an alternative to the suffocating matrix of the splace, the "alien" multitude – here again operating under the sign of the monstrous[80] – emerges from the recognition that the totality (the global common) emerges only by way of the singularity. As Hardt and Negri observe, attention to the local or singular does not suggest that "the world is merely a collection of incommunicable localities"; rather, in the very moment that we properly "recognize singularity, the common begins to emerge."[81]

Imagining long space

For Hardt and Negri (as for Singh), a primary factor in the emergent possibility of the global common, of the creation of *a world,* is the fact that "for the first time the majority of the planet's population lives in urban areas."[82] This "metropolitanization of the world" provides the condition for a variety of "aleatory encounters" along a vast continuum of scales, the complex overlays and interdependencies of which become visible, as "Hunger" demonstrates, only after the ideological field of the domestic has been exceeded. Indeed, once beyond the imaginative boundary of the home and its isomorphic extensions, we enter the chronotope that Peter Hitchcock theorizes as the "Long Space" of the postcolonial transnational. Hitchcock deploys the concept of this radically extensive space-time to correlate the durational and spatial interdependencies of colonialism to its purported "post."[83] Hitchcock urges Mikhail Bakhtin's familiar concept of the chronotope in the direction of the transnational in order to

> further discussion on time's claim on that which is presented as its superadequation. The idea that nations require time must be supplemented since this can be deployed to blunt transnationalism's history, one much longer than the term itself. I use postcolonialism within transnationalism to problematize this elision by introducing time/space coordinates into the latter's otherwise slick immediacy. The effect is not just one of catechresis but of slowing down, of marking duration with duration, of saving time by using it. Chronotopic critique, however, is not a means to fight speed and space: its strategy is to insinuate time/space coordinates in transnationalism, the better to specify what is living and dead in their conjunction.[84]

The aesthetic form taken by this impulse to save time by using it, and thereby to stage the "irruption of local history into the truncated temporalities of globalization and transnationalism in their hegemonic formations," is the extended novel (the trilogy or tetralogy), which, like Anderson's newspaper, "facilitates an experience of unbound seriality," though one that ultimately disrupts rather than secures national identifications.[85] Through its ability to strategically realize "agonistic creativity in a space where hegemony believes there is none," Hitchcock argues that transnationalist long fiction ("a resource of hope materially inscribed") articulates linkages between writers across spatial, cultural, and epistemological partitions "not because their histories are the same but because they speak to a logic of time that remains dissatisfied with 'posts' or 'eras' or linearity."[86] While Hitchcock's analysis prioritizes the long novel form,[87] he also indicates that long space is often "at odds with formal analysis" and does not so much codify a literary language capable of addressing the intricacies of the postcolonial within the transnational as it does mark a set of "specific symptoms in the problem of form without assuming a formal consistency or generic identity."[88] In fact, I want to suggest that the figuration of long space need not require the elongated narrative expanse of, for instance, Pramoedya Ananta Toer's majestic *Buru Quartet* but may be equally if not more dramatically realized in the formal demands of a work like Singh's *The Woman Who Thought She Was a Planet*, the organizational logic of which requires that its scrambled thematic and conceptual elements be reconstructed as the reader makes her way through the text, hazarding hypotheses and emending them in light of later developments, gathering the individuated narratives together toward some tentatively comprehensive set of conclusions that are construed not in the linear fashion of the extended novel but in the oscillatory relation of the overlapping temporalities and spaces of the otherwise discontinuous and completely self-contained stories in the collection.

While a drawn-out seriality resists the formal and spatiotemporal limits of the novelistic form, it cannot finally overcome them. The involutional organization of the collection provides, however, for an unlimited correlation of the "local" to the "global," of the private to the public, of the nation to the transnational, formally manifesting the book's foremost thematic content. Such formal demands (endemic to any collection of fiction but emphatically foregrounded here) more precisely and effectively throw into relief the convoluted spatial structures of globalization even as they contest the neatly synchronizing logic of "meanwhile" consciousness and encourage the reader to enact the composite creation of the transnational subject, who must likewise reconstruct a tenuous narrative of inclusion within and against the isolating, atomizing forces of late capital, which while positing a "one world" of capitalist development simultaneously inscribes a hierarchy of discrete, spatially defined temporalities.

From the delimiting vantage of the splace the intrusions of such transnationalist long space may appear as the spectral excess of a devitalized sociospatial organization. As Marx famously observes, "It is generally the fate of completely new historical creations to be mistaken for the counterpart of older and even defunct forms of social life."[89] I turn now to a story that figures the *site* of long space in precisely this hauntological sense. Immediately following upon the burgeoning spatio-ideological enlargements of "Hunger," "Delhi," explores the timescape of its titular "new old city," the architectonics of which stand not only as imbricated material reminders of a complex colonial history but also as the crystallization and critical historicization of its globalized present.[90] The story's "middle-class and educated" male protagonist, Aseem, is plagued by apparitions. As a child, he once believed them to be the spirits of the dead, but experience has revealed them to be the result of an exceptional sensitivity to temporal anomalies, to the "tangles produced when one part of the time-stream rubs up against another and the two cross for a moment."[91] The visions mark, in other words, points where past and present leak into and momentarily suspend one another, where the synchronizing field of homogenous empty time is disrupted by the confounding intrusion of the longue durée and what Derrida describes as the "*non-contemporaneity with itself of the living present.*"[92] If such disjointures, as Derrida instructs, are nothing less than "the very possibility of the other," then what difference is here?[93] Only for Aseem (and, we later discover, those few like him) do the nine distinct historical iterations of Delhi exist in simultaneity, the past and present collapsing into what we might recognize as the Benjaminian *Jetztzeit*, the radical now-time released from the determinate logic of historical causality, what Anderson describes as "a simultaneity of past and future in an instantaneous present."[94] Considering the British, for instance, whose lingering phantoms he occasionally encounters in the streets, Aseem is struck primarily by the ephemerality of the Raj relative to the seven earlier manifestations of the three-thousand year-old city:

> They built these great edifices, gracious buildings and fountains, but even they had to leave it all behind. Kings came and went, *goras* came and went, but the city lives on. Sometimes, he sees apparitions

> of the *goras*, the palefaces, walking by him or riding on horses. Each time he yells out to them: 'Your people are doomed. You will leave here. Your empire will crumble.' Once in a while they glance at him, startled, before they fade away.[95]

While Aseem sometimes entertains the thought after such encounters that he could somehow be personally responsible for the dissolution of the British Empire by sowing seeds of doubt in the past, he reasons that since he rarely encounters figures of any world-historical import, "he is simply deluding himself about his own significance" in such matters of historical causality.[96]

This gloomy resignation to History is soon challenged, however, by recurrent apparitions in the metro tunnel. Despite the unpredictable and singular nature of most spectral manifestations, Aseem "almost always sees people in the subway tunnels, floating through the train and the passengers on the platforms, dressed in tatters, their faces pale and unhealthy as though they had never beheld the sun."[97] Given the relative age of the subway system, he deduces that they must be specters from the future (which, Derrida insists, is the provenance of *all* specters), and their woeful, persistent appearance sharpens Aseem's sense of vocation while inspiring him to consider anew the possibility of allochronic intervention through the annihilation of linear time itself, through the convergence that marks the *Jetztzeit*. As Derrida suggests, despite our initial impulse to locate the source of the specter in either the past or future, "one must perhaps ask oneself whether the *spectrality effect* does not consist in undoing this opposition."[98] That is, if the effect of this spectral appearance of the future is the means to transform the present (and hence to alter the trajectory leading to that future), then Aseem might well have been responsible for the demise of the British Empire after all, and the present is instantly transformed from the attenuated mediator of an implacably determinate past and dedicated future to the site of an agential seizure that, according to Benjamin's famous formulation, fires at the dials and explodes the continuum of history altogether.[99] Singh thus conceives of history as Benjamin's "subject of a structure whose site is not homogeneous, empty time, but time filled with the presence of the now," vitalized by the animus of the revolutionary "tiger's leap" out of historicity's suffocating stringencies and into "the open air of history" itself.[100]

The story's (always tenuous, always qualified) utopian horizon of radical difference comes more clearly into view as the narrative doubles back to explain Aseem's relationship to the mysterious, never seen Pandit Vidyanath and his assistant Om Prakash as well as the circumstances of Aseem's lengthy suicide vigil over the city. Three years prior to the story's present action, Aseem, weary of the hauntings that have plagued him since boyhood, stands on the Yamuna bridge (both a decaying monument to the British imperial presence and the city's outer limit) and contemplates the turgid waters beneath as the answer to his suffering. Just as he positions himself to slide over the railing, a voice cries out, "Don't be a fool, don't do it," and a strange man emerges from the fog and presses a business card into Aseem's trembling hand.[101] The card, which bears a beehive logo and the legend "Worried About Your Future?" on its face, directs him to the "air-conditioned" office of Pandit Vidyanath where, he is promised, he will discover the purpose of his life.[102] Disappointed to find that the Pandit is not available (Aseem gradually comes to believe that there is no Pandit Vidyanath), he considers leaving until his eye is drawn to the swarming hive just outside the open office window: "... but the beehive fascinates him, how it is still and in motion all at once, and the way the bees seem to be in concert with one another, as though performing a complicated dance."[103] Eyeing with mild concern the bees crawling on the computer of Om Prakash, who appears little more than a "petty clerk," Aseem asks him how his computer can know the future. Prakash, gesturing at the bees, offers an opportunistic analogy: "A computer is like a beehive. Many bits and parts, none is by itself intelligent. Combine together, and you have something that can think."[104]

No less cryptically, Prakash offers Aseem a computer printout composed of a seemingly random pattern of x's that, when seen from a proper (indeed, a totalizing) distance, reveals the crude image of a woman's face. This, apart from a handful of business cards "to give other unfortunate souls," is the only instruction Aseem receives. After saving dozens of would-be suicides and distributing as many of Pandit Vidyanath's business cards (assiduously recording each encounter in a notebook), Aseem finally meets ("Or thinks he does") the face in the printout while wandering among the medieval ruins of Delhi Ridge, a forested area described as "a green lung" and a "warm, green womb" within the city boundaries.[105] The face belongs to a blind young girl who approaches Aseem for directions to Naya Diwas Lane, explaining that she must locate her sister there because, having misplaced her "papers," she risks being sent "to Neechi-Dilli with all the poor and the criminals."[106] Aseem tells her that he recognizes no such places and that she should simply go to the main road and ask directions. She thanks him for his assistance and, turning to go, adds that "she's heard many stories about the fabled city, and its tall, gem-studded minars that reach the sky, and the perfect gardens. And the ships, the silver *udankhatolas*, that fly across worlds."[107] She fades abruptly from view, and the full significance of the apparition's appearance and strange comments dawns on him. The specters in the Metro are indeed from the future, from *her* future:

> Lower Delhi – Neechi Dilli – that is what this must be: a city of the poor, the outcast, the criminal, in the still-to-be-carved tunnels underneath the Delhi that he knows. He thinks of the Metro, fallen into disuse in that distant future, its tunnels abandoned to the dispossessed, and the city above a delight of gardens and gracious buildings, and tall spires reaching through the clouds.[108]

Aseem recognizes in this bifurcated future Delhi the exaggeration of contemporary techniques of sociospatial engineering, "[l]ike when the foreign VIPs come to town and the policemen chase people like me out of the main roads,"[109] or, as during preparations for the 2010 Commonwealth Games, when more than a quarter of a million slum dwellers were displaced to accommodate new roads and elevated sections of the Metro as well as the controversial Commonwealth Games Village built along the occupied banks of the Yuma. In this future Delhi, however, the luxuries of the crystalline kingdom of freedom are predicated upon the *completely invisible* substratum of grim necessity in the tunnels of the condemned. No less significant is the fact that the young girl has lost her identification papers, recalling the plight of the global *sans papiers*, the undocumented laborer and the refugee in whom Badiou recognizes the internal exclusion that gives the lie to narratives of national cohesion.[110]

Believing that in his distracted moment of morose self-indulgence, he may have given the girl advice that will deliver her to imprisonment in the sunless bowels of the city without hope of release, Aseem returns to the office of Om Prakash and roughly interrogates him on the matter of destiny, demanding to know if his volitional actions have consequence or if he is "nothing but a strand in a web."[111] Prakash's response uncannily utilizes a natural metaphor that Aseem himself once considered as he stood trembling on the Yamuna bridge, that of the tenaciously resilient pipal tree, growing up irrepressibly from the cracks and fissures in the concrete and masonry of the urban landscape: "Whatever you do affects the world in some small way. Sometimes the effect remains small, sometimes it grows and grows like a pipal tree. Causality as we call it is only a first-order effect. Second-order causal loops jump from time to time, as in your visions, sir."[112] Linear temporality and the inexorable law of cause and effect conceal a deeper *Jetztzeit*, the effects of which are broadly cumulative and collective – like the concerted labor of the beehive or the slow, vegetable defiance of the pipal tree – rather than local, singular, or spectacular.

Finding himself again on the Yamuna bridge at the city's edge, Aseem is arrested this time by "a stranger who is not a stranger" but rather a scarred and bloody future self, who utters simply "Don't ..." before vanishing into the fog.[113] Faced with this spectral evidence of the desperate and perhaps futile "struggle that looms indistinctly ahead," Aseem once more contemplates suicide as a means of circumventing his destiny before recalling to mind a photograph he once saw as a boy: "a satellite image of Asia at night. On the dark bulge of the globe there were knots of light; like luminous fungi, he had thought at the time stretching tentacles into the dark."[114] Momentarily heartened by this magnificent image of a globality not globalization, he considers the possibility that "complexity and vastness are sufficient conditions for a slow awakening, a coming-to-consciousness."[115] This is what it means, then, "to work for the city":

> What he must do, he sees at last, is what he has been doing all along: looking out for his own kind, the poor and the desperate, and those who walk with death in their eyes. The city's needs are alien, unfathomable. It is an entity in its own right, expanding every day, swallowing the surrounding countryside, crossing the Yamuna which was once its boundary, spawning satellite children, infant towns that it will ultimately devour. Now it is burrowing into the earth, and even later it will reach long fingers toward the stars.[116]

Here, Singh's organic metaphor of global luminescence, of a burgeoning transnational collectivity, keeps pace with the blind sprawl of the omnivorous city, which, like globalization itself, sweeps aside every former border and barrier and insinuates itself into the capillary networks of what Rob Wilson and Wimal Dissanayake call a "transnational imaginary."[117] The global consciousness Singh evokes is thus not so much a simple refusal of the political imperatives or tectonic economic pressures of globalization as it is their paradoxical effect, a manifest expression of globalization's "polemical excess."[118] Refusing the identificatory consolations of home/city/nation, long used as strategic bulwarks against the tide of transnational capital, this "imaginary state" effects as the condition of its emergence an "'agonistic liminality' of alternative globalisms even within those worldly discourses like transnational capital that believe somehow the die is cast."[119] Restoring to the future its full potentiality and to the present a dynamic unfinishedness, "Delhi" concludes – as, Jameson observes, do most works of utopian modernism – with a self-reflexive meditation upon its own "impossible" narrative production.[120] Taking up once more the precious notebook cast aside in despair ("It feels strangely heavy in his hands"[121]), Aseem walks away from the bridge determined now to realize a possibility that he had formerly entertained only as passing fancy: "One day, he tells himself, he will write a history of the future."[122]

"The Tetrahedron" advances this sidelong glimpse into infinite multiplicity by imagining not only an inspired or anticipated departure from the structurings of the splace but the ruptural emergence of the site itself (in the appearance of a massive polyhedron already observed by the protagonist of "Infinities," another story offering a strikingly Badiouian ontology[123]). Establishing the incongruous object's delineation of the transnational in the very opening sentence, Singh writes that the "story of the Tetrahedron – its mysterious appearance in the middle of a busy street in New Delhi – is known in the remotest corners of the globe."[124] Most important for us here, however, "The Tetrahedron" culminates the collection's imaginative intervention by dialectically uniting its dominant thematic currents – the limits of the domestic splace *and* the intimation of the transnationalist site – in a manner that clears space for a politics (the Badiouian "art of the impossible") that is neither local nor the count-as-one algebraic agglomeration of globalization.

The story's protagonist, Maya, is a student at Delhi University facing the familiar dilemmas of domesticity. Engaged to "Mr. Perfect Kartick," Maya feels that the marriage represents the threshold of a final capitulation to the "demands of respectability" placed upon her by her parents and society.[125] Kartick's harsh criticisms and demands echo those of the collection's other bourgeois patriarchs and, like them, proceed under the familiar sigil of the imagined national community: "The *halwa* she had made for tea was a little too sweet, that sari was a little flashy – *and by the way, could she bring him the newspaper.*"[126] In the opening pages, then, we find already in place the tension between the national and the transnational. In fact, the very temptation to refuse these domestic expectations makes Maya feel "like a traitor."[127] However, as she sits contemplating the uncertainty of her immediate future, at "precisely 10:23 a.m. IST," the fabric of her former reality is rent irreparably by the obtrusive presentation of a void: "It came suddenly and incongruously into existence – a monstrous black thing, about two stories high, broad enough on its triangular base to span all four lanes of the road."[128] Its inscrutably opaque surfaces repel all symbolization, all efforts at inscription into the logic of the splace. Interpreted variously as signaling the arrival of the age of *Kaliyug*; the Christian Day of Judgment; a vaguely purposed "government ploy"; a secret weapon deployed by Pakistan, China, or even India itself; and a Martian invasion, "the Tetrahedron answered no questions or challenges" but simply "stood implacable, a question without an answer."[129]

Compelled "as if by an invisible string," Maya begins making daily visits to the site of the Tetrahedron, the unyielding mystery of which inspires her to consider "the pointlessness of a life lived small" and to question more boldly the direction her life is taking: "In a few years she would be like her sisters, plump and resigned, children running at her feet while Kartik gazed benignly at her from the sofa over the evening paper. 'Maya, you know that sari does not suit you. . .' Maya this and Maya that. Could she take a lifetime of it?"[130] Here again, Anderson's newspaper makes a conspicuous appearance in the domestic space, evoking the encompassing framework of nation and its "meanwhile" temporality. The two are further associated when, incensed at the narrowness of Kartik's parochial interpretation ("This time he was convinced China had something to do with it too. After all, why stop at Pakistan?"[131]), Maya insists on the Tetrahedron's unsymbolizable nonidentity: "China! Pakistan! Has it occurred to you that nobody – not anybody – can understand what that thing is? None of the foreign scientists, none of ours. Can't you see anything outside your own damned backyard?"[132] Kartik, it seems, cannot. Nor can Maya's own mother, who pleads with Kartik to be patient and dismisses her daughter's irrational outburst as owing to "that time of the month," naturalizing and thus neutralizing the Tetrahedron's estranging force.[133]

Despite such attempts to wrestle the alien object into a comprehensible, domestic horizon of signification, its immediate cultural impact is precisely the opposite. The site of the Tetrahedron is patrolled by a "now international team of soldiers," and "[f]oreign languages from all over the world mingled with radio music from the shops and live commentary from TV station crewmen."[134] Multinational capital moves in immediately—much to the chagrin of the "Western press" who are "unused to reporting anything but disasters and political unrest from the Third World"[135] – to appropriate the site in the form of hotels and gift shops hawking tawdry plastic replicas of the Tetrahedron, as Delhi rapidly becomes "one of the most popular travel destinations in the world."[136] Yet inasmuch as the site can be claimed as a general symbol of globalization itself (not unlike the precipitous rise of the ICT industry in Delhi or Bangalore), it also occasions the return of an authentically *public* space of encounter, in which "[r]ich businessmen rubbed shoulders with hippies and street urchins; Americans and Middle-Easterners, Japanese, Koreans, Kenyans all stood gawking and chattering in little groups."[137] With the sociospatial securities of the splace thus disrupted, Maya, like the thousands of others from all stations who gather daily at the site of the Tetradedron (and like all of Singh's protagonists for that matter), finds herself "waiting for something" that does not as yet have an intelligible designation.[138]

Maya's sensitivity to sociocultural difference, enhanced by the Tetrahedron's estranging effect, also begins to color her perspective on her budding friendship with Samir, a PhD student in astrophysics likewise obsessed with the Tetrahedron, with whom Maya (somewhat scandalously) begins spending afternoons. Though mesmerized by Samir's theories and the insights drawn from his disciplinary expertise, Maya begins to suffer considerable anxiety about the socio-economic gulf that apparently separates them. Enduring whispered taunts from Samir's friends about his "fraternizing with the proles," Maya experiences a profound coming-to-consciousness: "Abruptly Maya was aware of herself as hopelessly lower-middle-class, belonging to the petty-tradesmen-uncultured *bhainji* sub-culture with all its implications. She didn't know anything about Samir's life, nor he about hers – what was she doing here with him?"[139] Just as she is tempted to resign herself to this paralyzing narrative of class incommensurability, Samir introduces the theory of topology, a subject, unsurprisingly, of central importance for Badiou's project as well. For Badiou, the topological is distinctly opposed to the algebraic mathematical operation. In the latter, attention is directed to the relation between elements of a given set or a "provisory figure of the Whole."[140] Algebra thus presupposes homogeneity and requires a strict adherence to the law that governs the set and its elements just as it precludes asymptotic distortions of or departures from that law. The interests of topology, on the other hand, are kinetic, proximate, and immanently relational. Simply put, "The algebraic alterity is combinatory; the topological identity is differential."[141] Samir defines topology as the science of comparative spatial deformation, such that while a rectangular and a circular sheet of paper are topologically equivalent, a hole in one or the other alters this relation irreparably, changing the latter from a "simply connected two-dimensional surface" to one that is "multiply-connected."[142] Such a theory of spatial distortion, Samir explains, provides (in a "non-trivial, multiply connected" universe) the possibility of wormholes and extra-dimensional travel.[143] More important, it also suggests that, given the comparative dimensional privation of their own universe, the Tetrahedron might be of a structural complexity completely incomprehensible to them, in which prior "notions of in and out, edge and surface would be lost, or at least very confused."[144] Like other theorists of globalization's topographical dispensation such as Jean-Luc Nancy and Giorgio Agamben, Samir illustrates this exceptional space of infinite connectivity (the exception now the rule) with the Möbius strip.[145] Fashioning one from a scrap of paper, Samir has Maya run her finger along its outer edge: "You start at the outer surface and before you know it, you are inside! Except that inside and outside have lost their meaning in this case ... "[146] The collapsing of distinction between inner and outer entails that of the distinction between domestic and international as much as that between personal and political, as Maya's increasingly complicated relationship with Samir indicates: "It's not just space and time, she thought bitterly, that are multiply connected. If she could talk to Samir now, she'd tell him: outer space, inner space, both have unknown topologies. You couldn't look at the one at the expense of the other."[147] This dialectical perspective, I argue, is the book's key contribution to a "worlding" or *mondializing* political and imaginative imperative.

After the missing bicyclist and passenger bus displaced by the appearance of the Tetrahedron are discovered hundreds of miles away in the Thar desert, speaking "gibberish, or another language," Maya refines Samir's topological theory: "The world is like a cracked egg. ... Our world, I mean, where we live. Everything we know and see and understand is in this egg. But the cracks tell us that there are things outside – a world outside our understanding."[148] Yet this world "outside our understanding" may not be outside our world at all, but may rather be internal to it; that is, if the Tetrahedron, as perceived, is merely a glimpse of a vastly larger and more complex interdimensional object, perhaps this object extends for hundreds if not thousands of miles in all directions.[149] What appears as a uniform two-dimensional reality may in fact be one of multidimensional *connection*. But such theorizations are no comfort to Maya, who craves the vitalizing *experience* of such a reality, and a chance encounter with a significantly "motley" group of internationals at the site provides her the means: "They were all so different from each other that it took her a moment to realize they were a group – three elderly men, two young women who looked Japanese, a lean young man who could have been from the Middle East, and most incongruous of them all, an old lady in a beige *salwaar-kameez*."[150] Seemingly unaffected by the anxious energy of the masses thronging the Tetrahedron, there is "something indefinably different" about this ambiguously international group and, just as Maya begins to approach them, she notices a bird overhead fly directly into the impassive face of the monolith and vanish from sight.[151] Glancing back to the group, she finds the old woman looking straight at her with a countenance of benign and knowing serenity. The old woman, she learns, is from Mexico, and she extends Maya an oddly portentous invitation to join her eclectic group of international "tourists" when they depart the following day.[152]

Stealing away with the group, Maya enters the Tetrahedron through an invisible corridor, and once inside fully comprehends the poverty and aridity of her former two-dimensional worldview. Like "an Escher picture," walls, floors, and spiral stairways extend and converge in physically impossible ways.[153] The "outside world" is not distinguishable as such but is rather a part of the inside, which likewise extends at once into multiple dimensions. Most disconcerting of all, however, is the effect of this non-space on Maya and her companions. Examining her reflection, Maya finds "great crenellations and sweeping ridges that rose from her body as gracefully as the plates on a stegosaur's back."[154] Inspecting her hands, she discovers myriad other hands of all ages, all identifiably her own, branching off into infinity. Horrified at this monstrous transformation, she is patiently reassured by her *fellow travelers* that nothing has happened to her at all save that she now perceives herself in true multidimensionality, the scales of identitarian illusion having dropped suddenly away to reveal her authentic *transindividual* substance.[155] Like Abdul in "Infinities," she stands at the threshold of worlds, inhabiting the uninhabitable void; unlike Abdul, however, she is neither alone nor tempted to forsake fidelity to the event for mere *perseverance in being*. Imagining that she hears Lata Mangeshkar and Mohammad Rafi singing on the radio, "*'Chalo Dildaar, chalo, chand kepaar chalo. . .' Come, beloved, let us fly beyond the moon*," she announces resolvedly, "*Let's go further*."[156] This "Keep going!" is for Badiou the foremost principle of an ethical consistency and the credo of the faithful subject: "Keep going even when you have lost the thread, when you no longer feel 'caught up' in the process, when the event itself has become obscure, when its name is lost, or when it seems that it may have named a mistake, if not a simulacrum."[157]

But it is not only this inspiring expression of fidelity that sets "The Tetrahedron" somewhat apart from *The Woman Who Thought She Was a Planet*'s other stories. For the Tetrahedron itself is neither an alien technology nor a spaceship; nor is it merely an elaborate plot device providing Maya the convenience of escape from an undesirable marriage and domestic tedium – though it is certainly that as well. Above all, the Tetrahedron is an optic, a novum of scopic estrangement that reveals the multitudinous network of connections and interpenetrations *already present* in the homogenizing splace that defines our most immediate reality. What Maya witnesses in the Tetrahedron is neither a grotesque deformation of her unitary "self" nor a clever manipulation of actually existing space; it is the revelation that multidimensionality is the *truer* reality. "The Tetrahedron" differs from the other stories in that it not only offers an estranging critical perspective on the disciplinary boundaries of the present but also "does something to the real" by mapping an imaginary state, the long space of the transnational, *already obtaining within that present.* Grasping the nettle of globalization in a way that is structurally unavailable to realist or naturalist fictions, Singh fashions a *world* exclusively neither local nor global.

Finally, then, it is in the libratory structure and style of Singh's collection itself, oscillating ceaselessly between *splace* and *site*, home and world, individual and transindividual, domestic fiction and SF, that we trace the trajectory of this long space of the transnational, literary form becoming itself a space-time of infinite connectivity for which the vertical temporality of the Andersonian "meanwhile" is a woefully insufficient metric. Like Hitchcock's long space, Singh's short fiction also "cannot find solace in the simultaneity of the 'meanwhile'" but "must fight its prescriptions at every turn," which it manages through the complex concatenation of its heterogeneous "worlds" into a formal totality that can be grasped only after the fact in the thematic echoes and oblique self-references of the collection.[158] We might draw a further connection here between Singh's vision of a nameless, global/capillary solidarity to Derrida's call for a New International, which he defines as "a link of affinity, suffering, and hope" and, more importantly, an "untimely link, without status, without title, and without name, barely public even if it is not clandestine, without contract, 'out of joint,' without coordination, without party, without country, without national community (International before, across, and beyond any national determination)."[159] Or perhaps Singh directs us back to Marx's own original, no less universalizing definition of the proletariat itself, forged of "*radical chains*" that articulate a "universal character because its sufferings are universal, and which does not claim a *particular redress* because the wrong which is done to it is not a *particular wrong* but *wrong in general.*"[160] Defining such a *homeless* political ontology as the "*as-yet-unfigured* horizon of contemporary cultural production by which national spaces/identities of political allegiance and economic regulation are being undone" and in which the recognizable "imagined communities of modernity are being reshaped,"[161] Wilson and Dissanayake's evocation of a transnational *not-yet* equally resonates with the majestic conclusion to Bloch's magnum opus *The Principle of Hope*:

> *True Genesis is not at the beginning but at the end*, and it starts to begin only when society and existence become radical, i.e. grasp their roots. But the root of history is the working, creating human being who reshapes and overhauls the given facts. Once he has grasped himself and established what is his, without expropriation and alienation, in real democracy, there arises in the world something which shines into the childhood of all and in which no one has yet been: homeland.[162]

Liberating the contemporary Indian imaginary from both *home* (*domus*) and the hegemonic strictures of domestic fiction's nationalist horizon, Singh achieves the forceful occupation of this never seen, uninhabitable *homeland*, this no-place of the transnational imagination, not least because, as she observes, our post-millennial reality is now "such a complex beast that in order to comprehend it we need something larger than realist fiction."[163] What we require, her collection affirms, is a form capable of imagining into being a "common place of a totality of places," in short, a *world* – defined not by the homogenizing agglomerations of globalization, which merely extend into bad infinity the synchronic measure of the meanwhile, but by a common practice and field of action comprised of the shared "quantity of possible worlds" within it.[164] The revolutionary potential of speculative fiction, Singh's work admirably demonstrates, lies in its power to create such a world of worlds, the habitus for a new kind of subject.

4

Claiming the Futures That Are, or, The Cunning of History in Amitav Ghosh's *The Calcutta Chromosome* and Manjula Padmanabhan's "Gandhi-Toxin"

What subject inhabits and mobilizes the transnationalist solidarity imagined by Singh, and what is that subject's relation to the determinations of history? In his extended interrogation of the historicist assumptions that, in the twenty-first century, continue to define much of the discourse of postcolonial studies, Dipesh Chakrabarty argues that these secular metanarratives tend to posit a politics implicitly defined as "human sovereignty acted out in the context of a ceaseless unfolding of unitary historical time."[1] Rejecting this chronopolitical model as a viable "intellectual resource" for figuring the complexities of postcolonial cultural and political modernity, Chakrabarty recommends a move away from the determinate ontologies of traditional European historicisms, which ordain the a priori category of the *social*, and instead suggests a move toward the "plural normative horizons" that emerge from globally diverse ways of being-in-the-world.[2] Central to Chakrabarty's alternative is the concept of *heterotemporality*, an orientation to the present that resolutely refuses historicist assumptions of categorical anachronism, or the Fabianesque "denial of coevalness," to those life-worlds situated at the "margins" of modernity.[3] Taking Heidegger as his philosophical touchstone, Chakrabarty argues that such a heterotemporal sensibility conceives of time and its range of plural possibilities as neither the "not-yet" of the ripening fruit nor the additively totalizing "lack" that requires only adequate supplementation to achieve actualization. In either such approach, the potential of the "not yet" is impoverished as merely the "unrealized actual," that which is either waiting to become or is otherwise constitutionally incomplete.[4] Against this, he offers the seemingly paradoxical alternative that the "possible has to be thought of as that which already actually *is* but is present only as the 'not yet' of the actual," a locution that explicitly invokes the utopian thrust of Ernst Bloch's familiar theorization of the non-synchronous in the synchronous just as it likewise recalls Alain Badiou's concept of the void of the situation.[5]

Elucidating this notion of possibility as the already-existent-not-yet, Chakrabarty distinguishes two principal attitudes concerning the future. The first, the domain of persistent Enlightenment universals, anticipates a future that "will be," whereas the second, more heterodox futurity acknowledges the *futures that already are*, that is, the range of alternative lifeworlds that "do not lend themselves to being represented by a totalizing principle, and are not even always amenable to the objectifying procedures of history writing" and therefore register, if at all, as the impingement of the archaic or anachronistic onto the field of secular, historicist modernity.[6] In this way Chakrabarty accounts for persistent Marxist anxieties over a recrudescent pre-modernity, epitomized, for example, in Marx's descriptions of the Asiatic or ancient modes of production; his much-maligned rationalizations of imperialism as the agent of history; his comment in the preface to volume I of *Capital* that "[t]he country that is more developed industrially only shows, to the less developed, the image of its own future";[7] and his evocative, oft-quoted assertion in *The Eighteenth Brumaire* that "The tradition of all the dead generations weighs like a nightmare on the brain of the living."[8] Yet, Chakrabarty identifies a counter-current in Marx's historicism as well, which he nominates as "History 2," that views these "antecedent" forms as neither prior nor exterior to capital but as inhering in and interrupting or unsettling it from within.[9] Thus, Chakrabarty writes, these incompatible Marxist historicisms, "considered together, destroy the usual topological distinction of the outside and the inside that marks debates about whether or not the whole world can be properly said to have fallen under the sway of capital."[10] History 2, then, does not lie outside capitalist modernity as an antecedent form nor as a geospatial exception; rather, it "allows us to make room, in Marx's own analytic of capital, for the politics of human belonging and diversity."[11]

To illustrate the immanent nature of this counter-logic, Chakrabarty turns to the quintessential model of industrial labor itself: the factory worker. Between the hours of 8 and 5, say, the worker honors the wage contract and fulfills her obligations as the embodiment of productive labor. Inasmuch as she functions objectively as a "bearer of labor power," however, she also carries within herself "other pasts," memories, lifeworlds, and conscious practices that do not simply deny the universals of capital so much as expose their inherent limits. For although the objectifying tendencies of capital and its mechanistic, alienating disciplines would seem to desire a worker without the impediments of personal or collective histories, these histories (and the consciousness that mobilizes them) are in fact as necessary for the proper functioning and reproduction of the capitalist system as they are potentially threatening to it. Capital, as the privileged content of History 1, is therefore always reconfiguring itself both to accommodate and to obviate the demands and pressures of these alternative ways-of-being-human within it – or the disavowed content of History 2. Citing Marx's own distinction between the "productive labor" of the piano maker and the effectively dismissed "unproductive labor" of the piano player, Chakrabarty shows how traditional Marxist models occlude the content of History 2 by failing to recognize the "everyday, preanalytical, unobjectifying relationships we have with tools, relationships critical to making a world out of this earth."[12] The piano player's affective, *world-building* creation is not inscribed in the universals of History 1 and therefore exists as its excess or limit-point, just as the specific memories, hopes, and life-practices of the laborer are not tangibly recorded in the texture of her labor, though both serve to construct the communal relations and social conditions that sustain and reproduce capitalist universals even as they interrupt and contest them.

What becomes of this model, however, in our current moment of the *post-industrial* and *posthistorical*? Through this conceptualization of affective labor as one of the potential sites for revising conventional Marxist historicism (certainly a task of particular urgency in the moment of globalization), we might draw a productive conceptual parallel between Chakrabarty's project of "provincializing Europe" and Hardt and Negri's recent theorization of the revolutionary space of the *common*, in which, I offer, one can recognize a structural kinship to History 2. The common, Hardt and Negri argue, "provides a framework for breaking the epistemological impasse created by the opposition of the universal and the particular" by cutting diagonally across this opposition, neither replicating its asphyxiating binaries nor investing in some ultimately transcendent solution.[13] What is called for in the making of the common, they write, "is a shift of emphasis from knowing to doing, generating a multiplicity of beings constantly open to alterity that are revealed through the perspective of the body, which is an assemblage of affects or ways of being, which is to say, forms of life."[14] Immediately striking in this context is their definition of the common as an assemblage of life-practices and affects that manifest as present and *already immanent* alterities. Like Chakrabarty, Hardt and Negri dispense with the logic that posits an *exceptional* exterior from which an oppositional counter-hegemony can be mobilized and instead offer a way of avoiding the crippling impasse of identity and difference altogether by reorienting the "ethical horizon" from that of being or identity to that of becoming. The global subaltern, for instance, traditionally defined in terms of lack or exclusion, are for Hardt and Negri defined in terms of possibility and the dynamic production of political subjectivities in the already existent "futures" of the present. The production of alternative subjectivities is in fact the primary occupation of the modes of affective labor that characterize the grammar of globalization as well as its new ontologies of the *biopolitical*:

> The forms of intellectual, affective, and cognitive labor that are emerging in the central role in the contemporary economy cannot be controlled by the forms of discipline and command developed in the era of the factory society. We have argued elsewhere, in fact, that this transition toward the hegemony of biopolitical production was set in motion by the accumulation of struggles across the globe in the 1960s and 1970s against that imperialist and industrial disciplinary model of capitalist control.[15]

Of central importance to the theorization of this new subjectivity of biopolitics,[16] then, is its relation to the forces of modernity, which is to say, in part, its unique spatiotemporal orientation. Hardt and Negri first distinguish between two basic responses to the dilemmas of modernity: on the one hand are those like Jürgen Habermas or Ulrich Beck, who suggest that the cure for modernity's ills is simply a more robust and self-reflexive modernity that (at long last) makes good on its initial promise. This largely reformist trend Hardt and Negri identify as *hypermodernity*. On the other hand are those "liberatory antimodernities that challenge and subvert hierarchies by affirming the resistance and expanding the freedom of the subordinated."[17] Antimodernity, though in the end hamstrung by its strictly adversarial or reactionary relation to the modern, also engenders in its simultaneous production of both resistance and freedom an unassimilable (and therefore "monstrous") surplus that proves irreducible to the modernity/antimodernity binary and thus gestures toward the creative and dynamic response that they designate as *altermodernity*, a relation "defined not by opposition but by rupture and transformation."[18]

In addition, therefore, to the negation that is the primary characteristic of many anti- and even *post*modernities, altermodernity is, despite

Hardt and Negri's deep misgivings about the intellectual inheritance of the dialectic, marked chiefly by the dialectical negation of negation – or by the creation of new knowledges, new practices, and, indeed, new universals that do not define themselves simply in their resolute rejection of a normative modernity and its hegemonic standard. This generative dimension of altermodernity therefore shifts the responsibilities of the radical intellectual from ideology critique to active (utopian) invention. As Hardt and Negri contend, within altermodernity and its creation of the common, "the intellectual is charged with the task not only to denounce error and unmask illusion, and not only to incarnate the mechanisms of new practices of knowledge, but also, together with others in a process of co-research, to produce a new truth."[19] Fundamental to the production of alternative rationalities is a Foucauldian "insurrection of knowledge," which levels "a critique of the pretense of objectivity of the scientific tradition"[20] that does not depend, however, from a "search for an outside to that tradition" but rather emerges as modernity's in-dwelling point of failure.

The symmetries here between Hardt and Negri's altermodernity and Chakrabarty's radical decentering of European historicist and epistemic models – particularly inasmuch as the latter's project is influenced by the stridently anti-rationalist work of Ashis Nandy – are apparent. While each theorization remains largely abstract, however, I want to suggest that two recent works of postcolonial SF, Amitav Ghosh's novel *The Calcutta Chromosome* (1995) and Manjula Padmanabhan's short story "Gandhi-Toxin" (2004), undertake precisely this operation of insurrectionary knowledge production through the mapping of such alterior ontologies, thereby figuring agential models for the present that bear striking resemblance to that offered by Chakrabarty as well as that of Hardt and Negri.

Precarious space is the place: silence, exodus, and cunning in *The Calcutta Chromosome*

The historical shift from the formal to the real subsumption of capital that, along with the spatial displacement of production, is the foremost indicator of globalization, occasions the spatiotemporal paradox identified above in which the new global proletariat, whose function and identity are categorically expanded and relocated within now dramatically modified relations of production as the global "precariat," is wholly *within* the social totality of modern capital at the same time that it refuses and sets itself against it.[21] Traditional Marxist distinctions between necessary labor-time and surplus labor-time grow increasingly difficult to sustain under the pressures of this new spatiotemporal logic, just as technological and institutional innovations dissolve the barriers formerly separating *work* space-time from *life* space-time.[22] Thus, the old capitalist chronometric of discrete temporal units – assuming its most recognizable form in the locus of the factory or assembly line – and the traditional array of oppositional asynchronisms have now become "two alternatives on the same temporal horizon."[23] This transformation has important implications for contemporary resistance strategies as well, for as Hardt and Negri argue,

> revolution is no longer imaginable as an event separated from us in the future but has to live in the present, an "exceeding" present that in some sense already contains the future within it. Revolutionary movement resides on the same horizon of temporality with capitalist control, and its position of being within and against is manifest through a movement of exodus, which poses the exceeding productivity of the multitude against the exceptionality of capitalist command.[24]

Ghosh's *The Calcutta Chromosome*, winner of the 1995 Arthur C. Clarke Award for best science fiction novel, figures in its unique spatiotemporal dialectic precisely such radical futurity as the manifest excess of the present, one defined by the staging of its own universals and its own uniquely Hegelian "cunning of history" within and against the unprecendented space-time of globalization.

The novel's indefinitely near-future opening chapter introduces Antar, an Egyptian living in a mostly deserted Manhattan apartment from which he also works (indeed, in the novel's primary, twenty-first-century narrative, he never once physically leaves this space). His job is the tedious monitoring of an AVA IIe unit, an advanced artificial intelligence system created by the International Water Council, the imperialistic corporation that has annexed Antar's former employer, a non-profit global health consultancy named Lifewatch. "Ava" is charged with processing and inventorying "the endless detritus of twentieth-century officialdom," that is, with scanning and filing records of the countless companies and organizations that the International Water Council has absorbed.[25] As Ava's omnivorous digital archive entombs relics from the obsolete lifeworlds of the twentieth century, she occasionally encounters a piece of data, usually (and not insignificantly) in the form of a material object such as a novelty paperweight, whose meaning or function she cannot determine, at which point Antar is consulted to address the lacuna by supplementing Ava's databases with his own personal knowledge and life experience. Thus, in the novel's opening pages we find already in place the dialectic of History 1 and History 2[26] and, more important, a structural device for introducing the work's personification of the latter: L. Murugan, who makes his entrance as one such bone in the throat or indigestible data fragment within Ava's omnivorously hegemonizing narrative when his tattered Lifewatch ID card and chain appear on her screen. Not insignificantly, Antar is as much drawn to the stubborn materiality of the object[27] that has frustrated Ava's information flows as to the logical enigma that it presents: "Antar rubbed his fingertips, overcome by a tactile nostalgia, recalling the feel of those chains and those laminated plastic ID cards."[28] Identifying his former Lifewatch colleague as the owner of the card, Antar discovers that Murugan disappeared in Calcutta in 1995. Indeed, as he dimly recalls, Antar himself wrote this entry in Murugan's file. The discovery of the ID sets Antar on a quest to discover the truth of Murugan's disappearance, the mysterious circumstances of which surround yet another search for a suppressed narrative, this time the unrecorded shadow history of Ronald Ross' Nobel Prize-winning malaria research in India, which likewise serves as the point of convergence of several such eruptions of altermodernity onto the spatiotemporal continuum of the modern and, by the novel's conclusion, the postmodern as well.

In a brilliant deconstructionist treatment of *The Calcutta Chromosome*, Bishnupriya Ghosh[29] locates one such juxtaposition, via the Derridean analytic of *spectrology*, in the forced generic convergence of the medical thriller, the ghost story, and the vernacular Lakhaan stories, the latter of which receive only indirect (spectral) articulation through what she names the novel's tandem processes of "epistemological excavation (grafting)" and "ethical spectrology (ghosting)."[30] Hence, the medical mystery or detective narrative with which the reader is ostensibly presented quickly "fizzles out" – because, as B. Ghosh argues, "if we take seriously Ghosh's postcolonial unraveling of an established colonial truth, then the very *genre* of truth-telling must suffer" – as it is hijacked first by the ghost story, with that narrative's occultist preoccupations with spiritual transmigration, and ultimately by the intentional "silence" of the obliquely intrusive Laakhan stories.[31] While B. Ghosh's primary concern is "the stalking of the novel in English by vernacular Indian fiction," her reading has far broader implications, particularly in her brief excurses on the themes of embodiment as a valence of Ghosh's "restoration of a corpus/corpse of indigenous knowledge" and silence as the impossible articulation of "counterscientific knowledge from the proportions of rational discourse."[32] However, while she makes occasional reference throughout her analysis to "our current phase of 'empire,'" B. Ghosh remains predominantly interested, as have been most commentators, in the vexed relation of postcolonial knowledge production and historiography to the epistemological legacies of colonization. Indeed, in comparing Ghosh's "grafting of vernacular paradigms onto a literary tradition that ... references only its Anglo antecedents" to the attempts by celebrated Bengali authors Rabindranath Tagore and Phaniswarnath Renu to register the trauma of the colonial situation, B. Ghosh concludes that the epistemic, cultural, and economic violence recorded in the works of these latter are "replayed only a little differently" in the era of globalization.[33] This emphasis on continuity and on the "unearthing [of] these parallel histories" and counter-rationalities suppressed by prior colonial rule and its enduring hegemonic structures train the novel's critical energies on a colonial past despite B. Ghosh's efforts to connect this recovery of lost epistemologies to the task of today's progressive intellectuals, who must likewise "guard against a 'forgetting' facilitated by the current global hierarchies of knowledge."[34] Similarly, Suparno Banerjee contends that Ghosh exploits the hybridizing genre of SF to figure authentically subaltern alternatives to the hegemonic epistemes of both the West and the Vedic authority of the indigenous Brahminical elite.[35]

Building therefore upon Banerjee and B. Ghosh's respective insights into its formal hybridities and discontinuities, I want to explore further *The Calcutta Chromosome*'s dramatization and imaginative production of both space and time as encounters not with those aspects of globalization homologous to an earlier imperialism but rather with those new or heterologous elements for which no satisfactory conceptual model yet exists. By considering the novel's structural preference for spaces-within-spaces and coexistent temporalities against the politico-theoretical context enumerated above (displacing a general postcolonial hermeneutic with the more exact one of globalization), we can complicate B. Ghosh's assertions, based on a tacit center/periphery model, that "Ghosh can, in his fictional medium, imagine an 'outside' to these systems of exchange and commodity formation" or that Antar and Murugan themselves "are also 'guilty' of self-betrayal, of working for the 'babus' of globalization."[36] In each of these instances, a positive exterior to capital (both spatial and subjective) is suggested that belongs to an earlier, imperialist moment in the mode of production, a preoccupation with which, I suggest, both obscures the novel's critical engagement with its own complex present and fails to account for Ghosh's novel utilization of the genre of SF.

In a reading focused primarily on Ghosh's construction of an "alternate mode of being/knowledge that provides scope for third-world/women's agency," Suchitra Mathur directs our attention (if merely in passing) to the novel's multiple representations of spatial precarity, what she identifies as the "fringe space" that is "neither completely outside the gambit of the dominant socio-political structure, nor completely controlled by it."[37] Specifically, she calls attention to the "outhouses, anterooms, ramshackle houses under construction, and private apartments" that comprise the settings for the novel's primary action and, I argue here, its production of new political ontologies.[38]

Similarly, Barbara Romanik observes how, in navigating the uncertain spaces of the colonial cityscape, the characters of *The Calcutta Chromosome* utilize Michel de Certeau's opportunistic *tactics* of resistance to "redefine as well as reassert the categories of colonizer and colonized, British and Indian, powerful and powerless."[39] Like B. Ghosh, however, Romanik directs her analysis almost exclusively toward the novel's representations of Calcutta as a formerly colonized space, exploring its negotiation/recovery of a postcolonial metropolitan identity characterized by collaboration, interdependence, and a buzzing complex of destabilizing hybridities. A more satisfactory approach is offered by Jorge Luis Andrade Fernandes, who invokes the crucial Bakhtinian concept of the *chronotope* to investigate the way in which Ghosh and other recent postcolonial authors (like Amos Tutuola) "produce imaginative maps that offer great insights into a relational mode of being that transcends the strict domains of nationalism or cosmopolitanism."[40] Following the lead provided by Mathur, Romanik, and Fernandes, I offer that a closer inspection of the novel's production and juxtaposition of multiple space-times may reveal ways in which it may be said to dramatize the historical dialectic identified by Chakrabarty as it also registers the immanent potentiality of the biopolitical.

We have already observed the way in which the initial (and *enframing*) setting of Antar's abandoned Manhattan apartment building works to destabilize previous distinctions between inner and outer, work space and life space, a deterioration that is symptomatic of the more supple, internally striated authority of capital even as it reveals the burgeoning power of biopolitical production itself, the chief aim of which, Hardt and Negri remind us, is the creation of subjectivities:

> Production, in other words, is becoming "anthropogenetic," generating forms of life. From this trajectory of knowledge within economic production, two important facts follow. First, knowledge is no longer

> merely a means to the creation of value (in the commodity form), but rather the production of knowledge is itself value creation. Second, not only is this knowledge no longer a weapon of capitalist control, but also capital is in fact confronted with a paradoxical situation: the more it is forced to pursue valorization through knowledge production, the more that knowledge escapes its control.[41]

Forced to abandon the static organizational constraints of the factory, capitalist production, now confronted with the mobility and fluidity of increasingly biopolitical labor, now disperses itself "throughout the entire social territory," engages in a perpetual struggle "to rebuild borders, reterritorialize the laboring populations, and reconstruct the fixed dimensions of social space."[42]

We witness this struggle in the opening pages of the novel as Antar, whose daily life consists of subsidiary battles against the IWC for autonomy in his own home, reflects on previous instances in which Ava had failed to recognize an object ("the most trivial things usually") and had sought his assistance.[43] The first time it happened, he recalls, he had been reading via an "illegal" device that allowed him surreptitiously to project book pages on the apartment's far wall. So long as he maintained the correct bodily posture and tilt of the head and did not lose his rhythm in responding to Ava's insistent prompts, she was none the wiser. When delayed responses twice roused her attention, however, Antar received notice from the IWC that his pay had been docked for declining productivity and that future declines would impact his retirement benefits, after which he "stopped trying to get the better of Ava," returned the device to the Sudanese bank-teller from whom he borrowed it, and resumed his usual, mundane duties "staring patiently at those endless inventories, wondering what it was all for."[44] Here, *contra* Romanik's reading, Ghosh seems simultaneously to indicate the limits of de Certeau's transient tactics as either a strategic reclamation of autonomy or a satisfactory mode of resistance as well as the extreme measures to which capital is constrained to maintain productivity in the moment of globalization and its increased emphasis on the "labor of head and heart."[45] That is, Antar's relative autonomy is both necessary for the kind of immaterial labor that he performs at the same time that it threatens that very tenuous system of production, the frangibility of which is expressed in its anxious surveillance. Antar's labor is quite simply imaginative production itself, the crafting of narratives about people or objects that are appropriated by Ava toward the completion of her gradually accumulating master text. Her dependence on his creative/affective labor is thus a source of deep anxiety, a fact that his mild tactic of resistance entirely neglects to appreciate.

While we may be able homologically to associate de Certeau's relation of strategy/tactic with Chakrabarty's History 1/History 2 – the strategy assuming the visible place of proper officialdom, the tactic that of the covert discontinuities insinuated within this enframing public code – the tactic, while revealing the strategy's own disavowed contingency, finally leaves the latter structurally secure. In a passage relevant to the present context, de Certeau writes of the diminishing powers of the subject in the face of an accelerated technocratic expansion,

> Increasingly constrained, yet less and less concerned with these vast frameworks, the individual detaches himself from them without being able to escape them and can henceforth only try to outwit them, to pull tricks on them, to rediscover, within an electronicized and computerized megalopolis, the "art" of the hunters and rural folk of earlier days.[46]

These ludic manipulations, whereby de Certeau's trickster subject manifests "the fleeting and massive reality of a social activity at play with the order that contains it," do not finally contest the logic of that containment, just as Antar's inconsequential attempts at outwitting Ava do not productively acknowledge (and, indeed, tacitly deny) the growing power of the biopolitical and the reactionary contortions of capital (its exploitation of biopower) both to accommodate and restrain it.[47] As Hardt and Negri remind us, though, history is not "the horizon on which biopower configures reality through domination"; rather, "history is determined by the biopolitical antagonisms and resistances to biopower."[48] This reversal – from the mentality of "making do" to what I am tempted to call revolutionary consciousness – is the lesson that Antar must learn from his encounter with Murugan and, finally, the Mangala movement itself.

The novel's opening chapters adumbrate this trajectory by offering us the representation of a longed-for locus of the common in an age of unrelenting social atomization. As Ava undertakes the painstaking digital reconstruction of Murugan's card, Antar finds himself anticipating the genial warmth and easy camaraderie of the doughnut shop at Penn Station, which he visits as a kind of daily ritual. Though now somewhat habituated to his near-empty apartment building and the solitary tedium of his work, Antar finds himself drawn to the urbane chatter of the doughnut shop and its array of international patrons: "the

Sudanese bank-teller, the well-dressed Guyanese woman who worked in a Chelsea used-clothes store, the young Bangladeshi man from the subway newsstand."[49] Having been introduced earlier to the Sudanese bank-teller, we are not surprised to find that, in addition to the familiar comforts of "companionable silence" and the occasional viewing and discussion of international films, the patrons often exchange advice regarding what de Certeau would recognize as tactics, that is, information "about a gadget that was on sale somewhere, or some new scam for saving on subway tokens."[50] Antar's visits are motivated at least partially then by the consolations of and nostalgia for cultural and ethnic identity as well as by some tentative sense of defiance. We learn that he initially began patronizing the shop because the owner is also Egytpian and because the tea is "just like Antar remembered from his boyhood."[51] Weary of Ava's rootless (if utterly flawless) simulation of the Egyptian dialect he spoke as a child (having left his village at 14, he often has trouble following her in his native tongue), Antar longs for the lost assurances and predictabilities of a stable and coherent cultural enclosure:

> It was a relief to escape from those voices [Ava's] in the evening; to step out of that bleak, cold building, encaged in its scaffolding of rusty steel fire escapes; to get away from the metallic echo of its stairways and corridors. There was something enlivening, magical almost, about walking from that wind-blown street into the brilliantly lit passageways of Penn Station, about the surging crowds around the ticket counters, the rumble of trains under one's feet, the deep, bass hum of a busker's didgeridoo throbbing in the concrete like an amplified heartbeat.[52]

The novel summons this familiar vision of collectivity, yet, crucially, does not finally deliver it. Antar's visit to Penn Station is merely a recollection composite of past evenings. The refusal is significant, I argue, in that even as it expresses a desire for what Jenni G. Halpin lyrically names the book's construction of community "as gift,"[53] the novel denies Antar the narrow satisfactions of ethnic or nationalist affiliation and finally rejects its accompanying logic of *tactical* resistance. As Jameson reminds us, however, attendant global capital's culture of "minding the machines" and the concomitant "resituation of labor ... within some new space from which the opposition between private and public has disappeared" – wherein, one might add, mass culture assumes a valence very different from the grimmest diagnoses of the Frankfurt

School – is the possibility for even the most degraded, co-opted form of public expression to serve as the site for the well-nigh Utopian "enactment of collective sharing and participation."[54] For despite its reliance on the outmoded form of national or ethnic solidarity, Penn Station – as "unfinished" public space – functions as the reminder of an almost forgotten sense of collectivity, thus revealing the ideological function of Ava's simulated cultural/ethnic localities, the identification with which threatens to lull Antar and his innumerable global counterparts into an attenuating cultural identitarianism or, worse, a kind of demobbed complacency. Under the destabilizing pressures of a post-Fordist mode of production, as we have seen, private space becomes increasingly indistinguishable from labor space either through greater numbers of service workers entering the home or, as in the case of Antar, work conducted from the home itself, now a site of near-simultaneous (alienated) production and (private) consumption. The surging humanity and vectoral space of Penn Station, however much its appeal may rely on notions of peripheral "otherness," reminds Antar that in the moment of post-industrial capital, as Evan Watkins phrases it, "social space is anxious space," where the frictions and frissons of class identity can yet be witnessed and articulated, something Ava's alienating simulations of identity attempt to mediate and recontain.[55]

This still tentative anticipation of collectivity reappears in more emphatic form in the novel's other unfinished or public spatial settings, as when Sonali, searching for the missing Romen Haldar, stumbles upon Mangala and her followers mid-ritual in the mansion formerly inhabited by Ronald Ross himself – now undergoing major reconstruction as a hotel by the real estate-developing Haldar, metonymically charting the shift from imperialism to Empire. Peering down at the assembly from her precarious hiding place in the "narrow, flimsy-looking" minstrel gallery, a no-space between spaces, Sonali notes particularly the group's striking diversity, "some male, some female, young and old, packed in close together," consolidating a "strangely motley assortment of people: men in patched lungis, a handful of brightly painted women in cheap nylon saris, a few young students, several prim-looking middle-class women – people you would never expect to see together."[56]

Similarly, having followed Murugan to the liminal alleyway between the Ross Memorial Ward and the hospital's boundary wall, overlooking the outhouses that once served as the servant's quarter – where Mangala and Laakan would have dwelt – and the heavy traffic of the Lower Circular Road, Urmila is suddenly inspired to consider the role of space in the production of social reality and its concomitant management of subjectivities:

> How odd to think that all that separated them from her and Murugan was a paltry little wall, just one little wall, yet it did the job just as well as if it was the Great Wall of China, for they couldn't see her or him. In a way it was like being in a test tube: that was probably what it felt like, to know that something was going to happen on this side of the glass but not on the other; that there was a wall between you and everyone else, all those people in the buses and minibuses, hurrying to work from Kankurgachi and Beleghata and Bansdroni, after their morning rice, with the smell of dhal still buried deep in their fingernails; they were so far away, even though they were just on the other side of the wall.[57]

In addition to explicitly associating this insight with the subject-altering test-tube experiments of Mangala and Lakhaan, Ghosh also couples Urmila's acute recognition of the twin effect of civil and social engineering with its symbolic annihilation in her spontaneous sexual congress with Murugan, which itself achieves metaphoric effect as a transformative novum: "something new, something which she knew was going to change her ... something that was happening in ways that were entirely beyond her own imagining ..."[58]

Of the novel's several liminal or precarious spaces, however, none is more important or emblematic than the locus of Renupur, the way station occupying quite literally the middle of nowhere, the peculiar singularity of which Ghosh belabors almost to the point of stylistic absurdity:

> ... the platform at Renupur was a length of beaten earth, its surface covered in weeds and a few cracked paving stones. Two creaking signboards hung beside the track, separated by a hundred yards, each bearing the barely legible legend: "Renupur." Halfway between them, serving as a signal-room-cum-station-house, was a ramshackle tin-roofed structure, painted the usual railway red. There were no houses or huts anywhere in sight, no villagers, no railway guards, no staring rustics, no urchins, no food-vendors, no beggars, no sleeping travelers, not even the inevitable barking dog.
>
> Phulboni realized, looking around him, that the station was empty – absolutely empty. There was nobody, not a single human being anywhere in sight. The spectacle was so startling as literally to

> provoke disbelief....Phulboni, for all his gifts, was at a loss to think of a word to describe a station that was literally uninhabited and unpeopled.[59]

Beyond even the descriptive powers of Phulboni – who, following his harrowing experience at the station, devotes himself and his literary art to the service of Mangala and the "Silence" – Renupur marks the point of failure of the existing symbolic order and the no-place of potential or "future" ontologies. Exceeding familiar significations, it may be said to indicate the ambiguous site that Žižek (via Lacan) nominates the "place 'between two deaths,' a paradoxical locus of sublime beauty as well as terrifying monsters," where the ghostly echoes of an already dead order persist unaware of their demise[60] as well as where the unbounded and multifarious alternatives to that order issue forth with simultaneously terrifying and exultant promise.[61] Renupur is thus the space of anxious serial repetition as well as of the radical difference that emerges from this repetition, of exhilarating possibility and gnawing anxiety. Moreover, by resisting the metaphoric and practical value of the railroad as a technology of empire, one which "elucidate[s] and contain[s] the nation-state in contiguous and intelligible units," Renupur station confounds the tropological enumeration of the nation as a series of "contiguous and intelligible unities," an important point to which we must return.[62]

We are introduced to Renepur Station by way of Elijah Farley, a nineteenth-century malaria researcher who has come to India to investigate a revival of interest in the dubious hypothesis of Alphonse Laveran that the disease is borne by a blood parasite originating outside the body. Motivated by the boastful claims of novice researcher Ronald Ross that he has actually witnessed "Laveran's chimera," Farley visits the Calcutta laboratory supervised by D.D. Cunningham, who gives him access to microscope, slides, and, most important, a "chokra-boy" trained as an assistant. But before retrieving the slides, the young assistant surreptitiously consults with a "sweeper-woman," who appears to select the slides the young man delivers for inspection. After several fruitless hours, Farley grows increasingly suspicious of this arrangement and inquires of Cunningham how he came to employ the sweeper-woman, Mangala. Cunningham claims to have found her at the same place he hires all his bearers, the railway station, and says that it was she who suggested the hiring of the boy, who is likewise from her own part of the country near Renupur. Adamant in his pursuit of this mystery, Farley is finally allowed to see Laveran's parasite when Laakhan recommends that it can be found only in fresh blood, after which he is promised comprehensive disclosure upon journeying to the region of Laakhan and Mangala's birth. Last seen disembarking at Renupur station with a young man carrying his bags, Farley is never heard from again.

This scene is emphatically repeated some decades later with the arrival of the writer Phulboni, whose "first and only job" is with a British commercial firm dealing in household goods, "famous for its extensive distribution network, which reached into the smallest towns and villages."[63] As Phulboni discovers, however, his destination of Renupur village lies nearly three miles from the station that bears its name, which, because of railway regulations requiring a siding at regular intervals, "owed its existence more to the demands of engineering than to the requirements of the local population."[64] The station is thus non-purposive, a kind of spatially dislocated excrescence of the colonial bureaucratic order in a rural backwater, a singularity enisled by monsoon rains: "[Phulboni] had no idea where to go next. There was no road or pathway in sight. The station, perched on the railway embankment, was a little island in a sea of shimmering floodwater."[65] Like the manufactured island of More's King Utopus, the station realizes here the essential utopian (or at least heterotopian) characteristic of circumscription, the spatial secession from the world of the familiar (with its well-trod roads and pathways) within which multiple alternatives and divergent subjectivities may be made flesh.

A series of minor enigmas and curiosities culminates that night in Phulboni's near-death encounter with a phantom train whose arrival is punctuated by an "an inhuman howl" crying the name "Laakhan."[66] Pursued by the bobbing red signal lantern that had initially lured him out onto the tracks, Phulboni desperately retrieves his gun from the signal room, turns, and fires at the doorway, shattering the crimson window of the lantern and simultaneously knocking himself out with the recoil. Awakened by the stationmaster, who begins to confide the villagers' theories regarding the curious happenings at the station, Phulboni opens his eyes to reveal that this too is but a deceptive dream and that he is actually lying on the tracks with an "all too real" train hurtling toward him. As the bewildered engineers later inspect the curiously maintained siding and switch mechanisms, Phulboni offers that perhaps the stationmaster had pulled the switch by mistake, to which the chief engineer responds with "an odd smile": "There hasn't been a stationmaster at Renupur for more than thirty years."[67] The guard then confides in Phulboni that there had been other such incidents, the most recent in "'94," resulting in the death of someone reported to be "a foreigner," though his body was never positively identified.

As Phulboni's exchange with the guard also makes clear, Renupur marks the site of cleavage and overlap not only between non-synchronous temporalities but also between seemingly discontinuous or incommensurable epistemologies (indeed, in both instances the promised disclosure of clandestine knowledge functions as a kind of weapon). Told the story of the boy Laakhan, whose presence haunts the station, Phulboni asks why the guard didn't share this information earlier, before he disembarked, to which the man flatly replies, "But you would not have believed me. You would have laughed and said, 'These villagers, their heads are full of fantasies and superstitions.' Everyone knows that for city men like you such warnings have always had the opposite effect," an observation confirmed by the dismissive response of the unidentified foreign sahib in first class (Farley) whose body was discovered on the tracks many years before: "Oh, you villagers ..."[68] Moreover, the incredulity of both Farley and Phulboni is explicitly connected in either case to social class and proximity to the colonial/metropolitan center. While both the stationmaster and guard mockingly acknowledge Phulboni's status as a "big sahib" due to his employment with the British trading firm (whose expansive global network prefigures the more extensive one of the IWC), Laakhan, as hauntological agent, anticipates the properly *placeless* subjectivity that finds full hypostatization in the Calcutta chromosome.

Thus, it comes as no surprise to the reader to find that apart from the unexplained spatiotemporal disjuncture that enables his spectral presence to haunt the station long after his departure, we also learn that Laakhan's physical existence at Renupur Station was likewise decidedly precarious. Drifting in "from somewhere up the line," the boy made his home in the empty signal-room until the arrival of the new stationmaster, "an orthodox, upper-caste man" who "told the villagers that Laakhan was worse than an untouchable; that he carried contagion; that he was probably the child of a prostitute; that his misshapen left hand was a mark of hereditary disease."[69] To escape the incessant ire and abuse of the stationmaster, Laakhan constructs a "bamboo shack on the tracks of the unused siding," though his retreat to this markedly precarious shelter simply "drove the stationmaster into an even greater fury," such that one moonless night, he leads Laakhan out onto the unused tracks, then redirects a train toward him. As a virtuoso navigator of such vector spaces, however, Laakhan manages not only to survive but also to inveigle the stationmaster, who slips on the tracks before the oncoming train, in his own trap, providing, I want to argue, a grammar of resistance that metonymically recapitulates that of the novel more generally and, moreover, a logic that is structurally predicated on the cunning of the precarious subject and the dramatic device of the peripeteiac reversal.

The introduction of this liminal agent at Renupur Station in fact leads us back to Hardt and Negri, who identify as the "emblematic space" of the newly precarious capitalist order – with its "lack of guaranteed contracts, stable schedules, and secure employment, in which work time and life time blend together in the tasks and challenges of informal and changing jobs" – the ambiguous territory of the *banlieue*, the "poor metropolitan periphery" or suburban ghetto,[70] the inhabitants of which "are socially excluded at the same time that they are completely within the processes of economic and social production," a description that clearly resonates both with Mathur's suggestive discussion[71] of fringe space in Ghosh and Fernandes' recognition that the novel's unique chronotope allows Ghosh "to conceive of difference as always already within,"[72] both of which may be read against Jameson's recent discussion of the dialectical vocation as the exposure of "some ontological rift or gap in the world itself," of the detection "where common sense presumed a continuous field of uninterrupted phenomena in an unproblematic real world, of strange rifts or multiple dimensions, in which different laws and dynamics obtain."[73] Eschewing the vanguardism of traditional Marxist models, Hardt and Negri affirm the role of the urban ghetto and its diversity of capillary networks, hierarchies, and temporalities in expanding the terrain of resistance beyond national sovereignties to the unbounded domain of the global.[74] Such urban and/or peri-urban spaces, which increasingly define a "general planetary condition," are, in addition to being zones of pathologically uneven development, of privation and astonishing human misery, also zones of encounter, exchange, cooperation, and invention, spaces that consolidate and coordinate a *dispositif* of the biopolitical and a "factory for the production of the common."[75] Thus, the novel's strategic juxtaposition of diverse geographies and temporalities does not so much indicate a merely developmental shift (from colonial to postcolonial and so on) as it does dialectically produce – in the now-global space of exception – what Žižek calls "the seeds of the future," the universal and universalizing coalition of the "parts of no part," upon which we must now stake the "emancipatory wager."[76]

The novel's foremost expression of this precarious/emancipatory configuration is, of course, the titular "chromosome" itself, which Murugan describes as "a technology for interpersonal transference."[77] Dismantling intersubjective barriers, the chromosome unsettles conventional identitarian certainties and, as Fernandes argues, elaborates "radically new and contingent identities and modes of being-in-the-world."[78] In one memorable scene, Murugan illustrates to Antar the chromosome's destabilizing subjective effect by comparing distinct individual responses to unexpected stimuli – that is, by suddenly shouting "boo!" at both Antar and a passing waiter and noting their respective reactions:

> Same stimulus, different response: he says tamatar and you say tamatim. Now think, what if the "im" and the "ar" could be switched between you and him? What would you have then? You'd have him speaking in your voice, or the other way around. You wouldn't know whose voice it was. And isn't that the scariest thing there is, Ant? To hear something said, and not to know who's saying it? Not to know who's speaking? For if you don't know who's saying something, you don't know why they're saying it either.[79]

Tamatar is here the Hindi word for *tomato,* while *tamatim* is its Egyptian equivalent. Hence, the exchange to which Murugan refers is not merely personal-psychological-neurological but also historical-cultural-national. We have in fact already seen this erasure of previously stable identities through the dissociation of the cultural subject and its site of enunciation in Ava's ability to mimic with flawless precision any global dialect, reflective of globalization's simultaneous simulation and eradication of the "local." Fernandes contends that this interruption of the conventionally assumed continuity between national or cultural identity and language "challenges the conception of the local as geographically coherent linguistic and cultural practices"; and inasmuch as "the local draws a strict isomorphism between the geographical and the cultural-linguistic, *The Calcutta Chromosome*'s invocation of Ava as a singular example of the polyglot renders linguistic and cultural practices movable."[80] Demonstrating the decline of the statist problematic and tracing out nomadic lines of flight that defy a rigid politics of identity, Ghosh's novel, Fernandes contends, "challenges the local and national as sites of identity production" and submits to sustained interrogation "the technologies that produce individual identity narratives."[81] John Thieme perhaps puts it most succinctly when he argues that, far from producing a typical work of diasporic fiction "whose global interests obscure social and ideological specifics, Ghosh is concerned to excavate a labyrinthine network of traces, which foreground such specifics, while making it clear that essentialist versions of national and regional cultures, such as those inherent in Orientalist discourses, are insustainable" and, in so doing, to reveal more generally the "limitations of post-colonial theorizing" itself.[82] Thus, like many of the works surveyed here, *The Calcutta Chromosome* deploys the dialectical intelligence of SF to direct the postcolonial analytic toward the nettled problematic of globalization.

Indeed, only against the failure of these former (nationalist) identitarian narratives to produce agential political ontologies for a globalizing world are Ghosh's figurations of spatial and subjective precarity rendered legible. Ghosh does not, however, leave us at this point of mere critical negation but, as Hardt and Negri prescribe, takes up the generative task of utopian invention as well. In his deployment of SF (and the chromosome as novum), Ghosh leaves behind the vexed question of *being* that is the central concern of his previous novel *The Shadow Lines* (and perhaps of the postcolonial novelistic canon more generally) and directs the imaginative faculties of SF toward possibilities of an already existent *becoming*, that is, toward the futures that inhere in the present. In this way, the novel enacts a stunning reversal by way of the cunning of history in which, as Hegel has it, the universal World-Spirit manifests in the seemingly contingent phenomena of human history, the latter assuming the role of subsidiary actors bloodying one another on the gladiatorial field of time in pursuit of what they believe to be their own interests, while History itself "remains in the background, untouched and uninjured."[83] This historical cunning "sets the passions to work for itself, while that which develops its existence through such impulsion pays the penalty and suffers the loss."[84] That is, the supremacy of the rational/historical is secured through the mobilization and manipulation of apparently irrational or impassioned instruments. As Gosh's Murugan has it, "Someone's trying to get us to make some connections; they're trying to tell us something; something they don't want to put together themselves, so that when we get to the end we'll have a whole new story."[85]

Variations on this model underwrite the Marxist historicisms denounced by Chakrabarty, which are perhaps most notoriously represented in Marx's justification of the catalyzing role played by the colonization of India:

> We must not forget that these little communities were contaminated by distinctions of caste and by slavery, that they subjugated man to external circumstances instead of elevating man the sovereign of circumstances, that they transformed a self-developing social state into never changing natural destiny, and thus brought about a brutalizing worship of nature, exhibiting its degradation in the fact that man,

> the sovereign of nature, fell down on his knees in adoration of Kanuman, the monkey, and Sabbala, the cow.
>
> England, it is true, in causing a social revolution in Hindostan, was actuated only by the vilest interests, and was stupid in her manner of enforcing them. But that is not the question. The question is, can mankind fulfill its destiny without a fundamental revolution in the social state of Asia? If not, whatever may have been the crimes of England she was the unconscious tool of history in bringing about that revolution.[86]

As Partha Chatterjee observes, however, "Marx in his last years saw little regenerative value in the depredations of colonialism in Asian countries" and in fact later recognized in the Russia of the late nineteenth century "'the finest chance' in history for a country to pass into a phase of socialist development without first submitting to capital and thus 'committing suicide'."[87] For Chatterjee, arch-critic of the *derivative discourses* of an Indian nationalism beholden to the directives of capitalist universals, anti- and postcolonial national fidelities cannot outstrip the logic of capital and thus remain in thrall to its comprehensive historical cunning. Through the pre-emptive foreclusion of large-scale social/political possibility, third-world nationalism perforce preserves those antagonisms it cannot structurally resolve, then merely contains and redirects their expression in the form of "local" ethnic or cultural conflicts. The goal for any struggle against the disarticulating logic of global capital is therefore the acquisition or strategic production of "political-ideological resources" that match the universalizing impetus of capital and that link "the popular strength of those struggles with the consciousness of a new universality" beyond the delimiting form of the nation state and the interests it inevitably serves.[88]

Ghosh offers a figurative glimpse of this new form in outlining a political subjectivity that, existing beyond the enclosures of time and space sanctioned by the nation-state, expresses itself in the interstices, silences, and precarities of modernity (or, in Chakrabarty's terminology, in the narratives of History 2) and that, like Badiou's void, *inexists* in the totality of global capital and its privileged histories (as in the unrepresented vernacular stories of Laakhan) as its hauntingly illegible non-term. He does so, however, not simply by opposing this dominant with counter-narratives that might "fill" the intentional gaps of capital's hegemonic narrative with an oppositional content. As Chatterjee makes clear, such counter-hegemonic opposition, inasmuch as it remains within its conceptual horizons, merely reinforces the framework of that opposition without in any way disturbing its essential coordinates. Rather, I argue, what most distinguishes the revolutionary vision of *The Calcutta Chromosome* is its radical seizure of the Hegelian dialectical reversal (and thus of Marxist historicism itself) to imagine forth the alternative universal called for by Chatterjee. Subsuming the history of capital – from the imperial occupation of India to the octopine clutches of the multinational IWC – within the comprehensive horizon of an altogether different narrative continuum, the novel's peripeteiac inversion unmasks the imperializing discourses of rational science, the nation-state, and even of a triumphant, contemporary globalization itself as merely the impassioned instruments of a liberatory cunning, one whose encompassing logic has surreptitiously overseen the experiments of Ross and his predecessors just as it has engineered the cybernetic networking technology that allows Antar to be absorbed into the new political ontology of the no-place. Such a move radicalizes and expands Hegel's concept beyond the political formation that, from his own historical vantage, he privileges as History's absolute horizon:

> For Truth is the Unity of the universal and subjective Will; and the Universal is to be found in the State, in its laws, its universal and rational arrangements. The State is the Divine Idea as it exists on Earth. We have in it, therefore, the object of History in a more definite shape than before; that in which Freedom obtains objectivity, and lives in the enjoyment of this objectivity.[89]

Written in the immediate wake of Francis Fukuyama's controversial appropriation of Hegel in "The End of History?" (and the essay's subsequent book-length expansion), *The Calcutta Chromosome* wrests Hegel's hopeful contention in *The Philosophy of History* that "the History of the World is nothing but the development of the idea of Freedom" from the teleological terminus of the claim in *Elements of the Philosophy of Right* that "The State in-and-for-itself is the ethical whole, the actualization of Freedom."[90] Such a move retains the open-ended promise and dialectical dynamism that one associates with the young Hegel without foundering on the systemic ideology of a later *Hegelianism*.[91]

As the secret of the Mangala cult is unraveled, Murugan, the object of Antar's search, materializes before the sleeping Antar in holographic simulation, a reversal that John Thieme terms "the discoverer discovered," and offers to reveal to Antar the mystery in its entirety. Murugan indicates that all Antar need do is put on the Simultaneous Visualization (SimVis) headgear: "'You mean it's in there?' Antar gasped.

'But it can't be: nobody has access ...'."[92] Murugan's coolly understated reply obliquely acknowledges the expansive infiltrations of the Mangala group: "Guess we got in while the going was good."[93] Glancing at the SimVis system's start clock, however, Antar is stunned to find that the current program began loading at 5:25 p.m., the approximate moment that Ava "discovered" Murugan's lost ID card, a revelation that echoes the conclusion of Murugan's own search in Calcutta several years before. When Murugan and Sonali return to the home of Mrs Aratounian, who is revealed to be the current incarnation of Mangala, they discover that its contents have been emptied and the house itself already put up for sale, including Murugan's personal possessions, which are astonishingly itemized on an inventory dated exactly one year prior: "Murugan fell silent, staring at the clipboard, shaking his head in incomprehension. 'But this is insane,' he said. 'I mean – being here today wasn't even a glimmer in my eye a year ago'."[94] In each case, the apparently contingent and random – Murugan's impulsive decision to go to Calcutta, to stay in Mrs. Aratounian's guest house, even the personal possessions that he selects for the trip, and, later, the development of the IWC and the technology that supports its global empire – are shown to be unwittingly in service of an all-encompassing logic that reveals itself only in part and only at strategic moments.

Evident phenomena are thus transposed with (or are revealed already to have been) their very opposite. What appears in its immediacy as the absolute victory of the British Empire, western scientific discourse, or the "near-future" multinational corporation is transformed instantly, via perspectival shift, into their defeat; what seems an abject and insurmountable loss conversely becomes the instant of ultimate triumph. Such peripeteiac reversal, Jameson recently suggests, is simply the formal/narrative expression of none other than dialectical thought itself, which he explicitly identifies with Marx's appropriation of the cunning of history:

> Beginning with the *Grundrisse,* indeed, we can observe the emergence of a distinctive plot structure in which the very progress of a particular firm – in saturating the market with its product – at length brings about its stagnation as a business enterprise and its eventual collapse. Winner loses (and perhaps also loser wins) – the Sartrean version of this distinctive dialectical plot transforms the old bourgeois ideological categories of boom and bust, or prosperity and bankruptcy, beyond recognition (there is here also, no doubt, a relationship between this new narrative rhythm and the dialectical plot of the Hegelian period – the famous ruse of reason or history – in

which a narrative logic is transferred from individuals to collective forces unbeknownst to the former).[95]

The Calcutta Chromosome dramatizes precisely such a trajectory from the isolated individual dreaming of an outmoded collectivity – the consoling surface features of which are readily provided by multinational capital itself – to the realization of an utterly new form of mass political identification. At the novel's conclusion, as he awaits the promised revelation inside the SimVis headgear, Antar gradually becomes aware that other people have entered the room, that the secret he has been pursuing is in fact collectivity itself. Moving to take off the visor, he is gently restrained by someone he recognizes as his new neighbor, Tara, who whispers comfortingly in his ear, "Keep watching; we're here; we're all with you."[96] The acceptance of this reassurance – a faith in the unseen "we" – yields the gradually dawning awareness of an even grander collective: "There were voices everywhere now, in his room, in his head, in his ears, it was as though a crowd of people was in the room with him. They were saying: 'We're with you; you're not alone; we'll help you across'."[97] This "crossing" is not merely a withdrawal from or concession to the establishments of the present but rather "poses the exceeding productivity of the multitude against the exceptionality of capitalist command."[98] That is, Antar does not simply flee from his mundane, alienating duties with the IWC here. Rather, his crossing is an expression of what Hardt and Negri call *exodus*, which they define (again recalling Badiouian terminology) as "a process of *subtraction* from the relationsip with capital by means of actualizing the potential autonomy of labor-power."[99] Equating exodus to a kind of maroonage in the moment of the biopolitical, in which the new labor-power rejects the constraints placed upon its creative faculties by capital, they write:

> Like the slaves who collectively escape the chains of slavery to construct self-governing communities and quilombos, biopolitical labor-power subtracting from its relation to capital must discover and construct new social relationships, new forms of life that allow it to actualize its productive powers. But unlike that of the maroons, this exodus does not necessarily mean going elsewhere. We can pursue a line of flight while staying right here, by transforming the relations of production and mode of social organization under which we live.[100]

Lamenting the "sad indication of the wretched state of our political alternatives" in which the nation-state is deemed "the *only* community imaginable," Hardt and Negri thus offer the concept of exodus as an alternative social orientation that abjures the alienating prerogatives of capital without succumbing to the traps of nationalism enumerated by Chatterjee. Ghosh provides an abstract vision of this excessive biopolitical power, one no longer content with inherently cynical *tactics* of resistance, but one that rather acknowledges the full implications of Hardt and Negri's claim that "biopower is always 'subject' to the subjectivities it rules over" and that, by refusing further collaboration with capital, summons forth the new subject of biopolitics, who initiates ruptures in the capitalist continuum not by spectacular opposition from without, but by acting, as both Chakrabarty and Hardt and Negri suggest, *within and against.*

Hegel, peripeteia, and the infectious collective

If Ghosh's "loser wins" peripeteia remains somewhat evocative, a more recent example of Indian SF – one that bears more than a passing resemblance to *The Calcutta Chromosome* – provides a less ambiguous revolutionary conclusion that may be said to complete the imaginative trajectory of the former. Author and artist Manjula Padmanabhan, whose celebrated comic strip *Suki* appears in London's leftist Sunday *Observer* and whose science-fictional play *Harvest* was awarded the first Onassis Prize for Theatre in 1997, defends her preference for the genre in terms that we might recognize as dialectical:

> Some people dislike science fiction because of its anecdotal quality, often ending on a punchline and filled to the brim with weird, outlandish descriptions. What I like about the genre, however, is that it offers a writer the opportunity to go directly to the heart of an ironical or thought-provoking situation by setting up a theoretical world. Science fiction is a bit like writing a problem in mathematics, reducing reality to a tangle of pipes and cisterns or a group of three people travelling at varying speeds up a mountain, in order to reveal the relationships between matter, time and space.[101]

The three SF stories in Padmanabhan's otherwise realist narrative collection *Kleptomania* (2004) nicely demonstrate through such dialectical articulations of matter, time, and space the ways in which SF's critical abstractions can be appropriated for engaging the multiform problematic of globalization. Indeed, as she explains in the collection's introduction, the three stories were originally commissioned as non-fiction essays, but Padmanabhan found that the difficult topics of developments in gene technology, environmental concerns in Delhi, and Indian politics at the end of the millennium were all more productively approached by way of the estranging mechanisms of science fiction.

Of the three, none better exemplifies the genre's irrepressible utopian proclivities than the revolutionary fable "Gandhi-Toxin." Set in a distant, dystopian future in which the "MultiNations" achieve planetary supremacy by way of the genetic regulation programs under the authority of the United Gene Heritage and in which the "Fourth World is being devastated by battles being fought by clone troops of competing MultiNations," the brief story (just six pages) concerns a scientist, Gamma, who approaches the Supreme Command of the UGH claiming, first, that he is a distant genetic scion of Mohandas Gandhi and, second, that he has cloned the Mahatma's DNA and spliced it with his own in the form of a virus, a "blueprint for weapons-grade compassion!"[102] Fearing that through its power to disarm human "aggression vectors" the toxin could produce "catastrophic pacifism and widespread loss of the competitive urge," thereby dismantling the hegemonic mechanism whereby the MultiNations secure their rival global empires, the UGH detains Gamma, who is officially declared a "gene-hazard."

Perceiving, however, the means by which they might at last defeat their enemies, the UGH weaponizes the virus, renamed the Gandhi-Toxin, and delivers it through clouds of genetically manipulated mosquitoes. The toxin's effect is immediate and devastating:

> Beefy combat personnel, cloned from ten generations of war heroes, wilted on the battlefields. Cyber-fighters staggered away from their workstations in tears. Captains of Industry were reduced to whimpering heaps of guilt. A majority collapsed and died within minutes of being flooded with emotions lethal to their violent psyches. The few who recovered lost their muscle mass and became fantastically docile, unable to perform any tasks more hostile than tending organic herb gardens.[103]

From within his cell, Gamma hears rumors of the virus's effects and of the inevitable victories of the UGH. Within a year, however, disquieting reports of unanticipated side effects begin to surface. Asked by a fellow prisoner if he is aware that there is "a new kind of struggle going on," that those exposed to the toxin had become subversives, "dismantling commercial institutions and reorganizing marketplaces everywhere," Gamma serenely replies that perhaps it is simply a "new version" of a much older struggle.[104]

When he is accused by UGH leaders Isabella and Aidid, who have immured themselves within an impenetrable isolation shield, of destroying "the foundation of Civilization as we know it," Gamma calmly replies, "Not at all," and credits the UGH itself with the revolution's efficiency and scope:

> I cobbled together a handful of chromosomes and made them available to you. You did all the rest. You infected your competitors' troops more effectively than I could ever have done with my modest laboratory facilities. The mosquitoes, for instance! They were a stroke of genius. Because of them Gandhi's pacifism has gone planetary.[105]

Protected from the toxin's effects, Aidid remains both defiant and supremely confident in the self-replicating network of the Multinational empire, boasting that he has secured "self-dupes" in secret locations around the globe, each "tuned" to his bio-signature, such that upon his death the full datum of his person is instantly transferred to one of these automata: "And if that one dies, the next will take his place. And so on. You can't kill me! I'm immortal! I'm invincible."[106] If Aidid remains oblivious to the fact that the expansive mechanisms of this imperial network not only expedited but also made possible the revolution that has just expunged its authority, Isabella does not. Favoring the risks of the unknown to a life of solitary security within the isolation cell, Isabella switches off the protective field – much to Aidid's horror – and declares her belief that the potency of her character can overcome the toxin's pacific effect, after which, she predicts, "I'll have the market advantage over all you non-competitive sheep!"[107] Thus, it is Isabella's steadfast faith in her (and thus capital's) imperialist nature – not to mention her cynical disregard for revolution – that allows for the penetration of this final spatial enclave and its utopian transfiguration:

> Musical tones sounded behind them, as swarms of mosquitoes found their mark. A gentle smile distorted the usually frowning features of Aidad as he swooned under the influence of the bites. Isabella, tingling all over, lay back on the grass and, for the first time since childhood, slept without the aid of pills.[108]

Padmanabhan's iteration here of the utopian primacy of rest recalls almost exactly the lyrically anodyne (if yet ambiguous) concluding sentence of *The Calcutta Chromosome*, in which Antar likewise submits to the crossing and thus to the new biopolitical collective: "He sat back and sighed like he hadn't sighed in years."[109]

Beyond the obvious surface similarities (both mobilize a viral resistance – vectored by mosquito – against multinational corporate power) a deeper, structural symmetry is evident here as well: namely, the "loser wins" dialectical reversal of the peripeteia, or what we have identified as the Hegelian cunning of history. If Ghosh's vision remains intentionally inconclusive (its refusal of narrative closure itself formally indicative of a utopian content that cannot as yet be represented), juxtaposing it with Padmanabhan's "companion" story illuminates more fully the revolutionary drift of the former by staging the consequences of its large-scale "viral" transformation and clarifying its appropriation of Hegel. Even Padmanabhan's metaphorical deployment of viral transmission as a cipher for the revolutionary awakening of an alternative collective consciousness recalls Hegel's discussion of the inherently social force of even the most solitary utterance as *Ansteckung*, or infection: "The *I* that utters itself is *heard* or perceived; it is an infection in which it has immediately passed into unity with those for whom it is a real existence, and is a universal self-consciousness."[110] As Leela Gandhi convincingly demonstrates in a discussion of Ghosh's *In an Antique Land* (1992), Hegel is without doubt the author's most important interlocutor, providing the essential philosophical and historicist models that Ghosh variously repudiates, repurposes, or utterly reinvents in his fiction. In a brief SF overture of her own, Gandhi provides a useful thought experiment, half-facetiously qualified as "a scene from some amateurish late-postcolonial, faux-science-fiction, short film," in which the young author of the just-published *In an Antique Land* encounters and exhaustively debates Hegel himself, who has been inexplicably shunted into the future via "some perverse time-warp."[111] Following a lengthy exchange over tea in which Ghosh lends Hegel a copy of his recent novel and convinces the philosopher to reconsider the Eurocentric bent of his theory of history, the latter returns to the Berlin of 1831 and undertakes an ambitious (if uncompleted) revision of *The Phenomenology*, while Ghosh "commences work on a science-fiction narrative involving, in this case, a journey back in time from futuristic New York to late-nineteenth-century India."[112]

More than just an amusing moment of scholarly levity, Gandhi's brief science fictional prologue, defying the generic constraints of the academic essay it introduces,[113] functions effectively as an heuristic device helping to trace Ghosh's complex relation to Hegelian historicism. For if, as Gandhi suggests, Ghosh's celebrated work of ethnographic fiction[114] provides a qualifying rejoinder or critical supplement to both the master–slave dialectic and a teleological historicism, *The Calcutta Chromosome* emphatically demonstrates that Ghosh's encounter with Hegel is not entirely one-sided (nor, as Gandhi's time-travelling expedient itself implies, even unilinear), that the relation is perhaps not so much, as Gandhi formulates it in her title, the starkly antagonistic "Ghosh vs. Hegel" as it is the properly dialectical "Ghosh *avec* Hegel," in which the former is considered alongside the latter in dynamic, multidimensional tension.[115]

Ghosh's unique work of science fiction in fact provides us a glimpse of what Hegel's History looks like if carried beyond the notional extremities of the present and informed with new universals, where our forsaken futures are at once identified and inhabited, where the iron necessity of History is revealed as contingent, and where new necessities retroactively author the very conditions of their emergence. Such retroactive generation of an historical imperative, as Žižek contends (against conventional interpretation), is precisely what Hegel means by *totality* and, I suggest, its realization in the oft-maligned concept of the cunning of history, which, like Hegel's famous owl of Minerva, spreads its wings only with the falling of the dusk.[116] Or, as Jameson argues in defense of the dialectical method more generally, "totality is not something one ends with, but something one begins with."[117] Thus, Marx's controversial assessment of the role played by the British Empire in India need not be an apology for imperialism as the agent of an implacable, foreordained history, as a sequence in the adamantine chain of necessity binding a merely superficial historical contingency. On the contrary, what *The Calcutta Chromosome* demonstrates through its chronotopic dialecticism is the contingency of historical necessity itself, the positing of its own presuppositions, or the manner in which, as Marx famously has it, "[m]en make their own history but not in circumstances of their own choosing."[118] In this way, Ghosh joins the growing chorus of recent cultural theorists and philosophers (Žižek, Jameson, Susan Buck-Morss, Domenico Losurdo, and Badiou among its more audible voices) attempting both to reclaim a Hegelian intellectual inheritance and critically to reappropriate its much-criticized totalizations for a postmodern present. *The Calcutta Chromosome*'s foremost provocation might therefore be read as consonant with that of Buck-Morss's own audacious reconsideration of Hegel: "The project of universal history does not come to an end. It begins again, somewhere else" (151).[119] Indeed, Ghosh's *speculative* fiction – to return to that Heinleinian term now given the full weight of its implicitly Hegelian charge – suggests that such a history, despite all appearances to the contrary, is already underway, crafted by the multitudinous hands of a monstrous subjectivity.

5
Mob Zombies, Alien Nations, and Cities of the Undead: Monstrous Subjects and the Post-Millennial Nomos in *I am Legend* and *District 9*

The subject produced from this renewed historical cunning, or perhaps vice versa, is the properly monstrous political subject for whom existing social categories and agential determinations are demonstrably insufficient. From the scholarly collaborations of Michael Hardt and Antonio Negri, Peter Linebaugh and Marcus Rediker to the plethora of cinematic and televisual incarnations, the first decade of the new millennium has seen an acute resurgence of interest in – indeed, a well-nigh global obsession with – the reckoning of this monstrous subjectivity. Of especial prominence has been the return of the zombie and its phantasmagoric next-of-kin, the werewolf, the alien, and the vampire, all of which have increasingly assumed the key features of the former. In fact, the twenty-first-century zombie is easily distinguished from its Cold War, pop-culture predecessor by two fundamental characteristics: its proclivity for mass social organization and its disarming speed and power. While the first attribute has gone largely without notice, the second provoked vigorous online debate (weighing the merits of the "fast zombie" against the traditional "slow" one) following the release of Danny Boyle's British "viral zombie" film *28 Days Later* (2002) and Zack Snyder's much-anticipated remake of George Romero's classic satire of US consumerism *Dawn of the Dead* (2004), either of which might legitimately lay claim as the originator of this now *de rigueur* representation. Latter-day zombies eschew the standard (and perfectly logical) encumbrances of *rigor mortis* and in fact do not appear dead at all. On the contrary, they are possessed of an intolerable surfeit of life, an irrepressible surplus evident not only in their agility and strength but also in their unprecedented cunning and collective coordination, and it is this transgressive vitality (that which is in itself more than itself), rather than any customary decadence, that most accurately characterizes their threat to a beleaguered and desperate "humanity." The fast zombie's expression of an excessive or intolerable *verve* finds its objective correlative, I argue, in the yet-political possibilities of an allegedly post-political present. In the essay that follows, I explore two recent popular films that deploy in markedly distinct, if deeply related ways the contemporary monstrous subject (in both its "fast zombie" and "alien" variations) within the broad context of late capital's erosion of the state and the catastrophic reorganization of social space. First, I examine a representative first-world imaginative response in *I am Legend* (2007), a film that tentatively articulates but ultimately mystifies the deep structural relations undergirding the simultaneous rise of the slum city and the gated community in the evacuated space of the post-national. Second, I discuss the South African film *District 9* (2009), which, in a more satisfactorily dialectical meditation on contemporary spatiality, at once acknowledges and critically intervenes in the *nomos* of globalization.

In her pioneering case study of contemporary trends of spatial reconfiguration in the modern *polis*, Teresa P.R. Caldeira traces the rise of the fortified enclave community (in cities as seemingly remote as São Paulo and Los Angeles[1]) to the now-global supremacy of the neoliberalist economic order and its various sociocultural effects: the tumultuous installment of liberal democracy, the precarities of insertion into a new (increasingly virtual, increasingly volatile) global economy, and the decaying of the nation-state under the steady pressure of institutions like the IMF and World Bank, whose notorious structural adjustment programs hamstring developing nations with often debilitating reductions in government programs and oversight on the one hand and with the abolition of protectionary trade barriers, tariffs, and subsidies on the other. Furthermore, as Mike Davis observes, by eliminating the possibility for sustainable agricultural production, these IMF/World Bank policies (often including obligatory industrial mechanization) "continue[ ] to generate an exodus of surplus rural labor to urban slums even as cities cease[ ] to be job machines."[2] The result is the teeming multitude (well over a billion) who now inhabit the more than 200,000 peri-urban slums of the world, some of which, like Lagos, Nigeria, Dhaka, Bangladesh, and Karachi, Pakistan, are projected soon to be among the largest megacities in human history.

Strategically directing toward this politically evacuated and vulnerable space of the public the rhetoric of criminalization,

> [g]roups that feel threatened by the social order taking shape in these cities commonly build exclusive, fortified enclaves for their

> residence, work, leisure, and consumption. The discourses of fear that simultaneously help to legitimize this withdrawal and to reproduce fear find different references. Frequently, they are about crime, and especially violent crime. But they also incorporate racial and ethnic anxieties, class prejudices, and references to poor and marginalized groups.[3]

The new urbanism's simultaneous production of both enclave communities and the slums that Robert Neuwirth calls "shadow cities" signals at once an ongoing crisis in the global (re)conceptualization of democracy and a final renunciation of the political/cultural/spatial architectonics familiar to us as the constellation of *modernism*: "The new pattern of spatial segregation undermines the values of openness, accessibility, freedom of circulation, and equality that inspired the modern type of urban public space and creates instead a new public space that has inequality, separation, and control of boundaries as organizing values."[4] Opposing current practices of sociospatial dispersion to the public spaces of an erstwhile modernism, Caldeira also writes: "Privatization, enclosure, and distancing devices offer means not only of withdrawing from and undermining a certain space (modern) but also of creating another public sphere: one that is fragmented, articulated, and secured by separation and high-tech devices, and in which equality, openness, and accessibility are not organizing values."[5] What confronts us in the schismatic spatial management of the post-millennial megalopolis is therefore none other than the cultural logic of late capital itself, manifest in the transition from Le Corbusier's functionally utopian "machines for living"[6] to Robert Venturi's pococurante "less is bore."[7] While Caldeira's study remains largely unconcerned with the specific delineation of modernist or postmodernist typologies, she does invoke Edward Soja's explicit reading of this newly "polynucleated and decentralized" urban space as indeed "postmodern."[8]

Eroding the very conditions of possibility for an authentic *politics*, the compartmentalizing logic of the post-millennial *polis* disorganizes social space itself, circumscribing discrete, seemingly autonomous spatial monads, the deep structural correlations and interdependencies of which become increasingly and intentionally difficult to map. It is here, I argue, that the dialectical imaginary of science fiction productively intervenes. It perhaps comes as no surprise that sociologists and architects, critics and apologists alike turn to the genre to nominate the enigmatic effects of this novel urban re-spatialization. In his brilliant if sobering examination of the explosive growth of global slums and enclave communities over the last two decades, Mike Davis turns to the idiom of SF (specifically, to concepts and terminology engineered by Philip K. Dick) to represent the alienated spaces of postmodernity, noting that in their "quasi-utopian attempt to disengage from the suffocating matrix of poverty and social violence," the global elite construct increasingly self-contained *off worlds* such as "Utopia" and "Dreamland" in Cairo and "Alphaville" (after the 1965 Jean-Luc Godard dystopic sci-fi film) in São Paulo.[9] Others evoke identifications with the no less fantastical spaces of the first world: "Beverly Hills" in Cairo, "Orange County" and "Long Beach" in China, and "Palm Springs" in Hong Kong, where residents are surrounded by "live" Disney characters and neoclassical architecture. Dissociating their private *off worlds* from any recognizable form of polity, the urban elite, Jeremy Seabrook contends, effectively "cease to be citizens of their own country and become nomads belonging to, and owing allegiance to, a superterrestrial topography of money; they become patriots of wealth, nationalists of an elusive and golden nowhere."[10]

This "utopian" virtualization of the bourgeois state into discontinuous clusters of nomadic, semi-autonomous nuclei is perennially haunted, however, by its material/spectral complement in the sprawling, makeshift cities of the global poor. More than a million people, for instance, illegally inhabit the vast warren of tombs and mausoleums in Cairo's infamous Qarafa, or "City of the Dead," where they have ingeniously adapted the ancient structures as functional housing, constructing shelving and bedding from sepulchers of Egyptian nobility and pirating electricity from nearby lines to power lights, appliances, and television sets.[11] Similarly, the Congo Republic's own "city of the dead," Kinshasa, is popularly known by its increasingly desperate inhabitants as *cadavre*, *epavre*, or *Kin-la-poubelle*: "cadaver," "wreck," or "Kinshasa, the rubbish heap."[12] On the outskirts of Cairo one can also find Manshiyat Naser, better known as Garbage City, where inhabitants, the Zabbaleen, literally live on trash: collecting, sorting, recycling, or simply reselling about a third of the city's refuse. Even this precarious existence (which provides a much-needed, completely uncompensated service to the state) has been threatened in recent years by the ideology of privatization, with the Zabbaleen forced either to vie with international waste management companies for contracts on individual sectors of the city or to submit to wage-based employment with the winning contractors.[13]

The properly "ghoulish" material relation of cities like Qarafa and Kinshasa to their "virtual" gated counterparts – their literal as well as figurative status as necropoleis – is made disturbingly clear in the lucrative global organ market, in which the slums of the third world are increasingly mined by the urban elite as a source for much-needed human organs.[14] Davis writes of one such exploited slum city:

> In India, the impoverished periphery of Chennai (Madras) has become world renowned for its "kidney farms" ... The area's slum-dwellers were mostly drought refugees struggling to survive as rick-shaw pullers or day laborers. Journalists estimated that more than 500 people, or one person per family, had sold their kidneys for local transplants or for export to Malaysia; a majority of the donors were women, including "many deserted women ... forced to sell their kid-neys to raise money to support themselves and their children".[15]

For Trevor Harrison, the explosive growth in illegal organ trafficking since the 1980s "must be understood in the broader context of glo-balization, specifically the extension and intensification of a capitalist mode of exchange."[16] Under the reifying logic of capital, "all objects lose distinction" and are evaluated simply on the "basis of their relative equivalence;"[17] therefore, "wombs are rented; sperm is sold; and, finally, human organs 'harvested'."[18] The groundbreaking introduction of the immunosuppressant cyclosporine in the early 1980s decreased the risk of host rejection and spurred in the developed world an unprecedented demand for organs (mostly kidneys) that was met by the establish-ment of a network of unregulated transplant centers throughout the developing world.[19] By 1999, kidney transplants could earn the pro-vider between $10,000 and $30,000 with only $500–$2,000 of this amount going to the donor – even less in cases where donor organs were obtained either from cadavers or the forcibly coerced.[20] Due to the considerable cost as well as the legal and logistical complexity of this emergent international exchange, the initial "period of individual entrepeneurship soon gave way to corporations" who often work(ed) in collusion with state governments to procure the lucrative commodities retained in the bodies of their citizens.[21]

Unable otherwise to explain such unimaginable horrors and paradoxes of postmodern reality, inhabitants of these slum cities – like their first-world intellectual counterparts[22] – resort increasingly to the explanatory powers of the fantastic. For instance, in recent years Kinshasa has seen a "literal, perverse belief in Harry Potter ... leading to the mass-hysterical denunciation of thousands of child 'witches' and their expulsion in the streets, even their murder."[23] However, while Davis argues that "[t]he child witches of Kinshasa, like the organ-exporting slums of India and

Egypt, seem to take us to an existential ground zero beyond which there are only death camps, famine, and Kurtzian horror,"[24] Jean and John Comaroff offer an alternative perspective on the recent revival of popular third-world phantasms. Tracing the return of the zombie in South African popular culture to the "occult " economies of globalization, the Comaroffs contend that these preoccupations with the phantasmagoric must be read as attempts to reach "far beyond their orthodox rationalist frame in order to plumb the enigma of new social realities: harsh realities whose magicality, in the prevailing historical circumstances, does not permit the literary conceit of magical realism, demanding instead a deadly serious engagement with the actuality of enchantment."[25] Thus, the South African zombie is not merely some atavistic manifestation, the attempt to retreat from the discomforting aporias of modernity into the consolations of a familiar, native occult. Rather, it emerges as an attempt to fix with a legible signifier the illegible convolutions of the present:

> As the very conditions that call forth zombies erode the basis of a conventional politics of labor and place and public interest, we would do well to keep an open mind about the pragmatic possibilities of these creatures of collective dread: about the provocative manner in which they, perhaps more than anything or anybody else, are compelling the state to take note. Even to act.[26]

The Comaroffs specifically identify the zombie as a cipher for the dramatically increasing numbers of immigrant laborers in South Africa since the early 1990s, shadow citizens who, it is widely believed, disrupt local labor conditions, "usurp scarce jobs and resources, foster prostitution, and spread AIDS";[27] Like zombies, the Comaroffs argue, these immigrants are routinely cast in the role of "nightmare citizens, their rootlessness threatening to siphon off the remaining, rapidly diminishing prosperity of the indigenous population."[28] Summoned into existence by the dislocating velocities of global neoliberalism and its erosion of both national polities and local economies,

> [z]ombies, the ultimate nonstandard workers, take shape in the collective imaginary as figurations of these conditions. In their silence they give voice to a sense of dread about the human costs of intensified capitalist production; about the loss of control over the terms in which people alienate their labor power; about the demise of a moral economy in which wage employment, however distant and

> exploitative, had "always" been there to support both the founding of families and the well-being of communities.[29]

The zombie as subject is thus the "monstrous" remainder of the human in a posthuman world, the stubbornly unassimilable, spectral excess of the new world order's schismatic spatiosymbolic organization. Functioning as "standardized nightmares in a world of 'daylight reason,'" these monstrous subjects both recall us to an obscured material history at the same that they allow "free play to anger and anguish and desire."[30] As Hardt and Negri remind us, now more than ever, "[r]evolution is not for the faint of heart. It is for monsters."[31]

Privatopia and parallax in *I am Legend*

In Francis Lawrence's 2007 film adaptation of the 1954 Richard Matheson novel,[32] Will Smith portrays US Army Colonel Robert Neville, MD, the last man in a post-apocalyptic New York City and, we are initially led to believe, perhaps the United States if not the world. Departing, however, from the familiar dystopian vision of a metropolis reduced to rubble and a crumbling skyline providing the backdrop for the desperate activities of a subterranean social remnant, this near-future New York City is remarkably, even uncannily intact. In one of the few critical treatments of *I am Legend*, David L. Pike notes of the "achingly familiar setting" that the film's New York City is indeed "neither a terrifying urban underworld nor in ruins; it is deserted but basically unchanged from the city of 2007 – a fact the filmmakers stress with their choice to retain even the Times Square ads that were up when they filmed the backdrops for their digital effects."[33] Set only three years after a breakthrough viral cure for cancer has gone devastatingly awry – decimating the global population with a 90 per cent kill rate and transforming an estimated 588 million of the remaining planetary inhabitants into the monstrous "dark seekers" – the film features none of the genre's canonical privations. Looting stores, apartments, and even museums at his leisure, Neville (surprisingly tidily and tastefully) fills his immaculate four-story Washington Square townhouse with a superabundance of weapons, food, drugs, generators, medical and laboratory equipment, and even original Van Goghs apparently "liberated" from the Met. Such superfluity is emphasized in the redundancy of Neville's supplies: his home and lab are run (perhaps unrealistically) by a row of gas-powered generators; records of his scientific experiments are saved to six computer hard drives; and one brief but richly suggestive scene shows him take from a kitchen cabinet a jar of tomato sauce that he immediately replaces with another from a laden nearby counter. In fact, Neville's daylight hours are marked not, as we might expect, by the desperate exigencies of scarcity but by the conspicuous leisure of the solidly upper-middle class: hunting (not so much for meat as for sport, as we never see him take a deer, and his need for meat seems a minor concern); "shopping" in the homes and shops of Manhattan; fishing in a museum "pond"; exercising (we see him doing pull-ups and running vigorously on a tread mill in his home); golfing ("I'm gettin' good," he boasts, launching balls from the tail of a jet aboard the USS *Intrepid*); gardening (he leisurely gathers corn in Central Park from a stand that he has presumably planted, though the effect is that of spontaneous, cornucopian largess); selecting DVDs from a neighborhood video outlet (he has learned *Shrek* by rote); listening to music (the film's troubling appropriation of Bob Marley is, I hope to show, not insignificant); playing fetch at the pier with Sam, his loyal German Shepherd and singular companion; and driving a new sports car through the deserted city streets, even, when he likes, on the empty sidewalks (the fuel, advertized at $6 per gallon, is free).

Likening the ambivalent utopianism of Neville's casual daily routine to the Cold War "bunker fantasies" of the 1950s, Pike usefully observes that what is in one sense a nightmare scenario simultaneously functions as the imaginative expression or repository of "everything one wishes one's present life actually had but does not."[34] If Neville's nightmare is also the bourgeois dream come true, foremost among its fantasies is the eradication of the masses, the freeing of the individual and its subjective desires from the obstructions posed by community, government, and all that impedimentary humanity. Michael McKeon's observation regarding Crusoe's island, the obvious antecedent to Neville's New York City, is apropos: "Because it excludes all human society, it provides an arena in which the anti-social passions of avarice and domination can be indulged without suffering the consequences."[35] In a city from which the state has completely withdrawn Neville achieves a version of the neoliberalist utopia. Indeed, a glimpse into his impressively stocked hallway gun cabinet reveals that the virus has quite literally given him the keys to the city. We find similar imagery in many filmic incarnations of the postmodern zombie, even in satirical appropriations such as the otherwise irredeemable *Zombieland* (2009), which finds the four survivors of a zombifying super-virus looting and gleefully destroying merchandise from various outlets, driving a succession of increasingly massive luxury SUVs, and living the high life in an ostentatious Beverly Hills mansion (that of comedic actor Bill Murray), all of this while on their way to visit a Los Angeles theme park now ideally emptied of competing patrons. This emphasis on a liberal consumption unimpeded by the constraints of the social collective represents a drastic departure from the classic (what I am tempted here to call *modernist*[36]) Romero zombie films, in which the threat posed by the (slow and organizationally random) zombie hoard forcibly consolidates an often markedly heterogeneous remnant of the living, who, placed in discomforting and undeniable proximity to one another, transcend (or least manage) their differences to overcome the anomic zombie threat.

Films like *I am Legend,* however, participate in the bourgeois "privatopian" dream increasingly made reality in the world's contemporary urban agglomerates with the phenomenal rise of the gated community. The film expresses the structural schizophrenia of modern urban space in the bifurcation of Neville's lifeworld into day and night.[37] The price exacted for his daytime leisure and uncontested consumption is a hypervigilant security and paranoid anxiety. Neville's townhouse, occupying some of the most desirable and expensive real estate in the city with a view of the Washington Square Arch, is by day a well-lit, astonishingly clean, idyllic family home in a still-lovely neighborhood. At night, however, Neville withdraws to its pristine interior – assiduously masking with white vinegar any scent trails he may have left on the walk – secures all windows and doors with massive steel shutters and bars, and arms an elaborate remote-controlled security system complete with an outer perimeter of ultra-violet light-towers and an inner ring of military-grade explosives. In addition to a large foyer cabinet brimming with munitions, guns are stowed in every room of the home, and on the first nightfall depicted in the film, Neville sleeps in his capacious clawfoot bathtub, curled against Sam in the fetal position, cradling an assault rifle and listening with pained expression to the inhuman grunts and growls of the creatures prowling just outside his fortress. While Pike correctly suggests that the film might be read as a compendium of nested underground spaces – a figuratively "underground" New York City > Neville's fortified townhouse > the basement laboratory > the Plexiglass "safe room" > the underground coal hole > and the ultimate safe zone of the Vermont colony – we might more precisely situate its spatial play as a dramatization of the complexities and paradoxes of globalization and of the anxieties attending the withdrawal of the state, one that necessarily assumes the form of a Žižekian parallax: that is, both the "impossible" coexistence of mutually exclusive realities and the dialectical critical perspective that attempts to locate the fundamental antinomy of such an order and to lay bear this disavowed contradiction.

Thus, the terrifying nightworld of the seekers and Neville's sunlit world of untrammeled consumption are not simply irreducible parallel possibilities between which, following the creed of postmodern relativism, one may or must choose (as Neville continues falsely to believe) but are rather obverse sides of a singular problematic. Neither can exist without its structural counterpart.

While Pike also productively reads the film's spatial/temporal divide as that which "tropes the paradox of the modern city" (one, he suggests, that is familiar to "most of us"), I propose a somewhat broader referent, one made baldly explicit in what is perhaps the film's most emotionally harrowing and imagistically curious scene. When Sam recklessly pursues a deer into what appears to be a West Chelsea warehouse, Neville follows, refusing to abandon his only companion and link to his former life (Sam is entrusted to him by his daughter just moments before her death). Palming the beam from the flashlight affixed to his rifle, Neville nervously makes his way into the building's oppressive interior darkness, whispering desperate pleas to Sam. Following a suggestive bloodtrail spattered on the grimy, institutional-hued tile, Neville is relieved to find only a mutilated deer carcass near a stairwell, a discovery that, while momentarily heartening, is nonetheless a pointed reminder of his own comparative impotence next to the speed, strength, and sheer number of the seekers, who succeed where he and his high-tech weaponry cannot. Following the stairs, Neville finds himself in an interior room, where his search is dramatically arrested by the faint sounds of the creatures stirring and grunting. His carefully cupped beam reveals jail-like bars and a massive, steel vault-door. Directing the feeble light deeper into the room, Neville sees a group of seekers huddled in a tight circle. Their stirring, chanting activity here is ambiguous, though they appear to be either sleeping (a concession to their vampiric origins in Matheson's novel) or, inasmuch as the film functions as a 9/11 allegory, perhaps praying.[38] Most significant, however, are the bound stacks of now useless cash and bank documents that litter the floor of the room, a detail that catches the attention of both our protagonist and the camera, the gaze of each pausing fractionally over the incongruous sight even in this moment of mortal urgency. In fact, the odd scene offers a precise inversion of Neville's townhouse, a parallax representation of the reverse side of the Möbius strip which completes the film's dialectical representation of the postmodern present. Here, in the preternatural dark of the seeker's lare, the "safe zone" has already been violated, and the easy abundance of Neville's townhouse is liquefied into now-useless banknotes and the irreducible fact of the seeker's gruesome physicality, evidenced by the deer carcass, an image that recurs moments later as Neville locates Sam and sprints to safety. Closely pursued by a host of seekers in the shadows that stretch behind him, Neville races down a long hallway toward a distant beam of light radiating from a tiny hole in the blacked-out windows. As he flees, we perceive glimpses of the building's dim interior: a series of brass stanchions and velvet ropes, a lengthy polished wooden counter, and a United States flag, coupled with the vault seen earlier, suggest that what appeared from the exterior as a warehouse in an advanced state of disrepair is perhaps some kind of bank, a revelation that sutures Neville's alienated and unfettered consumption to material history even as it simultaneously bodies forth the nightmare of the increasingly precarious rich, in which the monstrous multitude has already penetrated the sanctum of capital and reduced its pristine order to rubbish. The scene therefore symbolically confirms both the diabolic threat of the seekers and Neville's status as embattled hero in relation to the current economic order.

However, in just this way the bourgeois privatopia of *I am Legend* likewise generates its authentically utopian counterpart or complement in the form of the vital mass movement that represents the intolerable "other side" of this contemporary global order, the latter's structurally immanent counter-agent. As Jameson teaches us in his model of the reification/utopia dialectic, in order to accomplish its ultimate ideological goal of containing this counterforce, the film (or other product of mass cultural expression) inevitably gives it form. We can perceive in Neville's consistent misrecognition of the seekers' purpose and nature the *fetishistic disavowal* that sustains his symbolic universe, an amnesiac suppression that, as Žižek describes it, generally takes the form of "I know it, but I refuse to fully assume the consequences of this knowledge, so that I can continue acting as if I don't know."[39] Perhaps the most significant of these pathological misrecognitions concerns Neville's failure to discern the creatures' relative *humanity*. Following his narrow escape from the warehouse-cum-bank, Neville rigs an elaborate snare using a broken vial of his own blood as bait, entrapping one of the creatures in a tarp and dragging it out of the warehouse into the daylight. As he prepares it for transport to the lab, one of the remaining creatures materializes from the shadows, roaring and glaring hatefully at him, unflinchingly pressing its face into the bar of sunlight just beyond the darkened doorway until its skin begins to sizzle. Observing this with a kind of repulsed pity, Neville later offers an astonishingly obtuse interpretation of the event in his assiduously maintained video records, one that, not insignificantly, assumes the form of mere afterthought or supplement to the primary entry: "Behavioral note: An infected male exposed himself to sunlight today. It's possible that decreased brain function or scarcity of food is causing them to ignore their basic survival instincts. Social de-evolution appears complete. Typical human behavior is now entirely absent." Neville's operative assumption of the creatures' inhumanity here precludes the recognition that this willful suspension of the self-preservation instinct might be fundamentally, even heroically human.[40]

Similarly, Neville fails to acknowledge the sophistication of the seekers' vengeful response to this event – a failure that ultimately actuates the film's ambivalent revolutionary expression/ re-containment in the storming of Neville's townhouse and the attempted rescue of the female seeker. On his way home after a day of sitting at the pier and fishing in the Sackler Wing of the Met, Neville is horrified to find that "Fred," one of the mannequins that he has positioned at the video store, is standing in the middle of Park Avenue just outside Grand Central Station. His ludicrous inability to deduce how Fred might have arrived here (one, the film's editorial cues ensure, not shared by the viewer) suggests a narrative tension, an implicit critical regard toward the perceptual limits of Neville's governing ideology: his premise that the seekers are no longer human. In the DVD "alternate version" of the film (to which I want presently to return), Neville's obliviousness is made stunningly obvious. Returning with Anna to inspect the site of his near capture and finding the seekers' elaborate snare, he says with less incredulity than dogmatic certainty, "The infected didn't do this. They can't. ... They have no higher brain function. They don't plan or hate. They don't love. They can't." When Anna asks if perhaps they could be following him, learning from his actions, adapting, he simply offers no response. What is more, the trap set by the seekers is infinitely more complex than Neville's technically competent, if conceptually simplistic snare. While Neville's trap appeals to what he perceives as the insuperable feral instinct and insatiable bloodlust of the creatures, the seekers' trap reveals a cerebral elegance and complexity borne of close observation and abstract psychology. That is, having observed his loneliness and noted his emotional vulnerabilities, they know how to press Neville's psychological buttons in such a way that his delimiting presuppositions render him incapable of reciprocating. As the sun begins to set and the dazed, badly wounded Neville extricates himself from the snare and attempts to drag himself to his vehicle, he sees standing in the smashed doorway of the station none other than the Alpha Male from the previous day, which confirms for the viewer both the intelligence and humanity of the seekers even as the presence of these qualities remains lost on Neville himself.

When Sam inevitably succumbs to the virus following the ensuing encounter with the seekers' infected dogs (which present further evidence of the creatures' instrumentalizing rationality), a grief-stricken Neville loses his stoic equilibrium, that very night recklessly driving his SUV (studded with UV lights) into an unsuspecting crowd of the creatures, attempting to take out as many as possible in a final stand before they ultimately kill him – which, if not for the fortuitous intervention of Anna, they would inevitably have done. Even this last-minute rescue ultimately fails, however, because Anna, unfamiliar with Neville's fastidious security protocol, neglects to disguise their scent on the walk, leading the seekers straight to the townhouse the following evening, where their swarming number and organized plan of attack effortlessly overwhelm Neville's high-tech security system.[41]

To the last, Neville remains astonishingly, pathologically unaware of the possibility made clear by the film that his actions are anything but righteous, that, via a parallactic focal shift, he might himself be seen as an agent of terror and perpetrator of incomprehensible violence. The film's representation of this moral myopia is captured most clearly in the panel of grisly photographs, all subjects of Neville's failed experiments, adorning the wall of his basement laboratory. The variously savage, mournful, or agonized countenances staring out from the columned display of headshots recall simultaneously, and thus in true parallax fashion, everything from the FBI's "Most Wanted Terrorists" list (released in late 2001) to the devastating display of portraits in Yad Vashem's Holocaust History Museum in Jerusalem (opened in 2004). "Did *all* of them die," asks Anna, eyes glistening with pity, to which Neville replies with a clipped and nonchalant "Yes." "My God," she says, sympathetically shaking her head. "God didn't do this, Anna. We did." Similarly, as Pike also observes, Neville appears wholly oblivious to the gender of his trapped test subject as well as to the probability that the aggressive male is her lover, rightfully enraged at seeing her kidnapped and subjected to Neville's torturous experiments (such as the burning of her skin with ultraviolet light to measure the efficacy of his serum) and thus wholly justified in his impassioned pursuit.[42]

Anna's presence crucially introduces a variant point of view, the contrast of which reveals the solipsistic limits of Neville's perspective. For instance, Anna's inquiry regarding Neville's experimental new procedure – augmenting the serum by packing the seeker's body in ice – marks the first time that the viewer, previously confined to

Neville's point of view, hears the creatures referenced as anything other than the pronominally objectifying "it": "Do you think it will cure *her*?" Neville's response, implicitly (perhaps unconsciously) corrective, insists, however, on the objectifying discourse of the practical/empirical: "No, this will almost certainly kill *it*, but it's possible that by drastically reducing the body temperature I can increase the compound's effectiveness." Entirely without malice, Neville has killed dozens of the seekers in an effort to cure them, though he recognizes neither violence nor contradiction in any of this, having embraced affirmatively the identity ambivalently assigned him on the caption of the *Time* magazine cover that adorns his well-stocked refrigerator: "Savior?" Žižek accounts for such perspectival blockage by distinguishing between two principal categories of violence: the sensational *subjective violence* that is "performed by a clearly visible agent" against the presumably neutral backdrop of a "non-violent zero level"; and the invisible *objective violence* that is "inherent to this 'normal' state of things."[43] That is, while the violence that founds and subtends a given order does not necessarily register as such to its inhabitants, any subsequent attempts to attack or destabilize that order can appear within its symbolic enclosure only as "'irrational' explosions of subjective violence."[44] What is required, therefore, is a critical distancing from the immediacy and transparency of this "neutral" background and the perspectival re-focusing of the sort suggested in Brecht's famous line from *The Threepenny Opera* (one frequently cited by Žižek): "What is the burgling of a bank to the founding of a bank? What is the murder of a man to the employment of a man?"[45] This properly dialectical or parallax perspective simultaneously takes into account the founding violence of the background while providing the previously occluded context for the subjective violence of the foreground.

Reading the film's deployment of fundamentalist allegory within Naomi Klein's now-familiar model of an opportunistic, crisis-based capitalism (and usefully juxtaposing it with Alfonso Cuaron's brilliant dystopian film *Children of Men* [2006]), Kirk Boyle suggests that in its favorable representation of "the winners of neoliberalization," *Legend* proffers "the moral palliatives of Christianity to allay and even justify the dubious workings of disaster capitalism."[46] Anna's estranging vantage thus reveals in full the film's ambivalent expression of an imminent threat or alternative to the neoliberal order, one that is finally re-contained in the anxious reversion to Christian allegory and the withdrawal to the sanctum of the final secured space: the "gated community" of the Vermont colony, which symbolically registers the "paradise" won by the blood of the film's ersatz savior even as it sanctifies his foundational misrecognition – re-affirming the diabolic role of the seekers in what can at last be read as an allegory of the West's (to the extent that it is also capital's) "salvation."

A comparable ideological mystification characterizes *Legend*'s appropriation of Bob Marley, whose presence is registered early during the film's first sunset as Neville bathes Sam and sings along to "Three Little Birds": "Don't worry about a thing/ 'Cause every little thing gonna be alright." One of the least overtly political songs comprising the cycle of Marley's posthumously compiled *Legend* (1984), "Birds" was originally released as a single from his incendiary 1977 masterpiece *Exodus*, the central theme of which is the (Garvey-inspired) repatriation of the motherland by the peoples of the African Diaspora.[47] "Birds," with its easily appropriable generic message of perseverance for the third-world *sufferah*, thus epitomizes both the radical decontextualization of the composite *Legend* album itself – a risk taken by any anthology, but one with particular significance given the demands of the western consumer for the exotic commodity purged of its radical political residue – as well as the film's crucial utilization of the album. For while the "legend" of Matheson's novel refers to the painful self-realization that in a world of vampires, Neville, who breaks into their homes and systematically murders them in their sleep, is himself the terrifying remainder of an obsolescent order (perhaps a progressive commentary on McCarthyism), the film exploits its incidental titular relation to Marley's *Legend* to circumvent this very recognition. Indeed, in a kind of cultural and political short-circuit, Smith's Neville simply assumes for himself Marley's cultural legacy as champion of the subaltern. Having named his daughter "Marley," Neville likewise claims the mantels of both victim and proxy for the victimized in order to sustain his narcissistic symbolic order. Fittingly, then, Marley's music achieves its supreme significance in the film just prior to the final standoff with the seekers. When Anna shows no sign of recognition at Neville's awkward rendition of "I Shot the Sherriff," he presents her the *Legend* CD case ("Best album ever made") and delivers a brief but solemn homily on Marley's cultural significance as "Stir it Up" plays quietly in the background:

> He had this idea; it was kind of a virologist's idea. He believed you could cure racism and hate, literally cure it, by injecting music and love into people's lives. One day, he was scheduled to perform at a peace rally. Gunmen came to his house and shot him down. Two days later, he walked out on that stage and sang. Somebody asked

> him why. He said, "The people who are trying to make this world worse are not taking a day off. How can I? Light up the darkness."

Just as with "Birds," however, the setting sun brings with it the hard realization that those "who are trying to make the world worse" will soon be stirring, and the scene is punctuated with the ominous clangor of the steel shutters, abruptly silencing the pacific rhythm of the music.

Generalizing Marley's message of resistance into a vaguely anti-racist endorsement of love (an interpretation reinforced by the casting of a black actor in the role of Neville), the film carefully extricates his legacy from its prevailing political and material situation. Though Marley was certainly an enemy of all forms of racism and hatred, as a devoted Rastafarian and supporter of Michael Manley's socialist People's National Party, he also did not hesitate to identify the material conditions of which these sentiments are themselves often symptomatic. Chary about politics and politicians, he nonetheless fully identified with Manley's socialist platform, as evidenced by comments made in an interview with Vivien Goldman just days before the "Smile Jamaica" free concert (which indirectly supported Manley) and just prior to his shooting:

> "People work for money, den dem don't want to split it. It's that kind of attitude," he continued scornfully. "So much guys have so much – too much – while so many have nothing at all. We don't feel like that is right, because it don't take a guy a hundred million dollars to keep him satisfied. Everybody have to live. Michael Manley say 'im wan' help poor people. ... We need a change from what was. It couldn't get any worse than that." Sounding more sure, he concluded fiercely, almost defiantly, "You *have* to share. I don't care if it sounds political or whatever it is, but people have to *share*."[48]

Such a philosophy, some argue, caught the attention of the CIA, who are thought to have supplied Manley's political opponent Edward Seaga (or, as some Jamaicans referred to him, Edward CIAga) and his ultraconservative Jamaica Labour Party with weapons and aide in distributing anti-PNP propaganda during the tumultuous period of the 1970s.[49] This fact, coupled with the revelation that the CIA had for some time prior considered Marley a political subversive and secretly maintained a file on him, spawned unsubstantiated, if persistent conspiracy theories that the US intelligence agency not only orchestrated the 1976 shooting but also later *successfully* assassinated Marley by surreptitiously injecting him with a carcinogen.[50] Such political context is artfully and absolutely occluded from Neville's sterilized multiculturalist version, which concludes with the obscure ethical imperative, "Light up the darkness," here given a pronounced evangelical inflection: Neville is the bearer of light who must, like the doomed Marley, sacrifice himself for the salvation of those who yet wander in darkness. Yet again, however, the problematic invocation of Marley, a figure so indelibly associated with cultural and political radicalism, produces an undeniable dissonance in the film's narrative fabric that, despite Neville's fetishized, glibly inspiring revision, does not fail to direct our attention to the suggestive hollow left by this act of historical suppression.

Legend's foreclusion of such alternate perspectives both indicates its obfuscatory ideological agenda as well as its structural inability to sustain the dialectical purview needed to register the paradoxes of postmodernity, a fact made especially clear in the controversial "alternate" ending. If Anna's butterfly tattoo functions as the quilting point that, as Boyle phrases it, "retroactively codif[ies] Neville's life as Christological" (its violent narrative imposition signaled by the voiceover of Neville's dead daughter), the alternate version reveals the tattoo's "true" function as the sign of an irreducible deadlock, that is, as the site of the unsymbolizable Real of history itself;[51] for the alternate ending, taking its cue from Matheson's novel, reverses the polarities of the theatrical version in Neville's ultimate realization that *he* is in fact the monster – the "legend" – preying on the now-dominant community of seekers. Having relocated from the arm of Anna to that of the captured female seeker, the revelatory tattoo (along with the voiceover) now foregrounds those elements conspicuously repressed in the theatrical version;[52] seeing for the first time the "humanity" in the eyes of the Alpha Male desperately flinging himself against the Plexiglass wall of the safe room, Neville realizes the violence inherent in his actions. By injecting the female seeker with the antidote to his serum and restoring her to her community, Neville satisfies the previously unacknowledged demands of the seekers, who then peacefully withdraw from his home. Thus, having "heroically" recognized the common humanity of the creatures, Neville, Anna, and her son leave Manhattan with surprising ease and drive toward the vanishing horizon and the promised utopia of the Vermont colony, which here remains unrepresented.

It is important to note, however, that despite its conventionally progressive sentiment of liberal humanist toleration, the alternate version of the film is no less ideologically charged than the theatrical. The "live and let live" philosophy to which it subscribes owes its generously permissive impetus to the disarticulating logic of postmodernity itself and therefore merely reinscribes the spatial grammar of the previous version by other means.[53] Under the guise of a moral reversal that would present the elided "truth" of the original, the alternate ending reaffirms the fragmentation of social space into discrete "worlds," the integrity of which is then maintained by an obsessive cultural toleration that honors (and thereby sustains) their mutual incommensurability. This version of the film simply displaces rather than rejects the defining framework of Hobbesian conflict allegorically resolved in the theatrical release. We might then recognize in the film's generation of wildly discrepant alternate versions (to which the viewer must retrospectively add the novel as well as the two earlier film adaptations) a typically postmodernist semiotic proliferation, the function of which is precisely the fetishistic disavowal of the constitutive contradiction or antagonism itself, the "hard kernel" of the unsymbolizable Real around which these contradictory narratives cluster as so many iterative symptoms. Citing Jameson's repudiation of those recent theories positing an array of culturally distinct "alternative modernities," Žižek contends that

> [t]he significance of this critique reaches far beyond the case of modernity – it concerns the fundamental limitation of nominalist historicizing. The recourse to multiplication ... is false not because it does not recognize a unique fixed "essence" of modernity, but because multiplication functions as the disavowal of the antagonism that inheres to the notion of modernity as such: the falsity of multiplication resides in the fact that it frees the universal notion of modernity of its antagonism, of the way it is embedded in the capitalist system, by relegating this aspect to just one of its historical subspecies.[54]

As he goes on to point out, even for Freud, the surest evidence of castration is the anxious generation of symbolic phalluses.[55] Thus, the perfectly diametric versions of *I am Legend* signal not so much the relativity of truth (that one version is justifiably preferable to the other depending on one's immediate subject position or mood) as the anxious attempt to paper over the principal point of animus where these ostensibly oppositional accounts coalesce. That is, in neither version of *Legend* does a perspective emerge with the critical capacity to map the city in its full sociospatial complexity as an expression of late capital or with the visionary potential to restore or reimagine the unbounded domain of the public within such a space.

So while the theatrical version forces the intolerable conflict to imaginary resolution in the crucible of fundamentalist fable, the latter version neutralizes conflict altogether through recourse to the no less ideological pieties of a familiar multiculturalism. Yet, as Žižek reminds us, "The only true solution is to tear down the *true* wall," which is neither chauvinism nor ethnocentrism per se nor the discourtesies of cultural intolerance, but rather the socio-economic conditions that motivate those, like Neville, who attempt to escape from reality while the wider world is reduced to cinders around them.[56] Such a possibility is, though indirectly acknowledged, finally refused in *I am Legend*, whose ideological strictures, like those of its protagonist, cannot sanction such ontological dynamism and must perforce reterritorialize it – in either version of the film – within the unassailable spatial and imaginative enclosures of the gated community.

States of exception and the dialectics of *District 9*

Instantly identified upon its release in 2009 as an "apartheid allegory (with aliens)," *District 9*, the first feature by South African filmmaker Neill Blomkamp, has achieved phenomenal critical and popular success as a fable rehearsing the conventional reverences of ethnic toleration and multicultural plurality – as the imaginative revisiting of a conflict now safely consigned to historical retrospect.[57] As such, however, the film's critical apparatus succumbs to the structural limits or inherent contradictions of this discourse, the chief assumption of which is that the gulf between self and other can be mediated or at least mitigated (as in the alternate conclusion of *I am Legend*) through either direct experiential knowledge or sustained sympathetic identification. But as our reading of *Legend* demonstrates, this rhetoric of multicultural tolerance ultimately collapses in on itself to reveal its fundamental opposite: that is, the compulsory "respect" paid the other becomes simply the positive articulation of (and implicit justification for) "his *intolerance* of my overproximity" and, therefore, finally of the assertion of one's own "*right not to be harassed*, which is a right to remain at a safe distance from others."[58] Indeed, it is worth recalling here Adam Kuper's critical reflection on the rise of "culture" as an analytic category in the discourses of anthropology and his claim that South African apartheid policy presented itself precisely in terms of such multicultural tolerance as the defender of tribal cultural integrity against assimilation within a dominant white culture.[59] Thus, multiculturalist discourse, emerging as what we might call the narcissistic cultural complement to contemporary forms of biopolitics,[60] reveals a somewhat paradoxical double-aspect: on the one hand, that of the assiduously revered subject of first-world sympathy; and on the other, that of Giorgio Agamben's *homo sacer*, who is both excluded from and subject to the sovereign order as the latter's foundational act in the abject jurido-political form of *bare life*.[61] As online reviewer David Korotky notes along similar lines, provided this standard interpretive frame, *District 9* replicates the canonical formula of popular liberal fantasies of cultural/ethnic otherness like *Dances with Wolves* or the more recent record-setting blockbuster *Avatar*:

> *District 9* is by and large a very good film and a very hard film to dislike, but here I have managed it. If only because *District 9* and James Cameron's *Avatar* are two versions of the same film. At the heart of both films is the phenomenon of interspecies transformation, which can easily be understood through the base ideology of racial/cultural transformation. In *Avatar* the transformation is from white man to noble savage. In *District 9* the transformation is from white man to poor black man. What is so startling about both films is that, in taking Kevin Costner's *Dances with Wolves* to its logical conclusion, the main character does not only assimilate the "alien" culture but rather transforms bodily into the "alien" itself.[62]

This conventional fantasy acts out not only the vague *ressentiment* expressed in the appropriation of the other's hidden knowledge but also the more insidious reduction of the truly alien experience of non-identity to a merely expanded knowledge of self. Inasmuch as we read the film as simply an allegorical retrospective on apartheid, we confine it to the paradoxical logic of this liberal colonization (and subtly violent neutralization) of categorical otherness, which not only simplifies the complex negotiations of cultural and racial identification but also obscures the prevailing material circumstances out of which they emerge. What if, however, *District 9*'s representation of the recognizable mise en scène of ethnic apartheid (particularly its logic of spatial partitioning) is no less allegorically deployed than its central conceit of an alien species stranded in Johannesburg? I suggest that attention to the film's conspicuous departure from the historical situation of apartheid allows us to reconsider it within a more immediate historical context as a mapping of the sociospatial dispensations of globalization in what Agamben identifies as the modern *nomos* of exception, or "the hidden paradigm of the political space of modernity," in *post*-apartheid Johannesburg.[63]

Deploying Carl Schmitt's influential theorization of the juridico-political concept of the *nomos* (traditionally rendered simply as *law* or *order*), Agamben likewise endorses Schmitt's important restoration of the term's "original spatial sense" as the "Greek word for the first measure of all subsequent measures, for the first land-appropriation understood as the first partition and classification of space."[64] Thus, for Schmitt (as for Agamben) sovereignty is founded on the originary act of spatial exclusion, on the demarcation of a free zone beyond declared "lines of amity" in which "force could be used freely and ruthlessly" without registering in the social Symbolic.[65] Originally designating zones of contestation between "land-appropriating Catholic powers and Protestant sea powers" of sixteenth and seventeenth-century Europe, the "space of exception" was associated first with the New World and later with India – then, in the nineteenth century, with the state of siege and the strategic suspension of the legal order during crisis response. The period between the sixteenth and twentieth century thus witnessed the codification of an international *jus publicum Europaeum* founded on the spatial binary of the European state and the anomic free space beyond it, a system of global linear organization ideologically buttressed by the Enlightenment precepts of "humanity" and "civilization." By the mid-twentieth century, this international order had fully succumbed to a gradual process of balkanization begun in the previous century and thence "dissolved into a spaceless universalism,"[66] the chief index of which was the rise of economic liberalism[67] and its partitioning of public (state) from private (non-state) zones of activity. Schmitt therefore outlines with startling prescience the recognizable contours of a nascent globalization:

> In short, over, under, and beside the state-political borders of what appeared to be a purely political international law between states spread a free, i.e., non-state sphere of economy permeating everything: a *global* economy. In the idea of a free global economy lay not only the overcoming of state-political borders, but also, as an essential precondition, a standard for the internal constitutions of individual member states of this order of international law; it presupposed that every member state would establish a minimum of *constitutional* order. This minimum standard consisted of the freedom – the separation – of the state-public sphere from the private sphere, above all, from the non-state sphere of property, trade, economy.[68]

This emergent "spaceless" universalism depends no less than its predecessor on a logic of spatial internment, albeit one that, rather than positing physical territories "beyond the line," folds in on itself and authorizes new zones of activity or degrees of participation liberated altogether from terrestrial boundaries and "certified by the standard of liberal constitutionalism – a line of free economy passing through the states."[69] It is at this important transitional moment in Schmitt's model that Agamben situates his own claim that "in our age, the state of exception comes more and more to the foreground as the fundamental political structure and ultimately begins to become the rule."[70] Thus, he argues, revising Foucault, that in the present age of the biopolitical "[t]he camp – and not the prison – is the space that corresponds to this originary structure of the *nomos*;"[71] moreover, it is the camp that functions as "the hidden matrix and *nomos* of the political space *in which we are still living*."[72] A "dislocating localization," the ambiguous site of the camp constitutes a "zone of indistinction between outside and inside, exception and rule, licit and illicit, in which the very concepts of subjective right and juridical protection no longer ma[k]e any sense."[73] The precarious subject/object of this exclusionary inclusion is *bare life*, the politicized inscription of life that complements in the present age the sovereign's traditional authority over death. Bare life is therefore a political ontology reducible neither to the Hobbesian state of nature nor to a proper humanity – that which is included in the sovereign order but without symbolic effect, which can be killed with impunity but neither murdered nor sacrificed.[74] Agamben's theorization of this new globalized order therefore replicates the bifurcating logic of Schmitt's European international order but in a radically diffuse, deterritorialized manner, such that *every* space (and therefore *every* subject) is internally fissured, becoming the site of law as well as of its suspension, simultaneously within and beyond the lines of amity. Therefore, Agamben can claim, when the state of exception becomes generalized as the normal order, we are *all* bare life – a realization, I argue, also at the very heart of *District 9*'s confrontation with the contemporary *nomos* of the earth.[75]

Indeed, such recognition defines the film's primary focal point: the metamorphosis of Wickus van de Merwe. Wickus, an obsequious, bumblingly congenial, low-level bureaucrat in the Multi-National United (MNU) corporation, finds his managerial ambitions realized when he is suddenly promoted to field officer for the relocation of the nearly two million alien inhabitants of District 9, a promotion Wickus describes as "[a]lmost as big as my wedding day." We soon realize, however, that the dubious legality of the operation explains in part Wickus' unheralded advancement, for District 9, the quintessential space of exception, has no discernible legal status, and the eviction of its legally precarious inhabitants is under the careful scrutiny of international humanitarian and watchdog organizations.[76] Echoing the descriptions of Rudolph Diels, former chief of the Gestapo (who testified that "[n]either an order nor an instruction exist[ed] for the origin of the camps: they were not instituted; one day they were there"[77]), the film's faux-documentary interviewees likewise acknowledge the precipitate appearance and juridical indiscernability of the alien district with observations like, "Before we knew it, it was a slum," or, "Well, the truth is nobody really knew what this place was." Beyond the legal lexicon of the nation-state, the non-space of District 9 can be managed only by its exceptional counterpart: the infinite sovereignty of the multinational corporation.

While the legal exceptionality of the film's alien internment might at first seem an allegory for the suspension of constitutional law during the officially declared South African State of Emergency in the latter days of apartheid policy (1985–1990), and the aliens' forced eviction the slum clearances that played such a prominent role in the National Party's political strategy (a way of both suppressing communist mobilization and inflating urban employment statistics), we should also recall that these actions were directly predicated on the state's centralized authority to designate discrete "'population groups' in order to create a legal framework for cultural separation and territorial partition."[78] Despite the fact that first contact with the aliens occurs in 1982, squarely in the midst of the National Party's reign, however, neither the party nor the state plays a significant role in the film, the eponymous slum of which is not cleared until *28 years later*, more than 15 years after the election of the African National Congress and the official end of the apartheid order; in fact, the absent South African state is significant only in the conspicuous ceding of its authority to MNU, and no representative of state power (neither human nor architectural nor symbolic) appears in the film. Explicitly directing our attention to this transference of sovereignty, Wickus observes during the preliminary briefing of his crew, "I think it's a great thing that it's not the military guys in charge this time," a point underscored in subsequent scenes depicting the sociopathic military officer Koobus happily taking orders from the MNU director.

So while the spatial logic of apartheid may have enduring relevance, both the field and the nature of its effect have significantly shifted in *District 9*. To overlook this key point is to duplicate the misplaced allegiances of our protagonist and to remain confined to the classical political distinctions of a moribund order, a perspective that, in its facile delineation of inner and outer, self and other, collapses into an orthodox multiculturalism that Žižek diagnoses as the "post-political ersatz" or the ideological culturalization of a properly political response to globalized capital.[79] To restore the film's *true* historical context, we must recall that immediately following the 1994 election of Nelson Mandela and the ANC, the new administration was faced with an extraordinary dilemma: how to balance the internal pressures of the political constituency in whose name it had declared itself a "disciplined force of the left" with the numerous external *and* internal demands that accompanied integration into the now-dominant neoliberal order. P. Eric Louw observes that if the primary obstacle facing the NP was the international demand for democratization, the defining issue of the post-1994 era was the ANC's capitulation to the forces of globalization and the "Pax Americana," a concession that also meant the abandonment of the party's defining ideals. For though the ANC entered the post-apartheid period with its "modernist" commitments to "rational planning, industrialism, and state interventionism/developmentalism" intact, it soon found these fidelities incommensurate with the structural imperatives of a postmodern world.[80] As Louw writes,

> The ANC and its constituency did not seem well placed to manage South Africa's transition into globalization, so South Africa's corporate sector, the IMF, World Bank, and diplomats launched a concerted exercise ... to "adjust" the ANC to the "realities" of globalized capitalism and shift their economic policies. The benefits of market economics, export-led growth, and trickle-down economics were promoted. The proselytizing exercise worked – the ANC was converted to the "Washington consensus" and abandoned the development state and socialism.[81]

The result, Louw contends, was the formation of an impotent South African state "constrained by a (mostly white) internal corporate sector that is allied to the powerful external forces of globalized capital."[82] Formally a "constitutional democracy," South Africa became in effect a "one-party dominant democracy, characterized by corporatism and elite pacting" and thereby the disenfranchisement of the vast majority of (mostly black, mostly poor) South Africans.[83]

In a more thorough anatomization of globalization's impact on South African political economy, Michael H. Allen describes the apartheid state of the NP as a hierarchically organized "collection of ethnic enclaves, with a rural subsistence for Africans, trading and plantation work for the Asians, commercial agriculture and skilled labor for the Afrikaners

English whites."[84] This "white nationalist capitalism" and its rigid division of labor proved insufficiently flexible and porous to accommodate international capital flows and thus generated resistance not only from an internal opposition to ethnic apartheid (one increasingly allied with "anticapitalist elements") but more importantly from the titans of international finance.[85] So while global economic authorities such as the IMF and World Bank had become, as early as the mid-1980s, sharply critical of apartheid (and of the national political economy it sustained), by the end of the Cold War, "it became even more feasible to press for a new governing coalition in South Africa that would be both postapartheid and post-national capitalist."[86] Thus, Allen suggests, while "American and European globalists wanted revolution," they wanted one that structurally precluded "the African revolution of the Freedom Charter."[87] Giving a new accent to the familiar liberal narrative of South African democratization buttressed by post-Cold War assurances, Allen concedes that "it was the globalization revolution that precipitated and set the context for the democratic revolution in South Africa";[88] however, he notes, "just as global markets had disciplined the Apartheid state into abandoning the nationalist form of capitalism, they were later to discipline the democratic state into abandoning economic restitution and social transformation."[89] What most distinguishes the South African *Uhuru* from its predecessors throughout the continent, then, is the emergence not of a familiar "radical national leadership" but of a compromised government "already recognizing the limits in the capabilities and authority of the state in the global mode of production, and already prepared to use the techniques of power and discourse appropriate to that ascendant mode," including submission to the loosely allied syndicate of global financial institutions and transnational corporations that would soon assimilate the ANC and rewrite its obsolescent model of political economy.[90]

While the ascendance of this comprador *corporati* in post-apartheid South Africa forms the historical backdrop for the film's action, *District 9* directs a more explicitly critical focus toward the liberal humanist social discourse that reinforces its political and cultural authority. Despite, for instance, their casual use of the pejorative "prawn" to refer to the aliens, MNU operatives assiduously observe the courtesies and discursive civilities of intercultural exchange even as they subject the aliens to unimaginable brutality. Crystallizing this contradiction, the sniper-equipped helicopters that circle the district emit recorded messages of amity ("We are here to assist you" and "MNU are your friends") even as Wickus and his "population control team" casually set fire to a nest of alien young and share a callous laugh over the "popcorn" sounds of the bursting egg pods. Faithful to the corporate directive ("always remember, a smile is cheaper than a bullet"), Wickus makes an heroic effort to preserve the veneer of congeniality and to characterize the conflict as one of symmetrical cross-cultural exchange: "The Prawn doesn't really understand the concept of ownership of property. So we have to come there and say 'Listen, this is our land. Please, will you go?'" Wickus' investment in social decorum soon begins to show the strain of contradiction, however, evident in his harsh reactions to the aliens' refusal to reciprocate such niceties. Confronted with an alien who protests his treatment by MNU representatives by openly urinating in their presence, Wickus exclaims, "That's bloody rude!" Gesturing toward the sniper in the nearby helicopter when the unrepentant alien resists, Wickus makes explicit the violence that subtends his friendly rhetoric: "You want to talk to them, or you want to talk to me?" After a frightened alien slams the door of his shack in Wickus' face, he likewise denounces the behavior as "rude" and "unacceptable" and has the alien dragged outside at gunpoint: "I tried to talk nicely to you," he says with exasperation. Similarly, when an alien child refuses Wickus' bribe of a lollipop by throwing it back at him, striking him in the face, his fury is matched only by his incredulity at such blatant discourtesy: "I tried to be fucking nice to you, man! Fuck! Is this your fucking little runt here? Teach him some manners."

The aliens' refusal to accept the implicitly consensual terms of civil discourse forces Wickus and the MNU to disclose their true intentions and to acknowledge the inherent violence of their "humanitarian" project. As one of the film's commentator's explains, "MNU is trying to move the aliens for humanitarian reasons, but the real focus, just as it has been right from the beginning, is weapons." The "second-largest weapons manufacturer in the world," MNU is primarily interested in obtaining alien weaponry and unlocking the mechanism of its uniquely designed interface with alien DNA. The ethical frangibility of this position accounts for the comparably obsessive observance of a superficial, infinitely pliable legality. In order to sanction the eviction and plunder of District 9, MNU has its residents sign "I-27" forms acknowledging receipt of the eviction notification. After one of the aliens angrily dashes the form from his hands, Wickus assures his colleague that the indentation left by the blow may be considered the alien's legally consensual "scrawl." When his armed accompaniment requests permission to shoot an alien child, Wickus quickly reminds him of the equivocal rules governing their engagement with the prawn: while destroying the alien eggs is acceptable, "You can't shoot it now, man. It's illegal." However, after the child's father, Christopher Johnson, dismisses the eviction notice as non-binding, Wickus again reveals the coercive nature of this thin legal fiction: "Sign the fucking paper. You don't have a choice in the matter. You have to sign the document." Acknowledging to colleagues that "[t]his guy's obviously a little sharper," Wickus kneels beside Johnson and quickly restores the tone of civility and its friendly presumption of equivalent exchange – "Hello. Seems like we didn't understand each other there properly, eh?" – as if all this unpleasantness might be remedied with a healthy measure of cross-cultural understanding. He then reintroduces the dubious legitimizing apparatus by inquiring whether Johnson has a permit for the youngling. When he replies in the affirmative, Wickus changes tact and gestures to the ubiquitous piles of trash: "You see this litter out here? This is dangerous conditions for your child. Article seventy-five says that because your child is living in dangerous conditions. ... I'm going to take him to child services."

Despite the self-conscious disingenuousness of such legal contrivances, however, Wickus remains compulsively devoted to this legalistic discourse for the majority of the film. Later shown the spaceship's lost command module beneath Johnson's shack, Wickus astonishingly upholds the principles of the very juridical order that arbitrarily suspended his own "human rights" and would have seen him flayed alive in the bowels of the MNU headquarters: "This is very illegal. This is a fine if they catch you with this." He makes a similarly pathetic appeal following his initial escape from MNU when, refused service at a local fast-food restaurant due to the propagandized claim that he has engaged in long-term sexual contact with aliens, he invokes the language of post-apartheid law: "You are legally obliged to serve me!"

I offer that it is precisely this ideological fidelity to the lawful order of the state and its guarantee of human rights that the film undertakes to deconstruct, for it relies on the logic of an outmoded juridico-political dispensation, the nation-state, whose definite lines of amity distinguish the inner from the outer, the human from the alien. Wickus' investment in this very order allows his manipulation by MNU, for Wickus (like *Legend*'s Neville) identifies himself with the interior space of the amity line, failing to recognize the generalization/interiorization of the exception to all spaces and all subjects under postmodernity. Thus, his metamorphosis does not so much create the conditions for an empathetic identification with the alien-as-ethnic-other as it does reveal that the exceptional space of District 9 extends well beyond its visible, obsessively guarded walls.

This generalization of the exception is made clear in the controversial presentation of MNU's structural counterpart, the Nigerian gang. "Where there's a slum," one of the film's interviewees observes, "there's crime. And District 9 was no exception." Nigerian gangsters exploit the lawlessness of the refugee camp, orchestrating a series of illegal ventures: the "cat food scam," in which the much-desired commodity is sold to the hapless aliens at exorbitant prices; interspecies prostitution; and, most important, the obtaining and trafficking of alien weaponry. The gangsters are led by Obesandjo, a cartoonishly sinister stereotype who, in addition to his desire for alien technology, has cultivated a perverse predilection for the consumption of alien bodies in part because, confined to a wheelchair, he believes that their vitalizing essence will restore the use of his legs. More than simply a racist perpetuation of the cannibal stereotype (though inarguably that), the obscene characterization of Obesandjo and the Nigerian gang actually serves to redirect our focus toward the hapless Wickus and the equivalent activities of MNU, who likewise bribe the aliens with cat food to secure their cooperation during the illegal eviction and, above all, to extract their technology. Moreover, as Wickus soon discovers, Obesandjo is far from being the sole or even the chief *devourer* of alien bodies. The parallel agendas of these equally exceptional agents in the lawless space of District 9 serve not only to imply the illegality of MNU's activities but to suggest that in the wider space of exception that is the postmodern nomos, corporate sovereignty is the supreme authority marking both the foundation of law and its limit.

Injured during his assignment and having unwittingly infected himself with the alien fluid that also powers their technology, Wickus collapses at a party celebrating his promotion (fittingly, he falls onto a cake decorated as the MNU building) and is admitted to the hospital. When doctors discover his transformed arm, the ward is evacuated, and MNU paramilitary thrust him into a black body bag for transport to corporate headquarters. Once there, Wickus is subjected to a battery of tests without explanation, without consent, and without anesthetic; the latter, it is explained, would dull his response to the electric drill used to gauge the "pain threshold" of his metamorphosing limb. Wheeled down the corridor and into a narrow room, Wickus perceives the gruesomely dismembered bodies of aliens (as well as what appears to be a humanoid fetus in a large jar, perhaps a failed attempt at a hybrid) roughly manipulated by teams of MNU workers in hazmat suits. His pleading inquiries regarding where he is and what is being done to the aliens go unacknowledged.

Once successful nerve fusion has been positively determined, Wickus is rushed directly to the firing range, where his status as bare life is made even more horrifyingly evident. With his transformed hand secured to a gun mount, an exhausted and battered Wickus is commanded to fire an alien assault rifle toward a pig carcass hung from a chain at the far end of the range, which, to the delight of the MNU scientists, explodes in a shower of shredded flesh when Wickus successfully discharges the weapon. A succession of alien guns are locked into the mount and fired until a tearful Wickus, pleading with his captors, refuses to cooperate, at which point he is jolted with a cattle prod to galvanize his obstinate muscles, and the experiment continues uninterrupted. Though screaming perfunctory curses of defiance, Wickus appears mostly resigned to his powerlessness until he notices that the pig carcass has been replaced by a trembling, handcuffed alien. Suddenly and desperately re-engaged, Wickus protests: "Hey, leave that fucking prawn, man. I'll shoot a pig. I'll shoot ... Sir ... Listen. I'll shoot a pig again for you. I'll pull the trigger but I'm not shooting that prawn, hear me?" The scientists do not respond; instead, they free his alien hand, secure his *human* one in the mount, jolt him again with the cattle prod, and note with muted satisfaction the lethal results: "Amazing ... AMR-B 21 test completed. All right, I think that's all we need." This astonishing exchanging of limbs (so subtle that it almost goes unnoticed by the viewer) can be said metonymically to encapsulate the film's ingenious dramatization of the contemporary state of exception, for it is not simply the aberrant alien appendage that is here manipulated with impunity or abjected from the normative order of law and the guarantee of human rights. The foulest deed is forcibly carried out by the *human* hand, which is simply revealed to be (as it has always been) an instrument of MNU, the bare life whose production is also the foundation for the latter's post-national sovereignty. The alien used for target practice is no more subject to the exclusionary/inclusionary ban than the instrumentalized, marionette-like finger that pulls the trigger – a point emphasized in the subsequent conversation among MNU executives, who determine that as Wickus' transformation accelerates, the window of opportunity for unlocking the DNA – weapon interface rapidly closes. To arrest the metamorphosis and preserve this unique DNA balance, MNU officials decide to collect it: "What happens to him isn't important. What's important is that we harvest from him what we can right now"; "This body represents hundreds of millions, maybe billions of dollars worth of biotechnology"; "We need everything: tissue, bone marrow, blood. The procedure is basically going to strip him down to nothing."

Recalling both the "Property of MNU" legend stenciled on the side of Christopher Johnson's head and the dismembered alien bodies of the previous scene, Wickus' reduction to what one interviewee calls "the most valuable business artifact on earth" demonstrates MNU's power to declare exemptions from the discourse of human rights and liberal democracy even as it reveals that such discourse functions as the handmaiden of sovereignty itself. As Agamben observes, the emergence of bare life as political subject can be traced to the earliest legal foundations of modern democracy itself in the form of the 1679 writ of *habeas corpus*, which provided for the inscription, assertion, and presentation of the body as subject of/subject to state (and, now, corporate) power.[91] The inner contradiction that distinguishes contemporary liberal democracy, Agamben writes, is that it

> does not abolish sacred life but rather shatters it and disseminates it into every individual body, making it into what is at stake in the political conflict. And the root of modern democracy's secret biopolitical calling lies here: he who will appear later as the bearer of rights and, according to a curious oxymoron, as the new sovereign subject ... can only be constituted as such through the repetition of the sovereign exception and the isolation of *corpus*, bare life, in himself. If it is true that law needs a body in order to be in force ... democracy responds to this desire by compelling law to assume the care of this body.[92]

Therefore, he contends, "it is time to stop regarding declarations of rights as proclamations of eternal, metajuridical values binding the legislator ... to respect eternal ethical principles."[93] Rather, it is precisely such declarations that "represent the originary figure of the inscription of natural life in the juridico-political order of the nation-state" and, as *District 9* demonstrates, that compromise our ability either to grasp or oppose the postnational sovereignty that has largely supplanted it.[94]

Thus, the refugee, that political shadow subject who abides in the twilight "between man and citizen, *nativity* and *nationality*," throws into crisis the "originary fiction of modern sovereignty" by illuminating the gap that exists "between birth and nation," exposing in the very liminality of his being the legal fiction of citizenship and the limits inherent to *human rights*.[95] The refugee marks the site of Agamben's (Benjaminian) "real state of exception," that which "makes it possible to clear the way for a long-overdue renewal of categories in service of a politics in which bare life is no longer separated and excepted, either in the state order or in the figure of human rights."[96] Identifying the refugee-as-bare-life with the liminal figure of the bandit, Agamben observes that Germanic and Anglo-Saxon legal documents of antiquity often identify the latter with the *wargus* or werewolf. Characterized in English sources as bearing a wolf's head, this monstrous legal subject occupies, like Wickus, the "threshold of indistinction and of passage between animal and man, *physis* and *nomos,* exclusion and inclusion: the life of the bandit is the life of the *loup garou,* the werewolf, who is precisely *neither man nor beast,* and who dwells paradoxically within both while belonging to neither."[97] It is at this threshold of the indeterminate, Agamben writes, that "the terms distinguished and kept united by the relation of ban (bare life and the form of law) abolish each other and enter into a new dimension."[98]

Such a utopian neutralization, however fleeting, is realized in *District 9*'s climactic scene. Operating one of the aliens' mechanized combat suits, Wickus surrenders his opportunity to reach the alien ship – and thus to obtain the cure that will allow him to reclaim his former existence – and returns instead to save Christopher Johnson and to ensure *his* escape. Only at this point in the film, fully neither human nor alien, does Wickus abjure his identification with his former life and its social and legal verities. Turning his weapons on Koobus and his men, Wickus fights until his battle suit is destroyed and he is expelled to the ground, wounded and vulnerable, his left eye grotesquely enlarged and visibly alien. Just as Koobus raises his sidearm to execute him, however, a group of aliens materialize from the surrounding debris and manually dismember Koobus and his soldiers in a liberal spray of gore.

At this important moment of mutual recognition, I argue, we must most emphatically resist the claims (however well-intentioned) of the liberalist interpretation and the culturalization of the film's political content. For to credit Wickus' physical metamorphosis (or the cultural/racial understanding that it allegedly engenders) for his decisive return is to lapse into an essentialism that mystifies the very political and economic contexts painstakingly elaborated in the film: the capitulation and withdrawal of the nation-state and the crisis of politics itself in the moment of postmodernity. Above all, we must recall here the crucial assessment of *entomologist* Clive Henderson, the film's "expert" on the alien species: "What we have stranded on Earth in this colony is basically the workers. They don't particularly think for themselves, they will take commands, they have no initiative." Once the standard allegorical reading (that "[i]n *District 9* the transformation is from white man to poor black man") is bracketed and sufficiently re-historicized, and our critical optic – like that of our protagonist – readjusted, we can clearly perceive that such a description is as applicable to the clumsily officious Wickus, dupe and disposable functionary of MNU, as to the refugee alien multitude. His transformation does not so much enable empathy with a racial or cultural other as it does restore a sense of collective class identity *across* racial, cultural, and national divisions – among those in the now-universal state of exception whom corporate sovereignty has reduced to bare life.[99] Put simply, Wickus, who formerly identified with the corporate masters he hoped one day to become, experiences a profound self-recognition of which his physical transformation is but the externalized symbolic expression; he consciously acknowledges what he has always been – a worker – and accedes to everything that designation continues to mean even in the epoch of posthistory. In fact, Wickus' physical appearance here recalls Jameson's vivid description of the contemporary dilemma of Utopia itself: "the Identity of a present confronting the immense unthinkable Difference of an impossible future, these two coexisting like eyeballs that each register a different kind of spectrum."[100] *District 9* thereby sustains the dialectical critical vision both circumvented and foreclosed by the discrepant versions of *I am Legend*. Holding together in *impossible* accord the incommensurable realities of slum city and gated suburb, human and alien, black and white, salaried professional and abject refugee under the monstrous sign of global class struggle, *District 9* outlines the emergent political subjectivity of the *real* state of exception, a solidarity without essence and without borders in which we are all refugees, in which we are all monsters.

6
Third-World Punks, or, Watch Out for the Worlds Behind You

According to influential cyberpunk commentator Larry McCaffery, the "cyberpunk controversy" of the 1980s is indicative of a more general postmodern turn in science fiction, postmodernity here defined as "a condition [that] derives its unique status above all from technological change."[1] Following Ernest Mandel's familiar theorization of "late capital" so critical to Jameson's reading of postmodernism, McCaffery suggests that the "unprecedented expansion" of global capitalism since WWII is "made possible specifically by the exponential growth of technology" and has "profoundly altered not only the daily textures of the world(s) we inhabit but the way we think about the world and ourselves in it."[2] These developments in telecommunications, surveillance, and weapons technologies have converged in the formation of vast networks of simulated experience or virtual reality. Such experiential novelty – which, McCaffery notes, has been theorized variously through the paradigms of Debord's spectacle, Baudrillard's simulacra, Cook and Kroker's hyperreality, or even William Gibson's cyberspace – is exclusively the provenance, however, of the first world, where "technological advancement, together with social and economic pressures, are most intense – particularly the United States and Japan, but also Western Europe."[3] Thus, McCaffery can unselfconsciously refer to the colonization of "*our* imaginations and desires, even *our* unconscious" as well as extend the unqualified generalization that "*people*" now often prefer such mediated and virtualized encounters over those more substantial experiences of reality implicitly identified with an "earlier" stage in the mode of production.[4] Cyberpunk might thus be regarded as the colonization of science fiction (SF) by globalization itself and of the exhaustion of the estranging capacities of the former. What happens to the genre, however, when the global saturation of capital and the techno-cultural formations that are at once the latter's conditions and foremost effects expand beyond the *developed/developing* binary that implicitly informs McCaffery's model? First, how does the emergence of postcolonial cyberpunk and its more recent derivatives (steampunk, dieselpunk, and so on) challenge accepted material and aesthetic premises of the form in its dominant mode: chiefly, the latter's ambivalent response to the virtualities of late capital; its philosophical accord with poststructuralist theory; and its cynical disregard for the agential subject of an erstwhile modernism. Second, if one accepts the rough accuracy of these broad and, admittedly, not unproblematic premises (bracketing momentarily the doubtless exceptions), how do these postcolonial "punks" reroute the neural pathways of the form and re-engineer its structural and conceptual anatomy for a renewed materialist engagement with what canonical cyberpunk insists is (and celebrates as) an increasingly *immaterial* present? Attention to two recent postcolonial innovators of the cyberpunk aesthetic, Lauren Beukes of South Africa and Tobias Buckell of Grenada, can yield productive insights in this regard and can perhaps be said to anticipate the convergent future trajectories of postcolonial and SF scholarship.

The thrill is gone? Lauren Beukes' *Moxyland* and South African cyberpunk

Among the acclamations that greeted Lauren Beukes' debut novel *Moxyland* (2008), including an approbatory nod from none other than William Gibson himself,[5] is the following by Hugo Award winner and third-generation cyberpunk writer[6] Charles Stross:

> It's what you get when you take your classic 80s deracinated corporate alienation sensibility, detonate about six kilos of semtex under it, and scatter the smoking wreckage across 21st century South Africa – full of unselfconscious spiky originality, the larval form of a new kind of SF munching its way out of the intestines of the wasp-paralysed caterpillar of cyberpunk.[7]

Hyperbolic excess aside, what is perhaps most striking about Stross' appraisal is its ambivalent identification/disidentification of *Moxyland* as cyberpunk, as a work that simultaneously liquidates and re-animates the tropes of this presumably depleted form toward the elaboration of a "new kind of SF." Eschewing the familiar politico-cultural zeitgeist of the West of the 1980s – which so evidently provides both the conditions for and enduring thematic contours of the cyberpunk aesthetic – Beukes, Stross implies, urges the genre beyond this moribund first-world cultural horizon toward a seismographic registering, as Jameson writes of Gibson's work, of "the geographic-cultural light spectrum and bandwidths of the new system" in the globalized post-millennium.[8] If the putatively anti-utopian impetus of cyberpunk, moored to a late-Cold War, Euro-American structure of feeling, generates a paradigm in which "[t]he only standard is thrill, the ability to 'light up the circuits' of the nervous matrix" and, indeed, in which "human beings have nothing left but thrill," Beukes' cyberpunk intervenes by exposing the ideological underpinnings of this nervous ecstasy from a perspective decidedly alternative to that of the still-globalizing first world.[9] She does so, however, not through simple or spectacular opposition to the cyberpunk aesthetic but through the acceleration of the form to its terminal velocity, through appropriating its penchant for cynicism, stereotype, and kinesis and carrying these to their perdurable limits. It is instructive to consider the movement from Beukes' first novel, often designated by reviewers as already "post-cyberpunk," to her Arthur C. Clarke Award-winning follow-up *Zoo City* (2010), which, perhaps most accurately categorized as urban fantasy, has also been called "the other side of cyberpunk."[10] What does it mean, then, to write cyberpunk in twenty-first-century South Africa, and is Beukes doing so?

As one reviewer notes, *Moxyland* is in most respects "a typical – in some ways even stereotypical – cyberpunk novel."[11] Indeed, the book scarcely departs from the humorous template prescribed by Csicsery-Ronay in which

> a self-destructive but sensitive young protagonist with an implant/prosthesis/telechtronic talent) that makes the evil (megacorporations/police states/criminal underworlds) pursue him through (wasted urban landscapes/elite luxury enclaves/eccentric space stations) full of grotesque (haircuts/clothes/self-mutilations/rock music/sexual hobbies/designer drugs/telechtronic gadgets/nasty new weapons/exteriorized hallucinations) representing the (mores/fashions) of modern civilization in terminal decline, ultimately hooks up with rebellious and tough-talking (youth/artificial intelligence/rock cults) who offer the alternative, not of (community/socialism/traditional values/transcendental vision), but of supreme, life affirming *hipness*. ...[12]

I want to suggest, however, that (Stross' assessment notwithstanding) Beukes' punctilious fidelity to the meme of cyberpunk is neither incidental nor merely derivative. For if, as Jameson observes, cyberpunk can productively be regarded as "a literature of the stereotypes thrown up by a system in full expansion," then the impassive technochromium cool of the late Cold-War moment certainly provides, from the vantage of millennial capital's global saturation, a set of tropes ripe for productive misappropriation.[13]

Yet, despite its evident rehearsal of/homage to what Suvin describes as cyberpunk's defining affiliation with "some fractions of the youth culture in the affluent North of our globe," *Moxyland*'s cagey hipness maintains an internally subversive awareness of its own formal and imaginative limits.[14] The novel's four main characters are little more than candidly undisguised *types* derived from the now careworn archive of an institutionalized cyberpunk imaginary, as indicated by their formulaic description on the novel's promotional website: Toby the "roguish slacker, living off his mom, streamcasting his daily blog, and carelessly dipping into an underworld of drugs, anarchy, video games and subversive revolution"; Kendra the "art school dropout, offered a second chance at cool by becoming a 'sponsorbaby'" for a corporation that implants her with nano-technology as part of its experimental dark marketing campaign; Tendeka the "hot-headed revolutionary, surviving below the corporate radar in the shacklands of the Sprawl" and ineffectually resisting cooptation by the very corporate entities he attempts to undermine; and Lerato the "brilliant corporate programmer and AIDSbaby" who is "just bored enough to risk everything by hacking the system that makes her privileged lifestyle possible."[15] What little plot is here concerns a loose corporate conspiracy that brings the four unique hipsters briefly into contact with one another through the pivotal character of Toby, the only member of the quartet who knows and personally interacts with the other three. This is a crucial detail in that, insufferable trust-fund smugness and mercenary venality notwithstanding, Toby is the group's sole surviving member at the novel's canonically bleak conclusion (Lerato lives but is fully incorporated into the very system that she tactically resists throughout).

While such a result is perhaps perfectly in accord with the posthumanism for which cyberpunk is variously lauded or condemned,[16] it likewise takes this conceit to its ultimate end: the least redeemable, most ethically vacuous character in the book is the last one standing by virtue of his utterly detached quick-thinking and virtuoso navigation of the bewildering spaces (urban and cyber alike) of a near-future Cape Town. Moreover, as the youngest and unquestionably hippest of the four main characters, Toby clearly exemplifies what Suvin decries as the form's distinctively adolescent sensibility.[17] Yet, as I hope to show, the novel likewise opens the possibility for a less derivative reading, one that proposes a somewhat more complicated relation to the genre in which it self-consciously participates. I suggest that through the character of Toby (and, more precisely, through his all-conquering, intolerable hipness – not to mention his whiteness) Beukes offers both a critique and a revision for the South African present of this adolescent genre consonant with that of Suvin's own deeply ambivalent assessment of cyberpunk's youthful orientation: "'Adolescent' does not necessarily mean invalid; indeed, it means very probably at least partially valid; but it also, finally, means untenable *à la longue*."[18]

But to understand *Moxyland*'s complex relationship to cyberpunk it is perhaps best to begin by approaching the novel according to the postmodern logic of the form itself, in which surface is depth and style substance and in which a near-compulsive nominalization (what Jameson simply refers to as "hyped-up name-dropping"[19]) takes on an enhanced, if not central significance. In the work of Gibson, Jameson argues, such brand referencing may be understood – in addition to its designation of capital's global reach and of an "encyclopaedic familiarity with the fashions of world space" – as a "joyous badge of group adherence," or as class identity achieved by way of epistemology – that is, through "knowing the score rather than [through] having money and power."[20] Gibson's characters and narrators creatively seize upon and reorder the alienated and alienating object-world around them, anchoring their own precarious place in its uncertain terrain through the recognition and recital of familiar corporate appellations: actually existing ones like Hitachi, Nikon, Braun as well as fictional ones like Ono-Sendai, Hosaka, and so on. Yet this strategic practice is clearly to be distinguished from the stylistic feature that is perhaps *Neuromancer*'s most recognizable and innovative feature: its jazz-like integration of hard-boiled noir and William S. Burroughs' hallucinogenic "viral" prose with drug-culture vernacular and cybernetics-derived neologism. For all the attention given to Gibson's supposedly depthless, low-affect, postmodern style, much of the novel's critical force derives from the dialogic collision of its various language worlds, from the tension between the flat and clichéd plane of corporatized media-speak (in which "everything is slowly being named"[21]) and the inventive and idiomatic richness of the speech of characters occupying the still-vital fringes of its rapidly homogenizing global continuum.

Moxyland, comprised exclusively of the four main characters' first-person narratives, seems on the other hand to strive to be a novel without such stylistic depths of contrast, or one in which the differential spaces of neologism or even of innovative bricolage, have collapsed into a fully reified language of monochromatic (very nearly monologic) immediacy, creatively attenuated and aridly inhospitable to spontaneous invention or even strategic instances of *détournement*. The speech of Beukes' characters is, like Gibson's, marked by the reflexive dropping of brand names; here, however, such corporate nominalizations have penetrated the semi-autonomous sphere of local vernacular production such that the "punk" slang of the counterculture is reduced to nothing more than the unimaginative recitation of globally familiar labels. It is not insignificant that such expressions are articulated almost exclusively by Toby: "Hey, easy now. Everything's sony;"[22] "You should come. It's going to be Toyota;"[23] "I've seen enough light tatts on the little trendies in the clubs to know, even at a glance, that this here is the coke."[24] Similarly, the act of "defusing," which describes the disciplinary delivery of a (usually) nonlethal voltage of current through the offender's cell phone (the favored behavioral management instrument of the novel's "government inc."), is more popularly known as "crisping" or "KFC": as in "Almost none of the protestors are KFC."[25] Such absence of invention defines a social space without relative horizon, where reification has penetrated to the quick of experiential reality and all expression is now trademarked. This collapsing of internal and external, public and private is, as we shall see, central to our understanding of Beukes' relation to Gibson as well as to the aesthetic of cyberpunk more generally.

This defining spatial problematic can most clearly be perceived in Gibson and Beukes' respective articulations of cyberpunk's celebrated internationalism. In his polemical introduction to the *Mirrorshades* anthology, Bruce Sterling avers that the cyberpunk era is one of "a new sophistication, a broader perspective" and that "cyberpunks aim for a wide-ranging, global point of view."[26] For Csicsery-Ronay, who maintains judicious skepticism of Sterling's claims for cyberpunk's "unholy alliance of the technical world and the world of organized dissent,"[27] the subgenre is less a development in one or more national SF literary traditions than a "legitimate international artistic style" buttressed by an accompanying philosophy, though the evidence given for its supposed global orientation (or what precisely is meant by "international" here) is only obliquely articulated.[28]

Suvin provides additional insight with his observation that stock cyberpunk protagonists (typically white males "between fifteen and thirty") are "totally immersed in – or, indeed, it would be more accurate to say that their sensibility is constituted by – the international pop culture."[29] This, it seems, is simply another way of saying that cyberpunk bears some meaningful relation to the cultural *flows* and exchanges of globalization more generally and to the first-world consumption of cultural otherness more specifically. Jameson certainly suggests as much when he notes that the Japanophilia characteristic of inaugural texts like *Neuromancer* and Ridley Scott's *Blade Runner* (1982) is the symptomatic marker of a shift in the global politico-economic order in which Japan occupies the role of "the great Other, who is perhaps our own future rather than our past, the putative winner of the coming struggle – whom we must therefore compulsively imitate."[30] Of course, Japan, the imminent future of the 1980s, has given way to today's China – a transition registered in the speech of *Moxyland*'s characters, for whom "china" functions as both a universal noun of direct address and a generally applicable exclamation. Alternatively, Suvin contends that the "nipponizing" style Gibson deploys in *Neuromancer* suggests an analogic relation between "Japanese feudal-style capitalism" and the "new feudalism of present-day corporate monopolies."[31] Neither of these explanations fully accounts, however, for cyberpunk's more comprehensive incorporation of global space and international cultures such as, in the case of *Neuromancer*, Istanbul and Zion, the latter an orbiting colony populated by Rastafarian laborers. For in these instances, cyberpunk's international hues are better read as coterminous with the simultaneous emergence of postmodernism[32] and the organization of fields like postcolonial studies (or other, less formal, first-world reconnaisances into cultures of Otherness) beginning in the late 1970s and early 1980s. Less the products of reciprocal cultural exchange in a McLuhanesque global village, such formations are more nearly, as Jameson describes them, symptoms of "the impoverishment of culture in a kind of standardized media society like this first world one, which is therefore tempted to reinvigorate itself perpetually and to restore its vitality by infusions of a more vital culture from the outside."[33] For an aesthetic that, as Sabine Heuser observes of cyberpunk, is "largely born and raised in the USA," such infusions are both desperately needed and in ever-diminishing supply.[34] Thus, in *Neuromancer*, "what is black, or 'African,' [i.e., the Rastafarians] comes to be idealized and exoticized as that which is natural, authentic, and true" over and against the bloodless alienations of the purely techno-cultural.[35]

The eclectic office décor of *Neuromancer*'s quasi-eternal Julius Deane (which, as Suvin also notes, offers the novel's first depiction of interior physical space) provides the prototypical example of this omnivorous appropriation and/or entombment of vital exterior forms. From the "Neo-Aztec bookcases gather[ing] dust against one wall of the room" and the Surrealist "Dali clock" slung languidly between them to the Kandinsky-inspired coffee table, whose simultaneous evocation and containment of a safely defunct modernism is completed by the "Disney-styled table lamps" that enframe it, Deane's office epitomizes a postmodernist compression of high and low, past and present, inside and outside – its hipness deriving as much from the museumification of these equally petrified cultural expressions as from the yet-perceivable incongruity of their perhaps excessively insouciant juxtaposition.

If in *Neuromancer* such displays are celebrated as instances of postmodernist pastiche, *Moxyland* revisits the scene of Deane's office with a decidedly more critical eye. Upon arriving at the corporate compound of Vulkani Media ("The name means 'Awake! Arise! Fight!,' which makes me wonder who they're supposed to be fighting"[36]) for enlistment in the nano-tech experiment that will make her an official "sponsorbaby" bearing the indelible mark of the corporate beast on her flesh (a green luminescent brand symbol for the soft drink Ghost), Kendra is ushered through a reception area decorated with "gold statuettes of African masks"[37] to the office of Andile, which is significantly described as

> colonized by an assortment of hip ephemera, a lot of it borderline illegal. The most blatant example is the low-fi subtech on his bookshelf, a cobbled-together satellite radio smuggled in from the Rural in defiance of the quarantines, which probably only makes it more valuable, more flauntable. It all goes with the creative director territory, along with the pink shirt and the tasteful metal plug in his right ear.[38]

Andile's collection, like Deane's, is composed of elements lent character by their suggestion of a former exterior now available for direct absorption and commodification, but in the "developing" world, that posited exterior is visibly and obviously classed, and the objects are not those, as in Gibson, bearing the identifying mark of a merely national or cultural exoticism but of a material resistance to the homogenizing forces of the corporate hegemony for which his office is itself symbolic. For this reason, Andile is particularly keen on obtaining a copy of the photograph (on actual film!) that Kendra surreptitiously snapped on her way into the building in spontaneous defiance of the "legal restrictions on documenting corporate space."[39] Beukes further contrasts the South African situation to the Western dilemma by positing an African internationalism that does not have the luxury of such invigorating infusions from a cultural exterior:

> Gaborone has all the soul and personality of a strip mall, or maybe the teenage blank-heads who hang out in strip malls all desperately trying to conform. ... This must be what Americans go through, the sour disappointment, expecting to encounter the exotic when it's all the same homogenous crap the world over.[40]

The adolescent "blank-heads," who purchase mass-produced uniforms of disaffection and nonconformist identity at the shopping mall, perhaps recall the hipster heroes of first-world cyberpunk. In such ways, Beukes takes severely to task the hipster internationalism of cyberpunk and reminds us that the eroding inside/outside distinction it (or its primary readership) implicitly celebrates is nevertheless exoticizing and perhaps not, as apologists like Bruce Sterling assert, necessarily indicative of a progressive political orientation.

As Andile's corporate appropriation of the "Vukani" slogan implies, the logic here is one of strategic subsumption or incorporation of dissent rather than of cultural revitalization or even liberal multicultural tourism. Such strategies of containment and neutralization also inform the novel's major plot developments, as when Lerato's multiple counts of "corporate sabotage" result in her surprising promotion to the office in Mumbai. This eventuality is adumbrated earlier in the novel by Tendeka in the urban legend-cum-cautionary tale of Hope Modise, a virtuoso 14-year-old hacker who, in the throes of a "dumb teenage crush" on her programming instructor, infiltrates the servers of Sonica Wireless and sends out a viral love message addressed to him in binary code, resulting in an estimated loss in productivity of $6.3 billion.[41] After receiving an unheard-of punishment of twenty years' disconnect ("We're talking relegated to homeless, out of society, cut from the commerce loop. . ."[42]), her sentence is commuted to three years in juvenile detention followed by exclusive employment with Sonica as a security agent "closing up loops and backdoors to stop the next gen of Hope Modises from getting through."[43] Her original message, subject to full commodification, remains available as "a fucking screensaver for your phone, a Valentine's download for geeks."[44] Even *Hope*, the heavy-handed allegory suggests, cannot long evade a reifying incorporation into a system that no longer entertains the antiquated notion of anything beyond its grasp.

Tendeka's case is especially significant as his spectacular street displays of spontaneous public resistance, tagging space, are forced to assume the form of corporate-sponsored electronic billboards and legally petitioned graffiti murals. Indeed, the smoldering indignation Tendeka feels at the inequity and injustice of his present is reduced to pathetically risible expression like the "real nasty" message he sends to an Italian firm that, initially interested in funding his graffiti project and filming his efforts for a documentary, backs out of what appears an unprofitable campaign: "I sent the hombres a real nasty email afterwards, telling them exactly what neo-colonial cocks they were, coming in here, raping our resources and fucking off again. ... I hate it when people fake being on the level, all global-village-ing when they're the ones raking in fat salaries, and we're the ones living hand-to-mouth ..."[45] This strategy of corporate-sponsored dissent, he notes, even bears a name: "Subvertising. Like what Levi's did when those kids in Brazil hacked their storefronts. Turned it into a challenge, a hacksibition, appropriating the street culture for their own twisted purposes."[46]

More significant than mere ideological compromise and appropriation, though, is Tendeka's central role in the corporate conspiracy into which each member of the hipster quartet is unwittingly drawn. Duped by the anonymous resistance agent known only as *skyward** (actually a duplicitous corporate construct), Tendeka is encouraged to organize an illegal protest against the "pass laws" that maintain the sociospatial compartmentalization of this future Cape Town – laws that discriminate no longer by race but by the economic information encoded on the SIM ID card of one's cell phone. The protest, Tendeka claims, "is going to be the ultimate, to demonstrate the divides in our society between the Emmies and the Zukos [i.e., the refugees, rurals, and street people] and the corporate with their gold-plated all-access passes and the things they do to keep us in our place."[47] Designed to coincide with *FallenCity Underworld*, a "meatspace" or alternate reality game with multimedia components involving collaborative as well as competitive interaction with other players in both gamespace and real-world situations, Tendeka's directive is to infiltrate the game's pass-restricted location in the Cape Town Underground with a group of activists and the homeless in order to force "the corporate and the cops so far over the line there's no coming back for them."[48] This illegal (mostly phoneless) assembly, in combination with the paintball guns carried by *FallenCity* players and the general hysteria of the surging underground, provides the occasion for the authorities to shower the crowd with the M7N1 Marburg virus – fatal within 48 hours of exposure unless the vaccine, available only at South African Police immunization centers, is administered. Toby, who is working the underground as a proxy for wealthy *FallenCity* players, believes that the virus is merely a ruse to lure protestors to the authorities, but Tendeka is less certain. When he arrives home that evening to consult *skyward**, he finds a package containing a new Nokia phone with messages from his ostensible comrade directing him to detonate bombs in various vaccination centers in order to call public attention to the police's brutal methods. Suppressing a momentary flash of unease ("I don't know how he knew where to find me"[49]), Tendeka does as he is instructed for the cause, believing the claim of *skyward** that the authorities plan to charge as terrorists those who report to vaccination centers, even the children, and to ship them to labor camps in the Rural from which they will never return. Naturally, the bombs are later credited to terrorists and merely legitimate the extended sovereignty of "government inc.," who then implement even more restrictive and authoritarian policies with the willing consent of a panicked, media-manipulated public. As corporate agent Stefan observes at the novel's conclusion, "any action is justified in a state under terrorist threat," to which the co-opted Lerato (now "[h]eading skywards") perspicaciously replies, "You just have to create your own terrorists."[50] Thus again, we find here no vitalizing exterior on which to draw, no uncolonized vantage to provide the perspectival alternative. The system generates and orchestrates its own resistance to overcome the impediments of its internal limits, just as Marx always claimed.

Indeed, in the one-dimensional, monochromatic future of *Moxyland*, even the liberatory promise of cyberspace has been foreclosed, its once thrilling capacity to provide "alternatives to conventional modalities of human existence" now exhausted and wholly incorporated.[51] Scott Bukatman, who emphasizes the utopian possibilities of cyberspace in his essential study *Terminal Identity* (1993), writes that "[w]hether a real space or a [Gibsonian] 'consensual hallucination,' cyberspace produces a unified experience of spatiality, and thus social being, in a culture that has become impossibly fragmented."[52] He further suggests that "the otherness of cyberspace abides as an ultimately *defining* metaphor, an attempt to recognize and overcome the technological estrangements of the electronic age, and a preliminary attempt to resituate the human as its fundamental force."[53] Attempting thus to restore to critical discourse an acknowledgement of cyberpunk's utopian deployment of cyberspace, Bukatman invokes Paul Arthur's observation that the latter bears much in common with the traditional pastoral, that it likewise "represents a new frontier, one that replaces an urban landscape desiccated by the pervasiveness of consumer dynamics."[54] Though it often "frequently recapitulates the complexities of the postmodern 'urban nonplace,'" cyberspace simultaneously "permits the subject a utopian and kinetic *liberation* from the very limits of urban existence."[55] Following Gibson's own lead, the unregulated expanses of cyberspace have frequently been seen as contemporary variations on the anarchic frontier of the American West, with the hacker undertaking a veritable civilizing mission, mediating and making habitable the often hostile or alien cybernetic matrices for a new form of community.[56]

Not all commentators have found what Gibson terms the "bodiless exultation of cyberspace" and its attendant "contempt for the flesh" quite so salubrious, however.[57] Urban historian M. Christine Boyer is archly skeptical of such claims, noting that the "thrill of constant travel in the unknown network of information without a centered focus or bounded domain" blunts our capacity for critical thought through its chaotic presentation of random and indeterminate motion: "Being constantly on the move in order to escape the repressive machines of disciplinary societies or to fully exploit the uncertain voyages of complexities in societies of control offers us no foundation on which to stand, to criticize, to remember the past, or to plan the future."[58] Boyer likewise cites the similar reservations of Sally Pryor, for whom the privileging of virtual space represents a "retreat from direct experience of the senses, the body, each other, and our (polluted) environment" and who argues that the "re-mapping [of] ourselves into digitally-mediated, synthetic fantasy worlds" is merely the turning of a capitulatory blind eye to materiality as such.[59] Hence, the *digerati's* ever-renewed faith in a posthuman gospel of technically achieved sublimity effectively translates the real of politics into mere technique and instrumental proficiency.[60] As Bukatman himself elsewhere concedes, cyberpunk's narrative of posthuman transcendence is at the same time "always a surrender."[61]

Cyberspace's pastoral and utopian compensations, however arguably emancipatory their function for the sprawling, undefined metroscapes of the post-industrial first world, assume a starkly different valence in the third. This is especially true of South Africa, where invocations of the pastoral bear a complex and heavily freighted history that cannot be articulated with the referential innocence that Arthur's model suggests. In *White Writing* (1988), J.M. Coetzee explores the "topos of the garden, the enclosed world entire to itself" traditionally evoked in the South African pastoral, observing that the form has historically been "assigned the task of asserting the virtues of the garden – simplicity, peace, immemorial usage – against the vices of the city: luxury, competitiveness, novelty."[62] Specifically, the pastoral provided a means of dual separation for a precariously positioned Afrikaner culture – from the undefined native wildness of the African land and peoples on the one hand and a degenerate urbanism, vicinity of both the British bourgeoisie and dislocated poor whites, on the other.[63] Like cyberspace, the pastoral marks a distinctive "dream topography" or "drifting habitation" seemingly "outside history, outside society" altogether, yet this exceptionalism is given, as Coetzee notes, only inasmuch as the colonized space itself may also be said to lie outside History proper as what we might call the former's unassimilable Real.[64] Thus, it is not surprising that a defining preoccupation of the South African pastoral is the vexed representation of labor, the differentiation of a nostalgic withdrawal from urbanism and commerce on the one hand from a mere decline into native "sensual sloth" and stereotypical indolence on the other.[65] For this reason, the pastoral pays an anxious "double tribute": "To satisfy critics of rural retreat, it must portray labour; to satisfy the critics of colonialism, it must portray white labour. What inevitably follows is the occlusion of black labour from the scene ..."[66] The presence of black labor thus haunts the pastoral form as a conspicuous lacuna, as the limit-point of its representational field. Imaginatively supplanting the ascendant British capitalist order with the preservation of traditional feudal or peasant values and social practices, the pastoral constructs a "lineal consciousness" in which legitimate possession of the land is demonstrated not through the vulgar quantifications of market exchange but through the "blood, sweat, and tears" of the family farmer, whose generations have lovingly redeemed the land from the desolation of the bush and its barbaric inhabitants, both of which are consigned to a primeval – and therefore unspeakable – past.[67]

This quasi-ancestral claim to the bones of the land falters, of course, at the edge of History's clearing, and the limits of the pastoral's nostalgic dream topography are delineated in its formal counterpart, the antipastoral. If the pastoral maintains a rigid distinction between urban and rural, inner and outer, the antipastoral collapses these spaces into indistinguishability; where the pastoral valorizes industry, the antipastoral reveals sloth; where the pastoral achieves a spatial succession from history and the world in the creation of its fecund and paradisical garden, the antipastoral cultivates only arid vastness without borders, "limitless plain beneath limitless sky."[68] The antipastoral thus opposes the naturalization of the farm and presents it rather as a violent impingement upon a blindly indifferent and incommensurable landscape. Where the pastoral elaborates a determinate semiotic matrix within which troublesome exotopic elements (like the black laboring body) are, however fitfully or contradictorily, ordered, contained, and neutralized, the antipastoral seizes upon such sites of erasure as the core of what Lacan might call an extimate identity construct that confounds the logic of discrete inner and outer spaces altogether.

We might therefore supplement Andries Visagie's useful location of *Moxyland* within the generic framework of the *critical dystopia*[69] with that of the post-contemporary antipastoral, one that specifically addresses the virtualities and cyber-realities of late capital's globalized spaces. The first such cyberspace utopia to receive Beukes' critically antipastoral treatment is *Pluslife*, a massive, user-created 3D virtual world (based closely on Linden Lab's *Second Life*) housing hundreds of millions of avatars. Even Tendeka, whom Toby sarcastically nominates a "Struggle revivalist" and "Steve Biko wannabe" born fifty years too late, is not above retreat into the bodiless consolations of the virtual. Tendeka's home in *Pluslife* is located in a region known as Avalon, "one of the world's favourite virtual escapes" with 59.3 million registered users, a population roughly equivalent to that of the United Kingdom.[70] While Tendeka finds a measure of satisfaction in the fact that less than half of the inhabitants in the "Asia-centric" gameworld speak English ("What's the point of escaping to Plus if the world is too close to the one you just left?"[71]), he also enjoys the opportunities that this language disparity affords to "make an okay living" in *Pluslife* by *teaching* English to its other users, a virtual income that Tendeka uses to spruce up his home, which represents for him both a kind of secure depository for and concrete expression of his deepest utopian longings:

> It's pretty humble, designed to be bio-friendly. All recyclable materials, solar panels on the ceiling, a wind farm in the garden. Not that you need to generate energy in-world, but it's the principle. It's a shining example to throw into contrast the kind of excesses the neighborhood attracts, which is why I chose this location specifically.[72]

The surrounding neighborhood is "a recreation of the L.A. hills, which pulls in celeb wannabes by the dumpload, all avatared to resemble their current favourites, living or deceased, the Cary Grants and Tupacs and Gwyneths and Engelica Ks."[73] Conflicts inevitably arise when two or more users select the same celebrity avatar, and "they get into this bullshit competitive crap about who's keeping it more real," a symptom, Tendeka avers, "of everything that's wrong with our culture."[74] The ever-earnest Tendeka resists the temptations of such avatar vanity and directly uploads and "skins" a photograph of himself, which is, he states without irony, "more honest."[75]

Yet a contradiction emerges here between Tendeka's committed idealism (his own version of "keeping it real") and the virtual spaces in which he is constrained to enact it. His *Pluslife* home, a utopian "shining example," he names "Monomotapa" after the Portuguese transliteration of "Mwenemutapa" (*chief* or *ruler of the conquered land*), Mutapa being the title of a powerful fifteenth-century tribal leader believed to have presided over an empire spanning much of southern Africa. The Monomotapa are reputed to have been advanced in metallurgy and architecture and are believed to have dug the first mines on the continent. The history of "Monomotapa" has been a subject of conjecture and dispute among European historians for hundreds of years, but investigations into its mysterious past reached a fever pitch among British scholars at the close of the nineteenth century as the British colonial presence in Africa became more prominent. In a book dedicated to none other than the notorious imperialist and gem mogul Cecil J. Rhodes, "who has been principally the means of giving a new empire to Britain and by whose advice and aid the researches into the history of Monomotapa were undertaken,"[76] Alexander Wilmot's self-proclaimed pioneering history (also featuring a substantial preface by the author of *King Solomon's Mines*, H. Rider Haggard) undertakes to restore the lost history of this "barbaric" empire, whose rise "stamped out whatever civilization, Christian or Mahommedan, still flickered in Monomotapa so completely that even native tradition is silent concerning it."[77] Conversely, the late nineteenth-century South African historian George McCall Theal observes what we might call the already virtual reality of this supposedly misnominated "empire":

> Some interest is attached to this word *Monomotapa*, inasmuch as it was placed on the maps of the day as if it was the name of a territory, not the title of a ruler, and soon it was applied to the entire region. ... Geographers who knew nothing of the country, wrote the word upon their charts, and one copied another until the belief became general that a people far advanced in civilization, and governed by a mighty emperor, occupied the whole of South-Eastern Africa.[78]

Despite widespread dissemination of the "fraudulent" theory among colonial historians and geographers, Theal claims that "[s]uch an empire never existed" as such; rather, the "foundation upon which imagination constructed it was nothing more than a Bantu tribe [the

Kalanga]."[79] Monomotapa thus marks the site of an historicist impasse: either Monomotapa did exist as a bloodthirsty empire that drove out Christianity and, with it, civilization, or it was an elaborate bugbear born of equal parts xenophobic dread, ideological expediency, and imperialist romanticism. No allowance is given by the late-Victorian intellectual for its actual, mundane existence in history, a history interrupted by successive European incursions, of which that of Rhodes and company is only the most recent and, as Beukes teaches us, certainly not the last. Tendeka's awareness of this history is a point left intentionally ambiguous, and whether the name is meant to evoke the idealistic puissance of a previously unified southern Africa, with its native wealth and majestic culture intact, or the lost city of gold and diamonds that came to be known among Europeans as the "African Eldorado," both the history and the name are largely inventions of the European imperial imagination.[80] More evidence of such historical absence can be found a few pages earlier in the chapter, where, in the course of a brief discussion of the failure of the state, the death of the local economy, and the unrelenting growth of the loxion sprawl, Tendeka laments the broken political commitments of a bygone era, though he isn't quite sure what the substance of those commitments actually were: "All the same shit they've been promising to fix since the 1955 Freedom Charter or whatever it was."[81] The subtle provincializing of this crucial pillar of South African political progressivism is telling indeed. For the raceless future for which the ANC once hoped has, in Beukes' vision, been largely achieved, yet the earlier abandonment of the Charter's other key principles (nationalization of industry and equitable land reform being the most crucial) has resulted in a world where even the nominalist historicizing usually found on street and building names (as in Hopkinson's Touissant) has given way to a succession of fleeting popular references pulled from the day's corporate-controlled media headlines. In other words, the idealized primal past Tendeka means to evoke through his virtual utopian home is already a commodity generated of the imperial imaginary and its conquest of Africa, just as his well-intentioned resistance against the corporate "neo-colonial cocks" is itself merely a maintenance function of the system he imagines himself to oppose.

The acute absence of history from Tendeka's pastoral vision is given broader significance when we consider that his Monomotapa stands amid an electronic simulation of a city that is itself already pure simulacrum. As Jean Baudrillard has it, unlike the Disneyland that it houses, "which is presented as imaginary in order to make us believe that the rest is real," the city of Los Angeles is "no longer real, but belongs to the hyperreal order and to the order of simulation."[82] Nourished by its orbiting circuit of "imaginary stations," Los Angeles conceals the fact that it is no more than a "network of incessant, unreal circulation – a city of incredible proportions but without space, without dimension."[83] What Baudrillard does not note, however, is that the city's ahistorical hyperreality (also that of North America more generally) is fundamentally an effect of the pastoral and frontier imagery that has long constituted its urban self-narrative. Taking up the strident petition of Fredrick Jackson Turner's stirring "frontier thesis," Los Angeles emphatically embraced unfettered mobility as its predominant organizing concept. With the official closure of the Western frontier preceding by three years his now-infamous address at the 1893 Chicago World's Fair, Turner made recourse to what Charles Scruggs calls "a second form of the pastoral" or to what we might recognize in the present context as the latter's virtualization.[84] Indeed, the national-spatial impasse facing Turner at the close of the nineteenth century is structurally analogous to the global-spatial one facing us at the close of the twentieth, and in either case, capital's answer – distinctly echoed in cyberpunk's privileging of cyberspace – is the same: *Keep moving!*

In his remarkable *The History of Forgetting*, Norman M. Klein considers LA's restless hyperreality alongside the systematic restructuration and erasure of ethnic and working-class neighborhoods (as well as the corollary phenomenon of civic amnesia) since the 1930s under the aegis of civic booster programs and promotional consumer campaigns. Exploring the way in which popular noir visions of the city (which may be read as collectively scripting a "mythos about white male panic"[85]) function as the cultural/ideological buttressing for ongoing political and economic programs of civic restructuration and privatization, Klein turns not only to archetypal LA noir artifacts of the interwar decades but also to the contemporary cyberpunk fictions of Gibson and Neal Stephenson, which equally construct a "topology of forgetfulness" and mobilize similar anxieties about a "barbaric amnesia replacing white civilization, in a city whose sky is the 'color of television tuned to a dead channel.'"[86] The pastoral promise of cyberspace, Klein suggests, provides not a critical superation of the present but merely its kinetic extension toward an ever-receding frontier, what Turner himself called "a gate of escape from the bondage of the past."[87] Citing William J. Mitchell's guide to life in the "cyburbs," Klein observes that the disembodied and fragmentary subjects of this rootless, placeless, and borderless alternative are simply "invited to escape into a cybernetic democracy that isn't really there."[88] Cyberspace reveals itself then as simply the most recent in a decades-long succession of civic booster stratagems:

> Like boosterism, it builds a social imaginary that distracts attention from the widening class structure and the global restructuring or economic power. Like earlier booster campaigns, it has master-planned millenarianism. It assumes that industrial decay will stop at the boundaries of the ghetto; that what happened to inner cities was historically unique, and could never infect the exburbs, much less the World Wide Web.[89]

Stross makes much the same comparison in his own ambivalent response to the traditional cyberpunk tendency to "romanticize cyberspace": "I can't tell whether or not there's going to be a Singularity. I don't really believe the rapture of the nerds stereotype – 'we're all going to cyber-heaven, hallelujah!' Rather boosterish."[90] Beukes' simulated LA might therefore be read as a repudiation of the residual frontierism that informs traditional cyberpunk's privileged spaces. In Avalon LA, stars are "brighter than realworld"; no evidence of material or class inequality is visible ("no gated communities, no Mexican labour riots"[91]); and one can enjoy the precise satisfactions of simulated agency: "There's a flickering on the horizon, and at first I think it's some bug in the software, but as it spreads, multi-coloured, I figure that someone has hacked the sky. It's doing a northern lights thing. And that's the beauty of Pluslife. That you can actually have an influence on the world."[92]

Tendeka soon discovers the naivety of this notion, however, when *skyward** hacks his enviro-friendly house and replaces it with "loxion shelters, the tinshacks appallingly incongruous among the mansions and manicured lawns."[93] Citing the material insufficiency of Tendeka's positive virtual example, *skyward** alludes to a distant relative of Tendeka's who once helped to shelter the eventually assassinated anti-apartheid activist and member of the South African Communist Party, Ruth First: "you ask that cousin about the effectiveness of politely asking for change, of peaceful demonstrations, the total pointlessness of street theatre of civil disobedience. or democracy."[94] Advocating shock tactics comparable to those used by the corporates themselves over more traditional modes of activist dissent, *skyward** argues that the old strategies no longer work because a media-fatigued public, sick with ennui, no longer has the sufficient attention span: "we're competing with media and advertising and promotions and pluslives, all helping people to avoid confronting reality."[95] *skyward**'s deeply cynical post-Frankfurt diagnosis leaves room for nothing save a spectacular jolt to awaken the masses: "we need to jar people from their apathy. we need spectacle. we need to fight the corporate on their own terms. Counter-exploitative."[96] What *skyward** intentionally omits here in this celebration of spectacular *détournement*, of course, is that oppositional stratagem's obverse correlate, what the Situationists called *recuperation* (or what Tendeka has already identified as corporate subvertising): the tapping and redirecting of oppositional or dissenting energies in service of capital, a strategic subsumption that *skyward** is in the very process of enacting.

Indeed, as the very presence of *skyward**'s "character" makes clear, in addition to the dubious pastoral assurances of a historyless frontier, Beukes also takes on cyberspace's vaunted liberation (and therefore privileging) of identity, the putatively empowering dissolution of the subject into the boundless telematic ontologies of the cyborg, characterized, as Donna Haraway has it, by the non-totalizing "profusion of spaces and identities and the permeability of boundaries in the personal body and in the body politic."[97] We find a tentative, though richly suggestive exploration of these conjoined themes in the virtual world from which the novel's title is ironically derived. "Moxyland" does not exist as such in the novel. The title refers rather to the character "Moxy" in *Kiwi Pop,* another of the games that Toby is hired to play as illegal proxy for wealthy game owners. *Kiwi Pop* is a children's game, and Toby is given the assignment by underground gamer coordinator Unathi partially because of his lack of recent gameplay experience and partially because of a playful animosity between the two: "'I got an order for a purple Blinka Stinka. It's worth two-eight. That's fourteen hundred to you. And yes, that means I'm taking 50%."[98] Easily circumventing the age protection feature with Unathi's hack, Toby enters the gameworld comprised of 1,487,763 other players, "99% of whom are in the eight-to-twelve demographic."[99] The remaining one percent, Toby estimates, is made up of "gatecrashers cashing in on the system, or maybe pedophiles looking to hook up"; of the two, he determines, "the former group may be the more evil."[100] Harried by two other players who repeatedly kill Toby's furry avatar as soon as it appears in the gameworld, he seeks assistance from Lerato, who quickly bypasses *Kiwi Pop*'s respawning programming by rerouting Toby's IP address through Melbourne and making him appear as a new character logging on from another continent. Once past the ambush, Toby easily obtains his contracted object, then backtracks to locate and kill the two ambushing players: "As a finishing touch, I put in a special request to Lerato to trace the little bastards' user names and get them banned from the gamespace for violating protocol. The pretext for locking them out is killer. Overage players."[101]

Its undeniable utility as a mascot and marketing aid aside (the paperback even includes a stencil instructing readers to make their own Moxy, "a symbol of defiance to the powers that be"), the significance of *Kiwi Pop* should not be overlooked, for Beukes reveals here that the intoxicating flux of postmodernism's "terminal identity" – wherein, Bukatman observes, our "myriad selves" and multitudinous realities are given unrestrained free play[102] – likewise allows for the co-optation or recuperation of that ludic space by the powers that be – to which Moxy is perhaps only a coyly winking acknowledgment. More disturbing, however, is the inescapable suggestion of the title that the novel's Cape Town is itself "Moxyland," an already virtual world of suspended identities and flickering cybernetic subjects for which there are no stable or exterior referents, a world already fully subsumed into vertiginous hyperreality.

For Visagie, this utter saturation or penetration of the real by the virtual suggests the inescapable vulnerabilities of life in a risk society where "it becomes unthinkable to find a consolidated position at a remove from the capitalist sphere of influence."[103] Even the space of the traditional arts has evidently been compromised and provides no effective critical vantage. Art, Visagie argues, is accorded a position of special ambiguity in the book, the integrity of its artists consistently "undermined by their inability to resist the seductions of corporate culture."[104] Even the novel's designated artist, Kendra, despite "deliberately us[ing] outdated photographic techniques" wears the corporate brand as material evidence of her hypocrisy.[105]

Yet I want to suggest that the novel's antipastoral (and authentically utopian) impetus finds its most emphatic expression precisely in the ekphrastic representation of Kendra's photography, specifically in her *Self-Portrait* and, more important, in the aesthetic that retroactively informs its composition. Printed from partially decayed film, the piece "came out entirely black," yet something in the failed project (like all great modernist failures) compels Kendra, and, despite the protests of her colleagues, she makes it the centerpiece of her first photographic installation, the void around which the other pieces, which she significantly describes as "hyper-realist," circulate.[106] Comparing *Self-Portrait* to a night dive she once took on the open ocean, she claims that the most unnerving part of the experience was not the enclosing darkness but rather the way submersion made the surrounding water seem overly immediate and visually available, encouraging a false sense of depth and of security: "Visibility limits your imagination of the ocean only as far as you can see, ten metres, fifteen at a stretch. But it's only in the utter black that you can feel the true scale, the volume and weight of that gaping unknowable drift between continents."[107] It is only fitting that immediacy and visibility are the very principles upon which the authority of "government inc." rests, as evidenced by the easy availability of police records and by incessant media saturation, but as Tendeka observes, "this is what's so truly fucked up, that government inc. thinks this level of transparency automatically rules out repression."[108] Beukes' government inc. has in fact mastered the ideological stratagem that Marcuse named "democratic domination," in which, as Bukatman glosses,

> an effectively functioning ideological state apparatus replaces the need for overt exercises of power by the repressive apparatus. "The perfection of power," Michel Foucault wrote, referring to the panoptic structures of the disciplinary society, "should tend to render its actual exercise unnecessary." Or, as William Burroughs observed, "A functioning police state needs no police."[109]

However, as Tendeka later observes, "transparency only works as a policy if you can still find a way to make the stuff you don't want people to see invisible – especially when it's out in the open."[110] The old modernist dilemmas of appearance and reality, of surface and depth, even of science and ideology thus return here in a unique, though strikingly familiar way. Surveying the secondary epidermal evidence of the cellular transformation happening within her, Kendra laments her inability fully to chronicle it: "If I could embed a camera inside my body, I would. But all I can do is document the cells mutating on the inside of my wrist, the pattern developing, spreading, fading up like an oldschool Polaroid."[111] That is, her documentation is at best a symptomatic reading (what Gibson would call *pattern recognition*) of a much more profound, subdermal event that can be represented only by the void, by the negative acknowledgement of the unseen.

Crucially, Beukes dramatizes the translation of this unfinished project from the media of the modern to that of the postmodern, from the film photography of Kendra to the "BabyStrange" of Toby, a passage the full significance of which will only be understood from the vantage of the novel's ambiguous conclusion. The key technology in the novel, Toby's BabyStrange is a hooded "chamo" jacket featuring thousands of microcameras sewn into its "smartfabric" surface, which also functions as a display screen. Having offended Kendra with the "gore-porn" that he projects as much for shock value as for social camouflage (for diverting unwanted attention by aggressively attracting it), Toby appears at the opening of her gallery installation with his BabyStrange set to black, a "little shout out to *Self-Portrait.*"[112] The ironic detachment and utter lack of sincerity with which Toby carries forward the content of Kendra's project in no way mitigates the substance of that project. While his primary motive lies in convincing Kendra to sleep with him, their love-making allows for the transference of the nano-tech from her body to his (and thus for the communication of its curious side-effect, to which we'll return momentarily).

It is here in the return of what we might recognize as the modernist quandary of representation that Beukes paradoxically both exceeds the cyberpunk aesthetic and, in doing so, is perhaps most faithful to it. In a brief critical reflection on Gibson's *Pattern Recognition* (2003), a novel that for many readers signaled the author's departure from cyberpunk if not from science fiction altogether, Jameson proffers the alternative that, inasmuch as cyberpunk's most salient priority has always been the "mapping of the new geopolitical Imaginary," this more recent work may in fact move Gibson "closer to the 'cyberpunk' with which he is often associated."[113] The novel's protagonist, Cayce Pollard (a nod to "Case" from *Neuromancer*), is a professional "coolhunter," whose special sensitivity to emergent sub-cultural expressions allows her to identify and subsequently to commodify the "next big thing" before it breaches surface and registers public attention. The novel's primary action concerns Cayce's efforts, under the sponsorship of a global advertising firm, to trace the source of a mysterious, discontinuous series of highly varied film clips and stills known collectively as "the footage."

Unrepresentable as such, the footage, Jameson contends, "makes *Pattern Recognition* over into something like Bloch's conception of the novel of the artist, which carries the unknown unrealized work of art inside itself like a black hole, the empty present of a future indeterminacy, the absent sublime within the everyday real."[114] The footage thus provides imaginative space within the wholly reified world of the novel's omnivorous, corporate-sponsored hipsterism for a radically neutralizing aesthetic whose "utter lack of style is an ontological relief, like black-and-white film after the conventional orgies of bad Technicolor, like the silence of solitude for the telepath whose mind is jammed with noisy voices all day long:"[115] indeed, Beukes describes Toby's BabyStrange tribute to *Self-Portrait* as "a relief" from the nauseating spectacle of his usual projections.[116] This symbolic "epoch of rest" Jameson further associates with the equally utopian "white writing" theorized by Roland Barthes, in which language approximates the final stage in its progression of metamorphosis and solidification, in which the writer rescinds the reified forms of a recognizable Literature and attempts rather to write the silence, the void of Literature's acute absence. Such a ruptural form, though inevitably subject to the corrosive forces of imitation and habituation and constrained to "borrow, from what it wants to destroy, the very image of what it wants to possess," nevertheless anticipates the uncorrupted language of Utopia itself.[117] Such strategic borrowing against a utopian future may be said to define postcolonial literature as such and certainly defines the South African literature of both Coetzee and Beukes.

In its resolute "silence," Kendra's *Self-Portrait* obviously resonates with this constellation of ideally emptied expressions, not least with that of Gibson's footage, particularly in the way it resists the commercialization to which the rest of her art (as well has her own person) is subjected. But I'd like to suggest that for Buekes, a white South African writer of science fiction, the stakes in such a representational gambit are both higher and more immediate, the borrowing to which Barthes refers more fraught. For the refusal of signification to which Jameson refers likewise recalls that other "white writing" discussed above in relation to the South African pastoral. As we have already seen, the necessary occlusion of black labor from the pastoral form leaves the irrevocable trace of its erasure, and it is here, in the void of an imaginative failure ("a failure to imagine a peopled landscape, an inability to conceive a society in South Africa in which there is a place for the self"[118]) that the antipastoral intervenes in the mythologized histories of the pastoral. Thus, Coetzee writes, "the art of the empty landscape is the pessimistic obverse of a wishful pastoral art that by the labor of hands makes the landscape speak, and peoples it with an ideal community," providing here a distilled description of the antipastoral impulse that informs his earlier revisionary novel *Foe* (1986) and that will achieve its highest expression in his masterpiece *Disgrace* (1999).[119] In Kendra's photograph, however, the obdurate silence is not only that of black labor, nor even of the black body per se, but more precisely that of a collectivity unable to receive annunciation, of a deep-dwelling alternative to present alienations of which we can register only the faintest and most indirect of symptomatic expressions or symbolic stirrings. In *Moxyland*, this unimaginable collectivity is marked by the loxion sprawl, which, though frequently gestured toward as a massive, metastasizing zone containing the vast majority of the city's desperate inhabitants, never receives direct representation. Its intractable material borders stand rather as the limit-point for the cybernetic ontologies and punchy hipsterisms fully as much as for the gaze of the educated, relatively affluent, white South African writer of science fiction, inheritor of the representational aporias that Coetzee identifies historically with the pastoral. As Coetzee has famously observed, "the white writer in South Africa is in an impossible position,"[120] one that must be acknowledged in the responsible work of art but that can be so only as void, as silence, as deference to what Gayatri Spivak poetically names the "guardian at the margin who will not inform."[121]

It is in this sense that Beukes' novel can be read as an instance of what Jameson terms cyberpunk's *dirty realism*. If cyberpunk may be said to mark the transformation of "a formerly futurological science fiction ... into mere 'realism' and an outright representation of the present,"[122] its *dirty* modification serves to invoke "the collective as such, the traces of mass, anonymous living and using" in a postmodern present.[123] The term, indirectly borrowed from Bill Buford (who coins it to describe the nostalgic minimalism of American writers like Raymond Carver), holds the antinomies of the postmodern in productive dialectical tension without letting them collapse back into indistinction; As Jameson writes, "the slogan carries its breach within itself."[124] Specifically, he notes the form's ability to register the postmodern abandonment of regional identification in favor of "some anonymous contemporary or future urbanization."[125] This is certainly true of *Moxyland* where, apart from the conspicuously occasional bursts of Afrikaans slang, few orienting landmarks are to be found, and its globalized Cape Town could be any post-industrial city along the immaterial currents of capital's global flow. But this anonymous globalism represents an even larger and enframing conceptual antinomy turning on the formal problem of "totality versus its parts," which likewise encloses a distinct but overlapping secondary dilemma, that of innovation versus replication.[126] In its repudiation of the modernist metanarratives of totality, postmodernism perforce abandons the Poundian injunction to innovation for serial replication and pastiche.

Dirty realism, while submitting to this aesthetic of replication on the one hand, nonetheless retains within it a stubborn commitment to totality, the distinctly modernist "will to include an entire world" within itself.[127] Thus, its replicated parts, drifting incommensurably in the void like organs without bodies, yet ignite "an impulse which, impossible of realization, evolves all the more, battening on its very frustration, into the sheer concept of transcoding itself," or of the translation of value, experience, and desire across seemingly immiscible dimensions that surpasses conventional (or even modernist) notions of organic restoration and begins to approximate that cyborg ontology outlined by Haraway – but with the crucial difference that the uncategorizable hybridizations of the former seek not the endless proliferation of decentered languages but instead the comprehension, however dimly provisional, of the totality of late capitalism itself and of a potential break with it.[128] Thus neutralizing the traditional antinomies upon which bourgeois or civil society is founded (private/public, inner/outer, self/other), cyberpunk invents the wholly new space beyond these, the "no-man's-land" that bears striking resemblance to what we have already called, by way of Agamben, the Benjaminian *real state of exception.* Turning, like Agamben, to the juridical delineation of this non-space, Jameson compares it to a fictional chamber directly beneath the Berlin wall, "a space beyond all national or political jurisdiction, in which the worst crimes can be committed with impunity and in which indeed the very social persona itself dissolves."[129] Yet, he insists, this non-space need not recall the familiar, nightmarish scenarios of "classical dystopian fantasy"; on the contrary, the "very freedom from state terror lends the violence of the no-man's-land the value of a distinctive kind of praxis, excitement rather than fear."[130]

In order to see how the novel achieves this valuation of excitement over fear, we must look to its seemingly cynical (and thus, canonical) conclusion. Watching over Tendeka as he succumbs to the excruciating latter stages of the M7N1 virus, Toby, who shows no symptoms of infection and whose utter self-absorption keeps him from fully accepting Tendeka's, pretends to streamcast at his request the dying man's testimony through the damaged BabyStrange. Unknowingly carrying Kendra's replicating nanotech, Toby is protected from the virus. When Tendeka proves too weak to complete his speech disclosing governmental/corporate brutality, the derisive Toby decides that the "deathbed" histrionics might be worth recording for his streamcast. What he captures, however, is precisely the damning evidence of human rights violation that Tendeka had intended as the latter expires violently and bloodily in his arms. The shaken Toby, vulnerable for the first time in the novel, considers setting his apartment ablaze, then realizes that he now possesses "the total sony exclusive on the untimely and grotesque death of a terrorist. Or a martyr. Depends on who's paying."[131] The novel thus concludes with an ambivalently utopian flourish: "I step out the door into a whole new bright world, feeling exhausted and exhilarated. And thirsty."[132] While Toby's unmitigated venality is well beyond either sympathy or redemption, he nonetheless bears witness in his own imperfect and deeply compromised way to that which would otherwise lapse soundlessly into the fissures of history. Just as he is earlier seen to embody (however briefly or ironically) the utopian void of Kendra's *Self-Portrait*, he now likewise bears into this "whole new bright world" of possibilities elements symbolic of each of the three characters: Tendeka's revolutionary dream, Kendra's cyborg ontology, and the VIMbot hacked and repurposed by the formerly subversive hacker Lerato.

Moreover, the nanotech he bears does much more than make him physically invulnerable, as indicated by Kendra's fleeting encounter with a liquor store thief earlier in the novel. Having witnessed the defusing of the perpetrator, a poor street woman, Kendra is physically compelled to intervene despite a habitually cultivated insensitivity to such matters. Kneeling beside her as the electricity-induced seizure passes, Kendra places a hand to the forehead of the woman, reviving her, and distracts the Aito (a nano-modified police dog) just long enough for the old woman to escape. While it is never made clear if Kendra's nano-tech actively restores the woman, Kendra senses something unusual about her, a "smell here, ozony cold and chemical" that recalls her own experience of nano-injection. The symbolic implication, left only as such, is a mutual recognition, across the class boundaries brutally enforced by the pass laws, of a fellow traveler, one in whom the insatiable thirst has likewise been aroused. She later explains to a colleague, "It wasn't empathy or altruism or anything. It was like I had to, like a real compulsion," intentionally neglecting to add, "The same way we're compelled to drink Ghost."[133] This symbolic giving way of discrete and individuated lifeworlds into a common project, however vaguely defined, is, I argue, the novel's utopian horizon, and its concluding declaration of thirst suggests at once the sign of corporate-manipulated subjects *and* of unmanageable appetites newly awakened. Thus are the nightmares of cyberpunk "also on the point of becoming celebrations of a new reality, a new reality-intensification, that cannot simply be dealt with by a reactivation of the older cultural and class attitudes."[134] Likewise are the fears used to regulate society ("Fear has to be managed. Fear has to be controlled. Like people."[135]) transformed into the irrepressible thrill of possibility.

We cannot be content to leave it here, however, and neither can Beukes; for in its embodiment of this radical project in the young, affluent, white hipster, her novel risks rushing headlong into the unavoidable limitations of the subgenre in which it participates: the investiture within a disengaged technophilic cool, oblivious to its own global seat of privilege, of the emancipatory yearning of utopia. Our lack of sympathy for the mercenary opportunist Toby matches our frustration at the novel's apparently deflationary, posthumanist conclusion in which the seemingly authentic revolutionary and artist are eliminated and the unscrupulous hacker and hipster rewarded. The availability of such a reading in part explains the novel's ambivalent ending and Toby's indecision about what to do with the footage he has acquired. That is, Toby's position at the novel's end, like that of the white writer in South Africa, is an impossible one, his speech always courting the danger of an illicit speaking for, his compromised bearing witness finally the bearing witness of the author herself, who likewise navigates the hieratic codes of a privileged form inaccessible to the masses on whose behalf it wages its precarious intervention. Such, however, is the necessary risk, as Coetzee's work vividly demonstrates, of the politically engaged white writer in South Africa and, I want to suggest, of the yet cosmopolitan genre of postcolonial science fiction. A brief excursus on the Caribbean steampunk of Grenadan native Tobias Buckell can perhaps offer additional insight here from another geospatial and (sub)generic vantage.

The dissidence engine: Tobias Buckell and Caribbean steampunk

Emerging as a retrofuturistic variant of 1980s cyberpunk,[136] steampunk may be said to have grown principally – though by no means exclusively – out of the fiction of American writer K.W. Jeter, whose *Morlock Night* (1979) established many of the conventions that authors like Tim Powers and James P. Blaylock (even Jeter himself) would later elaborate and extend into a coherent typology; set almost uniformly in the nineteenth century (with especial preference for Victorian and Edwardian England), much steampunk fiction demonstrates an intense nostalgia for and intertextual filiation with the early science fiction of Wells and Verne, both of whom the genre often reverentially reauthors. Thematically characterized by the centrality of pre-electric industrial technology, from whence the form derives its name, steampunk achieves much of its stylistic élan through the anachronistic reimagining of twentieth-century technical achievement within the preceding century's delimited mechanical horizon. The genre's commemorative neo- (or perhaps alter-) Victorian preoccupations rarely extend, however, to the realities of the material exploitation that enable this cultural and technological ferment (however imaginatively augmented). Steampunk, its critics argue, thus epitomizes that most paradigmatic of postmodern forms: an "historical" fiction in which a jettisoned material content has been replaced by depthless and baroque stylization. As the online enthusiast and self-described "Steampunk Scholar" most succinctly puts it, "Steampunk utilizes a look and feel *evocative* of the period between 1800 and 1914, unencumbered by rigorous historical accuracy."[137] Such costume historicity occludes nothing less than the substance of history itself, as a well-known critique by Charles Stross makes mordantly clear. Apart from his general discontent with the fact that the "category is filling up with trashy, derivative junk and also with good authors who damn well ought to know better than to jump on a bandwagon," Stross calls for a sober reassessment of the period that steampunk heedlessly romanticizes:

> But there's a dark side as well. We know about the real world of the era steampunk is riffing off. And the picture is not good. If the past is another country, you really wouldn't want to emigrate there. Life was mostly unpleasant, brutish, and short; the legal status of women in the UK or US was lower than it is in Iran today: politics was by any modern standard horribly corrupt and dominated by authoritarian psychopaths and inbred hereditary aristocrats: it was a priest-ridden era that had barely climbed out of the age of witch-burning, and bigotry and discrimination were ever popular sports: for most of the population starvation was an ever-present threat. I could continue at length. It's the world that bequeathed us the adjective "Dickensian", that gave us a fully worked example of the evils of a libertarian minarchist state, and that provoked Marx to write his great consolatory fantasy epic, *The Communist Manifesto*. It's the world that gave birth to the horrors of the Modern, and to the mass movements that built pyramids of skulls to mark the triumph of the will. It was a vile, oppressive, poverty-stricken and debased world *and we should shed no tears for its passing* (or the passing of that which came next).[138]

Perhaps no clearer index of such historical displacement/repression lies in the fact that the Victoriaphilic genre is, at least in its foundational expressions, the provenance of almost exclusively North American writers, though British voices have in more recent years also contributed – some, like Alan Moore's *League of Extraordinary Gentlemen* comics series, even delineating the subgenre's not inconsiderable potential for engaging a post-imperial crisis of British cultural and political identity and for measuring the contours of the previous century's imperial machinery against that of its more recent global incarnation.

Apologists of this enduringly and increasingly popular aesthetic point, however, to steampunk's strategic play of temporal juxtaposition and jarring anachronism as a clear sign of its contestatory attitude toward conventional (western, capitalist) narratives of progress. In a recent attempt to reclaim steampunk from the imputations of what seems a scholarly consensus regarding its feeble capacity for critical historicity, Margaret Rose suggests that we might rather

> look at steampunk as speculative fiction's revenge against such arguments, because steampunk is a fiction that places a premium on minutely accurate historical detail, within flamboyantly wrong imagined pasts, in order to explore the ways in which the conventional historical sensibility sometimes gets it wrong.[139]

The playful historical manipulation that we find in such works is not, Rose contends, the symptom of a reified or alienated historicity but rather a technical means to "explore the intersections and limitations of the various textual ways in which we access [history]."[140] Yet, even in the analysis of Rose's selected texts, we find no engagement with *material* history as such, but only the familiar postmodern emphasis on the complexity of historical narrativization and overdetermination and a suspicious regard for *all* expression bearing the mark of progressivism: "As often as not in steampunk, dreams of progress, both scientific and social, are revealed as dangerous drives to impose one's own order on others."[141] Offering James Morrow's dystopic steampunk story "Lady Witherspoon's Solution" as an exemplar of the genre's critical historicity, Rose suggests that the story presents us with a "most outrageous example" of a group of "feminist vigilantes" (The Hampstead Ladies' Croquet Club and Benevolent Society), who chemically devolve their erstwhile male oppressors into simian subhumans, who are forced to fight for the ladies' entertainment before being castrated and exiled from the female enclave. Critically revisiting the racializing tropes of Victorian social Darwinism, the story ultimately admonishes the reader against what Rose describes as "the potential for tyranny underlying the most benevolent of social projects."[142] Yet this explanation provides a rather incomplete accounting of the ways that Morrow's fiction engages its present; for while racism can hardly be said to have been eradicated in the twenty-first century, it certainly no longer comes draped in the antediluvian rhetoric of Darwinian theory (however misappropriated) – the latter now appearing in the current climate of anti-intellectualism rather as the blazon of social liberalism and enlightened toleration. That leaves us, then, with the work's primary theme, one that Rose's generous reading of the text conspicuously fails to countenance: its pronounced anxiety over feminism itself and, somewhat more damning, its reactionary extrapolation of a feminist politics into dystopian nightmare. That is, by resurrecting the obsolescent discursive strategies of a previous century's racism and ascribing it, however indirectly, to feminist politics as such, Morrow's story stimulates (at least in Rose's recounting of it) contemporary tolerationist attitudes and mobilizes them toward the foreclosure of progressive essays in the present. In both its artful circumvention of material history and its disregard for and indiscriminate assimilation of all forms of social progress, to say nothing of its fetishization of technology, steampunk therefore presents us, in the main, with an all too familiar cynicism narcissistically seeking its reflection in the imperial splendor of a bygone century, anxiously cathecting the energies of today's ever more precarious and diffuse imperial ambitions within a fantastical dominion on which the sun never need set.

Yet if western steampunk writers are, however tentatively or fitfully, already discerning ways in which the temporal and technical conjunctures of the form yield productive historicizations for and of the present, emergent voices like expatriate Grenadan writer Tobias Buckell offer signs of the genre's far from exhausted capacity to intervene in the problem of contemporary history from the latter's occluded or obverse side. In an ambivalent response to Stross' trenchant critique, Buckell concedes the ideological and representational hazards of steampunk while nevertheless reserving a measure of hope for the genre's critical potential:

> But ultimately, I share Stross's discomfort, which is why my steampunk plays have often been about adopting the style and nodding to the history. *Crystal Rain*, what I called a Caribbean steampunk novel, is about Caribbean peoples and the reconstituted Mexica (Azteca in the book) of old with a Victorian level of technology, using the clothing/symbols of steampunk, but making their artificiers black.[143]

Far from foregoing the material contexts and historical impedimenta that conventional steampunk romantically and stylishly evades, Buckell's "nod" to history serves, I want to suggest, much the same function as Chakrabarty's strategic provincialization of Europe. Deploying the familiar set pieces of generic standard, Buckell radically revises steampunk by relocating its geo-temporal coordinates from a first-world past to a third-world future, a structural inversion that transfigures the encumbering history casually shed by the former into the engrossing utopian destiny of the latter.

In *Crystal Rain* (2006), the inaugural installment of what will grow into the richly complex and ongoing "Xenowealth" series, Buckell introduces us to the planet of New Anagada or Nanagada (named for Anegada, "the drowned land," second largest of the British Virgin Islands). Having been colonized hundreds of years earlier by Antillean settlers from Earth (the "old-fathers"), who came through a wormhole seeking the solace of a new world in the mass exodus following what is cryptically described as the pacification of Earth, Nanagada is located at the terminus of the now-dead wormhole and, incompletely terraformed and stripped of an advanced technology now lost to living memory, has been isolated from the intergalactic network for more than 300 years.[144] Of this history, only vaguely folkloric traces remain:

> A long time ago, all we old-father them had work on a cold world with no ocean or palm tree. It was far, far from this world. It was far, far from them own world, call Earth! They had toil for Babylon. In return, Babylon oppress many people. And eventually them Babylon-oppress people ran away looking for a new world, a world far away from any other world so they could be left alone.[145]

Pursued into this new world by a tyrannical alien race, the *Teotl*, the humans send their warriors, the ragamuffins, to destroy the wormhole and thus prevent future invasions. While subsequent books in the series will gradually unfold a complex allegory of empire and resistance within the vertiginous, multidimensional flux of an interstellar space honeycombed with wormholes (in which the kingdoms of freedom and necessity, first worlds and third become ever more entangled and difficult to distinguish), *Crystal Rain* opens onto this "backwater" world, where the tether to such large-scale intrigues has apparently been severed and where history has long ceased to exist.

Indeed, the primary theme of the novel, as well as its foremost element of plot, is the painstaking rehabilitation of this lost spatiohistorical orientation. The only habitable portion of the planet consists of a wide, tapering peninsula divided from the mainland by the Wicked High Mountains north of which dwell the pan-Caribbean Nanagadans and south of which dwell the mysterious Azteca of Aztlan (the name for pre-Columbian Mexico taken up recently by Chicano nationlists), the latter a bellicose people under the tyrannical yoke of the bloodthirsty Teotl, the "gods" who live among them. Their lives extended by now-lost nanotechnology, the few remaining old-fathers remember, however, that the Teotl are not gods, but the remnant of an alien race with superior technology that still plot to enslave the planet and extract its resources. That is, those few secretly remaining old-fathers (still in possession of a now obscured history) know the broader contexts that inform a seemingly local conflict otherwise subject to a mystifying naturalization; the Azteca, it is believed in Nanagada, are both culturally and congenitally predisposed to violence. Yet Nanagada, too, is home to an alien race, the loa, revered by some as gods, who also intervene in the political affairs of the planet, albeit in a more obscurantist fashion than the Teotl. Thus, the two cultures uneasily coexist – in a fragment of a world seemingly cut off from the intergalactic imperial network, pawns in a war between the inscrutable alien interests that author their mutual realities – until the Azteca tunnel, secretly under construction for more than three centuries, is finally completed and full-scale invasion of Nanagada begins, history's return, as always, assuming the form of an acute punctum.

Among the first to fall to the Azteca *macuahuitl* is the coastal fishing village of Brungstun, home to John deBrun, a Nanagadan hero who some years before led an ill-fated expedition north, beyond the terraformed frontier of the peninsula, to seek out habitable land and to recover fragments of the legendary technologies of the old-fathers. Most of the expedition was lost and deBrun deprived of his left hand. Dragged ashore in Brungstun 27 years earlier with nothing save a silver pendant upon which his name is inscribed, deBrun remains in the village and works on sailboats in hopes that his memories will soon return. The restoration of deBrun's memory provides the characterological ballast for the novel's more comprehensive project of rehistoricism, for through deBrun's quest the novel undertakes an explicitly cartographic operation that recontextualizes local conflict in the world of Nanagada relative to the ongoing struggle of which it has always been, however unwittingly, entangled. It is therefore not insignificant that among the first intimations of deBrun's suppressed history is his inexplicable talent for what can only be called cognitive mapping. He discovers that despite his clear lack of experience in gauging tides and winds, he "could picture maps in his head as if they were before him. He could navigate by stars, sun, map, and with his eyes closed."[146] It is largely this talent that earns him the position as chief navigator on the tragic expedition north, the infamy of which makes John deBrun a reluctant legend throughout Nanagada. While his memories never return, his mapping ability remains, and he finds that he can, with practice, exercise fine control over its various functions. Delicately navigating the labyrinthine banks of deadly reefline that protect Salt Island, home to the "Frenchies," deBrun projects a "mental map" of the area: "Sharp, clear, and in his mind's eye he could rotate it around to examine it from different directions."[147] When the Azteca invasion separates him from his family and entrusts him to the care of the treacherous Azteca double-agent Oaxyctl – charged with the extraction from deBrun's repressed memory the access codes to a quasi-mythic machine of the old-fathers, the *Ma Wi Jung* – deBrun's cognitive mapping abilities allow them to circumnavigate trouble and to arrive safely in the northern citadel of Capitol City. From the besieged city, a second northern expedition is launched to recover the *Ma Wi Jung*, believed by Nanagadan historians, the Preservationists, to be a weapon powerful enough to turn back the Azteca forces. Given his history in the north and his unparalleled navigational talents, deBrun is tapped to lead it.

It is this last, desperate northern campaign that reveals to deBrun both his true identity and the conflict that defines Nanagadan reality. Encountering the deadly and mysterious warrior Pepper, who claims a familiarity with him from his period of lost memory, deBrun gradually accepts a dimly understood role in an even less intelligible struggle until, almost upon the point of death, he finds the site of the long-buried *Ma Wi Jung*, an interstellar ship of the ancestors that bears within it the secret of deBrun's identity as well as the lost history of Nanagada. Physically and mentally restored by the ship's interface with his own nanotech, deBrun discovers that he is one of the old-fathers, a pilot who helped enact the scorched earth closure of the wormhole and the self-sabotaging of Nanagadan technology in an effort to forestall the advancing Teotl. Trapped by the EMP blast in a slowly decaying orbit for hundreds of years, deBrun's nano-enhanced mind erected strategic cerebral firewalls to prevent complete insanity. When his ship finally breached the atmosphere and crashed into the sea, he was washed ashore and cultivated a private life of domestic satisfaction distinct from the *public* strife and devoid of the evident political stakes of his former existence.

In fact, it is the narrow ethos of individuated domesticity, as Vandana Singh readily demonstrates in her short fiction, that presents the greatest obstruction to the enlargement and repoliticization of deBrun's parochial worldview and thus to the retrieval of a personal history that is also inextricable from a collective one. But even the benumbing consolations of family cannot long forefend the inevitable and ruptural return of this repressed history, the "alienating necessities" of which,

Jameson famously reminds us, "will not forget us, however much we might prefer to ignore them."[148] Separated from his wife and son during the Azteca attack on Brunstun, deBrun's primary motivation throughout the novel is to have his family restored, this despite all evidence that they were likely killed in the invasion. However, as his expedition to seek the *Ma Wi Jung* approaches the fraught and mysterious north, an "alien land where the horizon never ended and the land constantly shifted and broke over itself," long-forgotten nightmares intrude upon this fortifying domestic vision:

> Alien world. That impression bubbled right up through John's subconscious. It was one of many different images and feelings that had been surfacing since the voyage started. He resented them, though. He had been trying to hold pictures of Shanta and Jerome in his head. The weird feelings stirring in his gut scared him.[149]

Much to deBrun's horror and despite his every conscious effort, he finds that "[e]very night the memories of Shanta and Jerome grew softer, shattered by the still-striking nightmares of images that had once haunted him before his family had come to him."[150] The most prominent of these haunting visions (threatening to crowd out his fading recollection of domestic contentment) is the image of a "spiked egg dripping water."[151] Recurring with increasing frequency and intensity as deBrun approaches the site of the sunken *Ma Wi Jung*, this obscure vision of the impaled egg, even prior to the revelation of its literal referent, figures the punctual violence that is the return to history and the resuscitation of political possibility in the leaden present. More literally, it recalls deBrun's 271-year imprisonment in the oviform space-pod and its eventual fiery crash into the sea, the final act in the traumatic sequence that sealed his memory and left him ensconced in the domestic pleasures of the alienated present. Most crucially, once he has assented to his true identity as one of the original ragamuffins, as a resistance fighter, deBrun finds that it need not displace his role as father and husband after all, that the former in fact complements and deepens the experience of the latter once it is freed from its enervating ideological bondage. In fact, the novel concludes with John's promise that once he has seen to his badly shaken son (with whom he has reunited) and once the *Ma Wi Jung* has been given sufficient time to repair itself, he will rejoin Pepper in the fight against the Teotl, though the battle, crucially, will no longer be for Nanagada alone, as he warns: "If we don't get help, if we don't warn other worlds, the Teotl will wash over all the worlds like a tide."[152] Thus, the novel ends with the symbolic evocation of a transnational solidarity and with the return to a properly global resistance against a foe that cultural nationalism and formal independence was once believed to have slain.

Buckell's subsequent novels, taking leave of the generic conventions of steampunk, pursue the broader implications of such an interplanetary (and intergalactic) struggle and thereby undertake a mapping of the spatial complexities and ideological complicities that characterize the unique problematic of globalization. Buckell, then, despite his ambivalent subject position as a white expatriate Grenadan writer of popular SF now living in the United States, re-encumbers steampunk with the terrific freight of historical remembrance, thereby activating the form's utopian formal possibilities and directing its creative energies from a vague imperial nostalgia to a trenchant critique of the new empire, from willed amnesia to impassioned remembrance, which, as Marcuse writes, is simply that utopian mode of historical reason that "recalls the terror and the hope that passed."[153] In squarely confronting the continued presence of the former, Buckell restores to steampunk, as Beukes to cyberpunk, the immanent potentialities of the latter, actualizing the admonitory promise of the lyric that Gibson once briefly considered as the epigraph for *Neuromancer*: "Watch out for the worlds behind you."[154]

Conclusion: Reimagining the Material

Thus, the "punk" variants of Beukes and Buckell, making good on Brooks Landon's claim that "[e]ven before it arrived, sparking and smoking like a cartoon anarchist's bowling ball bomb, cyberpunk fiction was headed somewhere else,"[1] can also offer considerable insight into the complexities and contradictions of the wider field of postcolonial science fiction (SF) itself. Despite their mutual limitations, both the white writer of South Africa and Grenada and the (typically) cosmopolitan writer of postcolonial SF summon the critical resources at hand, however partial or compromised, however imbricated within the cognitive and cultural architectures of hegemony, to illuminate and engage the brute necessities of the present. For despite claims such as Jameson's of the genre's relative marginalization in the West (claims which can perhaps no longer reasonably be sustained), SF's canonical thematics speak to an undeniably privileged access to a technorational and telecommunicational lexicon as well as a cache of cultural codes and imaginative resources strictly unavailable to the great majority of the global populace. Nonetheless, inasmuch as SF is uniquely endowed with the dialectical formal facilities commensurate to the reckoning of globalization's novel and emergent realities, postcolonial science fictions like those of Beukes, Buckell, and the other artists featured here might be said to realize the promise of SF not only as an historical genre but as a critical and utopian mode of thought as praxis. Announcing a decisive shift in register in a cosmopolitan "postcolonial" literature long privileged for a doctrinaire renunciation of the grand narratives of liberation and resistance as much as for a compulsive celebration of exile and hybridity, incommensurability and ambivalence, these works reclaim and revitalize the critical dialecticism of modernity's unfinished project and resume the radical and anti-essentialist labor of the third-world intellectual as once described by Edward Said.[2]

Positing the continuing existence and enduring relevance of those "grand narratives of emancipation and enlightenment" first articulated by pioneering thinkers like C.L.R. James, Samir Amin, and Anwar Abdel-Malek, Said suggests in 1995 that they are "at present in abeyance, deferred, or circumvented" through the dehistoricizing influence of a postmodernism that had assumed a well-nigh hegemonic status in postcolonial studies.[3] As he writes, "This crucial difference between the urgent historical and political imperatives of post-colonial and post-modernism's relative detachments makes for altogether different approaches and results"; invoking the historicizing vocation of the modernist artist (he specifically cites Pablo Neruda and Picasso), Said observes that the pressing task for such intellectuals is "explicitly to universalize the crisis, to give greater human scope to what a particular race or nation suffered, to associate that experience with the sufferings of others."[4] Such a totalizing exercise, bearing a close affinity with what Jameson calls transcoding, does not entail the abandonment of historical specificity so much as it "guards against the possibility that a lesson learned about oppression in one place will be forgotten or violated in another place or time."[5]

Exceeding the narrow determinations of geolinear space-time and mapping new ontologies sensitive to the discernment of the properly science fictional realities of denationalization and of the third worlds that now exist in the first as well as the first worlds that now exist in the third, postcolonial SF undertakes the urgent and totalizing recovery of what Neil Lazarus describes as postcolonial writing's "materialist heartbeat."[6] Postcolonial SF is, in this sense, simply "the attempt to think a material thought" within the alienating enclosures of global capital on the one hand and the corollary aestheticization of the political on the other.[7] The texts treated here, however selectively and partially, suggest a coherent materialist imaginative project, the scope of which has yet to be measured and the future of which is emphatically now.

Notes

Introduction: The Desire Called Postcolonial Science Fiction

1. J. Díaz (2007) *The Brief Wondrous Life of Oscar Wao* (New York: Riverhead), p. 6.
2. Perhaps the earliest book-length commentary on the genre's preoccupation with imperial themes is James Osler Bailey's *Pilgrims Through Space and Time: Trends and Patterns in Scientific and Utopian Fiction* (1947) in honor of which the Science Fiction Research Association named its Pilgrim Award for lifetime scholarly achievement. A more recent example of this line of inquiry is Patricia Kerslake's *Science Fiction and Empire* (2007).
3. J. Reider (2008) *Colonialism and the Emergence of Science Fiction* (Middletown: Wesleyan University Press), p. 3.
4. P. Kerslake (2007) *Science Fiction and Empire* (Liverpool: Liverpool University Press), p. 191.
5. I. Csicsery-Ronay (2002) "Dis-Imagined Communities: Science Fiction and the Future of Nations," *Edging into the Future: Science Fiction and Contemporary Cultural Transformation*, Eds. Veronica Hollinger and Joan Gordon (Philadelphia: University of Pennsylvania Press), pp. 215–37 (p. 231).
6. Reider, *Colonialism and the Emergence of Science Fiction*, p. 10.
7. C. Freedman (2000) *Critical Theory and Science Fiction* (Hanover, NH: Wesleyan), p. 17.
8. Ibid., p. 18.
9. Ibid., p. 20.
10. D. Suvin (1979) *Metamorphoses of Science Fiction* (New Haven: Yale University Press), p. 9.
11. Freedman, *Critical Theory*, p. 27.
12. Ibid., pp. 27–8.
13. Ibid., p. 40.
14. Ibid.
15. Ibid., p. 86.
16. F. Jameson (1971) *Marxism and Form: Twentieth-Century Dialectcal Theories of Literature* (Princeton: Princeton University Press), pp. 6, 8.
17. Ibid., p. 45.
18. D. Suvin (1994) "On Cognitive Emotions and Topological Imagination," *Versus*, LXVIII, 165–201 (191).
19. Csicsery-Ronay, "Dis-Imagined Communities", p. 237.
20. Ibid., p. 237.
21. Ibid., p. 218.
22. N. Hopkinson (2004) *So Long Been Dreaming: Postcolonial Science Fiction* (Vancouver: Arsenal), p. 9.
23. I. McDonald (2010) "Interview with Ian McDonald," SFFWorld.com, http://www.sffworld.com/interview/210p1.html, date accessed June 15, 2010.
24. Freedman, *Critical Theory*, pp. 48–9.
25. Ibid., p. 49.

26. Ibid.
27. F. Jameson (2005) *Archaeologies of the Future: The Desire Called Utopia and Other Science Fictions* (New York: Verso), p. 284.
28. Ibid., p. 284.
29. Ibid., pp. 285–6.
30. Ibid., p. 289.
31. F. Jameson (2002) *A Singular Modernity: Essay on the Ontology of the Present* (London: Verso), p. 159.
32. Ibid., pp. 180, 215.
33. Ibid., p. 215.
34. P.E. Wegner (2007) "Jameson's Modernisms; or, the Desire Called Utopia," *Diacritics*, XXXVII, Number 4, 2–20 (7).
35. Ibid., pp. 8, 9.
36. Ibid., p. 9.
37. A. Carpentier (1949) "On the Marvelous Real in America," *Magical Realism: Theory, History, Community* (Durham: Duke University Press, 1995), pp. 75–88 (p. 88).
38. Ibid., pp. 84–5.
39. Ibid., pp. 85–6.
40. F. Jameson (1986) "On Magic Realism in Film," *Critical Inquiry*, XII, p. 311.
41. Ibid.
42. D. Cooper (1998) *Magical Realism in West African Fiction: Seeing with a Third Eye* (New York: Routledge), p. 1.
43. M. Denning (2004) *Culture in the Age of Three Worlds* (London: Verso), p. 51.
44. See also C. *Miéville (2009) "Afterword: Cognition as Ideology: A Dialectic of SF Theory," Red Planets: Marxism and Science Fiction. Eds. Mark Bould and China Miéville* (Middletown, CT: Wesleyan), pp. 231–48.
45. J. Rieder (2010) "On Defining SF, or Not: Genre Theory, SF, and History," *Science Fiction Studies*, XXXVII, p. 193.
46. Ibid., p. 206.
47. I follow here Suvin's influential claim that "utopia is not a genre but the *sociopolitical subgenre of science fiction*" (*Metamorphoses*, p. 61).
48. R. Pordzik (2001) *The Quest for Postcolonial Utopia: A Comparative Introduction to the Utopian Novel in New English Literatures* (New York: Lang), pp. 149, 168. While several significant new studies have emerged, none have offered a comprehensive theorization of the form as I attempt it here. Nicholas Brown's *Utopian Generations: The Political Horizons of Twentieth Century Literature* (Princeton, NJ: Princeton University Press, 2005) uses the field of utopia to map the dialectical interrelation of British modernist and postcolonial African literary production; Amy J. Ransom's *Science Fictions from Quebec: A Postcolonial Study* (Jefferson, NC: McFarland, 2009), a regionally oriented examination of specifically francophone SF production, effectively establishes the validity of postcolonial analytic approaches to such works, but attempts no broader historicization; while the more recent essay collection edited by Ericka Hoagland and Reema Sarwal extends its foci to include postcolonial perspectives on canonical western SF writers like Heinlein and Butler. See E. Hoagland and R. Sarwal (eds) (2010) *Science Fiction, Imperialism and the Third World: Essays on Postcolonial Science Fiction* (Jefferson, NC: McFarland).
49. Ibid., p. 4.

50. Ibid., pp. 29, 9.
51. T. Moylan (2002) "Utopia, the Postcolonial, and the Postmodern," *Science Fiction Studies*, XXIX, 265–271 (267).
52. E. Hoagland and R. Sarwal (2010) *Science Fiction, Imperialism and the Third World: Essays on Postcolonial Literature and Film* (Jefferson, NC: Mcfarland), pp. 5–19 (p. 7).
53. Ibid., p. 8.
54. Ibid., pp. 9–10.
55. Ibid., p. 13.
56. Ibid., p. 14.
57. Ibid., p. 15.
58. N. Lazarus (2011) *The Postcolonial Unconscious* (New York: Cambridge University Press), p. 99.
59. Hoagland and Sarwal, *Science Fiction*, p. 10.
60. J. Langer (2011) *Postcolonial Science Fiction* (New York: Palgrave).
61. Lazarus, *The Postcolonial Unconscious*, p. 9.
62. N. Larsen (2005) "Imperialism, Colonialism, Postcolonialism," *A Companion to Postcolonial Studies*. Eds. H. Schwarz and S. Ray (Oxford: Blackwell), pp. 23–52 (p. 24).
63. Lazarus, *The Postcolonial Unconscious*, p. 106.
64. Ibid., p. 106.
65. F. Jameson (1992) *The Geopolitical Aesthetic: Cinema and Space in the World System* (Bloomington: Indiana University Press), p. 199.
66. D. Harvey (2000) *Spaces of Hope* (Berkeley, CA: University of California Press), p. 57.
67. For more on globalization as "denationalization," see S. Sassen (2006) *Territory, Authority, Rights: From Medieval to Global Assemblages* (Princeton, NJ: Princeton University Press).
68. Jameson, *Archaeologies*, pp. 312–13.
69. Harvey, *Spaces of Hope*, p. 57.
70. A. Badiou (1982) *Theory of the Subject*. Trans. Bruno Bosteels (London: Continuum, 2009), p. 280.

1 "Fictions Where a Man Could Live": Worldlessness Against the Void in Salman Rushdie's *Grimus*

1. M. Syed (1994) "Warped Mythologies: Salman Rushdie's *Grimus*," *ARIEL*, XXV, 135–51 (148).
2. Ibid.
3. C. Cundy (1992) "Rehearsing Voices: Salman Rushdie's *Grimus*," *Journal of Commonwealth Literature* XXVII, 128–38 (128).
4. Ibid., p. 128.
5. Ibid., pp. 137, 129. Cundy further suggests that *Grimus* figures a merely "nascent and tentative study of migrant identity ... a chaotic fantasy with no immediately discernable arguments of any import" (p. 131). The novel's fantastical "voyage of discovery," she claims, ultimately "buckles under the weight of the different elements it seeks to assimilate" (p. 131). Similarly, in his study of Rushdie (*Salman Rushdie* [New York: Twayne, 1992]), James

Harrison gives this developmentalist account a curious nuptial twist by claiming that the reader who first encounters *Grimus* "after reading any or all of Rushdie's next three novels will, like a newly married couple exploring each other's family albums, recognize the early stages of what they are familiar with in the later version" (p. 33). Harrison further maintains that in *Grimus* Rushdie "has not yet found either the theme or the style that will allow him to be the writer he will in time become," that his first novel "lacks energy, stylistic assertiveness, and confidence in what it is attempting to be, but the potential for most such qualities is there" (pp. 33, 40). The arch skepticism of these readings of the early 1990s can be traced in each case to the groundbreaking analysis of Timothy Brennan's *Salman Rushdie & the Third World* (London: Macmillan, 1989), the first scholarly monograph on the author and the first critical treatment to sound a timely note of caution regarding his cosmopolitan appeals to a modernist/postmodernist aestheticism as well as his ability to speak to third-world interests. For Brennan, the singularly fatal flaw of *Grimus* is its refusal to ground its profoundly dialogic narrative innovations in a definite national culture:

> It would be hard to find a novel that demonstrated better the truth of Fanon's claim that a culture that is not national is meaningless. For if novels do not necessarily have to be set in one location, or be resistantly pure to foreign importations, they must be anchored in a coherent "structure of feeling," which only actual communities can create. ... *Grimus* fails even though it is carried off with professional brilliance simply because it lacks a *habitus*. (p. 70)

As a result *Grimus*, Brennan goes on to assert in an oft-quoted passage, "doesn't know where it is and 'tries on' cultures like used clothing" (p. 71). The problem thus seems to be that the polyphonic excesses of the novel's complex tropology cannot be sensibly interpreted within a postcolonial hermeneutic and its now familiar taxonomy of binaries. Indeed, as Brennan phrases it, "If the conflict between Third World peoples and European colonizers is evident here, it is carried out in terms so metaphorical as to be unrecognizable" (p. 71).

6. A. Teverson (2007) "From Science Fiction to History: *Grimus* and *Midnight's Children*," *Salman Rushdie*. Contemporary World Writers. Ed. John Thieme (Manchester: Manchester University Press), p. 112.
7. Ibid., p. 111.
8. Ibid., p. 116.
9. Ibid., p. 116.
10. Ibid., p. 120.
11. Rushdie, *Grimus*, p. 66.
12. Ibid., p. 66.
13. Ibid., p. 66.
14. Teverson, "From Science Fiction to History: *Grimus* and *Midnight's Children*," p. 120.
15. S. Rushdie (1975) *Grimus* (London: Vintage, 1996), p. 218.
16. Rushdie, *Grimus*, p. 65.
17. Ibid., p. 65.

18. Ibid., p. 65.
19. Ibid., p. 65.
20. A. Badiou (1988) *Being and Event*. Trans. Oliver Feltham (London: Continuum, 2006), p. 55.
21. A. Badiou (1982) *Theory of the Subject*. Trans. Bruno Bosteels (London: Continuum, 2009), pp. 202–3.
22. O. Feltham (2008) *Alain Badiou: Live Theory* (London: Continuum), p. 55.
23. For Badiou, the political subject is never an individual but rather a configuration of multiples situated around the Event on the void's horizon. As Feltham explains, Badiou's "subject is not so much an agent as a series of meetings, tracts, protests and occupations of parliament," in essence a subject-effect (p. 111). In this sense, Eagle is not himself a subject but rather an allegorical placeholder for a future subjectivity.
24. While Badiou later revises in *Being and Event* certain peripheral aspects of the argument first advanced in *Theory of the Subject*, particularly those concerning the link he initially posits between destruction and the emergence of the new, I retain here the concept of "divine violence" as a form of what Louis Marin terms the imaginative neutralization (or subtraction) of the existent order necessary for authentic utopian figuration.
25. Rushdie, *Grimus*, p. 211.
26. Ibid., p. 211.
27. Badiou, *Theory of the Subject*, p. 54.
28. A. Badiou (1998) *Metapolitics*. Trans. Jason Barker (London: Verso, 2005), pp. 59, 63. As Badiou writes, "there is no theory of the subject in Althusser, nor could there ever be one" (p. 59). There are instead "only processes," and the subject is merely a product of the interpellating mechanisms of the State (pp. 59, 63).
29. R. Y. Clark (2001) "*Grimus*: Worlds upon Worlds," *Stranger Gods: Salman Rushdie's Other Worlds* (Montreal: McGill-Queen's University Press), pp. 30–60.
30. Ibid., p. 60.
31. Ibid.
32. E. Bloch (1986) *The Principle of Hope*. Trans. Neville Plaice, Stephen Plaice, and Paul Knight. Vol. 1 (Cambridge: MIT Press), p. 203.
33. This is an important formal element in that the novel's first chapter recounts the rescue of Flapping Eagle by Virgil and Dolores after he has already washed ashore on Calf Island. The descriptions in chapter two of the "real" world that Eagle has left behind are thus already at one remove from the world of the primary action, formally sealing off his past for the reader as a kind of insubstantial dream reality.
34. Rushdie, *Grimus*, p. 16.
35. Ibid.
36. Ibid.
37. Ibid.
38. Ibid., p. 21. It is perhaps not incidental that his first steps into the broader world also rehearse the anti-tribal, universalizing impulses of modernization itself.
39. Ibid., p. 52.
40. Ibid.
41. Ibid., p. 70.
42. Ibid., pp. 100–1.

43. Ibid., p. 77.
44. Clark, "*Grimus*: Worlds upon Worlds," p. 57.
45. Rushdie, *Grimus*, p. 78.
46. Ibid., p. 78.
47. Ibid., p. 79.
48. Ibid., p. 82.
49. Ibid., p. 123.
50. Ibid., p. 146.
51. Ibid., p. 129.
52. Ibid., p. 44.
53. F. Jameson (1991) *Postmodernism, or, the Cultural Logic of Late Capitalism* (Durham, NC: Duke University Press), p. 10.
54. Rushdie, *Grimus*, p. 44.
55. Ibid., p. 57.
56. Ibid., p. 101.
57. Jameson, *Postmodernism*, p. 48.
58. Rushdie, *Grimus*, p. 130.
59. Ibid., p. 237.
60. Indeed, As Michael Hardt and Antonio Negri suggest, "[f]rom the perspective of the United States," Vietnam might be said to mark "the final moment in the imperialist tendency and thus a point of passage to a new regime of the Constitution," a transition, from another point of view, from the now "impassable" model of a coercive European imperialism to the flexible hegemony of Empire (*Empire* [Cambridge: Harvard University Press, 2000], p. 178). And as they go on to argue, the Vietnam War crystallized, from the US perspective, the global "accumulation of struggles" that formed the "virtual unity of the international proletariat" (pp. 262–3). And though this virtual global proletariat never achieved actual political manifestation, the undeniable pressures it exerted in its shared struggle against international capital – causing in fact the crises of the late 1960s and early 1970s themselves – catalyzed the transformation of capital into its current form (p. 276).
61. Badiou, *Theory of the Subject*, p. 30.
62. Rushdie, *Grimus*, p. 142.
63. Ibid., p. 142.
64. See A. Badiou (2000) *Saint Paul: The Foundation of Universalism* (London: Verso), and S. Žižek (2003) *The Fragile Absolute or, Why is the Christian Legacy Worth Fighting For?* (Stanford: Stanford Univesity Press).
65. Rushdie, *Grimus*, p. 142.
66. Ibid., pp. 148, 150.
67. Ibid., p. 150.
68. Ibid., p. 150.
69. S. Žižek, J. Butler, and E. Laclau. (2000) *Contingency, Hegemony, Universality* (London: Verso), pp. 324–5.
70. Ibid., p. 325.
71. Ibid.
72. Ibid.
73. Her name, in another coded inscription of Grimus's presence, replicates in Roman numerals his "always-age."
74. Rushdie, *Grimus*, p. 224.
75. Jameson, *Postmodernism*, p. 42

76. Ibid., p. 44.
77. Rushdie, *Grimus*, p. 241.
78. Ibid., p. 191.
79. Ibid., p. 242.
80. Ibid., p. 242.
81. Hardt and Negri, *Empire*, p. 255.
82. Ibid., p. 25.
83. Ibid.
84. Ibid., p. 186.
85. Rushdie, *Grimus*, p. 233.
86. Ibid., p. 240.
87. Ibid., p. 239.
88. Ibid., p. 236.
89. S. Žižek (2008) *Violence* (New York: Picador), p. 216.
90. Ibid., pp. 216–17.
91. Rushdie, *Grimus*, p. 251.
92. Ibid., p. 252.
93. Ibid., p. 253.
94. L. Marin (1984) *Utopics: The Semiological Play of Textual Spaces*. Trans. Robert A. Vollroth (Amherst, NY: Humanity Books), p. 14.
95. Ibid., p. 16.
96. Badiou, *Theory of the Subject*, p. 164.
97. U. Parameswaran (1994) "New Dimensions Courtesy of the Whirling Demons Word-Play in *Grimus*," *Reading Rushdie: Perspectives on the Fiction of Salman Rushdie*, Ed. M.D. Fletcher (Atlanta, GA: Rodopi), pp. 35–44 (p. 36).
98. Rushdie, *Grimus*, pp. 74–5.
99. In his account of the progression toward a critical historical consciousness in Rushdie's work, Teverson likens the mature writer of *Midnight's Children* to the Walter Scott of the Waverley novels. As he notes, the two share remarkable structural tendencies as well as respective commitments to "exploring periods of cultural transition that resulted from colonial (particularly English colonial) activities" (p. 127). In detailing these parallels, Teverson draws upon influential theorizations of the novel offered by Avrom Fleishmann and Harry Shaw. Only once, however, and on the essay's final page, does he reference the work to which each of these theorizations ultimately traces its derivation: Georg Lukács' magisterial *The Historical Novel* (1962). If, however, we are to take seriously Rushdie's speculative turn, we must acknowledge the re-discovery of Lukács' privileged historical novel beneath the cosmic raiment of narrative SF. For more on this important generic transition, see Jameson's influential discussion in *Archaeologies of the Future* (New York: Verso, 2005) or Carl Freedman's *Critical Theory and Science Fiction* (Hanover: Wesleyan University Press, 2000).

2 "The Only Way Out is Through": Spaces of Narrative and the Narrative of Space in Nalo Hopkinson's *Midnight Robber*

1. With regard to the planet's non-specific racial/cultural demographic, the novel evokes a familiar syncretic model for Toussaint's cultural identity: "Taino Carib and Arawak; African; Asian; Indian; even the Euro, though

some wasn't too happy to acknowledge that-there bloodline" (*Midnight Robber*, New York: Aspect, 2000, p. 18). Gauri Viswanathan reminds us, however, that this model of easy cultural fusion (as epitomized by the "All of We is One" and "Out of Many, One People" slogans of Trinidadian and Jamaican nationalisms) often belies its more conservative tendency toward the submersion of cultural difference and the concealment of struggle and inequality ((1995) "Beyond Orientalism: Syncretism and the Politics of Knowledge," *Stanford Humanities Review*, V, 19–32 (23–4).

2. Hopkinson makes this spatial/psychological homology occasionally explicit, as in the following passage: "No words to speak about Tan-Tan the Robber Queen. That was another self, another dimension" (p. 311).
3. Jameson, *Archaeologies*, p. 283.
4. Ibid., p. 23. Similarly, Louis Marin writes of this crucial utopian formal requirement: "But what is this 'outside,' this 'place out of place'? Where can we utter a discourse on discourse that would avoid becoming the object it critiques? From what point can we theorize its contradiction and think out, circumscribe, the circle that encircles?" (Marin, *Utopics*, p. 7).
5. One might question here again the homogenizing ahistoricism at work in the celebratory formulation of a syncretic pan-Caribbean culture.
6. Hopkinson, *Midnight Robber*, p. 314.
7. Ibid., p. 315.
8. N. Hopkinson (2000) "A Conversation With Nalo Hopkinson," SF Site, http://www.sfsite.com/03b/nh77.htm, date accessed June 26 2007.
9. M. Beaumont (2005) *Utopia Ltd: Ideologies of Social Dreaming in England 1870–1900* (Boston: Brill), p. 89.
10. Marin, *Utopics*, p. 239.
11. Ibid., p. 277.
12. Jameson, *The Geopolitical Aesthetic*, p. 32.
13. Jameson, *Archaeologies*, pp. 288–9.
14. I. Thaler (2010) *Black Atlantic Speculative Fictions: Octavia E. Butler, Jewelle Gomez, and Nalo Hopkinson* (New York: Routledge). pp. 101–2.
15. N. Hopkinson (2001) "A Dialogue on SF and Utopian Fiction, Between Nalo Hopkinson and Elisabeth Vonarburg", *Foundation*, LXXXI, 40–7 (47).
16. L.T. Sargent (1975) "Utopia – The Problem of Definition", *Extrapolation*, 137–48 (142).
17. G. Collier (2003) "Spaceship Creole: Nalo Hopkinson, Canadian-Caribbean Fabulist Fiction, and Linguistic/Cultural Syncretism," *A Pepper-Pot of Cultures: Aspects of Creolization in the Caribbean*, Eds. Gordon Collier and Ulrich Fleischmann (New York: Rodopi), p. 453.
18. Ibid., p. 453.
19. Ibid.
20. Ibid.
21. Marin, *Utopics*, p. 274.
22. Jameson, *The Geopolitical Aesthetic*, p. 1.
23. F. Jameson (1991) *Postmodernism, or, the Cultural Logic of Late Capitalism* (Durham, NC: Duke University Press), p. 15.
24. Jameson, *Archaeologies*, p. 286.
25. Ibid.
26. Ibid., p. 313.

27. F. Jameson (1988) "Cognitive Mapping," *Marxism and the Interpretation of Culture*, Eds. Cary Nelson and Lawrence Grossberg (Urbana: University of Illinois Press), pp. 347–60 (p. 347).
28. Jameson, *Archaeologies*, p. 287.
29. E. Bloch (1986) *The Principle of Hope*. Trans. Neville Plaice, Stephen Plaice, and Paul Knight, vol. 1 (Cambridge: MIT Press), p. 180.
30. P. Ricoeur (1986) *Lectures on Ideology and Utopia* (New York: Columbia University Press), p. 309.
31. Jameson, "Cognitive Mapping," p. 356.
32. F. Jameson (1986) "Third World Literature in the Era of Multinational Capitalism," *Social Text*, XV, 65–88 (76, 81).
33. Ibid., p. 81.
34. P.E. Wegner (2003) "Soldierboys for Peace: Cognitive Mapping, Space, and Science Fiction as World Bank Literature," *World Bank Literature*, Ed. Amitava Kumar (Minneapolis: University of Minnesota Press), p. 285.
35. Ibid., p. 285.
36. A. Ahmad (1987) "Jameson's Rhetoric of Otherness and the National Allegory," *Social Text*, 65–88 (9, 10).
37. Wegner, "Soldierboys," p. 286.
38. Jameson, *The Geopolitical Aesthetic*, pp. 3–4.
39. B. Clemente (2004) "Tan-Tan's Exile and Odyssey in Nalo Hopkinson's *Midnight Robber*," *Foundation*, XCI, 10–24. p. 15.
40. Ibid., p. 15. Interestingly, Pordzik's study is likewise preoccupied with contemporary postcolonial writers' "ongoing struggle of coming to terms with the legacy of their colonial past" and their efforts to "liberate themselves from Old World domination and the influence of its cognitive patterns" to the exclusion of a detailed engagement with their neocolonial present and the very contemporary struggles within the New World Order (pp. 20, 169). This insistent emphasis on the past functions as both a result of and a precondition for Pordzik's focus on aestheticism: "It can be said that it has been one of the major projects of the representatives of this literary culture to address the changes and problems involved in the transformation of their societies *first and foremost* in terms of a reappraisal of the literature associated with *the dominating value system imposed upon them by the colonizers/settlers a few centuries ago*" (p. 19, emphasis added).
41. Hopkinson, *Midnight Robber*, p. 74.
42. The creature is typically defined as the goblin spirit of a child who dies before being baptized. Its deployment in the novel thus recapitulates the infantilizing techniques of colonial discourse.
43. Clemente, "Tan Tan's Exile," p. 14.
44. S. Homer (2006) "Narratives of History, Narratives of Time," *On Jameson*, Eds. Caren Irr and Ian Buchanan (Albany: SUNY Press), p. 77.
45. Clemente, "Tan Tan's Exile," p. 15.
46. Hopkinson, *Midnight Robber*, p. 2.
47. For instance, the *official* historical narrative of Toussaint is that the peaceful Douen are "No longer in this existence" in order "To make Toussaint safe for the people from the nation ships" (p. 33).
48. Ibid., p. 33.
49. Ibid.
50. Ibid., p. 94.

51. Ibid., p. 2.
52. Ibid., p. 247.
53. S. Žižek (2008) *In Defense of Lost Causes* (New York: Verso), p. 288.
54. Hopkinson, *Midnight Robber*, p. 27.
55. S. Žižek (1989) *The Sublime Object of Ideology* (New York: Verso), p. 163.
56. One inevitably recalls here Althusser's famous definition of ideology as "the subject's *Imaginary* relationship to his or her *Real* conditions of existence" ((1971) *Lenin and Philosophy and Other Essays*. Trans. Ben Brewster (New York: Monthly Review). p. 162).
57. Žižek, *Sublime Object*, p. 164.
58. Hopkinson, *Midnight Robber*, pp. 2–3.
59. Bloch, *Principle of Hope*, p. 18.
60. Ibid., p. 13.
61. N. Hopkinson (2000) "Highlights of Bear_Benford Conversation," with Kurt Lancaster, Connie Willis, and Michael Burstein, MIT, http://web.mit.edu/m-i-t/science_fiction/transcripts/hopkinson_willis.htm, date accessed 26 June 2007.
62. See W. Earl's (2005) *Obi; or, The History of Three-Fingered Jack, 1800* (New York: Broadview).
63. K.M. Bilby (2005) *True-Born Maroons* (Gainesville: University Press of Florida). p. 309.
64. Ibid., pp. 308–9.
65. Clemente, "Tan Tan's Exile," p. 20.
66. Hopkinson, *Midnight Robber*, p. 206.
67. Bloch, *Principle of Hope*, pp. 308–9.
68. Hopkinson, *Midnight* Robber, p. 198. Emphasis added.
69. Ibid., p. 198.
70. Bloch, *Principle of Hope*, p. 223.
71. Hopkinson, *Midnight* Robber, p. 207.
72. Ibid., p. 211.
73. Ibid., p. 8.
74. Ibid., pp. 127, 124.
75. Ibid., p. 135.
76. Ibid.
77. Jameson, *Postmodernism*, p. 53.
78. S. Colas (1992) "The Third World in Jameson's *Postmodernism, or, the Cultural Logic of Late Capitalism*," *Social Text*, XXXI, 258–70 (258).
79. Quoted in S. L. Russell-Brown (2003) "Labor Rights as Human Rights: The Situation of Women Workers in Jamaica's Export Free Zones," *Berkeley Journal of Employment and Labor Law*, XXIV, 180–201 (182).
80. Ibid., p. 183.
81. (2001) *Life & Debt*, Dir. Stephanie Black, New Yorker.
82. P.E. Wegner (2002) *Imaginary Communities* (Berkeley: University of California Press), p. 76.
83. *Life and Debt.*
84. Ibid.
85. Russell-Brown, "Labor Rights," p. 180.
86. Y. Troeung (2007) "Disciplinary Power, Transnational Labour, and the Politics of Representation in Stephanie Black's *Life and Debt*," *Politics and Culture*, issue 2, http://www.politicsandculture.org, date accessed June 26 2007.
87. Ibid., np.

88. Ibid., np.
89. *Life and Debt.*
90. Troeung, np.
91. A. Kumar (1999) "World Bank Literature: A New Name for Post-Colonial Studies in the Next Century," *College Literature*, XXVI, 195–204 (197).
92. Hopkinson, *Midnight Robber*, p. 256.
93. M. Hardt and A. Negri. (2000) *Empire* (Cambridge: Harvard University Press), p. 393.
94. Ibid., p. 357.
95. Ibid., p. 357.
96. Ibid., p. 357.
97. Ibid., p. 362.
98. A. Badiou (2001) *Ethics: An Essay on Understanding Evil*. Trans. Peter Hallward (New York: Verso). pp. 82–3.

    For more on the implications of Badiou's thought for cultural studies, see Phillip Wegner's provocative essay "We're Family: Monstrous Kinships, Fidelity, and the Event in *Buffy the Vampire Slayer* and Octavia Butler's *Parable* Novels" in *Living Between Two Deaths: Periodizing US Culture, 1989–2001* (Durham, NC, Duke University Press, 2009).
99. Žižek, *In Defense*, p. 404.
100. While I have focused on the spatial dynamic of the economic free zones here, one might also read New Halfway Tree as a figuration of the growing global crisis of sprawling squatter communities outlying urban centers, what Robert Neuwirth calls "shadow cities," whose inhabitants now number one billion, a figure that is expected to double in the next 25 years. See chapter 5.
101. References are also made to workers in the "pleasure industry," though we receive no significant details about them other than the disturbing fact of their existence in this supposedly utopian society.
102. Hardt and Negri, *Empire*, p. 354.
103. Hopkinson, *Midnight Robber*, p. 8.
104. Ibid., p. 8.
105. Ibid., p. 298.
106. The word "Sou-Sou" refers both to a Jamaican savings scheme in which members of a co-operative contribute weekly or monthly to a pool of money that is then shared by each of the members in turn *and* to the secretive exchanging of information through whispers or gossip.
107. Ibid., p. 9.
108. Ibid.
109. Hardt and Negri, *Empire*, p. 299.
110. Hopkinson, *Midnight Robber*, p. 173.
111. Ibid., pp. 234–5.
112. Ibid., pp. 2–3.
113. Ibid., p. 328.
114. Ibid., p. 72.
115. Ibid., p. 329.
116. As Marin observes, "The space in which [utopia] will be born cannot be another space separated from worldly societies by an unbridgeable *no man's land*" (*Utopics*, p. 276).

117. Quoted in Marin, *Utopics*, p. 278.
118. Hopkinson, *Midnight Robber*, p. 71.
119. It is perhaps not insignificant that *Midnight Robber* was published in 2000, the same year that saw the publication of both Harvey's *Spaces of Hope* and Hardt and Negri's *Empire*.
120. Harvey, *Spaces of Hope*, p. 196.

3 There's No Splace Like Home: Domesticity, Difference, and the "Long Space" of Short Fiction in Vandana Singh's *The Woman Who Thought She Was a Planet*

1. V. Singh (2008) *The Woman Who Thought She Was a Planet* (New Delhi: Penguin), p. 18.
2. B. Anderson (1983) *Imagined Communities: Reflections on the Origin and Spread of Nationalism* (New York: Verso).
3. H. Bhabha (1994) *The Location of Culture* (New York: Routledge), p. 158.
4. Ibid., p. 159.
5. Singh, *The Woman*, p. 202.
6. Ibid., p. 201.
7. Ibid., p. 202.
8. Ibid., p. 201.
9. D. Wiemann (2008) *Genres of Modernity: Contemporary Indian Novels in English* (New York: Rodopi), p. 207.
10. Ibid., p. 212.
11. Ibid., pp. 291–2.
12. Wiemann refers here to Vikram Seth's phenomenally popular *A Suitable Boy* (1993) which replicates, however self-reflexively, "the dead idiom of nineteenth-century realism" (p. 158).
13. Ibid., p. 158.
14. M. Douglas (1991) "The Idea of Home: A Kind of Space," *Social Research*, LVIII, p. 296.
15. Singh, *The Woman*, p. 2.
16. H. Lefebvre (1991) *The Production of Space*. Trans. Donald Nicholson-Smith (Malden, MA: Blackwell), p. 49.
17. Ibid., p. 121. For more on the politically motivated nature of the apolitical home in a European context, see Nancy Armstrong's *Desire and Domestic Fiction: A Political History of the Novel* (New York: Oxford University Press, 1990).
18. Ibid., p. 232.
19. Ibid., p. 363.
20. See my discussion of Badiou's theory of the subject in Chapter 1.
21. P.E. Wegner (2002) "Spatial Criticism," *Introducing Criticism at the 21st Century*. Ed. Julian Wolfreys. 179–201.
22. Singh, *The Woman*, p. 2.
23. Ibid., p. 2.
24. Ibid., p. 4.
25. Ibid., p. 12.
26. Ibid., pp. 17–18.

27. Jameson, *Archaeologies*, p. 120.
28. I distinguish here between Spivak's influential critique of *worlding* as the narrativization or conceptual consolidation of a "Third World" from outside its own semiotic and material authority and the practice that Jean-Luc Nancy calls *mondialization*, of which he writes, "*To create the world* means: immediately, without delay, reopening each possible struggle for a world, that is, for what must form the contrary of a global injustice against the background of general equivalence" (Nancy p. 54). See G. Spivak (1985) "Three Women's Texts and a Critique of Imperialism," *Critical Inquiry*, XII, p. 243.
29. Singh, *The Woman*, p. 89.
30. Ibid., p. 90.
31. Ibid., p. 90.
32. Ibid., p. 90.
33. Ibid., p. 99.
34. Ibid., p. 99.
35. Ibid., p. 99.
36. Ibid., p. 93.
37. Ibid., p. 93.
38. Ibid., p. 93.
39. Ibid., p. 91.
40. Ibid., p. 92.
41. Ibid., p. 90.
42. Ibid., p. 103.
43. Ibid., p. 104.
44. Ibid., pp. 104, 106.
45. Ibid., p. 107.
46. I should note that correspondence with the author reveals that it was not her intention to suggest Susheela's erotic attachment to the gardener, nor are we to assume that he is one of the Naga with whom Susheela mates. I want to maintain, however, that there is sufficient textual evidence to support just such a misreading.
47. Ibid., p. 108.
48. S. Delany (1986) "Of Triton and Other Matters," *Science Fiction Studies*, XVII, 295–324. As Delany famously comments, "There's often a literal side to SF language. There are many strings of words that can appear both in an SF text and in an ordinary text of naturalistic fiction. But when they appear in a naturalistic text we interpret them one way, and when they appear in an SF text we interpret them another. Let me illustrate this by some examples I've used many times before. The phrase 'her world exploded' in a naturalistic text will be a metaphor for a female character's emotional state; but in an SF text, if you had the same words – 'her world exploded' – you'd have to maintain the possibility that they meant: a planet belonging to a woman blew up. Similarly the phrase, 'he turned on his left side.' In a naturalistic text, it would most probably refer to a man's insomniac tossings. But in an SF text the phrase might easily mean a male reached down and flipped the switch activating his sinestral flank. Or even that he attacked his left side. Often what happens with specifically SF language is that the most literal meaning is valorized" ("Of Triton and Other Matters" p. 296).
49. Singh, *The Woman*, p. 106.

50. The progressive logic that I suggest here – "Hunger" and "Thirst" as companion stories that build toward the triumphant departure of the title story – is not, at first glance, strictly supported by the book's sequencing, which actually positions the latter between the two former and separates them with one story on each side: thus, their actual sequence is "Hunger," "Delhi," "The Woman Who Thought She Was a Planet," "Infinities," and "Thirst." An email discussion with the author confirms, however, that she intentionally uncoupled stories with an obvious thematic continuity and disrupted identifiably developmental patterns: "My editor and I simply wanted to avoid immersing the reader in too many successive stories that were similar. We wanted to avoid a thematic sequence so that each reader could make their own. Which is why a particular story might represent an abrupt change in scene and style and character from the one preceding or following it. I also realized while putting the stories together that perhaps too many of them involved women transforming into non-humans. I didn't want this theme to become too obvious in case it obscured other connections and patterns." The text's refusal to sustain such trajectories of thematic continuity, when considered alongside the formal capacities and/or limits of the short story genre that Singh employs here, suggest implications other than (if not wholly unrelated to) the editorial aim of mitigating readerly boredom or the immiscibility of the collection's component themes.
51. Singh, *The Woman*, pp. 39–40.
52. Ibid., p. 40.
53. Ibid., p. 40.
54. P. Chatterjee (1993) *The Nation and its Fragments: Colonial and Postcolonial* italicize (Princeton: University of Princeton Press), p. 116.
55. Chatterjee, *The Nation*, p. 132.
56. Ibid., p. 120.
57. Ibid., p. 147.
58. Wiemann, *Genres of Modernity*, p. 206.
59. Singh, *The Woman*, p. 41.
60. Chatterjee, *The Nation*, p. 116.
61. Ibid., p. 127.
62. Ibid., p. 39.
63. Chatterjee, *The Nation*, p. 129.
64. Ibid., p. 129.
65. Singh, *The Woman*, p. 41.
66. Ibid., p. 53.
67. Ibid., p. 42.
68. See Chapter 4.
69. For a discussion of *oscillation* as a useful paradigm for a renewed materialism, see P. Hitchcock's (1999) *Oscillate Wildly: Space, Body, and Spirit of Millennial Materialism* (Minneapolis: University of Minnesota Press).
70. Singh., *The Woman*, p. 46.
71. Ibid., p. 47.
72. Ibid., p. 49.
73. Ibid.
74. Ibid.
75. Ibid., p. 50.

76. Ibid.
77. Ibid., p. 52.
78. Ibid., p. 53.
79. Ibid., p. 54.
80. Suparno Banerjee likewise notes in an unpublished essay Singh's "use of the monster metaphor" in her depictions of the alienated desires of "urban Indian lower middle class women." Also recognizing the important role of literality in Singh's fiction, he observes that this desire for "escape into a parallel dimension is simply a literalization of a very commonplace metaphor in the Indian context." See S. Banerjee, "Native Aliens: Narratives of Immigration in Vandana Singh's *Distances*," International Conference on Fantastic in the Arts, Orlando, FL, March, 2011.
81. Hardt and Negri, *Multitude*, p. 128.
82. Ibid., p. 252.
83. P. Hitchcock (2009) *The Long Space: Transnationalism and Postcolonial Form* (Stanford: Stanford University Press), p. 4.
84. Ibid., p. 8.
85. Ibid., p. 9.
86. Ibid., p. 29.
87. Specifically, he engages the novels of Wilson Harris, Nuruddin Farah, Pramoedya Ananta Toer, and Assia Djebar.
88. Ibid., p. 49.
89. K. Marx. (1871) "Address of the General Council of the International Working Men's Association on the Civil War in France, 1871," *Civil War in France: The Paris Commune* (New York: International, 1993), p. 59.
90. Ranjana Sengupta observes that "[m]ore than any other Indian metropolis, because of its lack of a single culture, because of its different masters, Delhi is a city that is simultaneously many things to many people. It continuously evolves, mutates and reinvents; different Delhis coexist alongside one another, often wildly disparate, even contradictory. Looking merely at the outward forms – architecture is one example – it is possible to see structures four hundred years apart, wall to wall with each other" (2007) *Delhi Metropolitan: The Making of an Unlikely City* (New Delhi: Penguin), p. 19. For an illuminating discussion of temporal palimpest in "Delhi," see G. Hamilton (2010) "Organization and the Continuum: History in Vandana Singh's 'Delhi,'" *Science Fiction, Imperialism and the Third World: Essays on Postcolonial Literature and Film*. Eds. Ericka Hoagland and Reema Sarwal (Jefferson, NC: McFarland), pp. 65–76.
91. Singh, *The Woman*, p. 20.
92. J. Derrida (1994) *Specters of Marx: The State of Debt, the Work of Mourning, and the New International*. Trans. Peggy Kamuf (New York: Routledge), p. xix.
93. Ibid., p. 22.
94. B. Anderson (1983) *Imagined Communities: Reflections on the Origin and Spread of Nationalism* (New York: Verso, 2006), p. 24.
95. Singh, *The Woman*, p. 22.
96. Ibid., p. 22.
97. Ibid., p. 23.
98. Derrida, *Specters*, p. 40.
99. W. Benjamin (1969) *Illuminations: Essays and Reflections* (New York: Schocken), p. 262.

100. Ibid., p. 261.
101. Singh, *The Woman*, p. 27.
102. Ibid., p. 26.
103. Ibid., p. 28.
104. Ibid.
105. Ibid., p. 31.
106. Ibid., p. 32.
107. Ibid.
108. Ibid., p. 33.
109. Ibid., p. 34.
110. Badiou, *Theory of the Subject*, pp. 262–3.
111. Singh, *The Woman*, p. 34.
112. Ibid.
113. Ibid., p. 37.
114. Ibid., p. 38.
115. Ibid., p. 38.
116. Ibid., p. 38.
117. R. Wilson and W. Dissanayake (1996) "Introduction," *Global/Local: Cultural Production and the Transnational Imaginary* (Durham: Duke University Press), p. 6. Similarly, Nancy argues that in the current epoch of globalization, "it is no longer possible to identify either the city or the orb of the world in general. The city spreads and extends all the way to the point where, while it tends to cover the entire orb of the planet, it loses its properties as a city ..." (*The Creation of the World*, p. 33).
118. Hitchcock, *Imaginary States*, p. 17.
119. Ibid., p. 21.
120. Jameson, *Archaeologies*, p. 293.
121. Singh, *The Woman*, p. 38.
122. Ibid., p. 23.
123. While I haven't the space here to discuss this marvelous story at length, it is worth briefly noting its relation to both "The Tetrahedron" and the transnationalist theme I've identified here. If "infinity is another name for multiplicity as such" (A. Badiou (2004) *Theoretical Writings*. Trans. Ray Brassier and Alberto Toscano [London: Continuum], p. 45), Singh's "Infinities" effects a striking figuration of just such a politics that, like Badiou's, relies on a "thesis of the identity of mathematics and ontology" (Badiou, *Being and Event*, p. 9). Abdul Karim, instructor of mathematics at a small municipal school, "has a secret, an obsession, a passion that makes him different": namely, "He wants to see infinity" (p. 57). Like Aseem, Abdul too has suffered a lifetime of hauntings, of phantoms that flicker just at the edges of his field of vision. Also like Aseem, Abdul woefully misrecognizes these sightings: "In his childhood, he had thought them to be *farishte*, angelic beings keeping a watch over him" (p. 57). The apparitions persist throughout Abdul's life, until, driven by his febrile obsession, he begins consulting them on their knowledge of infinite: "Is the Riemann Hypothesis true. ... Are prime numbers the key to understanding infinity?" (p. 60). While the *farishte* mostly maintain their silence or flit instantly out of sight when so accosted, "sometimes, a hint, a whisper of a voice that speaks in his mind" seems to offer an unintelligible response (p. 60). Eventually, amid

a traumatic discharge of communalist violence, the creatures usher Abdul through a transdimensional portal: "All at once it seems as though numberless eyes are opening in the sky, one after the other, and as he turns, he sees all the other universes flashing past him. A kaleidoscope, vast beyond his imaginings. He is at the center of it all, in a space between all spaces. ... Slowly, he realizes that what he is seeing and feeling is part of a vast pattern" (p. 79). Upon returning to his own reality, though, Abdul is overcome with grief and cynicism and loses fidelity to the event of the non-place. It is precisely in relation to Abdul's failure, I argue, that Maya's heroic subjectivization may productively be read in "The Tetrahedron."

124. Ibid., p. 139.
125. Ibid., p. 140.
126. Ibid., p. 140. Emphasis added.
127. Ibid., p. 140.
128. Ibid., p. 141.
129. Ibid., pp. 141–2, 145.
130. Ibid., p. 145.
131. Ibid., p. 148.
132. Ibid., p. 148.
133. Ibid., p. 148.
134. Ibid., p. 146.
135. Ibid., p. 144.
136. Ibid., p. 146.
137. Ibid., p. 146.
138. Ibid., p. 145.
139. Ibid., p. 152.
140. Badiou, *Theory of the Subject*, p. 210.
141. Ibid., p. 211.
142. Singh, *The Woman*, p. 153.
143. Ibid., p. 153.
144. Ibid., p. 154.
145. Comparing the spatial logic of globalization to that of State sovereignty, Nancy writes, "The 'reverse of empire' does not designate the destruction of the Empire as was the case in the past for the destruction of the State ... but the necessity of thinking both one and the other" (*The Creation of the World*, p. 108). In a footnote to this passage, he observes that the two must now be conceptualized as a "Moebius strip, each side of which passes incessantly into the other" (p. 125). Similarly, in the exposition of his theory of sovereignty Agamben writes that the state of nature and the state of exception must likewise be thought of as "two sides of a single topological process in which what was presupposed as external (the state of nature) now reappears as in a Möbius strip or a Leyden jar, in the inside (as state of exception), and the sovereign power is this very impossibility of distinguishing between inside and outside, nature and exception, *physis* and *nomos*" (*Homo Sacer*, p. 37).
146. Singh, *The Woman*, p. 154.
147. Ibid., p. 162.
148. Ibid., p. 158.
149. Ibid., p. 159.

150. Ibid., p. 150.
151. Ibid., p. 150.
152. Ibid., p. 161.
153. Ibid., p. 165.
154. Ibid., p. 165.
155. I use *transindividual* here specifically in the sense of Etienne Balibar's theory of the *transindividual subject*, whose constitution is statically neither individual nor collective, but one born in the imaginary as a dynamic oscillation between the two. See E. Balibar's *Politics and the Other Scene* (New York: Verso, 2002).
156. Singh, *The Woman*, p. 166.
157. Badiou, *Ethics*, p. 79.
158. Hitchcock, *Long Space*, p. 143.
159. Derrida, *Specters*, p. 85.
160. K. Marx "Contribution to the Critique of Hegel's Philosophy of Right," in T. Bottomore (ed.), *Karl Marx: Early Writings* (London: McGraw-Hill, 1963), p. 58.
161. Wilson and Dissanayake, *Global/Local*, p. 6.
162. Bloch, *The Principle of Hope*, pp. 1375–6.
163. Singh, *The Woman*, p. 203.
164. Nancy, *The Creation of the World*, pp. 42, 46.

4 Claiming the Futures That Are, or, The Cunning of History in Amitav Ghosh's *The Calcutta Chromosome* and Manjula Padmanabhan's "Gandhi-Toxin"

1. Chakrabarty, *Provincializing Europe*, p. 15.
2. Ibid., pp. 20–1.
3. Ibid., p. 2143.
4. Ibid., p. 250.
5. Ibid., p. 250.
6. Ibid., p. 251.
7. K. Marx (1976) "Preface to the 1867 Edition," *Capital: A Critique of Political Economy Vol. I* (Penguin: London), p. 91.
8. K. Marx (1978) "The Eighteenth Brumaire of Louis Bonaparte," In *The Marx–Engels Reader* 2nd edn. Ed. Robert C. Tucker (New York: Norton), p. 595.
9. Derrida discusses in similar terms Blanchot's identification of the irreducible internal "*disjunction* of Marx's languages, their non-contemporaneity with themselves" (*Specters of Marx*, pp. 33–4).
10. Chakrabarty, *Provincializing Europe*, pp. 65–6.
11. Ibid., p. 67.
12. Ibid., p. 68.
13. Hardt and Negri, *Commonwealth*, p. 120.
14. Ibid., p. 124.
15. Ibid., p. 264.
16. Hardt and Negri enlarge or extend the standard Foucauldian definition of biopolitics as the subjugation of human life to the state and its epistemic apparatuses by connecting the biopolitical production of subjectivities to

Marx's claim in the *Grundrisse* that within bourgeois society "there arise relations of circulation as well as of production which are so many mines to explode it" (K. Marx (1973) *Grundrisse*. Trans. Martin Nicolaus (New York: Vintage). p. 159). Biopolitics therefore emerges for Hardt and Negri as that which resists biopower (or the state regulation of life) from within.

17. Hardt and Negri, *Commonwealth*, p. 101.
18. Ibid., p. 104.
19. Ibid., p. 118.
20. Such a critique of the rationalist discourses of science is clearly central to the concerns of *The Calcutta Chromosome*, as many critics have noted. See, for example, D. Nelson (2003) "A Social Science Fiction of Fevers, Delirium, and Discovery: *The Calcutta Chromosome*, the Colonial Laboratory, and the Postcolonial New Human," *Science Fiction Studies* XXX, 246–66; H. Thompson (2009) "The Colonial City as Inverted Laboratory in Baumgartner's Bombay and *The Calcutta Chromosome*," *Journal of Narrative Theory* XXXIV, 347–68; and C. Shinn (2008) "On Machines and Mosquitoes: Neuroscience, Bodies, and Cyborgs in Amitav Ghosh's *The Calcutta Chromosome*," *Melus* XXXIII, 145–66.
21. Hardt and Negri, *Commonwealth*, p. 290.
22. Ibid., p. 242.
23. Ibid., p. 242.
24. Hardt and Negri, *Commonwealth*, p. 243.
25. A. Ghosh (1995) *The Calcutta Chromosome* (New York: Perennial), p. 7.
26. Chakrabarty does not himself identify this negative relation as dialectical, but I proffer it as such following the lead of Slavoj Žižek, who likewise identifies in Chakrabarty's recent elaboration of a "universal history" (one made possible by the global climate crisis) a disavowed dialectical dimension: "Perhaps the key to the limitations of Chakrabarty's position lies in his simplified notion of the Hegelian dialectic. Is the idea of a 'negative universal history' really anti-Hegelian? On the contrary, is the idea of a multiplicity (of humans) totalized (brought together) through a negative external limit (a threat) not Hegelian *par excellence* ?" (*Living in the End Times*, p. 335).
27. In fact, as we learn in the book's first paragraph, it is the incongruous rusty chain and not the ID card that has stalled Ava's inventory.
28. Ghosh, *The Calcutta Chromosome*, p. 10.
29. To avoid ambiguity, Bishnupriya Ghosh is henceforth referred to as "B. Ghosh."
30. B. Ghosh (2004) "On Grafting the Vernacular: The Consequences of Postcolonial Spectrology," *boundary 2*, XXXI, 197–218 (198).
31. Ibid., pp. 198–9.
32. Ibid., pp. 197, 209, 211.
33. Ibid., p. 217.
34. Ibid., p. 201.
35. S. Banerjee (2010) "*The Calcutta Chromosome*: A Novel of Silence, Slippage, and Subversion," *Science Fiction, Imperialism and the Third World: Essays on Postcolonial Literature and Film* (Jefferson, NC: McFarland), p. 50.
36. Ibid., pp. 211, 217.
37. S. Mathur (2004) "Caught Between the Goddess and the Cyborg: Third-World Women and the Politics of Science in Three Works of Indian Science Fiction," *Journal of Commonwealth Literature*, XXXIX, 119–38 (133).

38. Ibid., p. 133.
39. B. Romanik (2005) "Transforming the Colonial City: Science and the Practice of Dwelling in *The Calcutta Chromosome*," *Mosaic*, XXXVIII, 41–57 (41).
40. J. L. A. Fernandes (2007) *Challenging Euro-America's Politics of Identity: The Return of the Native* (New York: Routledge), p. 101.
41. Hardt and Negri, *Commonwealth*, pp. 267–8.
42. Ibid., p. 244.
43. Ghosh, *The Calcutta Chromosome*, p. 4.
44. Ibid., p. 5.
45. Hardt and Negri, *Commonwealth*, p. 140.
46. M. de Certeau (1984) *The Practice of Everyday Life* (Berkeley, CA: University of California Press), p. xxiv.
47. Ibid., pp. xxiii–xxiv.
48. Hardt and Negri, *Commonwealth*, p. 31.
49. Ghosh, *The Calcutta Chromosome*, p. 14.
50. Ibid., p. 14.
51. Ibid., p. 15.
52. Ibid., p. 14.
53. J.G. Halpin (2009) "Gift Unpossessed: Community as 'Gift' in *The Calcutta Chromosome*," *ARIEL: A Review of International English Literature*, XL, 23–40.
54. F. Jameson (2010) *Valences of the Dialectic* (London: Verso), p. 429.
55. E. Watkins (1993) *Throwaways: Work Culture and Consumer Education* (Stanford, CA: Stanford University Press), p. 44.
56. Ghosh, *The Calcutta Chromosome*, pp. 165–6.
57. Ibid., pp. 220–1.
58. Ibid., p. 221.
59. Ibid., p. 260.
60. Elsewhere, Žižek compares this state to that of the cartoon coyote who, pursuing his prey, looks down to find that he has run off the edge of a cliff. Suspended in mid-air only by the fantasmatic support of his former reality, the coyote plummets to the ground only after this change in his material circumstances registers at the level of the symbolic.
61. Žižek, *The Sublime Object of Ideology*, p. 135.
62. Fernandes, *Challenging Euro-America's Politics of Identity*, p. 127.
63. Ghosh, *The Calcutta Chromosome*, p. 256.
64. Ibid., p. 258.
65. Ibid., p. 261.
66. Ibid., p. 274.
67. Ibid., p. 280.
68. Ibid., pp. 281, 283.
69. Ibid., pp. 281–2.
70. See chapter 5 for a discussion of the postmodern megalopolis under globalization.
71. Mathur, "Caught Between the Goddess and the Cyborg," p. 245.
72. Fernandes, *Challenging Euro-America's Politics of Identity*, p. 129.
73. Jameson, *Valences of the Dialectic*, p. 23.
74. Hardt and Negri, *Commonwealth*, pp. 246–7.
75. Ibid., p. 250.
76. Žižek, *The Parallax View*, p. 269.

77. Ghosh, *The Calcutta Chromosome*, p. 107.
78. Fernandes, *Challenging Euro-America's Politics of Identity*, p. 101.
79. Ghosh, *The Calcutta Chromosome*, p 108.
80. Fernandes, *Challenging Euro-America's Politics of Identity*, p. 107.
81. Ibid., p. 108.
82. J. Thieme (2003) "The Discoverer Discovered: Amitav Ghosh's *The Calcutta Chromosome*," *Amitav Ghosh: A Critical Companion*. Ed. Tabish Khair (Delhi: Permanent Black), pp. 128–41 (p. 129).
83. G.W.F. Hegel (1837) *Introduction to the Philosophy of History*. Trans. J. Sibree. Google Books Search. January 15, 2011. p. 33.
84. Ibid., p. 33.
85. A. Ghosh (1995) *The Calcutta Chromosome* (New York: Perennial), p. 217.
86. K. Marx (2003) "The British Rule in India," *Archives of Empire: From the East India Company to the Suez Canal*. Eds. M. Carter and B. Harlow (Durham: Duke University Press), pp. 117–23 (pp. 122–3).
87. P. Chatterjee (1986) *Nationalist Thought and the Colonial World: A Derivative Discourse* (Mineapolis: University of Minnesota Press), p. 170. For an account of this important transition in Marx's thought, see Kevin B. Anderson's (2010) *Marx at the Margins: On Nationalism, Ethnicity, and Non-Western Societies* (Chicago: University of Chicago Press).
88. Ibid., p. 170.
89. Hegel, *Introduction to the Philosophy of History*, p. 34.
90. Ibid., p. 568; G.W.F. Hegel (1991) *Elements of the Philosophy of Right*. Ed. A.W. Wood. Trans. H.B. Nisbet (Cambridge, UK: Cambridge University Press), p. 279.
91. Jameson offers the following periodization of Hegel's thought: "But in Hegel's case I will merely claim that, after the *Phenomenology*, it is Hegel himself who, with the later collaboration of his disciples, produces something we may call Hegelianism, in contrast to that rich practice of dialectical thinking we find in the first great 1807 masterpiece. Such a distinction will help us to understand that virtually all the varied contemporary attacks on Hegel are in reality so many indictments of Hegelianism as a philosophy, or, what amounts to the same thing, as an ideology" (*Valences of the Dialectic*, p. 8).
92. Ghosh, *The Calcutta Chromosome*, p. 310.
93. Ibid., p. 310.
94. Ibid., p. 303.
95. Jameson, *Valences of the Dialectic*, p. 562.
96. Ghosh, *The Calcutta Chromosome*, pp. 310–11.
97. Ibid., p. 311.
98. Hardt and Negri, *Commonwealth*, p. 243.
99. Ibid., p. 152.
100. Ibid., pp. 152–3.
101. M. Padmanabhan (2004) *Kleptomania; Ten Stories* (New Delhi: Penguin), p. viii.
102. Ibid., pp. 95, 94.
103. Ibid., p. 96.
104. Ibid., p. 96.
105. Ibid., p. 97.

106. Ibid., p. 98.
107. Ibid., p. 98.
108. Ibid., p. 98.
109. Ghosh, *The Calcutta Chromosome*, p. 311.
110. Hegel, *Philosophy of History*, pp. 308–9.
111. L. Gandhi (2003) "'A Choice of Histories': Ghosh vs. Hegel in an Antique Land," *New Literatures Review*, X, 7–32 (17).
112. Ibid., p. 18.
113. Indeed, so far does her SF prologue wander from scholarly convention that Gandhi concludes the introductory narrative with what amounts to its immediate dismissal: "It is time for us to get serious, and the following essay will, seriously, entertain a reading of Amitav Ghosh's *In an Antique Land* as an implicit critique of Hegelian historicism" (p. 18).
114. I have elsewhere recommended that it might more productively be read as a novel. See E.D. Smith (2007) "'Caught Straddling a Border': A Novelistic Reading of Amitav Ghosh's *In an Antique Land*," *JNT: Journal of Narrative Theory* XXXVII, pp. 447–72.
115. Phillip Wegner explores the dialectical formal dynamics of this (Lacanian) practice of reading a term X *with* a term Y in his 2009 essay "Greimas avec Lacan; or, From the Symbolic to the Real in Dialectical Criticism," *Criticism*, LI, 211–45.
116. Hegel (1991) *Elements of the Philosophy of Right*. Trans. Allen Wood. Google Books Search. Feb. 2, 2011. p. 23.
117. Jameson, *Valences of the Dialectic*, p. 15.
118. Marx, "The Eighteenth Brumaire." p. 595.
119. S. Buck-Morss (2009) *Hegel, Haiti, and Universal History* (Pittsburgh: Pittsburgh University Press), p. 151.

5 Mob Zombies, Alien Nations, and Cities of the Undead: Monstrous Subjects and the Post-Millennial Nomos in *I am Legend* and *District 9*

1. T.P.R. Caldeira (2001) *City of Walls: Crime, Segregation, and Citizenship in São Paulo* (Berkeley: University of California Press), p. 4. The global nature of this phenomenon in fact moves us well beyond the "postcolonial" problematic and its debates and squarely into those of globalization, as Caldeira observes: "the fact that private and fortified enclaves are as much a feature of Los Angeles and Orange County as Sao Paulo and Johannesburg should prevent us from classifying the new model as characteristic of postcolonial societies" (p. 4).
2. M. Davis (2006) *Planet of Slums* (London: Verso), p. 15.
3. Caldeira, *City of Walls*, p. 1.
4. Ibid., p. 16.
5. Ibid., p. 331.
6. Le Corbusier (2008) *Towards a New Architecture*. Trans. John Goodman (Los Angeles: Getty), p. 176.
7. Quoted in J. Roberts (1995) "Melancholy Meanings: Architecture, Postmodernity, and Philosophy," *The Postmodern Arts: An Introductory Reader*. Ed. Nigel Wheale (New York: Routledge), p. 135.

8. Caldeira, *City of Walls*, p. 324.
9. Davis, *Planet of Slums*, p. 119.
10. Quoted in ibid., p. 120.
11. Estimates of the necropolis's inhabitants vary widely according to source, ranging from as low as 30,000 to as high as five million. Davis estimates the number of tomb dwellers at approximately one million (p. 33).
12. Ibid., p. 191.
13. G. Kovach (2003) "Out With the Trash? – Cairo's Legendary 'Garbage People' Threatened," *New America Media*. Pacific News Service. Date Accessed 25 February 2010.
14. Davis, *Planet of Slums*, p. 190.
15. Ibid., p. 190.
16. T. Harrison (1999) "Globalization and the Trade in Human Body Parts," *Canadian Review of Sociology and Anthropology*, XXXVI, 21–35 (22).
17. Ibid., p. 26.
18. Ibid.
19. Ibid., p. 27.
20. Ibid., p. 28.
21. Ibid., p. 31.
22. In a brief but evocative deployment of the zombie as an heuristic for rethinking international policy, Daniel W. Drezner recently characterizes the creatures as "one of the fastest-growing concerns in international relations;" due to their ability to "spread across borders and threaten states and civilizations," he writes, "these zombies should command the attention of scholars and policymakers" ((2010) "Night of the Living Wonks: Toward an International Relations Theory of Zombies," *Foreign Policy*. 24 Jul. 2010. np). Similarly, Henry Giroux uses the figure of the zombie to interrogate contemporary American political and economic practices in *Zombie Politics and Culture in the Age of Casino Capitalism* (New York: Peter Lang, 2010).
23. Davis, *Planet of Slums*, p. 196.
24. Ibid., p. 198.
25. J. Comaroff and J. Comaroff, (2002) "Alien-Nation: Zombies, Immigrants, and Millennial Capitalism," *South Atlantic Quarterly*, CI , 779–805 (789). They write, "There can be no denying the latter-day preoccupation with zombies in rural South Africa. ... In recent times, respectable local newspapers have carried banner headlines like '"Zombie" Back from the Dead,' illustrating their stories with conventional, high-realist photographs; similarly, defense lawyers in provincial courts have sought, by forensic means, to have clients acquitted of murder on grounds of having been driven to their deadly deeds by the zombification of their kin; and illicit zombie workers have become an issue in large-scale labor disputes. Public culture is replete with invocations of the living dead, from popular songs and prime-time documentaries to national theatrical productions. Not even the state has remained aloof. The Commission of Inquiry into Witchcraft Violence and Ritual Murders, appointed in 1995 by the Northern Province administration to investigate an 'epidemic' of occult violence, reported widespread fear of the figure of the zombie" (p. 787).
26. Ibid., p. 799.
27. Ibid., p. 789.
28. Ibid.

29. Ibid., p. 798.
30. Ibid., p. 799.
31. Hardt and Negri, *Commonwealth*, pp. 339–40.
32. The two previous adaptations of Matheson's novel are Ubaldo Ragona and Sidney Salkow's *The Last Man on Earth* (1964) starring Vincent Price and Boris Sagal's *The Omega Man* (1971) starring Charlton Heston. Žižek fleetingly observes the "ideological regression" that characterizes this series of adaptations and likewise notes the Vermont colony's recollection of the gated community ((2010) *Living in the End Times* (London: Verso), p. 64).
33. D.L. Pike (2008) "A Boy and His Dog: On Will Smith, Apocalypse, and *I am Legend*," *Bright Lights Film Journal*, LIX. Web. 7 February 2010. np.
34. Ibid., np.
35. M. McKeon (2000) "Generic Transformation and Social Change: Rethinking the Rise of the Novel," *Theory of the Novel: A Historical Approach*. Ed. Michael McKeon (Baltimore: Johns Hopkins University Press), p. 394.
36. One might propose a periodizing schema for the zombie film subgenre following that of the dialectically triadic formula elaborated in Fredric Jameson's *Signatures of the Visible*, with the realist moment of primitive accumulation represented by the 1932 Bela Lugosi vehicle *White Zombie*; the self-referential postmodernist moment represented by films like *Zombieland* or *Shaun of the Dead* (2004); and the intervening utopian moment of modernism by the classic Romero films.
37. Pike, "A Boy and His Dog," np.
38. There are any number of oblique references to the events of 9/11 in the film, which, despite its otherwise near-comprehensive representation of New York City landmarks and Neville's insistence that the city is "ground zero," offers no direct reference to or representation of the site of the World Trade Center. But while the film can justifiably be read as an allegory about 9/11 itself, I suggest here a more comprehensive reading that might be said to encompass this interpretation as well.
39. Žižek, *Violence*, p. 53.
40. This is, of course, another point at which the film intervenes in post-9/11 discourse, demonstrating the ideological limits revealed in overly simplistic characterizations of the suicidal 9/11 terrorists as "cowards."
41. The alternate version seems to suggest that Neville himself, distracted by the day's unfamiliar domestic activities, is to blame, though the film lacks consistency on this point. While the alternate version features footage of Neville, Anna, and Ethan enjoying the city that day, the filmmakers chose to leave in the original scene where Neville accusingly asks Anna if it was dark when they returned the previous night.
42. It is a crucial point that we do not witness (in flashback or otherwise) the creatures consuming a human being, that we must rely wholly on Neville's subjective account of their terrific nature.
43. Žižek, *Violence*, pp. 1–2.
44. Ibid., p. 2.
45. B. Brecht (1949) *The Threepenny Opera*. Trans. Desmond Vesey (New York: Grove, 1960), p. 92.
46. K. Boyle (2009) "*Children of Men* and *I am Legend*: The Disaster-Capitalism Complex Hits Hollywood," *Jump Cut: A Review of Contemporary Media*, LI, np.

47. As we have already seen, Hardt and Negri recently appropriate the term for their own political theorization of resistance.
48. V. Goldman (2006) *The Book of Exodus: The Making and Meaning of Bob Marley and the Wailers' Album of the Century* (New York: Three Rivers), p. 63.
49. R. Iton (2008) *In Search of the Black Fantastic: Politics & Popular Culture in the Post-Civil Rights Era* (New York: Oxford Univesity Press), p. 232.
50. For an account of these rumors, see Timothy White's definitive biography *Catch a Fire: The Life of Bob Marley* (New York: Holt, 2006).
51. Boyle, "*Children of Men* and *I am Legend*." Boyle observes that the film's "final fifteen minutes quilt together the film's scrambled Christian allusions" and that the tattoo "'objectively' buttresses Anna's 'crazy' belief that divine reason undergirds all events, however coincidental they may appear to the theologically tone-deaf" (np).
52. In this case, the repression is quite literal, for unlike many DVD "alternate endings" that feature footage abridged from the theatrical release, that of *Legend* was completely reshot. Studio executives felt that Lawrence's original conclusion (released as the DVD "alternate ending") was not commercially viable and ordered him to replace it with what appears in the theatrical release.
53. Indeed, we might read the alternate version's multiculturalist resolution as an iteration of what Herbert Marcuse long ago called "repressive tolerance," which he describes as follows in a 1968 postscript to the original 1965 essay: "Under the conditions prevailing in this country, tolerance does not, and cannot, fulfill the civilizing function attributed to it by the liberal protagonists of democracy, namely, protection of dissent. The progressive historical force of tolerance lies in its extension to those modes and forms of dissent which are not committed to the status quo of society, and not confined to the institutional framework of the established society. Consequently, the idea of tolerance implies the necessity, for the dissenting group or individuals, to become illegitimate if and when the established legitimacy prevents and counteracts the development of dissent. This would be the case not only in a totalitarian society ... but also in a democracy ... where the majority does not result from the development of independent thought and opinion but rather from the monopolistic and oligopolistic administration of public opinion, without terror and (normally) without censorship" (H. Marcuse (1968) "Repressive Tolerance," *The Essential Marcuse*. Eds. Andrew Feenberg and William Leiss (Boston: Beacon), p. 55).
54. Žižek, *Parallax*, p. 34.
55. Ibid.
56. Žižek, *Violence*, p. 104.
57. J. Catsoulis (2009) "In 'District 9,' An Apartheid Allegory (With Aliens)," *NPR*. Date Accessed 15 February 2010.
58. Žižek, *Violence*, p. 41.
59. A. Kuper (2000) *Culture: The Anthropologists' Account* (Cambridge, MA: Harvard University Press), pp. xi–xv.
60. Taken here in the Foucauldian sense of the incorporation of the body and human life itself into the regulatory mechanisms of power, as distinguished from the emancipatory extension of this concept offered by Hardt and Negri.

61. Žižek, *Violence*, p. 42.
62. D. Korotky (2010) "On Neill Blomkamp's *District 9*," *Young Daguerreotypes*. Date Accessed 1 January 2011.
63. Agamben, *Homo Sacer*, p. 123.
64. C. Schmitt (2006) *The* Nomos *of the Earth in the International Law of the* Jus Publicum Europaeum. Trans. G.L. Ulmen (Ann Arbor, MI: Telos), p. 67.
65. Ibid., p. 94.
66. Ibid., p. 192.
67. Schmitt traces the emergence of this economic globalism to the Cobden-Chevalier Commercial Treaty of 1860, the Anglo-French trade agreement that reduced protective duties or tariffs between the two powers and established the precedent for subsequent European trade agreements (p. 235).
68. Ibid., p. 235.
69. Ibid., p. 236.
70. Agamben, *Homo Sacer*, p. 20. Further identifying his project with the historical moment of postmodernity and the deterioration of the nation-state, Agamben writes, "Today, now that the great State structures have entered into a process of dissolution and the emergency has, as Benjamin foresaw, become the rule, the time is ripe to place the problem of the originary structure and limits of the form of the State in a new perspective" (p. 12).
71. Ibid., p. 20.
72. Ibid., p. 166, emphasis added. In a recent critical commentary on Agamben's theoretical "mapping" of the Holocaust, Robert Eaglestone offers that more apposite as a paradigm for modernity than the camp and its Muselmann is the colony and its colonial subject ((2002) "On Girogio Agamben's Holocaust," *Paragraph*, XXV, 52–67 (60).
73. Agamben, *Homo Sacer*, p. 171.
74. Ibid., p. 8.
75. Ibid., p. 115.
76. Agamben reminds us, however, that the ultimate effect of such humanitarian intervention is merely the further inscription of bare life into the order of law and of sovereignty (pp. 186–7).
77. Quoted in Agamben, *Homo Sacer*, p. 169.
78. P.E. Louw (2004) *The Rise, Fall, and Legacy of Apartheid* (Westport, CT: Praeger), pp. 58–9.
79. Žižek, *Violence*, p. 140. I take Žižek's insight here not as a repudiation of the cultural as such nor as a blanket denouncement of "cultural studies" but of a reified and undialectical reckoning in which the cultural is substituted *tout court* for the material and thereby obscures the latter.
80. Louw, *Apartheid*, p. 197.
81. Ibid., p. 197.
82. Ibid., p. 195.
83. Ibid.
84. M.H. Allen (2006) *Globalization, Negotiation, and the Failure of Transformation in South Africa: Revolution at a Bargain?* (New York: Palgrave Macmillan), p. 27.
85. Ibid., p. 27.
86. Ibid., p. 25.
87. Ibid., p. 35.

88. Ibid., pp. 126–7.
89. Ibid., p. 183.
90. Ibid., p. 127.
91. Agamben, *Homo Sacer*, p. 123.
92. Ibid., p. 124.
93. Ibid., p. 127.
94. Ibid.
95. Ibid., p. 131.
96. Ibid., p. 134.
97. Ibid., p. 105.
98. Ibid., p. 55.
99. I refer here not to the "proletariat" in its classical form, which Agamben decries as "the reef on which the revolutions of our century have been shipwrecked" (p. 12), but to the radically inclusive and flexible collectivity of Hardt and Negri's multitude taking shape in "a world in which we can only understand ourselves as monsters" (*Commonwealth*, p. 194).
100. F. Jameson (1994) *Seeds of Time* (New York: Columbia University Press), p. 71.

6 Third-World Punks, or, Watch Out for the Worlds Behind You

1. L. McCaffery (1991) "Introduction: The Desert of the Real," *Storming the Reality Studio: A Casebook of Cyberpunk and Postmodern Fiction*. Ed. Larry McCaffery (Durham: Duke University Press), pp. 1–16 (p. 3).
2. Ibid., pp. 4–5.
3. Ibid.
4. Ibid., p. 4. Emphasis added.
5. Gibson contributes the following cover blurb: "*Moxyland* does lots of things, masterfully, that lots of sf never even guesses that it *could* be doing. Very, very good."
6. Stross characterizes his own work as an ongoing "dialogue" with the subgenre that attempts to "distill ... cyberpunk into something that works again" (in "Charles Stross: Exploring Distortions," Interview, *Locus: The Magazine of the Science Fiction and Fantasy Field* , 511 [August 2003], p. 86).
7. C. Stross, Moxyland.com, date accessed 16 June 2010.
8. Jameson, *Archaeologies*, p. 385.
9. I. Csicsery-Ronay (1991) "Cyberpunk and Neuromanticism," *Storming the Reality Studio: A Casebook of Cyberpunk and Postmodern Fiction*. Ed. Larry McCaffery (Durham: Duke University Press), pp. 182–93 (p. 191).
10. G. Jones (2011) "*Zoo City* by Lauren Beukes – review," *The Guardian*, date accessed June 16 2010.
11. J. Chappell (2011) "Moxyland Reaches One Step Beyond Standard Cyberpunk," http://barkingbookreviews.com/moxyland-lauren-beukes. Date accessed August 1 2011.
12. Csicsery-Ronay, "Cyberpunk", p. 184.
13. Jameson, *Archaeologies*, p. 385.

14. D. Suvin (1991) "On Gibson and Cyberpunk SF," *Storming the Reality Studio: A Casebook of Cyberpunk and Postmodern Fiction*. Ed. Larry McCaffery (Durham: Duke University Press), pp. 349–65 (p. 352).
15. Moxyland.com, date accessed June 16 2010.
16. I take as instructive here Thomas Foster's insight that cyberpunk's continuing relevance lies in its capacity to be read "not as the vanguard of a posthumanism assumed to be revolutionary in itself, but instead as an attempt to intervene in and diversify what posthumanism can mean" (T. Foster (2005) *The Souls of Cyberfolk: Posthumanism as Vernacular Theory* [Minneapolis: University of Minnesota Press], p. xiii).
17. Suvin, "On Gibson," p. 365.
18. Ibid., p. 365.
19. Jameson, *Archaeologies*, p. 386.
20. Ibid., pp. 387–8.
21. Ibid., p. 387.
22. L. Beukes (2008) *Moxyland* (Nottingham, UK: Angry Robot, 2010), p. 35.
23. Ibid., p. 76.
24. Ibid., p. 27.
25. Ibid., p. 260.
26. B. Sterling (1991) "Preface from *Mirrorshades*," *Storming the Reality Studio: A Casebook of Cyberpunk and Postmodern Fiction*. Ed. Larry McCaffery (Durham: Duke University Press), pp. 343–8, p. xiv.
27. Ibid., p. xii.
28. Csicsery-Ronay, "Cyberpunk," p. 185.
29. Suvin, "On Gibson," p. 352.
30. Jameson, *Seeds*, p. 155.
31. Suvin, "On Gibson," p. 353.
32. Jameson argues that the mapping operation of the conspiracy and the classic spy narrative has, by the late 1980s, "crystallized in a new type of science fiction, called *cyberpunk*, which is fully as much an expression of transnational corporate realities as it is of global paranoia itself" (*Postmodernism*, p. 38).
33. F. Jameson (2007) *Jameson on Jameson*. Ed. Ian Buchanan (Durham: Duke University Press), p. 103.
34. S. Heuser (2003) *Virtual Geographies: Cyberpunk and the Intersection of the Postmodern and Science Fiction* (B.V., Amsterdam: Rodopi), p. 19.
35. C. Freccero (1999) *Popular Culture: An Introduction* (New York: New York University Press), p. 110.
36. Ibid., p. 9. The term is likely meant to recall "Vukani Bantu!" the Zulu slogan used by the first indigenously owned and operated newspaper in Africa. South African government officials forced the paper to discontinue publication, citing the "dangerous and seditious invitation to rebellion" suggested by the "Vukani" banner. See A. Odendaal (1984) *Vukani Bantu!: The Beginnings of Black Protest Politics in South Africa* (Cape Town and Johannesburg: David Phillip), p. ix.
37. Beukes, *Moxyland*, p. 10.
38. Ibid., p. 11.
39. Ibid., p. 8.
40. Ibid., p. 60.
41. Ibid., p. 112.

42. Ibid., p. 113.
43. Ibid., p. 114.
44. Ibid.
45. Ibid., p. 47.
46. Ibid., p. 114.
47. Ibid., p. 231.
48. Ibid., p. 290.
49. Ibid., p. 292.
50. Ibid., p. 358.
51. V. Hollinger (1991) "Cybernetic Deconstructions: Cyberpunk and Postmodernism," *Storming the Reality Studio: A Casebook of Cyberpunk and Postmodern Fiction*. Ed. Larry McCaffery (Durham: Duke University Press), pp. 203–18 (p. 207).
52. S. Bukatman (1993) *Terminal Identities: The Virtual Subject in Postmodern Science Fiction* (Durham: Duke University Press), p. 156.
53. Ibid., p. 156.
54. Ibid., p. 145.
55. Ibid., p. 146.
56. See, for example, Thomas Michaud's discussion in "Science Fiction and Politics: Cyberpunk Science Fiction as Political Philosophy" in *New Boundaries in Political Science Fiction* (Columbia, SC: South Carolina University Press, 2008).
57. W. Gibson (1984) *Neuromancer* (New York: Ace), p. 6.
58. M.C. Boyer (1996) *Cybercities: Visual Perception in the Age of Electronic Communication* (New York: Princeton Architectural), p. 31.
59. Ibid., p. 118.
60. The authoritative historical account of this ceding of ground by politics to the promise of technical sublimity in the North American context is found in Leo Marx's *The Machine in the Garden: Technology and the Pastoral Ideal in America* (New York: Oxford University Press, 1964).
61. S. Bukatman (1991) "Postcards from the Posthuman Solar System," *Science Fiction Studies*, LV, Num. 18, n. pag., date accessed July 2 2011.
62. J.M. Coetzee (1988) *White Writing: On the Culture of Letters in South Africa* (New Haven: Yale University Press), pp. 3–4.
63. The discovery of gold and diamonds in the Transvaal region in the late nineteenth century spurred a massive trend toward urbanization as land speculation and rapidly transforming trends in agricultural production, such as the declining wool market, led to the displacement and impoverishment of many traditional small farmers. Natural phenomena such as drought and disease and historical eventualities like the war with the British converged to "create a class of 'poor whites,' or landless Afrikaners, who lived as sharecroppers and increasingly abandoned farming altogether, turning to the growing cities to make their fortunes." Between 1870 and 1911, the urban population of the Transvaal increased from 4,000 to more than 600,000, a trend that continued apace into the late 1930s. See J. Wenzel (2000) "The Pastoral Promise and the Political Imperative: The *Plaasroman* Tradition in an Era of Land Reform," *Modern Fiction Studies*, XLVI, num. 1, 90–113 (93).
64. Coetzee, *White Writing*, p. 4.

65. Ibid., p. 5.
66. Ibid., p. 5.
67. Ibid., p. 85.
68. Ibid., p. 64.
69. According to Tom Moylan and Raffaela Baccolini's substantial elaboration of the form (originally identified by Lyman Tower Sargent) in *Dark Horizons: Science Fiction and the Dystopian Imagination* (New York: Routledge, 2003), the *critical dystopia* emerges to address the late-twentieth-century reification of the utopian imagination as such and the attenuation of its hopeful content into merely individuated material acquisitiveness. Unlike the traditional dystopia, however, the critical dystopia manages to retain a clear measure of authentic utopian longing and so strikes a kind of balance between the two forms. As Moylan and Baccolini put it, these texts "negotiate the necessary pessimism of the generic dystopia with a millennial or utopian stance that not only breaks through the hegemonic enclosures of the text's alternative world but also self-reflexively refuses the anti-utopian temptation that lingers in every utopian account" (p. 7).
70. Beukes, *Moxyland*, p. 55.
71. Ibid., p. 55.
72. Ibid., pp. 55–6.
73. Ibid., p. 56.
74. Ibid.
75. Ibid., p. 55.
76. A. Wilmot (1896) *Monopotama (Rhodesia): Its Monuments, and its History from the most Ancient Times to the present Century* (London: T. Fisher Unwin). *Google Book Search*, date accessed June 23 2011.
77. H.R. Haggard (1896) "Preface," *Monopotama (Rhodesia): Its Monuments, and its History from the most Ancient Times to the present Century* (London: T. Fisher Unwin), pp. xiii–xxiv (p. xiv). *Google Book Search*, date accessed June 23 2011. Haggard alludes here to the death of the Portuguese Jesuit missionary da Silveira, whose efforts to convert Monomotapa to Christianity resulted in execution. Da Silveira's death legitimated the subsequent invasion by the Portuguese, who ruthlessly seized control of the region's mineral and ivory wealth.
78. G.M. Theall (1907) *History and Ethnography of Africa South of the Zambesi* (London: Swan Sonnenschein), p. 124. *Google Book Search*, date accessed June 23. 2011.
79. Ibid., p. 124.
80. See C. R. Boxer (1966) *An African Eldorado: Monomotapa and Mocambique 1498–1752* (Salisbury, Rhodesia: Central Africa Historical Association).
81. Beukes, *Moxyland*, p. 50.
82. J. Baudrillard (1994) *Simulacra and Simulation*. Trans. Sheila Faria Glaser (Ann Arbor: University of Michigan Press), p. 12.
83. Ibid., p. 13.
84. C. Scruggs (2004) "The Pastoral and the City in Carl Franklin's *One False Move*," *African American Review*, XXXVIII, Num. 2, 323–34 (325).
85. N. Klein (2008) *The History of Forgetting: Los Angeles and the Erasure of Memory*, 2nd edn (New York: Verso), p. 79.
86. Ibid., pp. 89, 90.

87. Scruggs, *The Pastoral*, p. 38. The bondage Turner refers to here is quite literal in that he credits the mobility of Westward expansion for the nation's overcoming of the merely regional or "sectional trait" of slavery (p. 29).
88. Klein, *The History of Forgetting*, p. 299.
89. Ibid., p. 299.
90. Stross, "Exploring Distortions," p. 86.
91. Beukes, *Moxyland*, p. 57.
92. Ibid., p. 58.
93. Ibid., p. 150.
94. Ibid., p. 151.
95. Ibid., p. 154.
96. Ibid., p. 155.
97. D. Haraway (1991) *Simians, Cyborgs, and Women: The Reinvention of Nature* (New York: Routledge), p. 170.
98. Beukes, *Moxyland*, p. 98.
99. Ibid., p. 137.
100. Ibid.
101. Ibid., p. 141.
102. Bukatman, *Terminal Identities*, p. 250.
103. A. Visagie (2011) "Global Capitalism and a Dystopian South Africa," *Criticism, Crisis, and Contemporary Narrative: Textual Horizons in an Age of Global Risk*. Ed. Paul Crosthwaite (New York: Routledge), pp. 95–109 (p. 107).
104. Ibid., p. 107.
105. Ibid.
106. Beukes, *Moxyland*, p. 38.
107. Ibid., p. 90.
108. Ibid., p. 45.
109. Bukatman, *Terminal Identities*, p. 38.
110. Beukes, *Moxyland*, p. 299.
111. Ibid., p. 16.
112. Ibid., p. 206.
113. Jameson, *Archaeologies*, p. 384.
114. Ibid., p. 388
115. Ibid., p. 391.
116. Beukes, *Moxyland*, p. 206.
117. R. Barthes (1968) *Writing Degree Zero*. Trans. Annette Lavers and Colin Smith (New York: Hill and Wang), pp. 87–8.
118. Coetzee, *White Writing*, p. 9.
119. Ibid., p. 9. For a discussion of Coetzee's extended engagement with the South African pastoral in *Foe*, see H. Flint (2011) "White Talk, White Writing: New Contexts for Examining Genre and Identity in J.M. Coetzee's *Foe*," *LIT: Literature Interpretation Theory*, XXII, Num. 4, pp. 336–53.
120. Quoted in Spivak, *From the Margins*, p. 195.
121. Ibid., p. 190.
122. Jameson, *Postmodernism*, p. 286.
123. Jameson, *Seeds of Time*, p. 158.
124. Ibid., p. 146.
125. Jameson, *Jameson on Jameson*, p. 130.
126. Ibid., p. 131.

127. Jameson, *Seeds of Time*, p. 134.
128. Ibid., p. 138.
129. Ibid., p. 159.
130. Ibid.
131. Ibid., p. 367.
132. Ibid.
133. Ibid., p. 212.
134. Jameson, *Seeds of Time*, p. 150.
135. Beukes, *Moxyland*, p. 358.
136. Steampunk in fact gains formal credibility, not to mention visibility, when sanctioned by cyberpunk pioneers Gibson and Sterling in their 1990 novel *The Difference Engine* (London: Victor Gollancz), which features an alternate history in which Charles Babbage's famously failed attempt to design and build a mechanical computer (dubbed the Babbage Engine) succeeds, thereby dramatically changing the course of nineteenth- and twentieth-century history.
137. http://www.antipope.org/charlie/blog-static/2010/10/the-hard-edge-of-empire.html://steampunkscholar.blogspot.com/p/steampunk-101.html.
138. Ibid.
139. M. Rose (2010) "Extraordinary Pasts: Steampunk as a Mode of Historical Representation," *Journal of the Fantastic in the Arts* 20.3 (2010): 319–33. *Academic OneFile*. Web. Date accessed October 3 2011.
140. Ibid.
141. Ibid.
142. Ibid.
143. T. Buckell, "Steampunk and Pastoralism." http://www.tobiasbuckell.com/2010/10/27/steampunk-and-pastoralism/, date accessed 5 November 2011.
144. T. Buckell (2006) *Crystal Rain* (New York: TOR), p. 314.
145. Ibid., p. 37.
146. Ibid., p. 16.
147. Ibid., p. 19.
148. Jameson, *The Political Unconscious*, p. 102.
149. Buckell, *Crystal Rain*, p. 220.
150. Ibid., p. 220.
151. Ibid., p. 221
152. Buckell, *Crystal Rain*, p. 354.
153. H. Marcuse (1964) *One-Dimensional Man: Studies in the Ideology of Advanced Industrial Society* (Boston: Beacon), p. 98.
154. Gibson, qtd. in McCaffery, p. 265.

Conclusion: Reimagining the Material

1. B. Landon (1991) "Bet on it: Cyber/video/punk performance," *Storming the Reality Studio: A Casebook of Cyberpunk and Postmodern Fiction*. Ed. Larry McCaffery (Durham: Duke University Press), pp. 239–44 (p. 239).
2. Among the most influential of those critics who have called into question the disciplinary tendency generally demonstrated by postcolonial studies

away from left-oriented nationalisms and toward the hybrid globality of cosmopolitanism writers is Tim Brennan. See T. Brennan (1997) *At Home in the World: Cosmopolitanism Now* (Cambridge, MA: Harvard University Press).
3. E. Said (1995) "East isn't East: The Impending End of the Age of Imperialism," *Times Literary Supplement* (London), date accessed June 22 2010.
4. E. Said (1996) *Representations of the Intellectual: The 1993 Reith Lectures* (New York: Vintage), p. 44
5. Ibid., p. 44.
6. N. Lazarus (2011) *The Postcolonial Unconscious* (Cambridge: Cambridge University Press), p. 79.
7. Jameson, F. *Postmodernism*, p. 129.

Selected Bibliography

Agamben, Giorgio. *Homo Sacer: Sovereign Power and Bare Life*. Trans. Daniel Heller-Roazen. Stanford: Stanford University Press, 1998.
Ahmad, Aijaz. "Jameson's Rhetoric of Otherness and the National Allegory." *Social Text* (1987): 65–88.
Allen, Michael H. *Globalization, Negotiation, and the Failure of Transformation in South Africa: Revolution at a Bargain?* New York: Palgrave Macmillan, 2006.
Althusser, Louis. "Ideology and Ideological State Aaratuses (Notes Toward an Investigation)." *Lenin and Philosophy and Other Essays*. Trans. Ben Brewster. New York: Monthly Review, 1971. 127–88.
Anderson, Benedict. *Imagined Communities: Reflections on the Origin and Spread of Nationalism*. 1983. New York: Verso, 2006.
Badiou, Alain. *Being and Event*. 1988. Trans. Oliver Feltham. London: Continuum, 2006.
——. *Ethics: An Essay on Understanding Evil*. Trans. Peter Hallward. New York: Verso, 2001.
——. *Ethics: An Essay on the Understanding of Evil*. 1998. Trans. Jason Barker. London: Verso, 2005.
——. *Theory of the Subject*. 1982. Trans. Bruno Bosteels. London: Continuum, 2009.
——. *Metapolitics*. 1998. Trans. Jason Barker. London: Verso, 2005.
Banerjee, Suparno. "*The Calcutta Chromosome*: A Novel of Silence, Slippage, and Subversion," *Science Fiction, Imperialism and the Third World: Essays on Postcolonial Literature and Film*. Jefferson, NC: McFarland, 2010.
Barnard, Rita. "J.M. Coetzee's Disgrace and the South African Pastoral." *Contemporary Literature* 44.2 (2003): 199–224.
Barthes, Roland. *Writing Degree Zero*. Trans. Annette Lavers and Colin Smith. New York: Hill and Wang, 1968.
Baudrillard, Jean. *Simulacra and Simulation*. Trans. Sheila Faria Glaser. Ann Arbor: University of Michigan Press, 1994.
Beaumont, Matthew. *Utopia Ltd: Ideologies of Social Dreaming in England 1870–1900*. Boston: Brill, 2005.
Benjamin, Walter. *Illuminations: Essays and Reflections*. New York: Schocken, 1969.
Beukes, Lauren. *Moxyland*. 2008. Nottingham, UK: Angry Robot, 2010.
Bhabha, Homi. *The Location of Culture*. New York: Routledge, 1994.
Bilby, Kenneth M. *True-Born Maroons*. Gainesville: University Press of Florida, 2005.
Bloch, Ernst. *The Principle of Hope*. Trans. Neville Plaice, Stephen Plaice, and Paul Knight. Vol. 1. Cambridge: MIT Press, 1986.
Boyer, M. Christine. *Cybercities: Visual Perception in the Age of Electronic Communication*. New York: Princeton Architectural, 1996.
Boyle, Kirk. "*Children of Men* and *I am Legend*: The Disaster-Capitalism Complex Hits Hollywood." *Jump Cut: A Review of Contemporary Media*, LI (2009): np.

Brecht, Bertolt. *The Threepenny Opera*. Trans. Desmond Vesey. New York: Grove, 1960.

Brennan, Timothy. *Salman Rushdie and the Third World: Myths of the Nation*. London, Macmillan, 1989.

Buckell, Tobias. *Crystal Rain*. New York: TOR, 2006.

——. "Steampunk and Pastoralism." (2010): http://www.tobiasbuckell.com/2010/10/27/steampunk-and-pastoralism/.

Buck-Morss, Susan. *Hegel, Haiti, and Universal History*. Pittsburgh: Pittsburgh University Press, 2009.

Bukatman, Scott. "Postcards from the Posthuman Solar System." *Science Fiction Studies* 55.18 (1991): n. pag.

——. *Terminal Identities: The Virtual Subject in Postmodern Science Fiction*. Durham: Duke University Press, 1993.

Caldeira, Teresa P. R. *City of Walls: Crime, Segregation, and Citizenship in São Paulo*. Berkeley: University of California Press, 2001.

Carpentier, Alejo. "On the Marvelous Real in America" (1949). *Magical Realism: Theory, History, Community*. Durham: Duke University Press, 1995.

Chakrabarty, Dipesh. *Provincializing Europe: Postcolonial Thought and Historical Difference*. Princeton: Princeton University Press, 2007.

Chatterjee, Partha. *Nationalist Thought and the Colonial World: A Derivative Discourse*. Minneapolis: University of Minnesota Press, 1986.

——. *The Nation and its Fragments: Colonial and Postcolonial Histories*. Princeton: University of Princeton Press, 1993.

Clark, Roger Y. "Grimus: Worlds upon Worlds." *Stranger Gods: Salman Rushdie's Other Worlds*. Montreal: McGill-Queen's University Press, 2001. 30–60.

Clemente, Bill. "Tan-Tan's Exile and Odyssey in Nalo Hopkinson's Midnight Robber." *Foundation* 91 (2004): 10–24.

Coetzee, J.M. *White Writing: On the Culture of Letters in South Africa*. New Haven: Yale University Press, 1988.

Colas, Santiago. "The Third World in Jameson's *Postmodernism, or, the Cultural Logic of Late Capitalism*." *Social Text* 31 (1992): 258–270.

Collier, Gordon. "Spaceship Creole: Nalo Hopkinson, Canadian-Caribbean Fabulist Fiction, and Linguistic/Cultural Syncretism." *A Peer-Pot of Cultures: Aspects of Creolization in the Caribbean*. Eds Gordon Collier and Ulrich Fleischmann. New York: Rodopi, 2003.

Comaroff, Jean and John Comaroff. "Alien-Nation: Zombies, Immigrants, and Millennial Capitalism." *South Atlantic Quarterly*, CI (2002): 779–805.

Cooper, Brenda. *Magical Realism in West African Fiction: Seeing with a Third Eye*. New York: Routledge, 1998.

Csicsery-Ronay, Istvan. "Cyberpunk and Neuromanticism." *Storming the Reality Studio: A Casebook of Cyberpunk and Postmodern Fiction*. Ed. Larry McCaffery. Durham: Duke University Press, 1991. 182–93.

——. "Dis-Imagined Communities: Science Fiction and the Future of Nations." *Edging into the Future: Science Fiction and Contemporary Cultural Transformation*. Eds Veronica Hollinger and Joan Gordon. Philadelphia: University of Pennsylvania Press, 2002. 215–37.

Cundy, Catherine. "Rehearsing Voices: Salman Rushdie's *Grimus*." *Journal of Commonwealth Literature* 27 (1992): 128–38.

Davis, Mike. *Planet of Slums*. London: Verso, 2006.

de Certeau, Michel. *The Practice of Everyday Life*. Berkeley, CA: University of California Press, 1984.
Delaney, Samuel R. "Of Triton and Other Matters: An Interview with Samuel R. Delaney." *Science Fiction Studies* 17.3 (1990): np.
Dell'Aversano, Carmen. "Worlds, Things, Words: Rushdie's Style from *Grimus* to *Midnight's Children*." *Coterminous Worlds: Magical Realism and Contemporary Post-Colonial Literature in English*. Eds Elsa Linguanti et al. Amsterdam: Rodopi, 1999. 61–81.
Denning, Michael. *Culture in the Age of Three Worlds*. London: Verso, 2004.
Derrida, Jacques. *Specters of Marx: The State of Debt, the Work of Mourning, and the New International*. Trans. Peggy Kamuf. New York: Routledge, 1994.
Dharker, Rani. "An Interview with Salman Rushdie." *New Quest* 42 (1983): 351–60.
Díaz, Junot. *The Brief Wondrous Life of Oscar Wao*. New York: Riverhead, 2007.
District 9. Dir. Neill Blomkamp. Tristar, 2009.
Douglas, Mary. "The Idea of a Home: A Kind of Space." *Social Research* 58 (1991): 287–307.
Drezner, Daniel W. "Night of the Living Wonks: Toward an International Relations Theory of Zombies." *Foreign Policy*. Jul. 2010.
Eaglestone, Robert. "On Giorgio Agamben's Holocaust." *Paragraph* 25 (2002): 52–67.
Feltham, Oliver. *Alain Badiou: Live Theory*. London: Continuum, 2008.
Fernandes, Jorge Luis Andrade. *Challenging Euro-America's Politics of Identity: The Return of the Native*. New York: Routledge, 2007.
Foster, Thomas. *The Souls of Cyberfolk: Posthumanism as Vernacular Theory*. Minneapolis: University of Minnesota Press, 2005.
Freccero, Carla. *Popular Culture: An Introduction*. New York: New York University Press, 1999.
Freedman, Carl. *Critical Theory and Science Fiction*. Hanover, NH: Wesleyan, 2000.
Ghandi, Leela. "'A Choice of Histories': Ghosh vs. Hegel in an Antique Land." *New Literatures Review* 40 (2003): 17–32.
Ghosh, Amitav. *The Calcutta Chromosome*. New York: Perennial, 1995.
Ghosh, Bishnupriya. "On Grafting the Vernacular: The Consequences of Postcolonial Spectrology." *boundary* 2 31 (2004): 197–218.
Gibson, William. *Neuromancer*. New York: Ace, 1984.
Goldman, Vivian. *The Book of Exodus: The Making and Meaning of Bob Marley and the Wailers' Album of the Century*. New York: Three Rivers, 2006.
Haggard, H. Rider. "Preface." *Monopotama (Rhodesia): Its Monuments, and its History from the most Ancient Times to the present Century*. London: T. Fisher Unwin, 1896.
Halpin, Jenny G. "Gift Unpossessed: Community as 'Gift' in The Calcutta Chromosome." *ARIEL* (2009): 23–39.
Haraway, Donna. *Simians, Cyborgs, and Women: The Reinvention of Nature*. New York: Routledge, 1991.
Hardt, Michael and Antonio Negri. *Commonwealth*. Cambridge, MA: Harvard University Press, 2009.
——. *Empire*. Cambridge: Harvard University Press, 2000.
Harrison, James. *Salman Rushdie*. New York, Twayne, 1992.

Harrison, Trevor. "Globalization and the Trade in Human Body Parts." *Canadian Review of Sociology and Anthropology* 36.1 (1999): 21–35.
Harvey, David. *Spaces of Hope*. Berkeley, University of California Press, 2000.
Hegel, G.W.F. *Elements of the Philosophy of Right*. 1820. Ed. Allen W. Wood. Trans. H.B. Nisbet. Cambridge, UK: Cambridge University Press, 1991.
——. *Introduction to the Philosophy of History*. 1837. Trans. J. Sibree. Google Books Search. January 15, 2011.
Heuser, Sabine. *Virtual Geographies: Cyberpunk and the Intersection of the Postmodern and Science Fiction*. B.V., Amsterdam: Rodopi, 2003.
Hitchcock, Peter. *Imaginary States: Studies in Cultural Transnationalism*. Chicago: University of Illinois Press, 2003.
——. *The Long Space: Transnationalism and Postcolonial Form*. Stanford, CA: Stanford University Press, 2010.
Hoagland, Ericka and Reema Sarwal. *Science Fiction, Imperialism and the Third World: Essays on Postcolonial Literature and Film*. Jefferson, NC: McFarland, 2010.
Hollinger, Veronica. "Cybernetic Deconstructions: Cyberpunk and Postmodernism." *Storming the Reality Studio: A Casebook of Cyberpunk and Postmodern Fiction*. Ed. Larry McCaffery. Durham: Duke University Press, 1991. 203–18.
Homer, Sean. "Narratives of History, Narratives of Time." *On Jameson*. Eds Caren Irr and Ian Buchanan. Albany: SUNY Press, 2006.
Hopkinson, Nalo. "A Conversation With Nalo Hopkinson." 2000. SF Site. June 26, 2007.http://www.sfsite.com/03b/nh77.htm.
——. *Midnight Robber*. New York: Aspect, 2000.
——. "A Dialogue on SF and Utopian Fiction, Between Nalo Hopkinson and Elisabeth Vonarburg." Eds Jennifer Burwell and Nancy Johnston. *Foundation* 81 (2001): 40–7.
——. "Highlights of Bear_Benford Conversation." With Kurt Lancaster, Connie Willis, and Michael Burstein. 2000. MIT. June 26, 2007. http://web.mit.edu/m-i-t/science_fiction/transcripts/hopkinson_willis.htm.
——. "Nalo Hopkinson Uses SF to Probe the Inner and Outer Worlds of Alienation." By David Soyka. *Science Fiction Weekly* Interview. 26 June 2007. http://www.scifi.com/sfw/issue232/interview2.htm.
I am Legend. Dir. Francis Lawrence. Warner Bros., 2007.
Iton, Richard. *In Search of the Black Fantastic: Politics & Popular Culture in the Post-Civil Rights Era*. New York: Oxford University Press, 2008.
Jameson, Fredric. *Archaeologies of the Future: The Desire Called Utopia and Other Science Fictions*. New York: Verso: 2005.
——. "Cognitive Maing." *Marxism and the Interpretation of Culture*. Eds. Cary Nelson and Lawrence Grossberg. Urbana: University of Illinois Press, 1988. 347–60.
——. *The Geopolitical Aesthetic: Cinema and Space in the World System*. Bloomington: Indiana University Press, 1992.
——. *Jameson on Jameson*. Ed. Ian Buchanan. Durham: Duke University Press, 2007.
——. *Marxism and Form: Twentieth-Century Dialectical Theories of Literature*. Princeton: Princeton University Press, 1971.
——. "On Magic Realism in Film," *Critical Inquiry*, XII, (1986): 301–25.

——. *Postmodernism, or, the Cultural Logic of Late Capitalism*. Durham, NC: Duke University Press, 1991.
——. *Seeds of Time*. New York: Columbia University Press, 1994.
——. *A Singular Modernity: Essay on the Ontology of the Present*. London: Verso, 2002.
——. "Third World Literature in the Era of Multinational Capitalism." *Social Text* 15 (1986): 65–88.
——. *Valences of the Dialectic*. London: Verso, 2010.
Johansen, Ib. "Flight From the Enchanter: Reflections on Salman Rushdie's *Grimus*." *Reading Rushdie*. Ed. M.D. Fletcher. Amsterdam: Rodopi, 1994.
Kerslake, Patricia. *Science Fiction and Empire*. Liverpool: Liverpool University Press, 2007.
Klein, Norman. *The History of Forgetting: Los Angeles and the Erasure of Memory*. 2nd edn. New York: Verso, 2008.
Korotky, David. "On Neill Blomkamp's District 9." *Young Daguerreotypes*. 30 June 2010.
Kovach, Gretel. "Out With the Trash? – Cairo's Legendary 'Garbage People' Threatened." *New America Media*. Pacific News Service. 17 February 2003.
Kumar, Amitava. "World Bank Literature: A New Name for Post-Colonial Studies in the Next Century." *College Literature* 26 (1999): 195–204.
Kuper, Adam. *Culture: The Anthropologists' Account*. Cambridge, MA: Harvard University Press, 2000.
Landon, Brooks. "Bet on it: Cyber/video/punk performance." *Storming the Reality Studio: A Casebook of Cyberpunk and Postmodern Fiction*. Ed. Larry McCaffery. Durham: Duke University Press, 1991. 239–44.
Langer, Jessica. *Postcolonialism and Science Fiction*. New York: Palgrave, 2011.
Larsen, Neil. "Imperialism, Colonialism, Postcolonialism." *A Companion to Postcolonial Studies*. Eds H. Schwarz and S. Ray. Oxford: Blackwell, 2005. 23–52.
Lazarus, Neil. *The Postcolonial Unconscious*. New York: Cambridge University Press, 2011.
Le Corbusier. *Towards a New Architecture*. Trans. John Goodman. Los Angeles: Getty, 2008.
Lefebvre, Henri. *The Production of Space*. Trans. Donald Nicholson-Smith. Malden, MA: Blackwell, 1991.
Life & Debt. Dir. Stephanie Black. New Yorker, 2001.
Louw, P. Eric. *The Rise, Fall, and Legacy of Apartheid*. Westport, CT: Praeger, 2004.
Lukacs, Georg. *The Historical Novel*. 1962. Trans. Hannah and Stanley Mitchell. Lincoln: University of Nebraska Press, 1983.
McCaffery, Larry. "Introduction: The Desert of the Real" *Storming the Reality Studio: A Casebook of Cyberpunk and Postmodern Fiction*. Ed. Larry McCaffery. Durham: Duke University Press, 1991. 1–16.
Marin, Louis. *Utopics: The Semiological Play of Textual Spaces*. Trans. Robert A. Vollroth. Amherst, NY: Humanity Books, 1984.
Marx, Karl. "Address of the General Council of the International Working Men's Association on the Civil War in France, 1871," *Civil War in France: The Paris Commune*. New York: International, 1993.
——. "The British Rule in India." *Archives of Empire: From the East India Company to the Suez Canal*. Eds. Mia Carter and Barbara Harlow. Durham: Duke UP, 2003. 117–23.

——. "Preface to the 1867 Edition," *Capital: A Critique of Political Economy Vol. I.* Penguin: London, 1976.
——. "Contribution to the Critique of Hegel's Philosophy of Right," in T. Bottomore, Ed., *Karl Marx: Early Writings*. London: Mcgraw-Hill, 1963.
——. "The Eighteenth Brumaire of Louis Bonaparte." In *The Marx-Engels Reader*, 2nd edn. Ed. Robert C. Tucker. New York: Norton, 1978. 594–617.
Mathur, Suchitra. "Caught Between the Goddess and the Cyborg: Third-World Women and the Politics of Science in Three Works of Indian Science Fiction." *Journal of Commonwealth Literature* 39 (2004): 119–38.
Marcuse, Herbert. *One-Dimensional Man: Studies in the Ideology of Advanced Industrial Society*. Boston: Beacon, 1964.
——. "Repressive Tolerance." *The Essential Marcuse*. Eds. Andrew Feenberg and William Leiss. Boston: Beacon, 2007.
McKeon, Michael. "Generic Transformation and Social Change: Rethinking the Rise of the Novel." *Theory of the Novel: A Historical Approach*. Ed. Michael McKeon. Baltimore: Johns Hopkins University Press, 2000.
Mosco, Vincent. *The Digital Sublime: Myth, Power, and Cyberspace*. Cambridge: MIT Press, 2004.
Moylan, Tom. "Utopia, the Postcolonial, and the Postmodern." *Science Fiction Studies* 29 (2002): 265.
Nancy, Jean-Luc. *The Creation of the World or Globalization*. Trans. Francois Rafoul and David Pettigrew New York: SUNY Press, 2007. Nandy, Ashis. *Time Treks: The Uncertain Future of Old and New Despotisms*. Salt Lake City: Seagull, 2008.
Neuwirth, Robert. *Shadow Cities: A Billion Squatters, a New Urban World*. New York: Routledge, 2006.
Padmanabhan, Manjula. "Ghandi-Toxin." *Kleptomania; Ten Stories*. New Delhi: Penguin, 2004. 93–8.
Parameswaran, Uma. "New Dimensions Courtesy of the Whirling Demons Word-Play in *Grimus*," *Reading Rushdie: Perspectives on the Fiction of Salman Rushdie*, Ed. M.D. Fletcher. Atlanta, GA: Rodopi, 1994. 35–44.
Pike, David L. "A Boy and His Dog: On Will Smith, Apocalypse, and I am Legend." *Bright Lights Film Journal* 59 (2008): n. pag.
Pordzik, Ralph. *The Quest for Postcolonial Utopia: A Comparative Introduction to the Utopian Novel in New English Literatures*. New York: Lang, 2001.
Reider, John. *Colonialism and the Emergence of Science Fiction*. Middletown: Wesleyan University Press, 2008.
——. "On Defining SF, or Not: Genre Theory, SF, and History," *Science Fiction Studies*, XXXVII (2010): 191–209.
Ricoeur, Paul. *Lectures on Ideology and Utopia*. New York: Columbia University Press, 1986.
Roberts, Julian. "Melancholy Meanings: Architecture, Postmodernity, and Philosophy." *The Postmodern Arts: An Introductory Reader*. Ed. Nigel Wheale. New York: Routledge, 1995. 130–49.
Romanik, Barbara. "Transforming the Colonial City: Science and the Practice of Dwelling in *The Calcutta Chromosome*." *Mosaic*, XXXVIII (2005): 41–57.
Rose, Margeret. "Extraordinary Pasts: Steampunk as a Mode of Historical Representation." *Journal of the Fantastic in the Arts* 20.3 (2010): 319–33.
Rushdie, Salman. *Grimus*. 1975. London: Vintage, 1996.

——. *Imaginary Homelands*. London: Granta, 1991.
——. Interview. *Scripsi* 3 (1985): 107–26.
Russel-Brown, Sherrie L. "Labor Rights as Human Rights: The Situation of Women Workers in Jamaica's Export Free Zones." *Berkeley Journal of Employment and Labor Law* 24 (2003): 180–201.
Said, Edward. "East isn't East: The Impending End of the Age of Imperialism." *Times Literary Supplement* (London): 1995.
——. *Representations of the Intellectual: The 1993 Reith Lectures*. New York: Vintage, 1996.
Sargent, Lyman Tower. "Utopia – The Problem of Definition." *Extrapolation* (1975): 137–48.
Schmitt, Carl. *The Nomos of the Earth in the International Law of the Jus Publicum Europaeum*. Trans. G.L. Ulmen. Ann Arbor, MI: Telos, 2006.
Scruggs, Charles. "The Pastoral and the City in Carl Franklin's *One False Move*." *African American Review* 38.2 (2004): 323–34.
Sengupta, Ranjana. *Delhi Metropolitan: The Making of an Unlikely City*. New Delhi: Penguin, 2007.
Singh, Vandana. *The Woman Who Thought She Was a Planet*. New Delhi: Penguin, 2008.
Sterling, Bruce. "Preface from *Mirrorshades*." *Storming the Reality Studio: A Casebook of Cyberpunk and Postmodern Fiction*. Ed. Larry McCaffery. Durham: Duke University Press, 1991. 343–8.
Stross, Charles. "Charles Stross: Exploring Distortions." Interview. *Locus: The Magazine of the Science Fiction and Fantasy Field* 511 (August 2003): 84–6.
Suvin, Darko. *Metamorphoses of Science Fiction*. New Haven: Yale University Press, 1979.
——. "On Cognitive Emotions and Topological Imagination." *Versus* 68 (1994): 165–201.
——. "On Gibson and Cyberpunk SF." *Storming the Reality Studio: A Casebook of Cyberpunk and Postmodern Fiction*. Ed. Larry McCaffery. Durham: Duke University Press, 1991. 349–65.
Syed, Mujeebuddin. "Warped Mythologies: Salman Rushdie's *Grimus*." *ARIEL* 25 (1994): 135–51.
Thaler, Ingrid. *Black Atlantic Speculative Fictions: Octavia E. Butler, Jewelle Gomez, and Nalo Hopkinson*. New York: Routledge, 2010.
Teverson, Andrew. "From Science Fiction to History: *Grimus* and *Midnight's Children*." *Salman Rushdie*. Contemporary World Writers. Ed. John Thieme. Manchester: Manchester University Press, 2007.
Theall, George McCall. *History and Ethnography of Africa South of the Zambesi*. London: Swan Sonnenschein, 1907.
Thieme, John. "The Discoverer Discovered: Amitav Ghosh's *The Calcutta Chromosome*." *Amitav Ghosh: A Critical Companion*. Ed. Tabish Khair. Delhi: Permanent Black, 2003. 128–41.
Troeung, Y-Dang. "Disciplinary Power, Transnational Labour, and the Politics of Representation in Stephanie Black's *Life and Debt*," *Politics and Culture*, issue 2 (2007): http://www.politicsandculture.org.
Visagie, Andries. "Global Capitalism and a Dystopian South Africa." *Criticism, Crisis, and Contemporary Narrative: Textual Horizons in an Age of Global Risk*. Ed. Paul Crosthwaite. New York: Routledge, 2011. 95–109.

Viswanathan, Gauri. "Beyond Orientalism: Syncretism and the Politics of Knowledge." *Stanford Humanities Review* 5.1 (1995): 19–32.

Watkins, Evan. *Throwaways: Work Culture and Consumer Education*. Stanford, CA: Stanford University Press, 1993.

Wegner, Phillip E. "Horizons, Figures, and Machines: The Dialectic of Utopia in the Work of Fredric Jameson." *Utopian Studies* 9 (1998): 58–74.

——. *Imaginary Communities: Utopia, the Nation, and the Spatial Histories of Modernity*. Berkeley: University of California Press, 2002.

——. "Jameson's Modernisms; or, The Desire Called Utopia." *Diacritics* 37 (2007): 3–20.

——. "Soldierboys for Peace: Cognitive Maing, Space, and Science Fiction as World Bank Literature." *World Bank Literature*. Ed. Amitava Kumar. Minneapolis: University of Minnesota Press, 2003.

——. "Spatial Criticism." *Introducing Criticism at the 21st Century*. Ed. Julian Wolfreys. 179–201.

Wertheim, Margaret. *The Pearly Gates of Cyberspace: A History of Space from Dante to the Internet*. New York: Norton, 1999.

Wiemann, Dirk. *Genres of Modernity: Contemporary Indian Novels in English*. New York: Rodopi, 2008.

Wilmot, Alexander. *Monopotama (Rhodesia): Its Monuments, and its History from the most Ancient Times to the present Century*. London: T. Fisher Unwin, 1896.

Wilson, Rob and Wimal Dissanayake. "Introduction," *Global/Local: Cultural Production and the Transnational Imaginary*. Durham: Duke University Press, 1996.

Žižek, Slavoj. *In Defense of Lost Causes*. New York: Verso, 2008.

——. *Living in the End Times*. London: Verso, 2010.

——. *The Parallax View*. Cambridge, MA: MIT Press, 2006.

——. *The Sublime Object of Ideology*. London: Verso, 1989.

——. *The Ticklish Subject*. New York: Verso, 1999.

——. *Violence*. New York: Picador, 2008.

——, Judith Butler and Ernesto Laclau. *Contingency, Hegemony, Universality*. London: Verso, 2000.

Index

CPSIA information can be obtained at www.ICGtesting.com
Printed in the USA
LVOW12*0936120814

398737LV00013B/622/P